CAROLINE'S
Locket

PETER CLARKE

First published in Australia by Aurora House
www.aurorahouse.com.au

This edition published 2024
Copyright © Peter Clarke 2024

Cover design: Donika Mishineva | www.artofdonika.com
Typesetting and e-book design: Amit Dey | amitdey2528@gmail.com

ISBN number: 978-1-922913-79-1 (Paperback)

A catalogue record for this book is available from the National Library of Australia

Distributed by: Ingram Content: www.ingramcontent.com
Australia: phone +613 9765 4800 |
email lsiaustralia@ingramcontent.com
Milton Keynes UK: phone +44 (0)845 121 4567 |
email enquiries@ingramcontent.com
La Vergne, TN USA: phone +1 800 509 4156 |
email inquiry@lightningsource.com

DEDICATION

To my mother and father and their parents.

To all those that came from distant lands and to all those who were already here.

It's impossible for us to imagine what they faced, how they coped and how they all learned to get on.

There's not a day goes by that I'm not grateful for what they all did.

ACKNOWLEDGEMENTS

This book is like others I have written in that it involves the NSW Gold Rush which began in May, 1851.

However, I also wanted it to shine a light on Sydney at the time. How the city looked, who the inhabitants were and how they lived.

It covers the rigours of a journey west and what the diggers had to face in their pursuit of a fortune they hoped was there for the taking.

Finally, and once again not surprisingly, it reflects on life in the goldfields and the people that lived it.

CONTENTS

1. A CHANCE MEETING

Caroline walked her horse slowly. It was hard to ride and balance her baby in front of her, so she didn't attempt to hurry. Looking nervously at the sky, she wished she hadn't set off to the store. It had been foolish and easy to regret now with hindsight. Tom was away carting goods again and she was sick of being stuck in the hut. It seemed he was always away leaving her to look after her baby and the animals, day in and day out.

It had started as a beautiful summer day, an unexpected chill in the air, no breeze to speak of and the promise of summer's sun. She'd hurried with the chores, had eaten a hasty breakfast, put on her best dress and set off for Guyong, more excited than she could remember to just get out of the hut.

Now, the sky was nearly black, heavy clouds rolling quickly across it, the wind increasing in strength and snatching at her clothes. Lizzie started to cry, increasing Caroline's anxiety. Lightning flashed in the distance. There were still a few miles to go and against her better judgement, she whispered to Kelly, her horse.

"We'd best get along. There's not much time to waste," and prodded him gently in the sides with her heels. Obediently, Kelly quickened his pace, but it wasn't long before Caroline slowed him again. It was too hard to keep her balance and hold Lizzie at the same time. There was no other choice than to slow down and endure the storm for the time it would take them to get home. Perhaps she should stop at one of her neighbours. Then, if she did, she might be stranded. No, best to keep going.

There was a small stand of trees up ahead. Mostly, trees were removed by the farmers to plant crops, or to create grazing for animals. However, some were left beside roads and creeks to provide shade where there was little point to their removal. Perhaps she could shelter there, for a few minutes anyway and see if the storm would pass. They often did. A summer storm could be like a rooster. All fuss and bother for a few minutes then meek as a lamb.

As she headed towards the stand, she realised there was a rider there already. Both horse and rider were still, watching her and Kelly with interest. The rain began to fall, large drops which hit her forcefully. She was close to the man now and had a better view of him. There was nothing she could see that gave her cause for alarm. He looked young and was badly dressed. His jacket, trousers and hat were worn and his saddle shabby. In sharp contrast, his horse was splendid.

"Come in out of the rain," he said quietly, his words shredded by the wind.

There was nothing else to do. She had no hope of escape if his intentions were to rob or hurt her.

As she drew near, she realised how little protection from the rain would be afforded by the stand and how foolish was his invitation to join him "out of the rain".

"Here, take my jacket," said the man. He didn't wait for an answer, removing his jacket and passing it to Caroline.

She didn't object. If nothing else, it would keep some of the rain off Lizzie. The jacket had an awful smell of body odour, but it was better for Lizzie and Caroline was sure her baby wouldn't object.

"What are you doing out here in this weather?" asked the man.

"I've been to the store. I wasn't expecting a storm."

"Do you live around here?"

"Not far."

The man laughed. Water poured off his hat, soaking his shirt. Caroline wondered what he found funny.

"Don't give much away, do you?" he said.

"There's not much to give away."

"How old's the baby?"

"Still a baby."

"You have nothing to fear from me."

Despite everything, Caroline felt relief. She should never have come and dreaded something might happen to Lizzie.

"What are you doing here? I haven't seen you before," she said.

"I'm not from around here. I'm from Carcoar. Well, I suppose I'm from Carcoar. I was there a few days ago."

"Carcoar? That's a pretty place. Where are you going?"

As soon as she spoke, Caroline regretted her words. It didn't pay to be a busy body, certainly not with a stranger, and certainly not with a baby in her arms.

"I'd better be going now," she said. She took the man's jacket off Lizzie and held it out.

"You keep it, missus," said the man. "It's old and ready to be replaced. Anyhow, without it your baby will get wet and might catch its death."

Caroline hesitated for a moment, then put it back around Lizzie. On the one hand, it was nice of the man, but on the other, she no longer felt safe and had a sudden impulse to leave.

"Thank you," she said and urged Kelly to continue their journey.

"Whoa," said the man. "Shouldn't you wait until the rain slows a little? There's an hour or so of daylight left."

"I need to be going. My husband will wonder where I am." Once again, the man laughed.

"He should take better care of you," he said.

"Thank you for the jacket," she said.

The man just tipped the brim of his hat. Caroline didn't look back, ignored her better judgement and kicked Kelly into a canter such that she was barely able to hold Lizzie and ride at speed.

It was a half hour before she arrived at the hut. The rain had fallen heavily all the way, and she was a bedraggled, soaked mess. Lizzie had cried most of the time, it was hard to ignore her, and her cries only added to her feelings of stupidity.

She stopped Kelly outside the hut, dismounted, and took extra care with Lizzie as though she could make amends. Sloshing through the mud and water, she put Lizzie and the things she had bought which she had put in a flour sack, inside the hut. It didn't take long to get the fire going. She always kept what she would need near at hand.

Then she took Kelly to the barn, gave him some oats, took off his saddle and bridle, rubbed him down quickly and returned to the hut, glancing back fearfully the way they had come in case she had been followed.

Lizzie had fallen asleep on the floor. Caroline was grateful to her father for the fact it was now wooden. It wouldn't do for Lizzie to fall asleep on a dirt floor, although Tom had said that worked perfectly well where he used to live outside Belfast. Thankful to be out of the rain, Caroline lit a lamp, then stripped off her own wet clothing, hoping that she hadn't ruined her good dress and hung it on a peg on the wall near the fireplace. With luck, it would dry out and be as good as new. She dressed quickly, then turned to Lizzie. Her heart stopped for a moment when she realised how still and quiet Lizzie had become, but alarm turned to relief when she felt Lizzie and found her to be warm despite being soaked. She quickly stripped and dressed her.

Children only survive if they're tough, she thought. *But only time will tell if I've done her any harm.* She cursed herself again for her stupidity.

She was tired herself, no doubt made more so by recriminations and anxiety. But there was no time for self-pity. She stoked the fire, every moment missing Tom and the help he could provide. Apart from the trip to the store, and being soaked by the storm, there was nothing to differentiate this day from any other. Never ending work and loneliness. She'd be glad when Lizzie would be older and would be help as well as company.

While waiting for the room to heat, Caroline fed Lizzie at the breast. It was almost time to wean her, but tonight wasn't that time. When she was done, she put Lizzie in her cradle and set about fixing some supper. She didn't fuss and was content with tea, bread and cheese.

When she was finished and had cleaned up, she checked on the things she had bought that day. Nothing exciting, it was more about the trip than the purchases. Fortunately, nothing would be ruined by the rain. She stacked the things, then as she moved past the bed, she noticed the man's jacket which had fallen to the floor. It was hard to dismiss the thought that he was up to no good, but nothing he had said, nor anything he had done suggested bad intent.

Stooping, she picked up the jacket. The rain had done nothing to improve its appearance. She held it in front of her, then realised it was upside down. Thinking to hang it on a peg, as Tom might find some use for it, she turned it the right way up and there was a *clunk!* as something fell from a pocket. She had to get the lamp to find the object on the floor. Putting the lamp back on the table, she sat down and studied the object by the light of the lamp.

It was a locket.

Caroline didn't own any, nor did she know much about them. It looked expensive to her untrained eye, but that was only because the metal looked like real gold. She pressed what looked like a button and exclaimed with delight when it opened and she could see a picture of a woman, but the poor light from the lamp didn't help to distinguish her features. Turning the locket over, she could see writing on the back, but it told her nothing since she couldn't read. She sat back and fondled the locket between her fingers. It felt good to do that even if it wasn't hers. Somehow, she'd need to return it even if she was wrong and it was worthless. She'd never seen the young man before and she doubted that without trying, she'd see him again, so that might be easier said than done. Still holding the locket, she settled back in the chair and fell asleep. She dreamt about the locket.

2. THE JEWELLER

The man hurried out of his shop. He was already late and there was no time to waste. After locking the door, he crossed to the other side of Castlereagh Street. The road around his shop had been metalled, but not yet kerbed and guttered, so there were still many puddles left after last night's rain and he needed to walk carefully, not only because of the puddles, but to avoid the moving vehicles. There weren't many, but what there was always moved too fast for his liking. People riding horses were the worst. They were always in a hurry.

After crossing the road and being urged by a rider to be more careful, he turned left and walked the short distance to King Street. The Liverpool Arms Hotel on the corner of Pitt and King Streets was his destination. He went to the area often for one reason or another and if time didn't matter, he'd go right once he crossed the road outside his shop, go down Hunter Street and back along Pitt. It was about twice as far to walk, but the houses were better in Hunter Street, and he liked the glimpses of the harbour near Bridge Street. The best houses were up the hill in Macquarie Street. He intended to live up there one day.

My days are running out, he thought regretfully. *The way I'm going, I'll spend the rest of my life in a rented room in Surry Hills.*

His client had written to say he would be in Sydney on that day and if possible, he'd still like to have lunch together and collect the locket. The jeweller knew the Liverpool Arms well. He used to go there all the time.

When he had first opened his shop, he didn't have many clients and used to go for lunch at the Liverpool Arms every day. In the beginning, he didn't stay long. Just lunch and maybe one or two drinks. Then, when he got to know people, there was always someone to drink with and after a few months, he rarely came back to the shop in the afternoon.

Whisky had become a problem and he tried to avoid it now. He loved to drink, but the drink didn't love him. It ruined his work and of course, his reputation. Business had all but vanished when he came to his senses. It had been a long and hard journey back. Many was the time he had told his landlord that he hadn't the ten shillings for his weekly shop-rent. He was lucky the landlord was a good, patient and tolerant man. Somehow, he always found the money and it was probably the embarrassment of being always broke and begging forgiveness that set him back on the right track.

His client had come into the shop about two months ago, had given him a locket and had asked him to change the lettering. He'd known the client for a few years but had lost contact with him until this sudden visit. The man was short with a Scottish brogue that always amused if not entertained the jeweller. He always wore matching coat, waistcoat and trousers, and had large mutton-chop sideburns and a moustache. His shirt had a high, upstanding collar, tied at the neck with a large, brightly coloured bowtie. The jeweller also liked that the man never wore his top hat indoors, showing his flame red, bushy hair. Someone had once told him the man was a surgeon.

He had said the locket was a family heirloom, that he was soon to be married and wanted to give the locket to his intended.

"I can do it all right," had said the jeweller, "but it will take time. I'll need to build up the gold again and conceal the old lettering. It'll cost more than the locket is worth."

"Not at all," had protested the client. "My father gave it to my mother. I've brought it all the way from Scotland, and I've been keeping it to give it to my wife when I get married. It has great sentimental value. The cost is not important. Can you do it?"

"Of course. When do you want it?"

"Is a month enough time?"

"When are you getting married?"

"Two months' time."

The jeweller had thought for a moment. Time wasn't the problem.

"I'll need to buy some gold," he had said.

"Do you want some money now?"

"If you can advance me some, it would help."

"Have you fallen on hard times?" the client asked, looking around the shop, as if noticing for the first time that there was very little stock for sale.

"I've not been well."

"Will five pounds be enough? I know I can trust you, so ask for what you need. I want you to do a good job. No, the best job you can. My fiancée deserves the best."

"She's beautiful," had said the jeweller, looking at the portrait again.

"Yes, she is," had said the client proudly, as though he had something to do with her looks.

"Yes, five pounds is enough. I won't know the final amount until I finish the job."

"That's all right," had said the client, taking five pounds out of his pocketbook and handing it over.

The jeweller had put it in his own pocket and had looked at the portrait again.

"She's young," he had said.

"Yes," had said the client, "but that's no reason not to give me a receipt."

"Sorry," had said the jeweller, embarrassed. "My mistake."

He had written one out quickly and had passed it over.

"I'll be back in Sydney in about a month's time. I'll write to you and confirm when I'll be here. Perhaps we can have lunch together at the Liverpool Arms?"

"Best lunches in Sydney."

"I think so. Don't worry. I'll pay."

The jeweller had smiled, and the client left.

Still chastened by the abuse from the rider, as he continued his walk, he fingered the locket in his coat pocket, through the cloth, to dwell on happier matters. He thought how pleased his client would be with it. Smiling to himself, he thought he might even have a whisky over lunch to celebrate. He'd done work for this client years before and the client wasn't aware of his recent troubles; however, it seemed he'd never be aware of them, as those problems were now behind him. He smiled again as he thought that if this locket wasn't the best work he'd done, then it was close to it.

He hadn't yet worked out how much to charge. On the one hand, being his best work, he thought he should charge a little more. On the other, he had so little work he wanted the client to tell his friends that the work was not only excellent, it was inexpensive. He had folded a blank invoice into his pocket and thought it best to discuss the matter with his client.

Made wary by his recent experience with the rider, he stood on the north-east corner of King and Pitt Streets, diagonally opposite the Liverpool Arms. He looked carefully in all four directions and could see nothing coming that posed any danger. People didn't always follow the few rules of the road, sometimes doing what they thought most expedient. Both roads were metalled, kerbed and guttered and well presented. The Liverpool Arms too was impressive with its fine glass windows overlooking both King and Pitt Streets. It was a two-storey stone building and his client could well be staying there in the rooms provided on the second floor. He looked up and gazed in wonder that after all the times he'd been there, he'd not ever seen the accommodation.

He was about to step out when he heard, "Look out!"

A young rider was coming at pace along King Street from the west. It was he who had called out. His horse was out of control, running at full pace and there seemed nothing the young rider could do to control it. The jeweller became aware of the noise of the horse galloping, other traffic shouting warnings and mayhem at the intersection. There was a cart, heavily laden with crates of what might be bottles, heading south along Pitt Street and obviously turning left into King. The driver had seen the rider and rather than stopping, he was moving the cart closer to the kerb to avoid him. The jeweller looked to his left to assess what might happen once the rider crossed the inter-section, could see nothing and looked back just in time to see the left side of the cart strike an awning post. The jolt loosened two of the large crates at the top, and the last thing the jeweller saw was the crates falling towards him.

3. THE DRIVER

The cart driver told anyone with the patience to listen that it wasn't his fault. He was near to tears and kept muttering that it was the fault of the rider who should have kept control of his horse. Only a few people stood to listen, interested to know what had happened. One man who said he was a doctor checked the body and assured those still looking that it was lifeless.

"You say it's not your fault," said the doctor to the cart driver, "but you're the only one here that can take care of the body."

"Me? Why me?" declared the driver, still close to tears. "I'm late with the delivery already."

"Has anyone called the police?" asked another by-stander.

"Why do you want the police?" demanded the driver. "It was an accident."

"The coroner will do an inquest," said the doctor. "It's best if the police take a statement from anyone that saw the accident."

As soon as he said that everyone except the doctor and the driver walked away.

"I'll wait with the body, if you like," said the doctor. "The police are over in Bathurst Street. It won't take you long to get them."

"Why do I have to go? Why don't you go?"

"It's none of my business," said the doctor. "I didn't even see the accident. I only stopped to see if I could help the man, but there's no help for him. I think he died immediately. You should have asked the others to help. The ones that saw the accident, I mean."

"It wasn't my fault," said the driver again.

"What's in the bottles?"

"Soda water," said the driver, looking surprised at the question. "It's made by Bossely's. They're on the other side of Bridge Street. I came from there. I deliver a lot of it."

"Where are you taking it?" asked the doctor.

"To the Infirmary."

"The Infirmary? Why don't you take the body too? They'll take a body. They do that now. It'll be easy. You can tell them what happened. Leave the body there and the coroner can do the inquest at the hospital. I'm sure your sense of responsibility will sit well with the police and the coroner. I'll help you put it on the cart."

Between them, they got the body onto the cart. It wasn't easy, as the doctor was only of slight build, and the driver squeamish about the blood that was evident on the clothes of the jeweller. The driver also loaded what was left of the crates and bottles that had fallen on the man.

"It's strange there was no one with him," said the doctor, perspiring from his exertions.

"I didn't see anyone. I think he was standing on his own."

"Which way was he walking?"

"Why?"

"He might have been meeting someone at the Liverpool Arms."

"I'm sure if he was, they would have come out. Anyway, I'm late. I must get going. Thanks for your help."

"Do you want my name and address?"

"What for?"

"In case the police ask for it."

"Why would they? You said you didn't see anything."

"All right, but I'll go by the police office in Bathurst Street later and give them my details."

"If you wish and if you think they'll want them."

The driver looked back as he drove off and saw the doctor standing on the corner, watching. He was already thinking that he might just tell them at the hospital that he found the body in the street. Even as he formed the idea, he realised the stupidity of it. There was no way he would find a body at the corner of Pitt and King Streets in the middle of the day. Still, he was worried that the court would find him at fault. The doctor was right. He should have found the name and address of someone that saw the accident happen, someone that could confirm it was the rider's fault. How was it possible that no one cared about a person being killed?

When he arrived at the hospital, he had some trouble convincing them that he had a body in addition to the soda water and that there'd been an accident. They made him sign a paper taking responsibility for the bottles when they noticed that some were broken.

"What will you do with the body?" he asked.

"We'll keep it here. The coroner will want to inspect it. He'll probably hold the hearing at the hospital. He always does when there's an inquest into a death at the hospital."

"Should I see the police?"

"Haven't you done that already?"

"I met a doctor. He said to bring the body here."

"You should have taken it to the police."

"Should I do that now?"

"No. Not now. Leave it with us but go and see the police and tell them what happened."

The driver left with a sinking heart. He wished he'd taken the doctor's offer to wait while he fetched the police. As he drove away, he saw them load the body into a hand cart. He cursed the fact that he made regular deliveries there and they knew him.

4. THE WARDSMAN

The wardsman wheeled the man along in the handcart. Looking down, he saw a slightly balding, badly dressed, middle-aged man. His face showed not only the marks where he'd been injured, but red lines and blush as evidence of a fondness for the bottle.

Too young to die, he thought. *What bad luck for him. Wrong place at the wrong time.*

He'd heard the discussion with the driver and knew that the man had been delivered as an unnamed body. As he pushed him down the passageway to the dead house, he wondered if the man carried any identification and decided to check as soon as he reached his destination. He didn't like the dead house. It smelled even if there were no bodies and was nothing more than a room with a table on which bodies were placed. It hardly merited the title of 'house'. Nonetheless, he'd delivered bodies there before, both when people had died in the hospital, or been delivered from the street as in this case. Mostly the bodies from the street were in worse state than this one and had usually died from exposure, alcoholism or starvation. There was the odd one that had been bashed to death.

As he pushed the cart into the room, he saw there was no one else there, nor were there any other bodies. Putting the body on the table, he rummaged through the pockets to see if the man could be identified. There was no pocketbook, but there was a key, a blank invoice, a gold locket, a few pounds and some loose change.

The blank invoice must mean something, but it had only a description of the locket on it. There were no details of the buyer, the seller and no price. It was odd and suggested to the wardsman that the man had probably stolen the locket, no doubt from the place where one would gain access using the key. Looking at the wounded face, the wardsman decided the man could not be a thief. Not only did he not look like one, but he also had some money in his pocket. He wasn't sure why that granted the man the status of honesty. He picked up the locket and after studying it for a few moments, pressed the clasp on the side. The locket popped open.

There was a portrait of a young woman and despite the fact the portrait was quite small, it was obvious the woman was beautiful. The locket was new, and the words easily read.

To my beloved.
From your heart.
William.

Was this William? This poor, lifeless body on the table? What will his beloved think when she finds that he's dead? He doesn't look like a William. No, William was someone else. Whoever this is, it's not William.

He checked the hands. The man was not a tradesman and probably worked at a desk. There'd be more calluses on his backside than on his hands.

The wardsman looked around quickly and wasn't sure why he had done so. He would have heard anyone coming, so he didn't need to worry about anyone else. The coroner would call for an autopsy, and it wouldn't be unusual for there to be nothing in the pockets of an unknown man. Looking around again, making sure no one was watching, he slipped the locket and the blank invoice into the pocket of his own jacket. He left the money. A thief would take everything, so the fact that some money was left meant there'd been no theft.

Taking the cart, he left the room before he could change his mind. Once he left the room, the locket was stolen. If they ever asked him about it, he would say he knew nothing. The body would be handled by more people before being placed in the grave and any one of them could well have stolen the locket.

When he left work at the end of the day, he had made his mind up about what to do. He'd stop for a drink on the way home and hopefully sell the locket. There was no point in keeping it. He had no one to give it to, nor any use for it himself. And it was dangerous to keep it.

He always went home the same way. Along Macquarie Street until he reached Hunter Street, then down Hunter until he reached George Street, and along George until he reached the Rocks where he rented a room in Gloucester Street. If he had the time, the inclination and the money, he'd stop for a drink at the Fortune of War Hotel, not far from where he lived.

On his walk, he would admire some of the newer Chapels and Churches and the older Legislative Assembly buildings in Macquarie Street. In the summer, if it was still light enough when he left, he could see some of the fancy homes and buildings in the Domain and the impressive Government House and Botanic Gardens in the distance before he turned into Hunter Street. The City Council faced an uphill battle to maintain the roads in serviceable condition. Major roads like Macquarie, Pitt, George and parts of Hunter were surfaced, kerbed and guttered, but the materials used were often inferior, so the work would often deteriorate quickly after it was done, and pedestrian and vehicular traffic would have to deviate around ruts and potholes.

There were many shops and some fine houses in Hunter Street, although the best were closer to Macquarie where they could enjoy views of the harbour and the fresh breeze that blew most of the time from the Northeast. There were fine houses too in Elizabeth Street, many owned by the legal profession who wished to live close to the Supreme Court which wasn't far away at the corner of Elizabeth and King Streets. He could see those as he crossed Elizabeth on his way down Hunter.

Walking down Hunter, he would sometimes stop and look into the shop windows, interspersed among the houses, admiring the produce that he lacked the money to buy. There were clothing stores, bakeries, jewellers, druggists, butchers and even the offices of the publisher of "Bell's Life", a weekly newspaper that he liked to read if someone else bought it. As much as he enjoyed it, the price of sixpence was beyond him. The buildings were mostly weather board front, stone back and side walls, but sometimes the commercial buildings were multi-storey and all stone, providing a greater sense of permanence.

The worst part of the walk was crossing the stone arch over the Tank Stream in Hunter Street. The old tanks that were dug into the sandstone to hold water were still visible from the arch to the right but had long since been disused and now held all manner of things that found its way into the stream. The stream was now nothing more than an open sewer and smelled like it. There was talk that it would soon be covered entirely and the sooner the better as far as he was concerned.

He felt safe enough on the walk, although when it was dark, he fretted when walking through the poorly lit areas, of which there were many. The City Council was always adding more gas lighting, but mostly in the streets and areas frequented by the well-to-do. He'd read about robberies and murders, particularly around the Tank Stream in Hunter Street that always made him nervous. It was only a few years before that a fellow called O'Brien had pursued Dr Meyrick in Hunter Street, chasing him about and shooting him twice before killing the poor man. And not long before that, another fellow called Wilkes, thankfully now in Cockatoo Island prison had murderously assaulted a Mrs Wells. There were still parts of Sydney that were not for the faint-hearted. Still, it was the best and quickest place to cross, but he'd always breathe a sigh of relief when he reached George Street.

This evening, it was a double sigh of relief because he carried the locket. He was sure that he looked like he wouldn't carry anything valuable, so he would hardly be a target for a thief. But he would be pleased to sell it and get some money that he could stash in his room, using a little at a time to avoid any suspicion.

It was only a ten-minute walk down George from Hunter to the Fortune of War. As he walked, he pondered the problem of how to sell the locket. He'd not ever done such a thing and didn't know how to start. Perhaps the best idea was to ask

Robert, the publican. Robert was not much older than himself, around twenty-five, but married with children and successful as a publican and businessman. People often involved publicans in matters of holding money or goods where they had been illegally obtained on the pretext that it would only be for a short time. He knew that Robert was a straight as a die and if he thought the locket had been illegally obtained, he would immediately involve the police. Discretion would be necessary.

When he arrived at the Fortune of War, it was nearly dark, but still warm, so he was glad to finish the walk and step inside. The building was quite a few years old, of brick, narrow and three storeys. The wardsman was well known, so it was easy to stand at the bar and order a whisky, passing the time of day with other patrons some of whom looked like they had been there for a while. There was no sign of Robert. It would be out of character for the wardsman to ask after him, so he decided it best to sip his whisky and continue to chat with the others.

Time passed quickly and it seemed like only an hour or so when the barman said they would be closing soon.

"Whersh Robert?" asked the wardsman, struggling with the words. He hadn't realised how drunk he had become, chatting with the patron beside him about the cricket and races at the Hyde Park Racecourse. They'd been matching drinks for most of the evening and while they understood each other, communication with others was now a problem.

"Not coming in tonight," said the barman after thinking about the question for a few moments.

"T'morrer night?" slurred the wardsman, a trace of query in his voice.

"Think so," said the barman, unsure of the question. "Anyway, finish those and leave. Both of you."

The men finished their drinks, and left the pub. They stopped outside, thanked each other for the evening's companionship and headed in their respective directions, both making hard work of it.

I'll just have to hang onto the locket until tomorrow night, thought the wardsman, shaking his head sadly. It would have been better if he'd been able to get rid of it sooner rather than later.

He started up the steps on the walk to Gloucester Street, slipping and falling several times. On reaching the house where he rented a room, he stopped to piss on the street outside, then using his keys, let himself into the house and into his room, being careful not to wake anyone. Closing the door behind him, he fell onto his bed, fully clothed and was asleep in seconds. He woke sometime during the night, took a few moments to orient himself and upon checking for the locket in his pocket, with distress and dismay found that it was no longer there.

5. THE BOY

That morning, a young boy taking a short cut to the National School in Fort Street and using the steps to Gloucester Street, noticed the locket glinting in the early morning sun. He stooped and picked it up, looking at it closely before checking to see if anyone was about. It could belong to someone who had just dropped it, but not seeing anyone and being in a hurry, he put it in his pocket to check later. He'd only started school that year and was afraid the school bell would strike before he arrived. It wouldn't do to get in anyone's bad books. His father told him it cost four pence a week for his education, and he didn't want that money to be wasted.

He was an only child, living with his mother and father in a weatherboard cottage in Cambridge Street, not far from the school. His father who worked on the wharves, was a big man with a huge, black beard and a belly that wobbled when he laughed which was often.

"Freddie," has father used to say when Freddie was little, "please don't pull my beard."

Freddie would pull it and his father would howl in fake pain. It was a great game. His mother, father and himself would make such a fuss that the neighbours would object. The street was crowded with houses packed tightly and his father used to say that you didn't need good ears to hear people snoring at night all up and down the street.

It was a good street, with many children and families, but people lived too close to each other, some sharing privies, with others just going where they could. There was no kerbing or guttering and water hung about in stagnant, smelly pools. The street had more than its fair share of lodging houses, which were frequented by people who couldn't care less how they treated the area. Everyone worried about cholera, dysentery and smallpox, but it seemed all they could ever do was worry. His mother said other areas always seemed to merit more attention from the Council.

His mother used to be a teacher and she always encouraged Freddie with numbers and letters, such that he looked forward to going to school. His mother was delighted when they converted the Military Hospital in Fort Street into a National School and Freddie would be able to walk to school. Not that his mother didn't have time to take him. She took in washing and did some cleaning, but most of the time she looked after their house and did cooking, washing and cleaning for her family. His father didn't want him going to a school run by anyone other than the state and the only other available schools were in Crown and Riley Streets, too far for a comfortable walk.

Thankfully, he arrived at school in time and took his place among the many students shuffling to their classrooms. The school was a big, two-storey brick building, not really designed to be a school. However, somehow it had been converted such that the children could be distributed across its ample rooms. It didn't surprise him that there were so many children as he'd heard that there were nearly five hundred at the school. Some came from wealthy families, but most came from poor families like his own. His father had seized the opportunity when the National School had opened, telling his mother that he wouldn't send their son to a school run by religious people who would fill their son's head with nonsense.

Fred had his own desk, slate and slate pencil. The slate and the pencil were kept on a single shelf accessed by lifting the lid on the top of the desk. Lucky for him he was only small and could fit easily into the seat. The desk was a single piece, and it wasn't possible to move the seat if there wasn't enough room. Some of the other bigger children had to squeeze themselves into the available space.

The best part of school was meeting Anna. He didn't know her other name yet. There was plenty of time. Just sitting next to her during recess was enough. He didn't know how or why, but he was sat next to her at recess on the first day when school started a few weeks back and the arrangement hadn't been changed. They were both good students and competed to be the best in their class. The boys were on the ground floor and the girls on the first and while they couldn't attend the same class, they talked about what they learned. He liked that she was a girl. She had a nice laugh and they sometimes shared stories about things that had happened in their families since school the previous day. It turned out that she lived down in High Street, so she came to school from the other direction. There was disappointment in the news. He'd hoped they could walk to and from school together. There might still be a way to do it, but he'd have to lie about where he lived. Still pondering the problem, he'd been vague about where he lived, but knew he was running out of time to tell her some place that would suit his purpose.

She was a little distant when they met before class this morning and it dawned on him that she was flirting with another boy. This was a dreadful development and he wondered how it might have happened. They'd been all right when they went their respective ways on the previous afternoon. He tried unsuccessfully to get her attention, but the bell rang, and the classes were called to start.

The teacher, Mr Mills started on the morning's lesson, and it was easy for Fred. Just the endless repetition of the times tables. Not needing to pay attention, he thought again how to get Anna's attention. Mr Mills seemed absorbed by the chanting, had his head cocked to one side as though listening to something very interesting and possibly not of this world.

Mr Mills was a young man who always wore a vest and a bow tie, grey flannel trousers, shiny brown shoes, glasses and slicked his dark hair down so that it stayed that way all day. The girls in Anna's class said he was handsome, most of the boys said he wasn't, and no one could agree on his age.

Every now and again, Fred stole a look at the locket. There was nothing else for it. Fred took the locket from his pocket and moved it carefully between his fingers. It would certainly get her attention and he imagined himself smiling at her and whispering, "For you." He was absorbed and enchanted by the image.

"Stop!" shouted Mr Mills. The room froze and the chanting stopped abruptly.

"You! Fred!" shouted Mr Mills. Fred looked up, stricken with guilt.

Will they throw him out of the school?

"Me?" he asked, meekly.

"Well, I don't mean David Copperfield!"

"Who's David Copperfield?" asked Fred.

"You'll find out soon enough. What do you have there?"

"Me, sir?" said Fred. "Nothing."

"No? What do you have in your hand?"

"This, sir," said Fred, holding up the locket with a clumsy, shaking hand.

The teacher took it and pressed it between his fingers.

"Where did you get it?" he asked, looking at Fred.

"I found it."

"Where?"

"On the steps."

"What steps?"

"Between Cambridge Street and Gloucester Street."

Fred's short life passed before his eyes. He'd only been at school for a few weeks, and he was about to be thrown out.

What would his father say?

He started to cry. He'd never been in such trouble. The other boys laughed.

"There, there, lad," said the teacher, first looking sternly at the other boys, then at Fred, his face softening. "It's nothing to cry about. We'll talk about it later, before lunch."

He walked back to the front of the class and recommenced the times tables where they had left off. Fred felt better that Mr Mills had offered comfort, but he couldn't focus or wait for the morning to finish. He wanted only to know what would happen and didn't dare imagine what his father would say.

The other lessons dragged on endlessly until finally, it was twelve o'clock and the lunch break arrived. Mr Mills dismissed the rest of the class and told Fred to wait while the others left.

Now that the time of reckoning had arrived, Fred wanted the floor to open up and swallow him. He sat in miserable silence, shaking with fear and staring at Mr Mills.

Once everyone had left the room, the teacher sat behind his desk, took the locket from his pocket and said, "Come here, Fred."

Fred waited while Mr Mills continued to roll the locket between his fingers, then snipped the clasp at the side and the locket opened. Fred stared in astonishment.

"How did you do that?" he asked in a voice filled with wonder, all thought of retribution gone with the discovery.

"That's what they're for," said Mr Mills. "There's usually something inside, like a piece of hair or a portrait."

He motioned for Fred to come closer.

"See, here," he said, showing the locket to Fred, "there's a portrait."

They both studied the portrait.

"She's pretty," said Fred.

"Yes," said Mr Mills. "She is."

Fred lost all his nervousness. It was like he and Mr Mills were both involved now, equal partners in an adventure.

"What'll we do?" asked Fred.

"We?" snapped Mr Mills.

All Fred's confidence vanished, and he was once again a boy without a school and without a future. He started to cry.

"I'm sorry, Fred. I didn't mean to snap. I'll tell you what we'll do. I'll keep the locket and try to find who owns it. I don't recognise the lady in the portrait, but the portrait might be the key to finding the owner."

"But I found it! It's mine!"

"I suppose, but if I can find who owns it, it's better to give it back, isn't it? It might have a lot of value to them. What if you lost something? Wouldn't you want it back if someone found it?"

"I suppose," said Fred, miserable that he couldn't give it to Anna.

"I'll tell you what, Fred. If I can't find who owns it, I'll give it back to you."

Fred brightened. All was not lost.

"You can go now. Join the others."

"How long will it take to find who owns it? Can I have it back tomorrow?'

"It might take longer than one day. Leave it with me, Fred. You be off now. Don't worry, I'll try to find them as soon as I can."

"All right," said Fred, face down cast and miserable. There was still the problem of Anna to solve and without the locket, no immediate solution was available. Going back to his desk, he picked up his lunch bag and left the room

The teacher put the locket in his pocket, also picked up his lunch bag and went to join the other teachers.

6. THE TEACHER

The other teachers were already seated in a room set aside for them. Mills was uncertain as to the original use of the room, but he heard that it had been a storeroom. He wasn't sure what you could store in it, but whatever it was, it had to be small. There was an empty place on one of the benches and he took it to enjoy his lunch. The lunch was usually made up from what was left from dinner the previous evening, or if not, it was bread and cheese. Mills lived with a family not far from the school. Board and lodging cost him fifteen shillings a week which left him about the same amount for other things. He didn't drink alcohol, use tobacco or gamble, so aside from what he judged to be ridiculous prices for clothing, he was able to save much of his money. He didn't yet know for what yet, but was happy to bide his time.

He was from Edinburgh in Scotland. His father was a minister in the Church of Scotland with strong views on morality and was very committed to the teachings of his church. The family had moved briefly to London, then when Mills was in his early teens, they had moved to Dublin. While Mills agreed with the teachings in a broad sense, he thought there had to be more to life than self-discipline and denial. He and his father could never see eye-to-eye and he'd realised early that it would be best if he found anywhere but Dublin to live. It was only an idle thought until his last year at school. He was a brilliant student, much praised by his teachers, one of whom recommended that he attend teacher training in the Model School System based in Dublin. His teacher had remarked, with a smile and a twinkle in his eye that "not only was the system excellent training for teachers, but it was also non-denominational". It was unusual for pupil-teachers to be selected from outside the Model School System, but Mills' teacher had pulled some strings, called in some favours, wrote fulsome letters of recommendation and Mills was selected.

The idea had a lot of appeal, but the fact it was non-denominational would give his father an excuse to veto it. Besides, his father maintained that they had excellent teaching programs in the Church. His mother had stood up to his father for the only time in her life, threatening to make his father's life a "misery unless he saw his way clear to supporting their son". He had no idea how much more miserable his father's life could be than it already seemed, but the threat was enough to enable him to attend the school. At the time, Mills didn't care what he did, provided it gave him an opportunity to move away from home.

Upon graduation, he worked in the National School System for two years, then completely by chance saw an advertisement asking for applications for a teaching post in Australia in the National School where "graduates of the Irish Model School teacher training would be preferred". He applied more out of curiosity and was astonished to eventually be accepted. Knowing little about Sydney and less about Australia, he thought long and hard about the opportunity before taking it. His mother was terribly upset, blaming herself for helping him to become a teacher. On the other hand, his father saw the move as an opportunity for his son to spread the word of his Church to Australia. Mills said little about that, preferring not to have an argument on the eve of his departure.

He booked the cheapest passage possible to Sydney, taking a steamer from Dublin to Liverpool, then a clipper ship to Melbourne and a coastal steamer to Sydney. Promising his mother that he would come home as often as possible, the trials and difficulties of the journey left him with the feeling that a lifetime may not be enough to recover such that he would ever return. Until he was ready, letters would have to suffice. He wrote to his mother often and dreaded her letters in reply, pleading with him to come home.

His letters tried to downplay how much he loved Sydney. The weather, the people, the theatre, the walks all wove their spell such that he doubted he would ever leave. He even loved teaching and fitted well into his new role, being popular with both students and the other teachers. Still, he didn't need to say so to his mother and kept all those details to himself.

Lost in his own thoughts, he realised with a start that the lunch break was nearly over and he hadn't yet decided what to do with the locket. Someone had fetched a pot of tea from the kitchen and put it on a table in the corner. Lifting the pot, he was pleased to note there was still some left.

"Might be cold by now," said Peggy, a teacher sitting beside him.

"Doesn't matter," he said. "I like it as much. Anyway, I think it's better cold on a hot day."

"You're funny," she said. "No one else thinks like you do."

Peggy was about his age and taught the young girls. Most of the teachers were men, but a few like Peggy taught domestic tasks like sewing and cooking. She was a plain girl and one that his mother would say was "big boned". Mills was always surprised she was so big when she seemed to eat so little. Her hair was cut in a fashion that looked like she put a bowl on her head and cut any hair poking out from under it. She lived with her parents and a sister in a nice house in Kent Street, at Millers Point, not far from the school. Mills thought her dull as well as plain and tried to avoid her, but it wasn't always possible, and this was one of those times.

"That might be a good thing," he replied, not wanting to be rude.

She chuckled, a pleasant sound. He thought that if she spent some time on her appearance, she might even be attractive. On the spur of the moment, he showed her the locket.

"Oh, that's pretty," she said, rolling it between her fingers. "Thanks so much. I've always wanted one."

"Oh, no," he said quickly, "I didn't mean …"

"I know," she said. "I was just having some fun."

She smiled at him and looked at the locket again.

Mills was flustered and must have looked it.

"I didn't mean to embarrass you," she said, regret in her voice. "Where did you get it?"

"One of the boys in my class. He said he found it."

"Lucky him. Why have you got it?"

"I thought I might be able to find out who owns it."

"How will you do that? Is there a name on it?"

"Just 'William', but there's a portrait inside."

"Inside?"

"Yes," he said, taking the locket back. He pressed the clip and the locket sprung open.

"Oh," she said, "I didn't know you could do that."

He showed her the portrait.

"Oh, isn't she beautiful!" she exclaimed. "I wish I looked like that."

Mills was embarrassed by his thoughts about Peggy, feeling badly about thinking her plain and dull. Lost for words, he sat silently.

"There's a jeweller in York Street," she said. "Near the Old Burial Ground."

"A jeweller?"

"Yes. You could show it to him. He might recognise the workmanship. It looks new."

"That's a good idea. The Old Burial Ground? Near Park Street?"

"Yes. Near there."

"That's a long walk."

"It's not that far. You could go after school. I could come with you. Show you where it is, I mean."

Mills looked quickly around the room.

"They've all gone," she said.

"Oh. I was just looking to see if anyone else might be here and might know of a closer jeweller," he said. The excuse sounded weak. It was clear to Mills they both knew he was checking to make sure no one else would know they might see each other outside the school. He was brought up to believe such interactions were frowned upon. *You don't get your meat at the baker's shop* was the expression often used by his father.

Just then the bell sounded to commence the afternoon's classes. He got up quickly.

She looked at him with her head cocked to one side.

"I don't bite," she said.

"I know, but I'll be all right. I'll find it easily enough. And there's probably others in York Street that I might see on the way."

"I'd like to come, too. The jeweller is a family friend and I know he'll be more helpful if I'm there. It's up to you, of course. I'd like to know more about the locket. I do like mysteries."

"Mysteries? What do you mean?"

"I read a lot of mystery books."

"All right. We must hurry back to class. If you do decide to come, I'll meet you on the corner of Cumberland Road and Charlotte Place. Then, we won't be seen leaving the school together."

"What wrong with us leaving the school together?" she said, an edge to her voice.

"I don't think they like us seeing each other outside school."

"First, I've heard of it. Did you make that up? We're only inquiring about the lost locket, not running away together."

She stood up and looked at him, an expression of sadness in her face.

"I thought you might have been made of sterner stuff," she said.

Mills was both shocked and embarrassed. He'd gone from thinking Peggy plain and boring to now thinking he had to defend his courage. Realising that Peggy was not at all what she had seemed, he capitulated and wanted to know more.

"Shall we meet here? After the last class?"

Peggy smiled quickly and perhaps a little smugly.

"Of course," she said, picking up her lunch bag, "see you then."

On his way back to class, Mills decided he would see the headmaster and tell him what he and Peggy planned to do after class. That way, it would be up to the headmaster, and he could either sanction or veto the proposed adventure.

Surprisingly, he was enthusiastic.

"Yes, I know that jeweller," said the headmaster. "Peggy has sent me to him. He's very good. It's best if Peggy goes with you. She went with me. Well done. Good plan, good plan."

Mills decided to not tell Peggy that the project had the headmaster's blessing. At least Peggy might still think him made of sterner stuff. They met as arranged and walked quickly out of the school grounds, turning right into Upper Fort Street and shortly after into Princes Street. They crossed Charlotte Place, then crossed York Street to walk down the right side as they headed south along it. They passed the St Phillip's Anglican Church and School building on the corner of York and Charlotte. It was still under construction; the old stone church being torn down and replaced. Peggy told Mills that many people thought the old church building a monstrosity, being built from terrible materials, so they were pleased when the decision was made to replace it. Some men were still working on the site and stopped to look at Peggy. She noticed and put her hand lightly on Mills' arm, to make it look as though she was taken. Mills was both surprised and thrilled at the touch.

They crossed Margaret, Erskine, King and Market Streets, passing many small businesses and cottages. It was a reasonably well-to-do area and being still autumn, the day was warm, and people were out and about, some shopping and others going to or from their homes. There was some vehicular traffic too, but nothing like George Street that carried much of the traffic in and out of Sydney. York Street wasn't yet kerbed and guttered or surfaced, so dust rose at every step and soon Mills' shoes were shiny no more.

Peggy chatted gaily about all manner of things to do with the school and her class. It was obvious she was enjoying herself. She kept her hand on Mills' arm as though it was the most natural thing. They looked like any other couple out for an afternoon stroll.

As they neared the markets, the street and footpath were paved, traffic increased and horses and carts were parked along the market building, collecting and delivering produce.

"Have you been to the markets?" asked Peggy.

She stopped and looked around. Mills stopped too, looking at the buildings which he could see were made of wood. They covered the block between George, Market and York Streets and almost to Druitt Street. Two large market buildings fronted Market Street and there were large entrances to accommodate horses and carts. The markets had double pitched roofs undoubtedly to let odours escape, and walls about twenty-five to thirty feet high. The police station and court building were partly of stone, backed close to the market complex and fronted Druitt Street. The building looked as if it might have once served the markets.

"No," he said. "Shouldn't we be getting along?"

Peggy looked further along the west side of York Street.

"I can see the shop from here and it's still open."

She looked back at the markets.

"I think they're exciting," she said. "If you like, we could come on Saturday night."

"They're open on Saturday night?"

"Yes. Saturday night is more for the common people. People like us. There are stalls that sell all sorts of things and entertainment, too. I think you'd like it. Anyway, you don't have to answer now. Let's see about the locket and we can talk about it on the way home."

She looked at Mills and smiled.

"C'mon," she said, taking his hand as though they'd been together all their lives. She led him into a shop, not twenty feet away. It was one of several shops in a substantial stone building. There were panelled glass windows on both sides of the door and some merchandise on display.

"Uncle doesn't put much in the window," said Peggy, noting Mills' frown. "He doesn't like to attract thieves."

"Uncle?"

"Yes. He's my uncle. I don't tell people when I recommend the store. I don't want them to think they're being tricked."

"Oh, Peggy!" shouted a man when they entered the door. "And who is this fine young man?"

The man looked to be in his fifties, dressed completely in black. He had a vest with a watch and chain, a black optical visor, gold rimmed glasses and a very small, tidy grey beard. Coming out from behind the counter, he shook Mills' hand warmly.

Clocks abounded on the walls of the shop, in all sizes and types, merrily marking time and ticking away people's lives. There were cabinets at waist height with rings, brooches, chains, lockets and many other types of jewellery.

"This is Henry Mills," said Peggy. "He's a teacher at the school. Henry, this is Gustave, my uncle."

"Henry. You are very welcome," said Gustave, still holding Mills' hand.

"Nice to meet you," said Mills, trying to shake his hand loose.

"What can I do for you both?" asked Gustave, finally dropping Mills's hand and returning to his place behind the counter.

Mills took out the locket and passed it over.

"That's a very nice locket," said Gustave. "Good workmanship, too."

He popped the locket open.

"She's pretty. Friend of yours?" asked Gustave, looking at Mills.

Mills shook his head.

"No. One of my students found it in the street. I'm hoping to return it to its rightful owner."

"How can I be of help?" said Gustave, looking from Mills to Peggy to Mills.

"I thought you might recognise the workmanship," said Mills, uncertainty in his voice.

"I said you might be able to help. I suggested we come here. It's my idea," said Peggy.

Mills thought it was nice of her to step in, make him look better than he felt.

Gustave looked at the locket, studying the portrait for some time.

"She looks familiar," he said. "But I can't place her. It might just be that most portraits look like this, so that might be why she's familiar. The locket looks old, too, as though someone has reworked it."

"What do you mean, reworked it?" asked Peggy.

"It looks as if it might have had other letters that have been filled and the new writing put on it. Like it's an heirloom and passed down the family."

"That's sad," said Peggy. "Whoever has lost it must be very upset."

Gustave turned the locket in his hands.

"William? I wonder who William is. Unfortunately, there's lots of Williams. Gustave would be better," he said, laughing. "Good workmanship, but you can't tell who made it by looking at it. They're all made the same way, so there's nothing distinctive about it. All I can say is that William, whoever he is, isn't poor."

"What do you think it's worth?" asked Peggy.

"Eight, maybe ten pounds."

"What should we do?" asked Mills, finally joining the discussion.

"Peggy's right. Someone would be keen to get it back. Where did the boy find it?"

"He said he found it on the steps between Cambridge Street and Gloucester Street."

"I'm not familiar with them. Not my part of town. I suppose your William lives someone near to there. You could knock on a few doors, asking for either William or if they own it."

"There's lots of people live in that area. Not all of them honest, either," said Peggy. "The first dishonest person would claim it."

"You could take it to the police," said Gustave, but there was hesitancy in his voice.

"You don't sound convinced that's a good idea," said Peggy. Mills was glad she did. He wanted to say the same thing but didn't want to be rude.

"Well, I don't like to say it, but they're a rum lot. It could go missing."

He gazed at the locket in the palm of his hand.

"It's a pity," he said, shaking his head. "Poor William. Still, it could be either William or his love that lost the locket. He may not have given it to her yet, of course."

"He might have lost it on the way to give it to her," said Peggy.

"If that's the case, he lives near the area where it was found," said Gustave.

"Or, she does," said Mills. "Perhaps your idea of a door-knock is the best idea."

"I don't think it'll last past the first dishonest person," said Peggy.

"I'll tell you what I'll do," said Gustave, looking at one of the clocks on the wall. "It's getting late, and it'll be dark soon. My favourite niece has to get home, but I'm sure you'll see to that young man. The police office is just on the corner. I'll take it to the police in the morning and I'll get a receipt, so if they lose it, they'll have to pay for it. Does that help?"

Peggy looked at Mills who nodded.

"That's wonderful, Uncle. Thank you so much."

"If the police can't find the owner, will we get it back?" asked Mills. "I promised the boy that if I couldn't find the owner, he could keep it."

"I'll do my best," said Gustave. "But, there's no guarantee. In the meantime, check the papers. Someone might place an advertisement with a reward if the locket is found. I'm sure the boy would find that just as valuable."

"I suppose we could place an advertisement that we found it," said Mills.

"Same problem as the doorknock," said Peggy. "Every dishonest person will claim it."

"You're right, of course," said Mills. "Let's leave it with your Uncle Gustave and see what develops."

7. THE CONSTABLE

The constable stood inside the doors of the courthouse. He was shortly to give evidence in a case of petty theft and had arrived early walking across to the court in Druitt Street from Brickfield Hill. It was a pleasant walk, the early morning not too warm, and the breeze not yet too strong, although he could see some storm heads gathering in the south-west. He'd walked down from his rented house in Goulburn Street, crossed over George Street, dodging in and out of the early morning traffic, and walked along the western side of George, crossing Liverpool, Bathurst and Druitt streets. Most of the time the sun was at his right and strong enough to promise another warm autumn day.

The central Sydney watch-house stood on the corner of Druitt and George streets, and he passed it just before turning left into the Court House. No doubt his prisoner would shortly be brought from there by a conductor. Thankfully, giving evidence meant he had no contact with the prisoner and that was to his liking. He was glad to arrive early. The Court would start around 10am, but it wasn't always punctual. It would give him a chance to cool down. He was always nervous before appearing in court. The law was inevitably on his side, but that didn't stop him being nervous. The formality, the magistrates' frequent short temper, and the fact that some poor person would soon face legal punishment on his evidence always contributed to his nervousness.

He felt hot and uncomfortable in his new uniform. He'd only had it about a year, and still felt proud when he put it on. Blue coat with silver buttons, blue pants with a red cord and a blue cap also with a red cord. The police had worn all manner of clothes before the new shipment had arrived, so at least they all now looked the same. It meant that thieves and criminals could spot the police easily enough, so sudden confrontations were less frequent. It was the same uniform worn by the London Metropolitan Police and not in any way suited to Sydney conditions. He'd heard police in the bush where it was hotter in the summer mostly still wore their own clothes and there was trouble brewing between them and the magistrates who wanted police to at least look like police.

The odd assortment of people standing around was always confronting. Police, witnesses, lawyers, conductors and offenders gathered in small groups. Everyone always looked nervous, no matter their side of the law. It was easy to identify the reporters from the papers by their scruffy, badly fitting suits, pencil and paper in hand, moving from group to group, always hopeful but never satisfied. Fortunately, a policeman standing on his own was of no interest to anyone.

A man came up the few steps, through the doors and into the area before the court room. He was smartly dressed in black and stopped at the top of the stairs, looking completely out of place. He didn't look nervous, just bewildered, so the constable decided he had nothing to do with the matters at hand, unlike the others gathered in the room. The constable liked watching people, it helped to pass the time. Curiosity getting the better of him, he walked over to the man and asked if he could help.

"I hope so," said the man. "Is there someone I can talk to about some lost property?"

"Have you lost something?"

"No, quite the opposite. I've found something. Well, someone I know has found something."

"Why have you come to the court?"

"I thought this is the Central Police Office?"

"You're right, of course," said the constable, laughing.

"Why is that funny?" said the man, looking serious.

"The building is both, but these people are here for the court. I presumed you would be here for the court, too. I thought it funny that you're not."

"I'm in a hurry," said the man, staring at the constable and obviously not sharing his sense of humour.

"What have you found?"

"This locket," said the man, taking a gold locket from his coat pocket and passing it to the constable.

"It's beautiful," said the constable, holding the locket and in the palm of his hand.

"Yes, it's a very nice piece of work," said the man, looking less serious and more thoughtful.

"Where was it found?"

"In the Rocks."

"Why didn't you take it to the police there?"

"I'm a jeweller. My shop is across the road in York Street. It was brought to me there in the hope I might recognise it. I don't, of course. If it should go to the police in the Rocks, perhaps you'll send it there?"

The constable was about to shake his head. He looked at the man.

"You're in a hurry, you say?"

"Yes," said the man. "I've left my shop to come here. I should have come earlier. I need to get back."

"All right," said the constable. "Leave it with me. I'll see that it gets to the Rocks."

"Can I have a receipt for it?"

"A receipt? Why do you want a receipt?"

"If you can't find the owner, I'd like it back."

The constable nodded and said, "Of course. I'll have to have one made up. Come back later. Ask at the office. They'll have it for you."

"Can't I get one now?" said the man, hopefully.

"It's busy at the moment. Court starts soon, so everyone is busy. There's a lot to do."

"Perhaps, when I come back, I can ask for you? If you have one prepared, then you can keep it until I come back."

"No. I have to go back on street duty. I won't be here. Like I say, ask at the office."

"How will they know who I am?"

"Tell them you're the jeweller from across the street who handed in a lost locket."

"All right," said the man, still reluctant. "If that's the best way."

The constable held out the locket.

"Perhaps you should take it with you and bring it back later when we're not so busy."

The man hesitated and looked at the constable as though assessing his character.

"No, it's all right," he said. "I'd have to explain everything again to someone else. You keep it and I'll come back and get the receipt later."

The man turned and walked back through the door.

That was easy, thought the constable.

He'd done that sort of thing before. People always wanted to have done with a matter. He'd gambled that the man wouldn't want to take the locket away and have to come back again. Of course, the man should have hung onto the locket and simply put an advertisement in the paper like most people.

Looking down he admired the locket again and ran it between his fingers.

"What do you have there?" said a voice from behind him. Startled, he dropped the locket and looked before bending to pick it up. It was a constable from the local lock-up. He didn't know him well, but presumed like most of the police he had little time for honesty.

"It's a locket," he said. "A man just handed it in. Said it's lost."

He looked at the other constable. There were now two in the conspiracy, or the locket would be handed in as the man had expected. The matter was now in God's hands and the outcome would depend on the other constable's honesty.

"Let me see it," said the other constable.

Taking it, he ran it between his fingers.

"Nice. Looks new. Found it, you said?"

"That's what he said."

"Does he know who you are?"

"No. What do you think I should do?" said the constable, shaking his head.

"I'd keep it if I were you. If you don't want to, I will."

"It's nothing to do with you," said the constable, quietly, but felt like shouting.

"It's everything to do with me. I know you've got it and I know how you came by it. If you keep it, you have me to deal with. On the other hand, if you hand it in, you're a fool."

The constable was aghast. He'd dealt easily with the man, but the constable was another matter.

"Be reasonable," he said. "I don't know what it's worth, but I expect not a lot. I'm sure there's not enough for both of us to share."

"I think it's worth a few pounds and that's a lot when you earn about three bob a day."

"I don't care what you think. Give it back, or I'll take it back."

The other constable smiled and put the locket in his pocket.

"You will, will you? And how do you propose to do that?"

"Like this!" shouted the first constable, angrier than he could remember. He reached for the other constable's pocket, but the other constable was too quick and easily stepped to one side. However, in doing so he fell into a group nearby.

"Steady on," shouted one of the men in the group.

"What's going on here?" bellowed a huge voice.

Startled and distracted from their confrontation, both constables turned to see a police sergeant moving quickly towards them.

"That man pushed me!" shouted a woman in the group beside the constables, her voice shrill and filled with indignation.

"Did he now?" said the sergeant. "Well, we'll see about that. My apologies, madam. I trust you are unhurt?"

"I'm all right," said the woman. "This is a beastly place at the best of times. The behaviour of your men only makes it worse."

"I'll get to the bottom of it, madam," said the sergeant, touching his hat lightly with his finger and bowing slightly. "Good day to you all."

The group moved away, and the sergeant turned to the two constables.

"You. I don't know you. What your name?" he asked, addressing the constable who had bumped the lady.

"It wasn't me! He pushed me!" exclaimed the man and pointed at the other constable.

"Pat," said the sergeant, nodding at the constable. "What's this about?"

"Sergeant. It's a private matter."

"Don't try my patience, Pat. The public's opinion of the police is low enough as it is without such rough-house behaviour. Out with it, or I'll put you both on a charge."

"I was given a locket for safekeeping. He took it from me," said Pat, pointing at the other constable. "I was trying to get it back."

"What's your name and watch-house?" asked the sergeant, turning to the other constable.

"Joseph Dole. Druitt Street."

"Is what he says correct?"

Pat watched on helplessly. A few minutes ago, he'd managed to gain a very fine locket. Now, he had lost the locket, he might be on a charge and even lose his job. Once again, everything depended on the other constable.

"It is," said Joseph, "but I was only having fun."

"Give me the locket," said the sergeant, holding out his hand. As he took the locket, he realised a small group had gathered around them, no doubt more interested as it took their minds of more serious issues. Now, they all had to be careful.

"Who gave it to you, Pat?"

"A man. He said he found it. Thought if he turned it in to us, we'd find the owner."

The small crowd nodded approvingly.

"I'll see to it," said the sergeant. "I'll make sure it's restored to its rightful owner."

Just then, the doors to the court opened.

"I have to go, sergeant," said Pat.

"Me, too," said Joseph.

"Fair enough," said the sergeant. He put the locket in his coat pocket. The constables and the group around them headed for the court.

"Pat," called the sergeant.

Pat Riddell stopped and looked back.

"We'll have a talk when we're both next at Bathurst Street."

"All right," said Pat and turned back to the court. It clearly wasn't over. He wished he'd never seen the locket.

8. THE SERGEANT

The sergeant watched Pat walk away.

I wonder what's really happening?

All his dealing with Pat so far had been good. They'd only worked together for a few months. Pat had been at Harrington Street watch-house until it was closed in 1847, then he'd transferred to Cumberland Street and recently to Bathurst Street. The sergeant had always been at Bathurst Street. Some of the police were ex-convicts, but neither the sergeant nor Pat had that dubious honour. He'd seen the other constable before but didn't know his name until that morning. Still, he was confident Pat would tell him the truth when the time came.

There were still some people standing and sitting in the court anteroom, certainly waiting their turn. The sergeant glanced around. It was a depressing place. The structure itself was dark and gloomy, being originally part of the markets next door. Noise and offensive smells came from the markets, adding to the odious nature of the place. The sergeant had been here many times in his professional capacity but could never wait to get out. He only came this morning because his Inspector had asked it of him. The Inspector was meant to check on all the patrolling constables, making sure they covered all their territory in a timely fashion. Druitt Street wasn't part of his territory, but the sergeant knew Pat was here and thought if he checked on Pat, he could say that he'd been diligent standing in for the Inspector.

He headed for the doorway and stepped out into the weather. The southerly that had recently come up was still blowing and there was enough rain to be uncomfortable. Already he'd had enough of the rain and was glad of his knee-high boots as he strode across the flag stones outside the court. It was obvious why the Inspector had asked him to do the patrol. He smiled to himself. There was a lot of competition to be an Inspector and he hoped that by doing favours for the Inspector he might improve his chances.

Coming out the York Street entrance of the Court he looked across the road and saw a jeweller's shop. Momentarily, he entertained the idea of getting the locket valued, then dismissed the idea as foolish. It didn't matter what it was worth, the main idea would be to return it to its rightful owner. The area around the markets had long been flagged, but the rain still managed to lie in puddles. His boots meant that the puddles mattered little, it was more other refuse and rubbish that lay about in piles that needed to be avoided. He supposed the City Council did their best to maintain the streets, but there was no doubt it was a battle. On the spur of the moment, he decided to return to the watch-house in Bathurst Street. It was unlikely there would be much criminal activity on such a miserable day, so checking on the constables seemed unnecessary.

He walked along York Street, heading towards the Old Burial Ground on the corner of George and Druitt streets. St Andrew's Cathedral was visible through the rain and mist on the other side of the ground. For some reason, there was a wall around the Burial Ground. The sergeant was never sure if the wall was meant to keep the living out or the dead in.

When he reached Druitt Street, he crossed it and turned right, heading down the hill towards Darling Harbour. The low-hanging cloud made it hard to see the harbour, although there were occasional glimpses of ship masts when the wind tore the clouds away. Water poured down the gutters in Druitt Street, churning up the recently laid kerbing and guttering. It was obvious they needed a better system than the flag stones and timber being used. He turned left at Kent Street and walked along until he passed the Baptist Chapel on the corner of Kent and Bathurst, crossed Bathurst and stepped into the watch-house with a sigh of relief. One of the best features of the watch-house was that it had no prisoners, only police and their administration, so it had none of the smells and sounds associated with human misery.

He stepped into a small room, built to the usual type of watch-house design. Two cells and an area with some chairs and a few tables. A stove against the back wall and a door at the back that led to the privy. The cells weren't normally used as detainees were taken to Druitt Street, although they had been used a few times when a riot or such had occasioned an unusual number of detainees. The room didn't require much space as the constables were meant to be out maintaining law and order. The building was designed to house prisoners, but holding prisoners cost money and it was easier to walk them up the street.

Pulling off his Macintosh water-proof cloak he hung it on a peg on the wall near to the door, ignoring the water that fell to the floor. It wasn't police issue and there was often criticism of anyone that wore them, but it was better than getting wet.

Grateful that the room was empty, he walked over and checked the teapot on the table near the still-warm stove. He pulled off the lid and peered in, pleased to notice there was still some tea in it. No doubt it had been there for a while, but a hand placed on the side determined it was warm, so he poured some into a pannikin, added four spoonful's of sugar, stirred it absently and sat at the table. He was still wet from the rain, so he pulled his chair closer to the stove after throwing in a few more lumps of coal from the scuttle nearby. The stove was kept going all day both summer and winter to make tea. It would burn more fiercely when the colder months arrived.

The rooms were always neat and tidy. A woman came by and cleaned the stove and the floor. There wasn't much else to do as the men weren't there most of the time. He'd seen her a few times. She was really old, and he always felt sorry for her, helping her with anything that needed to be lifted or carried. If there was no one else there, she would sometimes chat with him. He supposed she did that with everyone. She said she was a widow and lived on her own down in Sussex Street, not far away.

Once, she'd been a farmer's wife at Windsor, living out in the Hawkesbury with him and her two children. She'd been born in Sydney, where she had met and married her husband. He'd been transported as a convict, eventually becoming a ticket-of-leave man due to his good behaviour. Her father was a prosperous importer, so she'd had a good upbringing and a good education. It wasn't surprising that her parents disagreed with her choice and would have nothing to do with her and her husband.

"Where did you meet?" asked the sergeant, curious.

"He was a gardener at Government House, and we lived near to there. He was always very nice to me. There weren't many nice men in the Colony."

"Was he older than you?"

"Of course. But not that much. He couldn't read or write and didn't know how old he was. It didn't matter."

She'd tried to convince her parents that they were wrong, but nothing she said made any difference, so they married anyway. Not long after, her husband had been allocated to a farmer in the Hawkesbury and they'd gone out soon after the area was first settled.

They'd been happy there she said, had five children, but the first three had died very young. He asked why, but she didn't know. She wasn't alone, she said. Many children died when they were only little.

The last two, a boy and a girl grew up and they were wonderful children, part of a happy family. Eventually, her husband became a free man, but they liked Windsor and were part of the community. They stayed with the farmer.

Then her husband had died. Her voice trembled as she talked about it.

"It was the start of my trouble," she said. "First, he died, the next year my boy was drowned on the floods, trying to cross a bridge. I thought the farmer would send us away, but he didn't. My daughter and I tried to work like men, so he'd keep us, but it wasn't easy. It must have been too hard for her. One day, she took ill and never recovered. She was sick for about six months. I couldn't stay there after she died. I'd lost everything. I came back to Sydney. I was lucky to get the job here."

Confident that he wouldn't be disturbed, he pulled the locket from his pocket and rolled it between his fingers. Not having looked at it before, he was struck with the workmanship.

What did Pat say? Someone had found it and given it to him? For safekeeping?

He sighed and slipped it back into his pocket. It was a mistake to tell Pat that they'd have a talk later at the watch-house. Pat would not be in a hurry to come back. Something had gone on between Pat and the other constable, but the sergeant wouldn't find out what until he talked with Pat. There was a process to manage property reclaimed from thieves where the police advertised such property and sought the owners. Of course, the locket may have been stolen and subsequently lost. The sergeant decided it was best to leave the matter until he could talk with Pat.

Picking up his pannikin, he realised he'd finished his tea. He'd been so preoccupied; he'd not even taken time to enjoy it. Not yet ready to go back out on patrol, he thought to pour another cup, but the teapot was cold and almost empty. He took the teapot out the front of the building and emptied the leaves into the gutter. The rainwater flushed them away quickly, taking them on their short journey to the harbour a few hundred feet away.

Stepping back into the watch-house, he went to the water-tub to add more water to the teapot to rinse away the remaining leaves, only to discover it empty. He picked up the water-bucket and walked in the rain the few hundred yards to the fountain at the corner of Kent and Market Streets. The rain had reduced to a drizzle, but the wind was still strong from the south and the walk most unpleasant. Still, he felt more useful than sitting in the watch-house, contemplating the locket. Normally, he would make several trips and fill the tub, but the weather was such that he wasn't in the least motivated by service to his fellow policemen. There'd be more than enough water in the bucket to suit his purposes.

He'd filled the bucket to the brim and had to swap hands several times on the return journey due to its weight. It was a relief to get back to the watch-house. Filling the kettle, he put it on the stove and sat back in the chair waiting for the water to boil.

A short time later, a shadow filled the doorway. It was Pat.

"Marcus," said Pat.

"Hearing over?" said Marcus.

"All done. Guilty. Five years hard labour."

Marcus shrugged.

"Any tea in that?" asked Pat, pointing at the teapot.

Marcus shook his head at the same time as the kettle started to bubble, indicating the water was ready.

"I'll make it," said Pat and picked up the teapot, heading for the door. He stopped, feeling the weight of the teapot.

"No need to empty it," said Marcus. "That's all done. Just needs tea and water."

Pat made the tea and put it on the table to settle. He retrieved a pannikin and sat beside Marcus.

"All right," said Marcus. "Tell me about the locket."

"Nothing to tell," said Pat, shrugging.

Marcus stared at him.

"All right," said Pat. "Feller came into the court. Said he'd been asked to return it to the owner if possible. That's all."

"Why'd he come to the court?"

"Said he was looking for the police. I told him to take it next door."

"How come you had it then?"

"Well, he asked me to help. I said I would."

"What did he want you to do?"

"Like I said, return it to the owner."

"Pat. Don't make this harder than it needs to be. There's only an hour or so before we knock off and I don't want to waste the time in word games. Just tell me what Joseph had to do with it."

"All right," said Pat. "He took it from me. Said he was going to keep it."

"Why did you care?"

Pat shifted uncomfortably in the chair, before picking up the tea and pouring it into the pannikins. Both men put sugar in the tea and stirred it.

Marcus waited, saying nothing. Pat shifted uncomfortably again.

"All right," said Pat, exhaling and slumping his shoulders. "I was wondering if I should keep it. Then Joseph took it, put it in his own pocket and suggested that we sell it and share the money."

"What was wrong with that idea?"

"Are you serious?" asked Pat, staring open faced at Marcus. "What do you mean? Do you think it was a good idea?"

"No, but I wonder why you didn't."

"I don't trust Joseph. I decided that he'd betray me somehow."

Marcus nodded. It was an honest answer. Marcus didn't trust Joseph either.

"I'll tell you what," said Marcus. "I'll keep it and make sure it's returned to its rightful owner."

"Are you going to report me?"

Marcus stared at Pat who shifted uneasily under the stare.

"What's to report?" said Marcus. "I can't report you for an idea. Let's leave sleeping dogs lie. I'll worry about it from here."

Marcus stood up and pressed a hand on Pat's shoulder.

"Don't worry, lad. They can't send you to gaol for what you're thinking."

Pat looked relieved and smiled.

"Thanks, Marcus."

Marcus resumed his seat, and they finished their tea in silence.

"Time to go," said Marcus, getting up from his chair and fetching his Macintosh from its hook. Pulling it on, he stopped in the doorway, looking out before stepping out into the gathering darkness.

9. THE WIFE

Marcus set out along Kent Street. He lived with his wife, Sally and baby son near Millers Point, almost the full length of Kent Street away to the north. The walk took twenty to thirty minutes, the time taken depending on whether he hurried or not. Kent Street was in good condition for the first few blocks, kerbed guttered and surfaced and buildings on both sides. Then it gave way to more open areas where there were no buildings yet, although Darling Harbour with its buildings on the wharves, anchored ships and busy local traffic was clearly visible to his left. As he drew closer to his rented home, worker's cottages like his own and made of timber appeared. There was talk some of them would be pulled down to make way for stone terraces, but Marcus doubted it would ever happen.

Reaching his cottage, Marcus could see the Lord Nelson Hotel not far away and briefly thought to go for a drink before going home but decided against it. There were many reasons not to do it, not the least of which was he couldn't afford it. Even before he pushed the door open, he could hear the baby screaming. That's all he ever did. They'd been to see some doctors, but none could find anything wrong. Yet, the constant screaming was hard to endure, and Marcus wondered how his wife could stand it.

The four-roomed cottage was comfortable for the three of them, although some of the neighbours had four and five people living in similar circumstances. The main advantage for Marcus and his wife was that being a little run-down, the rent was only three shillings a week and was manageable, although the recent doctor's bills had been difficult to accommodate.

Sally looked up helplessly when he stepped into the room. Marcus felt the familiar surge of resentment when he looked at her and the baby.

Why did he have to endure this? Other men's wives coped with their baby. Why not his?

As soon as the feeling rose, he suppressed it. At heart, he knew it wasn't her fault, but the sadness and unfairness of it all was becoming too much to handle. Sally was still young and very pretty. She could be the woman in the locket, but of course she wasn't. However, it might brighten the moment if he showed it to her. Something to take both their minds off the difficulty of parenthood.

"He won't feed," she said, "I've tried and tried. He just screams all the time as though he's hungry but doesn't want to feed. Oh, Marcus, I've no idea what's to be done."

Their son lay in a basket on the floor, red in the face and screaming. Marcus was sure the scene hadn't changed for hours.

"There, there," he said, sitting beside her and holding her, trying to find words to comfort her.

Sally started to cry too; little sobs drowned out by the cries of the baby. Marcus was momentarily crushed by his inadequacies as head of the family.

"Don't cry," was all he could think to say.

"I've had enough, Marcus. I don't know what to do. I had no idea it would be so hard to be a wife and mother," she sobbed.

He looked at her helplessly for a few moments, watching her sob.

"Here, look at this," he then said and passed her the locket.

"Oh, it's beautiful," she gasped between sobs.

Sally fondled it for a moment, pressed the clasp and studied the portrait.

"Is that me?" she gasped, momentary pleasure in her voice. "Where did you get it? What does it say?"

"No, it's not, but it does look like you. That's why I gave it to you to look at," he said, ignoring the question about the words.

"Is it mine? Can I keep it?" she asked, hopefully, all thought of tears forgotten.

"No, somebody passed it in and asked us to find the owner."

"Why do you have it here? Shouldn't it be at the watch-house or the headquarters?"

"I haven't had a chance to turn it in yet," he lied. It was too much to explain the full story.

"If no one knows about it, why don't we keep it?"

"There's a few people know about it. The man that turned it in and two police constables."

"Tell them you've given it back to the owner. Who's to know differently?"

"I don't know why you want to keep it. You can't wear it."

"I don't want to keep it. I want to sell it."

"Sell it?"

"We need money to buy some laudanum for the baby. The doctor said it might help."

"Doctor?"

"I went and saw another doctor today. I know there's something wrong with him." She waved a hand towards the baby.

She only ever called the baby him. Marcus wished she would use the baby's name. It was as though he wasn't a person yet.

"Why don't you use his name?"

She looked at the baby and whispered, "I don't know."

"Perhaps he doesn't feel welcome," said Marcus without thinking.

"Do you think it's my fault? Is that it? Why don't you say it?"

"No, no," he said quickly, "that's not what I think at all."

She stared at him for a few moments, red in the face from anger and crying.

Why does it always go like this? Her saying what she thinks I think and me denying it? Why can't we be happy?

"What's laudanum?" he asked.

"The doctor said it would help him sleep."

"How much is it?" he asked.

"A shilling an ounce," she said matter-of-factly, as though they'd not even discussed their baby.

"How much do you need?"

"The doctor said two or three ounces. He said to give some to him every time he cries."

"I could get some other work. Earn the money."

She stared at him, saying nothing. She didn't have to.

"All right, all right," he said, "let me think about it."

"Don't take too long, Marcus. I can't take this much longer."

He nodded dumbly and went out back to wash up before supper.

Supper that night was a terrible interlude between getting home and going to bed. Not a word passed between them, and Marcus thought it better to say nothing as Sally tried several times to feed the baby. He wanted no more arguments that night.

Removing his uniform and hanging it behind the door gave him an opportunity to study the locket again. The portrait did look like Sally, so they could say it was his except for the three people that knew it wasn't. He sat on the bed and studied the words by the light of the candle. They made no sense to him, but he didn't doubt they would not help them to claim the locket. Perhaps Sally was right. The best thing to do was to sell it and use the money for medicine for the baby. He had a feeling that his marriage was the cost of being honest.

He woke several times in the night to the baby crying and Sally trying to feed him.

There must get some value in what she does, or the poor mite wouldn't be alive.

Once he was woken by the sound of a neighbour pounding on the wall.

Don't worry. I'd stop it if I could.

A rooster heralded the dawn, and he got out of bed, dressed in his uniform and made some tea and porridge for breakfast.

Sally joined him at the table. He raised an eyebrow.

"Asleep," she said, "but it won't last long. Have you decided what to do?"

"Not yet. I need another day. It's risky. I've not ever broken the law and I don't like the idea of doing it."

"If you can't get the money, you have no other choice."

"I could lose my job."

"That's not all you could lose."

"All right, all right. We'll talk about it again tonight."

He let himself out the front door, nodding briefly to the neighbour who had pounded on the wall.

"Restless night?" said the neighbour. "You should take that baby to a doctor. Babies shouldn't cry all night."

"We have."

"There's something wrong with him. If the doctor didn't say so, take him to another doctor."

"My family is none of your business."

"If it stops me gettin' a good night's sleep, it is. If you don't do somethin' about it, there's a few of us'll get you thrown out."

"I'm sorry, mate. We're working on it."

"Well, get a bloody move on. I can't take too many more nights like that one."

"All right, all right," he said for the second time that day.

He set off down Kent Street. The day was a little better, the wind was still from the south, but had dropped. A glance skyward revealed a leaden sky with the promise of more rain.

There's got to be more to life than this.

He was halfway to Bathurst Street when he realised, he'd left the locket on the bedside table.

No matter. It'll be safe there.

10. THE PAWNBROKER

Marcus had a horrible day. He didn't see either Pat or Joseph, but his mind was occupied all day with the idea of keeping the locket. The reasons to keep it were obvious, but so was the reason not to do so. He decided for and against all day. By the end of the day, he was exhausted, but still hadn't decided.

It was nearly dark when he stepped into the front room of the house. Sally was sitting in a chair, the baby lying quietly on a blanket at her feet. Marcus was both stunned and relieved.

Perhaps they wouldn't need the laudanum after all.

Sally smiled one of those happy smiles that he had forgotten.

"See, just like I told you," she said.

"Told me what?" he asked, relief in his voice.

"Like the doctor said, he just needed some laudanum."

"Laudanum? What do you mean? Have you given him some?"

"Yes," she replied, her voice a little nervous this time.

"Where did you get it? I thought we couldn't afford it."

"I pawned the locket," she whispered.

"You what!" he shouted, all the blood draining from his face. He stared at his wife, incredulous. The baby continued to sleep.

It was done now. He'd been worrying about it all day, and it had happened anyway.

All the things that could go wrong flooded his mind. They'd be found out and he'd lose his job. He'd be branded a thief, might even go to gaol. The police sometimes talked about what happened at the hands of other prisoners to policemen in gaol.

He pulled out the chair beside her and slumped into it, his mind racing with terrible thoughts of what might now happen.

"Oh, Marcus," she said and placed a hand on his arm. "I knew you couldn't do it, but it had to be done. See? It's worked. He's been like that since I first gave him some."

"I'm a thief," he said, disbelief and resignation in his voice.

"No, you're not. I pawned it. But I'm not a thief. You found it. I think that means it's yours."

"No, Sally. I didn't find it. Someone else found it and asked me to return it to the owner."

"Who said you didn't? Don't you see? You're worried about nothing. Just say you returned it to the original owner."

"And who shall I say is the original owner?"

"It doesn't matter. You forget. You've got a lot on your mind."

Marcus thought about what she'd said.

"Which pawnbroker did you use?"

"The one in Kent Street. Near to the watch-house."

"How did you know to use that one?"

"You've talked about him. You said he's sly."

"Did you give him your name?"

"Yes."

"Did you wonder why he might ask for it?"

"No. I just assumed he needed it."

"Do you know what they do with it?"

"No," she said, fearfully, as though she knew what might be coming.

"And your address?"

This time she just nodded.

"I have to get it back," he said. "They can trace it back to you."

"Trace it back to me?" she said in a soft, trembling voice.

"Yes. There were some changes to the Pawnbroker Act a few years back. Now they must keep a record of any items that are pledged. Oh Sally, how could you have been so foolish?"

"I didn't know," she wailed. "I only did it for us, for the baby."

The baby made some slurping sounds.

The doctor was right, thought Marcus, marvelling at the transformation.

"Can you redeem it?" asked Sally. "He said I could redeem it."

"I have to find some money. How much did he give you for it?"

"Two pounds," she said, a hint of pride in her voice.

"I don't know how I'll get two pounds."

"I didn't spend it all."

Marcus just nodded, overwhelmed by the size of the problem and the lack of options.

"Maybe I can see him and ask for it back? We could owe him the money," she said, tentatively, but without a shred of confidence.

"Maybe," he said, his voice trailing off.

They sat for a while without talking, listening to the baby.

"Be grateful for small mercies," his mother used to say.

Well, Sally was right to get the medicine, so now it was his problem to resolve how to pay for it. No one would investigate the locket for a few days, so he had some time to work out how to retrieve the locket.

"Let's have supper," said Sally.

Marcus nodded absently, trying to work out what to do.

11. BLACKMAIL

Once again, Marcus spent his days at the watch-house fretting about anything but police business. On the third day he'd decided he would have to have a plan before the next day.

Just after noon, Joe Dole came into the Bathurst Street watch-house. Marcus was about to leave. He thought he might walk down Kent Street and stop at home for a few moments to see if his wife was all right. She'd been out of sorts that morning and he had left without even saying goodbye.

"Joe," said Marcus, nodding to acknowledge him.

"Leaving?" queried Joe.

"Just about to. What are you doing here? I thought you were from Druitt Street?"

"Can you stay for a few moments?"

"If you want. What's up?"

"Had a funny thing happen this morning."

"Funny?"

"Interesting."

"All right. What was it?"

"I was told to check on the pawnbroker in Kent Street."

Marcus tried to keep a neutral expression, but already his stomach flipped.

Joe stared at him, saying nothing. Marcus stared back, afraid that if he said something, it would only make matters worse.

"I found this," said Joe and put the locket on the table.

"What's this?" asked Marcus, staring at the locket with a look he hoped could be interpreted as disbelief.

"Pick it up. Check it out. See what you think."

Marcus fingered it. "It looks like the one that you and Pat gave me the other day in the court."

"Is it?"

"How can it be?"

"That's what I thought."

"All right, Joe. What's going on? What are you up to?"

"I was going to ask you that."

The men stared at each other for a few moments. The conversation had reached a stalemate. Marcus didn't want to say anything and lose whatever advantage he had left. He knew Joe was after something, but Marcus had decided he'd make him work for it.

Joe broke. "I thought you were going to return it to its rightful owner. What's it doing in the pawn shop?"

"It's not in the pawn shop."

"That's where I got this."

"What makes you think this is the locket you gave to me and what are you doing with this locket anyway? How did you get it from the pawnbroker?"

"I liberated it," said Joe with a small smile.

"Liberated? Took? Stole? What do you mean? How did you get it?"

"Is it the one you took the other day?"

"How can it be? I'm still trying to find the owner. Tell me about how you got this one."

Marcus still held the locket.

"I saw it in the pawn shop. It looks just like the one you took the other day. Same portrait, same words."

"What do the words say?"

"Don't you know?"

"No."

"They say, 'To my beloved. From your heart. William.'"

"Why did the pawnbroker give it to you?"

Joe coloured slightly and stammered, "He didn't. I took it."

"You stole it?"

"Borrowed it. I plan to take it back."

"Take it back?"

"Yes, I only borrowed it."

"Let me get this straight. You think this is the same locket as the one the other day and you decided to borrow it. Why?"

"The pawnbroker wants to make a deal."

"A deal?"

"Yes," Joe stammered, "a deal."

"All right, Joe. I'll give you all the time you need. Tell me about the deal."

"The pawnbroker said he'd pay us to leave him alone. A few pounds a week. I noticed the locket in his shop. I asked to see it, he showed me. I told him it looked like the one that had been found the other day. He said it had been pledged by a woman, said her name was in the books and he'd get it for me. I told him not to bother."

"Why did you tell him not to bother?"

"I knew it would be you."

"You think I look like a woman?"

"No, but I knew you would have arranged someone else to pledge it."

"And why would I have done that?"

"I'm guessing that because his shop is not far away, and he'd know you."

"Wouldn't you think I'd take it somewhere that I wasn't known?"

"He doesn't care if people that pledge property don't own it."

"He takes stolen goods?"

"If that's how you want to put it."

"Why didn't you arrest him?"

Joe stood silently as though wanting to be sure he wasn't about to make a big mistake.

"He wants to make a deal."

"Why are you telling me?"

"You pawned the locket. You might want in on the deal. You came across so high and mighty the other day, but you're the same as the rest of us. You're not afraid to make a bit on the side when you can."

"Is that so?" asked Marcus quietly.

"Yes," said Joe, but all the confidence had fled from his voice.

"Joe, I still have the locket I liberated, as you call it from you and Pat the other day. I'm not interested in making any deals and you aren't either. Take this locket back to the pawn-broker right now and if he wants to make a deal, or has any stolen property on his premises, arrest him."

Joe stared blankly, clearly afraid of Marcus.

"Am I clear?"

Joe nodded.

"Say something. Am I clear?"

"Yes, you're clear."

Joe continued to stand.

"Do it!" shouted Marcus. "Do it now!"

Joe took the locket and left the watch-house. Marcus sat and buried his head in his hands. After a few moments, he got up, adjusted his clothing and set off down Kent Street in the fading light of an autumn afternoon, his walk slow and his heart heavy.

What now?

12. THE MISTAKE

As he walked down Kent Street, he realised everything had moved beyond his control. He had to get the locket back and turn it in at Cumberland Street watch-house. There'd be time elapsed before he could do so, but he could always maintain that he'd kept the locket at home before turning it in. That Joe had found the locket at the pawnbroker's was a damning development, but if Marcus could get it back, all was not lost. His anger against his wife grew with every step. Sure, he'd brought the locket home, but she had no right to take it and pawn it.

Damn the woman!

Getting angry wasn't going to help. He had to come up with a plan to get the locket back.

Should he wait and confirm with Joe that it had been returned? No, there wasn't that kind of time available. He had to get it back tonight and turn it into the police first thing in the morning. How? He could redeem it, but that would cost two pounds.

How? How?

There was only one way and that was to take it back? What had Joe said? Liberate it?

Before he got home, he resolved to go the pawnbroker's after dark, break in, collect the locket and turn it in at Cumberland Street in the morning. He tried to console himself that he wasn't stealing, he was only retrieving his own property and even though his wife had received money for the locket, the pawnbroker was a thief anyway.

Stepping through his doorway and closing the door behind him, he resolved to say nothing to his wife. He would supress his anger and hope that the whole mess would just go away.

The room was nearly dark.

"Darling? Are you here?" he called. There was no answer, nor any sound from their child.

Now, where could she be?

Before he could light a candle, there was a knock at the door. He opened it. In the remaining light of the day, he saw Joe.

"Joe? What the hell are you doing?"

"I came to see you."

"Just a minute. I have to light a candle."

Marcus went back to the room, lit a candle and carried it to the door.

"What do you want?"

Joe seemed to sway, but Marcus couldn't smell alcohol. It must be the light from the candle.

"Can I come in?"

"If you wish," said Marcus and stood to one side to let him in. "Well?"

"I don't believe you," said Joe and Marcus had the impression that he continued to dance in the light of the candle as the flame moved about.

"About what?"

"That you still have the locket."

"Of course, I've still got the locket! What is this insanity? Have you been drinking?"

"No but show me the locket. If you still have it, show me."

"I'll do no such thing and you have no right to ask me."

Marcus struggled to control his anger.

"How dare you come to my home and question me? Make allegations! Tell me I'm a liar!"

"Then show me! Show me the locket! You say you've got it. Show me!"

"You've taken leave of your senses, Joe. What are you trying to do?"

"I think you've pawned the locket. I took the locket back to the pawnbroker. He was angry that I had taken it, accused me of stealing. I told him why I took it. He told me there could only be one and told me to tell you that you're a thief and a liar. If you don't show me the locket right now, we either strike a deal with the pawnbroker or I'm going to the inspector."

"The inspector? You're going to the inspector? What do you plan to tell him?"

"That you stole the locket and pawned it."

"You fool! The inspector doesn't even know about the locket! Why do you think he'll give a damn?"

Joe stared at Marcus, a look of triumph briefly crossing his face.

"I think when I tell him about the locket and he asks you to show it to him, he'll give a damn. I think you will too."

"You're testing my patience, Joe. If you don't leave immediately, I'll throw you out!"

Joe looked at Marcus briefly, shaking his head as if in disbelief.

"Your choice, Marcus. You and I leave and see the pawn-broker, or I leave and see the inspector."

"Get out of my house! I don't care what you do!"

Joe left and Marcus collapsed into a chair. He had no choice now and had to retrieve the locket from the pawnbro-ker's. But how? He couldn't just ask for it. If they could find the money, he could get his wife to get it back, but there was no way to do that before the morning. The inspector may not be interested, but that was too big a gamble.

Where the hell was Sally? This was as much her problem as his. After all, she'd pawned the damned locket!

As he sat there, a plan began to form.

The locket was in the shop somewhere, so he'd need time to find it. He could go and see the pawnbroker, demand to see the locket and then he'd know where it was kept. Later, well after dark, he could go back and steal it. Of course, if he was caught robbing the shop, it would all be over, but that was better than being confronted by the inspector and be unable to show him the locket.

Wearily, Marcus rose from his chair, blew out the candle and went to the pawnbroker's. He had to walk almost the full length of Kent Street, so there was plenty of time to draft a plan. The pawnbroker was known to him as he'd inspected the shop before, usually finding some irregularity, but he couldn't come up with a reason to ask about the locket. Joe had said he'd told the pawnbroker that Marcus had stolen it, so the pawnbroker would be suspicious of any request by Marcus to see the locket.

When he reached the shop, he was both surprised and grateful to see it was still open. He knew the pawnbroker lived at the back, but dreaded the idea of pounding on the door if the shop was closed. Pushing the door, he stepped inside and was immediately recognised.

"What brings you here so late in the day?" queried the pawnbroker.

"I've come to see about the locket."

"Of course, you have. Where's Joe? I thought he'd be with you."

"No, he's not with me."

"He'll need to be here."

"Why?"

"A deal is only a deal if it involves the three of us."

"We're not doing any deal."

"Then it's your funeral."

"Not if there's two lockets."

"Have you got one?"

"Yes. I want to compare them to see if they're the same."

"What is it with the police? I turned my back and Joe stole it. How do I know you won't do the same?"

"I just want to see it. You can hold it if you want."

"Fair enough."

The pawnbroker reached into a drawer, pulled out the locket and put it on the counter.

"Let's see yours too."

Marcus picked up the locket and pretended to study it.

"They're not the same," he said.

"Well, let's see yours."

"I don't have it with me. I didn't bring it, being close on dark. I didn't want to be robbed."

"A policeman? Not wanting to be robbed? That's a good one," muttered the pawnbroker, returning the locket to the drawer.

"I trust that's the end of this nonsense. As I told Joe, I've a good mind to arrest you both."

"On what charge?"

"Interfering with the police in the execution of their duties."

"You'll have trouble proving it."

"That's why I'm not arresting you. However, take this as a warning. Any more of either you or Joe talking about a deal, and I will arrest you."

"All right, all right," muttered the pawnbroker. "Still, Joe said he was going to see you and tell you that if you didn't have a locket, he would see the inspector."

"He saw me, I showed him the locket and I told him what I'm telling you," said Marcus and turned to leave the shop. "Like I said, that's an end to it. Good night."

As he walked off into the gathering darkness, he reasoned the lie about Joe was worth it. It added credibility to his story, and it would be unlikely that Joe and the pawnbroker would collude once Marcus gave the locket to the inspector in the morning. He'd decided that was best and he could say he was turning the locket in to be returned to its rightful owner, that he'd been planning to take it to Cumberland Street but felt confident the inspector would better see the matter addressed.

He wandered the streets for an hour or so, being careful to stay away from the Bathurst Street watch-house. It wouldn't matter if he was seen, but he'd have to concoct a story as to why he was there and thought one lie for the day was enough.

Eventually, he was back in Kent Street and saw the pawnbroker's shop in darkness. It wasn't a good time to think over what he was about to do, but after a few moments, he again reached the conclusion that he had no choice. He hated the predicament, hated breaking the law, and hated having no other choice.

The gas streetlights cast long shadows about the building, and he waited until he was sure he was the only person in the area. He crossed the street; gravel crunching under his boots and approached the door of the shop. Breaking glass would attract undue attention and he hoped he'd be able to force the door without making any noise. He reached the door, gripped the handle and tried to push it open and as he did so, he wished he'd come better prepared. A piece of iron or steel would be better than simply pushing or pulling at the door, so he'd need to find one. He wasn't concerned about walking away at this point as he could simply say he'd been testing the door to make sure it was locked. Enacting the pretence, he turned the handle and to his astonishment, the door opened. The pawnbroker must have forgotten to lock it!

Without thinking, he pushed the door open and stepped inside. It was easy to find the counter, open the drawer and find the locket. There was a noise behind him, the sound of a striking match and light from an oil lamp flickered in the room.

"I thought you'd be back," said the pawnbroker.

Marcus turned and saw the pawnbroker, no longer in shadows and standing at the end of the counter. The light from the lamp showed the triumphant look on his face and the revolver he held, pointing at Marcus.

"Perhaps I should call the police," said the pawnbroker. "What do you think? Would that be a good idea?"

Cursing himself for his stupidity, Marcus tried to keep any emotion from his face. He was trapped and he knew it. There was no way to explain his presence there, nor the fact he held the locket in his hand. Still, if he could get away, it would be the pawnbroker's word against his and who would believe a sly pawnbroker? He put the locket on the counter.

"I'm going to walk out of here and you're not going to stop me."

"Sergeant, you've got guts, there's no doubt about that. However, this gun is loaded and I'm not afraid to use it. You're on my premises and I'm entitled to protect my shop."

"I'm not sure how you'd explain an injured policeman."

"Dead policeman."

Marcus felt a stab of fear. He hadn't thought the pawnbroker would use the weapon.

"I can walk out the door and everything goes back to how it was."

"Not everything," said another voice from the shadows near the back wall.

Marcus peered into the darkness. Joe stepped out.

"I think you might be ready to discuss that deal now," he said.

Marcus looked from one to the other. The pawnbroker was one thing, Joe was another entirely.

"All right," said Marcus, stalling for time. "You can put that gun down. I never discuss deals with anyone pointing a gun at me."

The pawnbroker put the gun on the counter. It wasn't that far away, only a foot or so. The thought crossed Marcus's mind that he might be able to get to it.

"What's this deal?" asked Marcus, resting his elbow on the counter and leaning forward, as though interested. "And you, Joe, come over here too. I can't talk to you while you're back there."

"That's better," said Joe, "now we're getting somewhere."
He came over and stood beside the pawnbroker.

"You two tell me about the deal," said Marcus, his voice
soft and friendly. "I suppose I have to be interested now."

The pawnbroker and Joe looked at each other as though to
work out who would describe the deal. In that instant, Marcus
pounced.

13. THE MURDER

Marcus got his hand on the revolver, but the pawnbroker was almost as quick and seized Marcus's wrist. Joe stared in disbelief as though the unthinkable had happened. Marcus launched himself forward and crashed into both the pawnbroker and Joe. All three fell to the floor.

Joe screamed, "Stop! Stop! We don't need to fight about this!" while Marcus and the pawnbroker fought over the gun. Marcus held the revolver while the pawnbroker held his wrist, yelling all the while, "Joe! Joe! For God's sake help me! Take the gun from him!"

The lamp on the counter was next to useless to help the antagonists determine who was where. The area behind the counter was in darkness, so Marcus worked entirely on feeling. He reasoned where the pawnbroker's face was from where his hand held Marcus's wrist, so Marcus launched a flurry of blows as hard as he could with his free hand. He thought he was hitting flesh and decided he was probably right when the hand holding his wrist began to lose its grip. At the same time, he kicked as hard as he could with his feet. In the tangle of bodies, he had no idea of a target, just hoped he could inflict some damage.

"For Christ's sake, Marcus, stop fighting!" shouted Joe. "Before someone gets hurt!"

"You fool!" shouted the pawnbroker, "I'm already hurt!"

Marcus now had the gun, but the pawnbroker or Joe was lying across him and he couldn't get his arm free.

"I've got the gun now!" he shouted, "get off me before I use it!"

Marcus felt a hand move across his that held the gun. He managed to get a better grip on the gun, but it was a waste of time. The hand covered his now and a finger went into the trigger guard and the next moment, squeezed the trigger. The noise of the gun in the confines of the room was shockingly loud.

"I'm hit!" shouted someone. "You bastard, Marcus! You've shot me!"

Marcus had no idea who had pulled the trigger, nor who had been shot. It was not what he'd expected, and certainly not what he wanted.

"All right, all right!" he shouted, "let the gun go and I'll do the same!"

The grip of the hand on the gun didn't lessen at all.

"I can't let it go while you've a hand on it!" he shouted.

He felt a blow to the side of his head, then another and he was afraid he'd lose consciousness.

"Marcus, it's Joe. You've shot the pawnbroker. I think he's dead. Don't move. I'll get the lamp."

"Joe? Is it you that's hit me?"

"No."

"Then the pawnbroker's not dead."

"Off course I'm not dead, but that's no help to you. You've shot me though and you'll pay for that!"

Marcus felt another blow to his head and released the gun.

Joe held the lamp above them, and Marcus could see the pawnbroker sitting on the floor, leaning against the counter. His face and shirt were bloody, and he held the gun in his hand, pointed at Marcus.

"You've shot me Marcus, you clumsy fool!" shouted the pawnbroker and coughed blood.

"I'll get a doctor!" shouted Joe. "You look like you need one too, Marcus. Your head is bloody."

Marcus couldn't speak and nodded weakly. He was still dizzy from the blows and could feel blood running down his face.

"Leave the lamp, Joe. I want to watch this bastard," said the pawnbroker.

Joe put the lamp on the floor between the two men and left the shop.

Marcus looked at the pawnbroker and knew he was the more seriously hurt. He hoped Joe would hurry and he didn't want to add murder to the charge of stealing. Not that anyone would know he was a thief. It was the pawnbroker's and Joe's word against his, but the whole story was now very messy, and he doubted he'd emerge from the event with his career intact.

"You shouldna shot me," said the pawnbroker weakly. "You didn't need to."

"I didn't. Someone put their hand over mine and pulled the trigger."

"Do you expect me to believe that?"

"It doesn't matter. That's what happened. Anyway, you're not that injured that you couldn't hit me. What did you use?"

"This," said the pawnbroker and held up a clock in his other hand. "I hope Joe hurries. I think I'm dying."

"Then you'd better give me this," said Marcus and reached for the gun.

"And have you shoot me again? Not likely."

Marcus watched the pawnbroker. There was no doubt he was dying and probably would do so soon. The hand holding the gun was unsteady and the barrel dipped towards the floor several times before the pawnbroker rallied and pointed it towards Marcus.

"Take it easy," said Marcus. "We don't want it going off accidentally."

"It won't go off accidentally. If it goes off, it's because I mean it to."

After a few minutes, the pawnbroker slumped against the counter and the gun hand fell to the floor. Marcus reached forward to retrieve the gun. He gripped the barrel and pulled it towards himself. It went off.

14. A SHOCKING OUTCOME

Joe returned to the shop without a doctor. He knew there was one in Bridge Street, but it was too far to go to fetch him. After checking several places where he thought a doctor lived, he asked a passer-by with a cart if he could help him move some injured men to a doctor's premises in Bridge Street. The man reluctantly agreed to help, and they drove together to the pawnbroker's.

When they pulled up outside, Joe jumped down and told the man to follow him. They stepped into the store and Joe called, "Marcus?"

There was no sound and Joe peered around the corner of the counter. The pawnbroker was slumped against the counter and Marcus lay on the floor in front of him.

"Jesus!" shouted the man behind him. "They look dead!"

Joe checked.

"They are," he said. "They were alive when I left them."

"Did that feller with the blood in his shirt shoot the other one? Looks like they had a fight."

They stared at the men on the floor.

"There's no help for them now," said the man. "Do you still want to take them to Bridge Street?"

"No," said Joe. "You're right. There's no help for them there."

"You don't need me anymore, do you? I mean, you being a trap and all. Sorry. Policeman. I'd rather not be a witness if that's all right with you."

"No, I don't. Thanks for your help. Sorry to trouble you. I'll take care of this."

The man muttered his thanks and left.

Joe slumped onto a chair that had clearly been used often by the pawnbroker and surveyed the scene.

What had happened? Did the pawnbroker shoot Marcus as soon as Joe left?

Joe shook his head sadly. He'd never know. The light from the lamp cast long shadows on the walls. The flame flickered a little but was largely protected by its glass surrounds.

The flame is like a life. There one minute, and flickered out the next.

It was hard to think. This was not at all what was meant to happen. Originally it had been a good way to make a little money. He shouldn't have pushed Marcus so hard and should have known that Marcus wouldn't go along with it. He'd been so accustomed to the police being either corrupt or corruptible that he had presumed the outcome. Well, it was done now and couldn't be undone.

How would he explain this? Why would a policeman shoot a pawnbroker or vice versa? How did Marcus shoot the pawnbroker while holding the barrel?

Then it occurred to Joe that he didn't need to explain it at all. He had simply to leave and let circumstances take their course. There was the deliveryman to worry about, but Joe doubted he'd come forward. The papers would be full of the story, but chances were the delivery man couldn't read and wouldn't come forward to talk about the other policeman at the scene.

He got up to leave. There was nothing more to do here and he would be better not to be found. Then he thought, perhaps he should turn the lamp off? It might be easier for people to believe that a shooting would take place in the dark. He picked up the lamp and put it back on the counter. As he did, he saw the locket. Marcus must have put it there after getting it from the drawer.

Joe permitted himself a smile. The pawnbroker had said Marcus would come and they should wait until the drawer was opened and give Marcus a chance to get the locket before they announced their presence. It could have stopped there, even if Marcus didn't go along with what they wanted. God knows why Marcus started the fight. If he'd succeeded in getting the gun, what was he hoping to do? Arrest them both? His word against theirs? Joe only wanted to stop the fight. He'd thought by pulling the trigger, the gun would fire harmlessly into the counter, the sound would cause them to stop fighting and they'd get Marcus to see reason.

Turning off the lamp, he slipped the locket into his pocket, stepped out into the night and pulled the door closed behind him. He looked quickly up and down the street and seeing nothing, headed home.

15. THE DECISION TO LEAVE

Joe arrived for his shift at Druitt Street watch-house the next morning and the two other constables were quick to tell him that a sergeant and a pawnbroker had been found dead in the pawnbroker's shop. It looked like the pawnbroker had shot the sergeant, but there was only one gun and the pawnbroker himself had been shot. Even if the sergeant had gone to arrest the pawnbroker, he wouldn't have carried the gun, so the gun must have belonged to the pawnbroker or to someone else.

They decided there'd been a robbery, the sergeant passing by had gone to help and had been shot for his trouble. That didn't explain why the pawnbroker still held the gun, unless he and the sergeant had managed to get it from the thief after he'd shot the pawnbroker and the sergeant. The other odd thing was that the sergeant had his hand on the barrel, as though trying to take the gun from the pawnbroker. Nevertheless, it would take a few days to determine if anything was stolen as they'd have to compare the books against the articles in the shop, so everything was conjecture until then.

When asked if he knew the sergeant, Joe said that he'd met him a few days earlier when he'd been at the court. He didn't know him well and expressed sympathy when he heard that the sergeant had a wife and child. Similarly, he said he knew the pawnbroker and had inspected his premises several times. They all agreed the pawnbroker was known to be sly, so there could be any number of explanations for the shootings.

Things settled down and not much happened for the next few days. Joe worried that if the papers carried a story about a missing locket, there might be any number of people to come forward, not the least being the man that handed the locket to Pat Riddel, or even Pat himself. Only Pat could associate the locket with Joe, but if enough people started talking about it, it could lead back to Joe and he would have to deny any further knowledge of it. There was no chance it would be found in his possession as he'd hidden it away carefully, but Pat would certainly remember that he gave it to Marcus and conjecture would begin as to why that was the only item stolen from the shop.

"Oh, what tangled webs we weave,

When first we practise to deceive."

His mother used to say that when he was a boy. She would say it if she caught him lying which he did often enough. He worked on the principle that if he was caught out telling a lie, he told a bigger one. His mother used the lines to remind him of the foolishness of his principle. He thought the lines clever and his mother even cleverer, but they rarely changed his behaviour. In his youth he found that he could often avoid punishment by lying, but he also often found there was a limited period for which the lie would hold. Other circumstances would come to light that would reveal he had told a lie.

It was too late now to tell the inspector that he'd been at the scene of the crime. He could probably have come up with a credible and reasonable excuse for being there, but a man with nothing to hide would have notified his involvement immediately, so now it was a matter of waiting to see if he'd be found out, or his pretence would prevail.

On the following Tuesday morning, he came to his shift to hear that the police had identified that the only item stolen was a locket. There was a description of the locket in the pawnbroker's books and the police planned to advertise in the hope someone would recognise it and assist them to find the murderer. Interest in the case was rekindled in the watch-house and his fellow officers all agreed that the locket was the only item of interest, and it was key to the murderer's intent.

Time was no longer on his side, but fate was.

There was a headline in the Sydney Morning Herald the next morning that said "Discovery of An Extensive Gold Field" and the article went on to describe that a feller called Hargreaves had recently met with some others at an inn in Bathurst and confirmed the discovery of gold in several places west of Bathurst. Joe gasped when he read, "Mr. Hargraves states as the result of his observations that from the foot of the Big Hill to a considerable distance below Wellington, on the Macquarie, is one vast gold field that he has actually discovered the precious metal in numberless places, and that indications of its existence are to be seen in every direction. Indeed, so satisfied is he on this point, that he has established a company of nine working miners, who are now actively employed, digging at a point of the Summer Hill Creek near its junction with the Macquarie, about fifty miles from Bathurst, and thirty from Guyong. Ophir is the name given to these diggins."

The public had been aware for some time that gold had been found in a number of places in New South Wales, but there was little excitement as a result. The authorities had downplayed the finds as they were afraid every convict and outlaw would be encouraged to exploit the finds to their own advantage and police would be unable to contain the lawlessness.

Joe realised that this article and surely others to follow would excite the community and everyone would head west to make a fortune. He'd been handed the perfect opportunity and he'd be a fool not to take it. Several of the other constables asked what he was reading, and he explained it in glowing terms. He wanted to inspire them all with the desire for gold in the hope that it would be more than just himself that would head to the new gold fields. If several of them left, their sudden departure would be associated with the gold rush, and little would be made of it. He had no doubt that the road west would be clogged in the coming days with men of all walks and professions hoping to make a fortune. Everyone had heard of poor men becoming rich in California, that gold had recently been discovered in Victoria and some people had gone there.

In the afternoon, some of the men discussed if they should tell anyone, or just leave. Most of the men thought it best to just leave and Joe encouraged them. He already planned to tell his sergeant that he was leaving to seek his fortune thinking that more likely to show a clear conscience. The other men simply leaving would muddy the waters a little which he thought to his advantage.

His sergeant came by later in the afternoon and laughed when Joe told him he was planning to seek his fortune. It turned out the sergeant knew some men who had gone to Victoria and as far as he was aware, had found little or nothing.

"Don't let me talk you out of it," the sergeant said, patting him on the shoulder. "You'll be one of many, no doubt. Many will go and few will get rich. Still, you might be one of the ones that gets rich, so good luck."

"What will happen to my job?"

"If the digging doesn't work out, get a job in the west. They're always looking for police out there and who knows? If there's a lot of gold, I'll bet there'll be more bushrangers than flies and they'll be needing fellers like you."

"I mean, what will happen here?"

"What do you care? They'll manage somehow. Might even put the wages up so we stay. I suppose you might be doing us a favour."

Joe tried to look concerned, as though his role mattered, and he was a good policeman.

"It's a credit to you that you care. Most wouldn't. I'll make a note on your file. Might make it easier if you decide to come back."

"I'm planning to leave tonight. I'm probably owed some money for this week."

"Go and see the office now. They'll prepare it for you."

"Thanks Edward. You've been a good sergeant."

"That's my job," said the sergeant, obviously pleased at the compliment. "See me if you fail and come back. Like I said, you might stay out there, but if you come back, I'd be happy to take you on again. Good luck."

The sergeant shook Joe's hand and walked out.

Joe went to the office and told them he was leaving at the end of the day. They said they owed him eleven shillings and threepence and he should come back and collect it when he left. When he walked out of the building at the end of the day he was still dressed as a policeman because he owned the uniform, but he was no longer in the force.

16. THE JOURNEY

It turned out it was easier to leave the police force than it was to get to Ophir.

Joe knew nothing about looking for gold, what he should wear or how he would get to the gold fields. When he returned to his rented room in Brickfield Hill, he told his landlady over supper he'd be leaving the next morning. She looked surprised and asked why. He told her and she laughed.

"A few of my tenants are doing the same," she said. "You'll be sorry. There's no shortage of tenants and not many rooms, so don't expect to get yours back."

A small family rented the only other room in the house and their small boy looked excited when he heard the reason for Joe's departure.

"Do you think you'll find some?" he asked.

"Wouldn't be goin' if he wasn't," said the boy's mother and clipped him across the ear. "Mind yer own business. None of yours that Joe is goin'."

"Leave him be," said Joe. "I'm happy to tell him."

"You mind yer own business too, then. None of yours what I tell my boy."

Joe looked at the father who carefully studied his supper, as though he might find gold in there.

"Don't go lookin' at 'im either," said the mother. "None of 'is business. 'e earns the money and I bring up the boy. All got our jobs and our jobs is our own business."

Joe thought it might be good to get away. The boy and the father were all right, but the mother was another matter.

The next morning, he packed his bag and settled up with the landlady. She wanted to charge him the full day because he'd stayed overnight, but eventually they compromised on a half day. He'd decided during a restless night that he'd get to Bathurst and work out how to find gold once he got there. There was no doubt he'd pay more for what he'd need, but it was better than not knowing what to buy, buying the wrong equipment and carrying it all the way to Bathurst, only to throw it away once he got there.

As he stepped out the gate onto Parramatta Street, he felt a moment of misgiving. His plan was to go Stewart's Horse Bazaar in Pitt Street. Sales were mostly conducted on a Saturday, but he might find a horse there and be able to negotiate a fair price. He hoped owners might be bringing stock by for the next sale. He knew a little about horses, enough that he couldn't or wouldn't be cheated. The misgiving related more to the enormity of his step, but he consoled himself with the thought that he had no choice. He'd made all the right moves and received all the right assurances from the sergeant, but he was better off a long way from Sydney when someone came forward about the locket. He sighed, a long, introspective sigh. Freedom always came at a price.

He wanted to stay away from Bathurst and Druitt Streets, so he walked up the hill before turning right into Goulburn Street and then left when he reached Pitt Street. Buildings, kerbing, guttering and street lighting all improved as he headed down Pitt towards the Bazaar. He had a brown, leather carry-all bag which wasn't heavy, so he continued to walk comfortably. Autumn was underway and he often thought of this as the best time of year in Sydney. The air was crisp and clear, the winter winds had not yet arrived and the temperature made for easy walking.

It was a gentle slope up Pitt Street before he reached the level area crossing Bathurst, Park and Market Streets after which he found the Bazaar on the right. The buildings he passed were mostly commercial or pubs, some looking very modern and prosperous. He presumed the Bazaar was located there because of the proximity of the horse races in Hyde Park. It wasn't the only one of course. There were a few places where horses and equipment were traded, but Joe had heard that John Stewart was a veterinarian, so he thought his horses might be in better condition. It really didn't matter, because he couldn't afford to pay more than six pounds for a horse he could ride to Bathurst.

When he arrived at the Bazaar, there wasn't a lot of activity, and his heart sank. It seemed as if he'd made the trip for nothing. Still, someone might be able to help him with a place he could go. He was told the man who ran it wasn't John Stewart, but someone called Sydney Burt.

"Can I see him?" asked Joe.

"Why?"

"I want to buy a horse."

"Tomorrer. Come back tomorrer. Sales are tomorrer."

"I can't come back tomorrow. I must leave today."

"You lookin' fer gold?" asked the man. He was a thickset fellow, wearing a heavy leather apron, heavy boots, a much worn felt hat and a very broad smile. It was hard not to like him.

Joe nodded.

"Bin a few of you fellers by this week. Word's out I s'pose."

"I suppose," said Joe, not sure what he was supposing about.

"There's a feller in Strawberry Hills. He'll have what yer after. I've sent a few fellers there. No one's come back, so I s'pose it's worked out. Anyway, walk down Elizabeth Street. You won't be able to miss 'im. First place you see that sells 'orses once you get to Strawberry Hills."

"Do you know how much?"

"How much what?"

"How much for the horse?"

"You want a saddle and bridle?"

Joe nodded.

"No more than five pounds. Make sure 'e's shod, too. Ask 'im for a geldin'. You can't go wrong with a geldin'."

"Can I say who sent me?"

"If you want, but it won't make any difference. A horse is a horse, and the price is the price."

"All right. Thanks," said Joe and turned back the way he had come.

"Good luck," called the man.

"With the horse?" called Joe, turning to face the man.

The man laughed. "No, with the gold!"

It took Joe a half hour to get to Strawberry Hills. He walked up Market to get to Elizabeth and walked past Hyde Park on the left all the way down the hill after Park Street, then up the hill on the other side past the new burial ground on the right. The road was little more than a track, with potholes and wash-aways all along its length. Walking was harder and he wished he'd done some investigation to avoid the wasted trip in the opposite direction.

Like the man had said, the coper was easy to see. There was a sign to announce the purpose of his place and a small paddock with several horses. The business premises was a dilapidated bark and pole humpy that looked like it was an afterthought. There was a forge nearby and a man working at it, bashing horse hooves with so much energy it looked like he was trying to flatten them out of existence. The man was huge, with massive arms and head. Like the man at the Bazaar, he wore a leather apron that covered most of his body.

Joe walked up to him, but the man took no notice.

"I'm after a horse," said Joe, eventually.

The man simply nodded.

"I'd like to get one this morning, if I can," said Joe after another few minutes, struggling to keep the irritation out of his voice.

"Be done soon," said the man. "Find somewhere to sit. If you can't, find somewhere to stand."

Joe moved away and waited. He looked over at the horses, wondering if they were for sale. One looked at him, ears flicking back and forth. The horse seemed to say, "He takes no notice of us either." Joe smiled; the horse snickered.

"A gelding," said Joe quietly, walking to the post and rail fence and the horse did the same, probably expecting to be fed. The horse started searching Joe through the rails, snuffling and pushing at Joe. He wasn't a tall horse, about sixteen hands, but he had what Joe thought were good lines and a nice roan colour. Some might call him splendid.

"What do you want a horse for?" a voice said, and Joe turned to see the man standing near to him.

"I'm going to Bathurst."

The man stared at Joe for a minute or so, shook his head sadly as though dealing with someone of limited intelligence and said, "Do you want 'im to pull somethin', or do you want to ride 'im?"

"Saddle horse. Gelding."

"Only got one of those."

"I only need one. How much?"

"Do you need a saddle?"

"And bridle."

"Goes without sayin'."

"All right. Horse and saddle. How much?"

"Six pounds."

"I'm told five pounds."

"Who told you that?"

"Man at Stewart's Bazaar."

"He'd know."

"Then it's five?"

"I said six."

"Five pounds ten shillings?"

"Done."

The man turned and went back to the forge.

"Which horse is it?" called Joe.

"That one," said the man, pointing at the horse at the fence.

"What about the saddle?"

"You got eyes?"

"What does that mean?'

"On the fence," said the man, pointing at some saddles on a fence nearby.

"They're saddles?"

"Well, they're not boots. What's the problem?"

Joe walked over and inspected the saddles. There were three and all were in an advanced state of disrepair.

"I can't use those! They're not fit for use!"

"All right. Just the horse. Five pounds and five shillings."

"I can't use the horse without a saddle!"

"Then you've got a problem. If you want to leave your horse while you find a saddle, it'll be six pence a day."

"Six pence a day!" shouted Joe.

"No need to shout," said the man looking affronted. "I can hear well enough."

"Anyway," said Joe, "I don't have time to find a saddle."

"Then your problem is only gettin' worse."

"Do you have any other saddles?"

"Yes, but they cost more'n five shillin's."

"How much more?"

"For you? A man with a problem that's hard to solve? Why, I'd say a pound more."

"That's robbery!"

"I guess you'd know about robbery, bein' a policeman."

"How do you know that?"

"Your boots. Only traps wear 'em."

"I don't have another pound!"

"Sure you do. But I'll tell you what. What're you goin' to do with that carry-all?"

"What do you mean?"

"Where're you goin' to put it on the horse? Tie it somewhere?"

"I suppose."

"You give me the carry-all and ten shillin's, and I'll give you a better saddle, a bridle and some saddle bags. How does that sound?"

"I want to see it all first."

"Fair enough", said the man and went into the bark humpy, coming back moments later with a saddle in better condition and put it on a fence rail.

"What about the saddle bags?"

"Just a minute. I can't carry all that stuff at once."

He went back and came with some saddle bags and a bridle all of which he draped across the fence.

"There you go. Now, empty your carry-all into the saddle bags, give me my money, saddle your horse and bugger off. I've got work to do."

"I'll need a blanket."

"Take one of those sacks. That'll do 'till you can find better."

"Where can I buy some supplies?"

The man looked up at the sun, then at his forge. "Be good to get this done today," he said. "The way you're goin', I'll run out of daylight."

"Only take you a minute to answer."

"And then?"

"And then what?"

"Will you go?"

"Yes, I'll go."

"Parramatta," said the man. "Find the Australian Arms Hotel. Coaches go from there to Bathurst, so you might find someone that's been to the gold fields."

"Gold fields?"

The man nodded.

"How do you know I'm going to the gold fields?"

"You still here?" asked the man and went back to forging the horseshoes.

Horseshoes! I forgot to check if he's shod! Too late now!

Joe fetched one of the sacks and went into the yard. It had been sometime since he'd last saddled a horse and he had no doubt he'd be able to do it but dreaded now making a fool of himself in front of the man. To his astonishment, the horse stood still while he set the saddle in place, tightened the girth and adjusted the stirrups. He also had to make some adjustments to the bridle, but it wasn't long before he was ready to go. At one point, he glanced at the man who was still busy with the shoes.

He led the horse out of the yard, mounted and set off. As he went into the street, the man called, "Good luck!" Joe ignored him, fed up with the man's strange ways. He rode back along Elizabeth Street, then turned left into Devonshire Street, past the Benevolent Asylum on the right and the Government Paddock on the left where a station was being constructed to service the railway line. Construction had started the year before and most people marvelled that it wouldn't be long before Sydney was serviced by a railway to the south and west, although the project was already bedevilled by delays. Carts and wagons that brought goods to Sydney were still drawn up in the paddock and the animals that pulled them grazed nearby.

Turning left onto the road to Parramatta, he reckoned he had about six hours of daylight left. It should be enough to get to Parramatta where he'd have to find somewhere to stay overnight. He already wished he'd spent more time planning the journey and hoped the man was right and he'd find someone to tell him the ropes. There would no doubt be many challenges before he reached Ophir.

17. PARRAMATTA

Joe sat on his horse on a ridge overlooking the diggins at Ophir, several hundred feet above a creek. It was mid-afternoon and still too cold to be comfortable. He'd lost track of time since leaving Sydney and thought it nothing short of a miracle that he'd reached Ophir at all. Pulling his horse to one side to allow others to pass, he surveyed the scene below. It was nothing like he'd expected. For a start, there weren't many diggers. He'd been led to believe there would be thousands, but he reckoned on there being no more than a few hundred. The sound of digging came to him clearly, mostly metal against stone. He could see men swinging picks in holes beside the water and moving dirt with shovels. The ground was all torn up, both beside the water and in the ridges overlooking it.

"C'mon mate, get that bloody thing outa the road," shouted a voice. He looked to see a man driving a heavily laden cart with four large horses. The track was narrow at this point where it turned on itself to leave the top of the ridge and descend to the creek below. Others were on the road as well and all seemed in a hurry to continue their journey now that the prize was in sight. There was nowhere to go to be out of everyone's way, so Joe had no other choice than to tap his horse lightly in the sides with his heels and move on down the hill.

He tried to peer through the gums that grew thickly to assess the diggins. His horse was steady and picked its way along carefully. The track bent and twisted like a snake as it wound its way down. The man with the cart took things even more carefully and it wasn't long before he was left behind. Once Joe reached the bottom, he saw a ford and what must be Ophir on the other side. The ford was about twenty yards wide, looked about knee deep and the water flowed swiftly. He'd heard that gold was to be found at the junction of two creeks and could only guess the ford crossed one of them. He could only see one and wondered if he had the right place at all. Still, the people digging probably knew more about it than him and they couldn't all be wrong.

The horse didn't hesitate, stepping into the water and heading for the other side. Others who were walking also entered the water and their loud gasps signalled that the creek water was cold. Once he had crossed the ford, there was more room between the creek and the hill, and he was able to stop and take in his surroundings.

Joe moved his horse towards the township where only a few buildings and many tents were standing. He'd try to find a place to buy a drink and ask what to do next.

When he'd pulled up at the Australian Arms saddle-sore and weary late in the afternoon four days ago, it had been easy to get a room to stay and to find someone in the bar to join him for a whisky. The problem had been finding someone who knew about the gold fields. People told him they knew a little about the gold rush, but mostly could only talk about the excitement, or repeat what Joe judged to be exaggerated tales of success. Of course, he didn't really know other than what he'd read in the paper, but stories about people finding gold lying on the ground didn't make sense. Nevertheless, he couldn't suppress excitement at the very prospect of looking for and hopefully finding gold.

After an hour or so he tired of making small talk and sat on his own at a table in the corner. His failure to find out what he'd need, how to get there and what he would find was dispiriting and he thought a few moments alone might revive his enthusiasm. He stared at the remnants of his whisky. There wasn't much left, and it might be time to take supper. He was conscious of someone standing near to him. He looked up and nearly fell from his chair.

A very good-looking, well dressed young woman was standing there, smiling at him.

"Hello," she said with a distinctly Scottish accent. "My name's Margaret McKay. They tell me you're on your way to the gold fields."

Joe stood rapidly, nearly knocking his chair over in his haste.

"That's right," he said, unsure of the source of his embarrassment. He wasn't sure if it was that a good-looking young woman would approach him, or that she was aware that he'd been trying to find out about gold.

"Please sit," she said. "I'll join you for a few moments if you like. Perhaps I can help you."

"I'm Joe. Can I buy you a drink?" asked Joe, more interested in the woman than in gold.

"No. I don't drink."

Joe must have looked perplexed, as she added, "I'm the innkeeper."

"Oh, I'm sorry."

She laughed. "Don't be. I'm not."

After studying Joe for a few moments, she asked, "What do you want to know?"

"Everything. What do I need to take? How long to get there? How do I look for gold?"

"I know a little. People talk. If you want to talk to someone that's been there, your best chance is tomorrow morning when the coach arrives from Bathurst."

"They go at night?" asked Joe, unable to keep the astonishment out of his voice. He knew his statement showed he knew little about the ways of the Western Road.

"They do, both ways. The one to Bathurst left on Monday evening. It leaves here around six at night."

"It must be a good road."

"It's a terrible road. Everyone complains about it, but it's the only road for coaches. Riders and walkers can also go through Windsor."

"Do you expect there'll be someone on the coach that knows about digging?"

"Yes, there will be tomorrow."

"What time does it arrive?"

"Early in the morning. Depends on all going well."

She looked at Joe, perhaps wondering if she should continue.

"We got off the topic," she said. "You'll need a tarpaulin, a cooking pot, a pick, shovel and wash pan, some supplies and endless patience. It's cold out there too, so you'll need a coat and blankets. There's talk too that you'll need a gun."

"A gun? Why a gun?"

"There's bushrangers about."

"I have nothing they'd want."

"You could try holding up a sign to tell them, but they might still want to find out what you have. Going out, you'll have money and coming back, you might have gold,"

"I was told I can buy what I need here in Parramatta."

"You can get the supplies as you leave. There's a good grocer in Church Street. I doubt you'll be able to buy the digging equipment. I expect you'll have to get that in Bathurst."

"It might be expensive."

"If you find gold, then that won't matter."

Joe laughed. He'd forgotten how much he enjoyed a woman's company.

"What else do you need to know," she asked.

"Has anyone talked about how you find the gold?"

"One man said they were digging for it along the creeks. Some men use what they call a cradle, and others a wash pan."

"What's a cradle?"

"I don't know. That's just what he said."

"I thought the wash pan was for me."

"Maybe, but they say you use it to separate the gold and the dirt."

"I'll feel silly if I go all the way out there and find there was something I should have taken with me."

Margaret bristled a little and said, "I'm telling you what I know. I can't tell you more."

"I'm sorry," said Joe quickly. "I didn't mean to offend you."

She stood up. "Look for me when you come for supper. I'll see if I can put you with someone who knows more."

"Thank you," said Joe, standing as she left. He was disappointed the conversation had finished on a poor note. He liked her, regretted his clumsy statement and wished the conversation hadn't ended.

Joe took his time with the remaining few sips of whisky. He hoped she might come back, but decided after some time that she was busy elsewhere, and it was time to go for supper. Margaret spotted Joe as he walked into the dining room and put him with a couple who not only knew nothing about gold, but they also weren't the least bit interested in it. He decided he was being punished for his rudeness, so he finished his supper quickly and went to his room, hoping to get a good night's sleep and be ready for the coach from Bathurst when it arrived in the morning.

After a restless night, Joe went down for breakfast and found he was too early. There were a couple of people pottering in the kitchen, but they told him to come back in an hour. He went out onto the street and wondered how to fill in the time. The air was fresh, and a slight breeze blew from the south. There was no point in trying to find a shop to buy what he needed, none of them would be open yet. He wandered around, never going far from the hotel and was again amazed at the number of hotels in Parramatta. There seemed to be one on every available corner, the number causing him difficulty finding the Australian Arms the day before.

The sound of a shrill steam whistle disturbed his peace. He looked in the direction where he thought it came from and saw people hurrying along the road. Following them, he came upon a solid stone bridge across the river and to its right, a wharf with a steamer that looked ready for a trip he supposed to Sydney. It didn't look like it could go further up the river as the low bridge would doubtless prevent it from doing so. Some of the passengers seemed panicked and he could hear barked instructions to them and between them. No doubt the departure of the steamer was imminent. As if to confirm his thought, he watched it pull away from the wharf, its smoke drifting off to the north on the wind as it headed down river. It might have been a better way to come. Steamer to Parramatta and coach to Bathurst. Too late now.

It was probably time to head back. He hadn't gone far when he saw a coach pull up outside the hotel with a rattle of harness and a clatter of hooves.

The coach was a sight to behold. Passengers were both inside and outside, those on the outside looking cold, dishevelled and far from comfortable. The four horses were lathered and panting as though they'd been pushed hard. The coach itself looked too flimsy for the purpose, the wheels, spokes and coach probably made for easier roads and loads. Goods were stacked wherever possible and the whole image was one of a group of refugees fleeing a battle.

Quickening his pace, he arrived back to help the passengers unload from the coach. There was a couple who refused his help, two young men that did the same and one older man who expressed his gratitude. The coachman just looked at him and shook his head.

"Have you been at Ophir?" asked Joe of the only man that wanted help.

"Yes," nodded the man, wearily.

"Digging?"

"No. Newspaper reporter. Are you wondering why I'm grateful for help?" he asked, smiling.

"Perhaps," agreed Joe.

"It's a long trip. There's no sleep on the coach. I don't know that I do it again. You're bounced about. The road's not worth a damn."

The man stuck out his hand and shook Joe's furiously.

"Name's Jacob," he said. "I hope you don't mind taking that bag."

Joe picked up the bag and followed a limping Jacob who to Joe's surprise, carried nothing. Once through the doors they met Margaret.

"Jacob," she said, handing him a key. "Welcome back. Your room is ready. Will you have breakfast now?"

"Yes. I'd like to."

"Perhaps Joe here could join you?"

"If he'd like to."

Margaret looked at Joe who nodded.

Over breakfast Jacob told Joe that he'd spent three miserable days at Ophir camping by the creek.

"There's been rumours for some time that gold had been found in the area. I went to a lecture by Hargreaves in Bathurst in early May. He showed us pieces of gold that he said had been found in Ophir. I decided to go and look for myself."

"Who's Hargreaves?"

"You know. The feller they say found the first payable gold in Australia."

"Of course, of course. I'd forgotten. Please go on."

Joe listened eagerly, still wondering why the man had agreed to breakfast.

"I borrowed a horse and rode out to where Hargreaves said I'd find gold."

"How long did it take?"

"Two days, but part of that was because I kept getting lost. You can do it in one if you set out early enough and you know where you're going."

"What's it like?"

"What's what like?"

"The journey."

"Easy at first. Then, when you get near to Ophir, the hills are steeper and the gullies deeper and rougher. Once you reach Lewis Ponds creek you follow the creek most of the time, but where it's rocky or heavily timbered, you have to climb the ridges. Of course, when you do it's easy to lose your way. I had to double back sometimes and make sure I was still following the creek. It's easier now, I think. There's a track because people are going there every day."

"Did you look for gold yourself?"

"No, just talked to people. Most of them were looking."

"How many people?"

"Couple of hundred. Might be thousands there now."

"Are they finding gold?"

"Most of them."

"Much?"

"Depends."

"On what?"

"Luck."

"Why luck?"

"There's a lot more dirt than gold."

"Where are the lucky ones looking?"

The man sat back and studied Joe.

"That's the funny thing," he said. "There's no rhyme or reason. Well, that I can see anyway. They're finding it along the creeks and along the hills. Hargreaves said it looks like gold country because it looks like California, so I suppose there's such a thing as a place to find gold. It'd be better if there was a sign saying 'dig here'. The people at Ophir are only guessing and even when they dig within a few feet of each other, one group would find a lot of gold and the other very little."

"Where did you stay?"

"I took a tarpaulin and blanket and slept under the stars. There's nothing there. There's a shepherd's hut, but Hargreaves's men are using that."

"Hargreaves's men?"

"He's hired some fellers to dig for him. I tried to talk to them, but they weren't very friendly."

"I thought he'd do the work himself."

"He's more interested in the reward for discovering the gold field."

"What are you going to do now?"

"I told Mrs McKay that I'd speak tonight at a meeting she's arranged."

"Mrs McKay?"

"Yes, Margaret."

"I didn't know she was a Mrs."

"Disappointed, eh?"

"No. Not at all. I just didn't know."

"It doesn't matter. Her husband is dead. Died about a year ago. She's kept going with the inn."

"She talked to me last night about Ophir. Told me as much as she knew. I liked her."

"Everyone does. She's very popular."

"So, you're practising on me before you talk to the meeting tonight?"

"Bit of that. I got sick of talking to grumpy people at Ophir. Besides, I slipped and hurt my leg while I was there, and I was grateful for your help this morning."

"I didn't do much."

"You didn't need to do much. They don't let you take a big bag on the coach, so there wasn't much to carry."

"What do you think I should do?"

"Are you serious about looking for gold?"

"I think so."

"That's not a good start. You have to be very serious and very committed. Don't worry that you don't know what you're doing. Most don't know what they're doing. They set out with great hope and finish with great disappointment. Having said that, some do find gold, and some get rich. It's all about luck, so if you're lucky then give it a go."

"Should I go on the coach?"

"Have you got a horse?"

Joe nodded.

"Use your horse. You'll need it once you get to Bathurst."

"How long will it take to get to Ophir?"

"Three or four days to Bathurst, depending on how hard you ride. I'd take it easy if I were you. The road over the Blue Mountains is difficult and dangerous in parts."

"Are there places to stay?"

"There are, but it will cost you money. Besides, you'll need to practise with your tarpaulin and see if you're ready to endure the rigours of life outdoors."

"How long should I go for?"

"Take supplies for a month. There's talk of them setting up stores at Ophir, but go prepared. You should be able to take enough to last a month."

"Where should I get them?"

"What do you mean?"

"Margaret said to buy what I need here in Parramatta."

"It'll be cheaper here, but you've got to get it to Bathurst. Your horse will struggle to carry everything, so you're better to get what you can in Bathurst, so you won't have to carry it so far. Buy clothes, blankets and supplies to get to Bathurst here, but buy whatever else you need once you get there."

"Won't it be more expensive?"

"Yes, but that can't be helped, unless you join some others with a cart. I'd go on my own if I were you. Get enough to get you to Bathurst then get what you'll need for the rest."

"What about my horse?"

"Good question. You'll need to take some oats, but you won't carry enough to feed him. You'll need to find somewhere there you can let him graze."

"What did you do?"

"Took enough oats."

"What did the diggers do?"

"There's a feller there looking after their horses. Maybe you could use him."

"Where should I dig?"

"Fellers that are there are digging where they like and hoping for the best. There's talk you'll need a licence. If that happens, you'll need to stake a claim and you won't be able to dig wherever takes your fancy."

"I don't know anything about it, so fancy doesn't come into it."

"That's not the point. You tell the Commissioner where you want to dig, he'll mark the area for you and that's the only place you can dig."

"I wouldn't know where to tell him!"

Jacob leant back and laughed.

Joe was embarrassed. He didn't think what he'd said that was funny.

"That's right," said Jacob. "Like I said, there's no signs 'dig here'. Everyone's the same. It's all about luck."

"Where did you see people finding gold?" asked Joe after a few moments.

Jacob was suddenly serious.

"All right. Listen carefully. I'll tell you what I think, but I might be wrong. I decided the gold starts on the tops of the hills. Might have been left there millions of years ago. From there, it's washed down to the creeks. It's heavier than anything else, so it falls through and gets left on mud or rock. So, you either look on the top of a hill that hasn't been weathered yet, or down by the creek where you dig through the sand and gravel until you get to clay or mud."

"Is it mostly in Ophir?"

"Ophir's just the name of a place near the junction of Summerhill and Lewis Ponds creeks. I think there's gold in the hills and creeks all around there, but like I said, you've mostly got to do a lot of digging to find it."

Joe was about to ask another question, but Jacob stood up.

"I'm tired," he said, standing and smiling broadly, "no sleep at all last night, so I'm off to bed. I hope I've helped. Good luck and remember me if you become rich."

"I will," said Joe. "Let me pay for breakfast. Least I can do."

"As you wish," said Jacob and limped out of the room.

Joe finished his tea slowly, thinking about all he had learned. None of it sounded easy and all of it unlike anything he'd ever done. He had no experience at living outdoors, certainly not on the ground under a tarpaulin. For a moment, he thought about going back to Sydney, re-joining the police and hope there was no repercussion from the incident in Kent Street.

He sensed a presence and looked up to see Margaret standing nearby.

"Do you mind if I sit?"

"I'd be delighted if you did. I came looking for you last night to apologise for my thoughtless comment."

Margaret sat.

"Don't worry about it. What do you think now you've spoken to Jacob?"

Joe laughed.

"You're right to ask. Nervous, excited and a little afraid. I've never done anything like it."

"Like what?" she asked, smiling.

"Ridden a horse for over a hundred miles, lived in the open under a tarpaulin and tried to find a fortune by digging a hole in the ground."

"What have you got to lose by trying?"

"Nothing," he said shaking his head. "It's not what I've got to lose, it's what I've got to gain."

"Are people finding gold?"

"Jacob said some are."

"I heard that too. No one really knows if they'll find a lot of gold, but if they do and you had a chance and didn't take it, you'll regret it for the rest of your life."

"You sound like you're speaking from experience."

"Maybe, but I see a lot of people. I think you have more than one reason to go west, and I think if the price of an opportunity to become rich is some nights outdoors, then it's worth it."

"If I'm not gone too long, will you be here when I get back?"

"I'm not planning on going anywhere."

Margaret got up and left without another word. Joe finished his tea, went to his room and fetched his bag. He settled his account for the room and lodging but didn't see any more of Margaret.

Joe went and got his horse from the paddock nearby and visited three stores on the way out of town to buy a tarpaulin, a coat, some blankets and some supplies. By the time he arranged it all on his horse, he thought he looked like a gypsy.

18. PENRITH

Joe rode out to Penrith on the Western Road. He'd decided not to go through Windsor but hadn't put much thought into the decision. It just seemed like a better idea to go the way more frequented. If something went wrong, he'd be more likely to get help.

He was surprised by a toll just outside Parramatta. He'd already paid a toll on the road between Sydney and Parramatta and was annoyed to pay more. When he told the tollkeeper as much, the man laughed and told him to get used to it.

Another surprise was the number of people and vehicles on the road. There seemed to be many different types of vehicles, pulled along by horses, oxen and mules and even some people walking. Some were carrying picks and shovels, so he decided most were going to the gold field. He felt an urge to hurry, to beat them all there, but decided that if it took four to five days, he'd beat anyone in a wheeled vehicle and certainly anyone that was walking.

It was late afternoon and there were a few people gathered around when he reached the punt at Penrith which would take him across the Nepean River. When the punt arrived, it easily accommodated all those waiting. It was about forty feet long, sixteen wide and over two feet deep. Joe was glad there were only riders and pedestrian traffic because even though the man assured him the punt could easily accommodate two teams, he was pleased none wanted to cross. The cost was six pence and the man told him he could return for free provided he came back within a day.

"Can I cross for threepence if I don't come back in a day?"

"Not how it works. Sorry," said the man. "C'mon, a few of you men, help pull on this rope. We'll cross faster if you do."

Joe and some other men pulled on a rope that passed across the ferry and connected it to both shores. The ferry moved easily across the river, and they reached the other side in no time. There were three riders in the group that had crossed and the other two pulled up at an inn not far from the ferry. Joe continued to ride and one of the men called out, "You not stoppin'? You should. Be dark soon."

"No," said Joe. "There's somewhere that I need to be."

"Up to you," said the man, "but you'll need to be careful. There're bushrangers about."

19. BUSHRANGERS

Joe hadn't gone far when he realised the stupidity of his action. He had no water, had no idea of where creeks might be, where he could camp for the night, hadn't even tried to use his tarpaulin to make a tent and it was already getting hard to see. Any bushrangers would be upon him before he would see them.

The road wandered around the side of a narrow valley, and he could hear a creek perhaps a hundred feet below on the right and even in the fading light, he could sense rocky overhangs to his left and above him where the road had been carved out of the side of the escarpment. Approaching what he sensed to be a sandstone bridge, he tried to make out other shapes ahead, but thought they were only shadows caused by the gathering darkness.

Sounds of birds and the rustling of animals came to him on the still evening air. They settled his nerves a little. He thought everything would be quiet if there was danger about.

"What have we here?" queried a soft voice from the darkness to the side of the road. Joe had been so focused on the bridge he hadn't seen the rider until he spoke.

"A rider," said Joe.

"I can see that. What kind of a rider?"

"A horse rider."

The man laughed. It was a pleasant sound, humourful and without malice.

"Well, I can see that too. Although, I didn't expect a rider to be on anything else."

"What do you want? It's dark and I'm cold and hungry. I'd like to be on my way."

"Where are you going?"

"None of your business."

"I'm making it my business," said the stranger, all the friendliness gone from his voice.

"That doesn't change anything," said Joe, softly and firmly. He wanted to tell the stranger that he was out of patience but was nervous despite the calmness of his voice. There was no doubt he was on his own in the event of trouble.

"No, it doesn't, but this might," said a voice behind him. Joe glanced back and could just make out a man, standing a few feet away and holding a gun. It was too dark to see any detail of either man, so Joe still didn't know what he was up against.

"It does," said Joe, and turned back to the rider, "but it makes me no more interested in talking. What is it you want?"

"Where are you going?"

"It's still none of your business."

"I'm finished with this," said the voice behind him. "Get off your horse!"

Joe was in a real dilemma. He knew that if he got off his horse, he would certainly be robbed and possibly killed. On the other hand, he could try to ride away, but was still a good target for the man with the pistol despite the darkness.

Without thinking of the consequences, he kicked his horse hard in the sides and rode towards the mounted man. As he did, he hunched in the saddle and braced for the impact. He knew his horse wouldn't deliberately ride into the other horse and would swerve to avoid an impact, but the horses would still collide in some fashion. There might be enough confusion that any shot from behind would miss and once he was entangled with the other rider, the marksman would no longer have a clean shot. Sure enough, his horse tried to stop as he neared the other rider, but Joe threw himself from the saddle, grabbed the other man as best he could and dragged him to the ground. The sound of a gun firing was background noise to the squeals of the horses as they collided.

The men hit the ground hard and were immediately kicked several times by the horses prancing about, trying to avoid the wrestling men. If Joe was trying to create confusion, he got everything he wanted. His opponent seemed to be trying to work out what had happened and was throwing wild punches, not at all sure of where Joe was. Joe realised he was still holding his horse's reins, so not only could his horse not get away, but he was also prancing about above the men on the ground. He thought to let them go, then realised the horse was more dangerous than anything that Joe could do, and it was better to run the risk that he could be hurt by his own horse.

"I can't see a bloody thing!" called the man's companion. "Get out of the way! Let me get a clear shot!"

"Shoot the damn horse!" shouted the man on the ground, not realising his voice told Joe where to find the man's head. He swung the best punch he could to the man's head and the man stopped moving. Joe realised the danger. The man was no longer moving and the other man with the gun now had a target. Joe pulled hard on the horse's reins, and he pulled back hard, dragging Joe to his feet. The man with the gun didn't fire and it was clear to Joe that he wasn't sure if the man pulled to his feet was Joe or his companion. Unfortunately for him, he'd come in too close to get a shot and was now in Joe's reach.

Joe grabbed the man's gun arm and wrenched it skywards. The gun fired again, and Joe knew he'd had a lucky escape. There may not be any more. He let go of the reins and threw himself at his assailant. They fell to the ground and Joe knew he was once again on the ground with an armed man and unable to see well enough to find the gun. It was the last time he'd carry his in his saddle bag. Well, if he lived that long. He needn't have worried. The man tried to bring his gun to bear, so Joe now knew where it was. He grabbed the man's arm and the gun fired again. If he could get hold of the barrel, he might be able to break the man's trigger finger. The man's other fist punched Joe repeatedly, but none of the blows hurt enough to cause Joe to lose focus on the gun. They were short, jabbing blows and probably gave the man comfort that he might be doing damage. Joe sensed the man was losing strength and taking a chance, he used his free hand and reached for where he hoped the barrel might be. He was gratified to feel the barrel in his fist and despite it being hot after being fired, he wrenched it upwards and threw his weight with it.

There was a loud scream from the other man, so Joe knew he'd done some damage and could only hope it was enough to stop the fight. It was a short-lived hope. He'd fallen beside the man, and he could feel fingers grasping for his face. He opened his mouth and kept it open until he felt a finger nearby, pushed his head forward and bit down hard. The man screamed again, and the fingers stopped probing.

One hand still held the barrel and the other the man's arm. He tried to turn the barrel towards where he thought the man might be and hoped that the man might try to fire again. The man started to punch again, short jabbing blows, but lacking any of the previous effect. The bite might have done some damage.

Joe decided his only hope was either to get the man to shoot himself, or to take the gun from him. He reached up from the man's arm, found the finger around the trigger and pushed it. The roar of the gun was shocking so close to his head. Doubtless, it would be the same for his assailant. Despite the man holding the gun, Joe's grip on the barrel and his hand around the trigger meant that he had full control of the weapon. He pushed the man's finger, continuing to fire the gun until it was empty. When he heard the click, he smashed the gun as hard as he could onto the ground. The man released his hold on the weapon and Joe tore it from his grasp.

"Oh, no!" he heard the man groan.

Once again, the words told him where the head was and Joe smashed the gun at it with all his might. The man lay still. Afraid that the man might be pretending to be hurt, Joe struck two more times with all his might.

Joe lay still for a moment. He was exhausted, but knew he had to check on the man's partner. The partner was probably still unconscious, or he would have tried to help his friend, but Joe had to be sure. Still holding the gun, he sat up and tried to get his bearings. He could make out the shadows of the horses standing nearby, the still form of the man lying beside him, and after a few moments the form of another man lying beside the low wall running the length of the bridge.

Still holding the gun, he struggled to his feet and approached the other form.

"All right," he said, "get up."

The man didn't move. If he was conscious, he'd know the gun was empty. If Joe got too close, the fight would be on again. Uncertain, he stood staring at the shape on the ground. Then he fretted he was only giving them both time to recover. A better plan would be to get on his horse, go back the way he'd come, find some accommodation and tell the local police about the attack in the morning.

He squatted beside the man and prodded him with the gun. The man groaned.

"I've got the gun," Joe said.

"What gun?" asked the man, groggily.

"Your friend's gun."

"Where's he?"

"Over there," said Joe, indicating with his head, even though he knew the man wouldn't see the movement.

"Is he dead?"

"Probably."

Sensing a movement behind him, he stood and tried to look back but before he did, he was attacked by a weight on his shoulders and an arm around his neck. The man that he thought was unconscious had jumped him. The man in front of him struggled to his feet, facing them, his legs against the wall and his hands on top of it, but he was too close and only hindered his companion. Joe and his assailant fell to the ground and as they did, they pushed the other man off the bridge. There was a short, sharp scream, a thud and a splash. Under his attacker, on the ground Joe swung the gun in a wide arc and this time made sure to connect with the man's head. He went limp. Joe rolled him off, got onto his knees and belted the man as hard as he could once more on the head with the gun. This time there was no mistake. Joe peered over the parapet but could see nothing in the darkness.

The fight was finally over, and Joe knew he was lucky to be alive. He didn't know why other than it wasn't his first fight ever and he supposed he'd learnt a thing or two. Returning to the figure on the ground, he felt for a pulse and found none. It would have been better if the blow had been successful the first time. At least his companion would still be alive. Deciding to take advantage of the turn of events, Joe threw the gun off the bridge, then picked the man up and threw him off too.

Joe was used to death. He saw it often enough as a policeman, so there was no regret or guilt about the men's demise. The only fear he had was being found out, but he knew there was nothing that he'd left behind, nor any reason that he'd be associated with the men. Their death could have happened any time before or after he got to the bridge.

It took a few moments to find the horses. His own and that of the man he'd ridden into. They weren't far away and stood silently, looking in the direction of the bridge as though marvelling at the humans and their ridiculous behaviour.

Joe mounted his horse and continued with his journey. The other horse followed for a few moments, then turned back as though realising its loyalties lay elsewhere. There was doubtless another horse back there to keep it company. It was completely dark now and Joe knew he would have to find somewhere to stay soon, or he would have to turn back towards the ferry. He was sore from his fight with the men but didn't expect he'd show any evidence of it so he could deny any knowledge of the events at the bridge if ever asked. As far as he knew, he carried no obvious physical injuries from the fight.

20. LAPSTONE

He was about to turn back when he saw an inn, or what he hoped would be an inn. As he rode up, he could see the building was single storey with a veranda, a half dozen doors and windows and the same number of veranda posts. Breathing a sigh of relief, he pulled up outside, dropped the reins and went into the building using a door that he hoped would be the main one. As he pushed the door, he could hear sounds of merriment which he took to be confirmation it was an inn.

The room became suddenly silent when he pushed open the door and stepped in. There were about ten people in the room, mostly sitting at tables, but one man was standing behind what looked like a bar. It was so small, there was barely enough room for him to stand behind it. Candles burned on every table and in several places around the walls. The candle flames moved slightly as Joe closed the door behind him. There was a fire burning brightly in a fireplace to his right and the people nearby had moved their tables and chairs away from it. No doubt the fire was too hot for those up close.

"What're you after?" asked the man behind the bar as all the others stared at Joe with unified curiosity.

"Not much," said Joe. "A drink, a meal, a bed and somewhere for my horse."

"Use one of the lanterns out front," said the man, "and put yer 'orse in the paddock. Put the saddle and bridle in the stable. You'll find it easy enough. Then come back and we'll see to the rest."

Joe did as he was told and returned in about ten minutes. No one was interested in him when he returned. He warmed his hands by the fire for a few moments before joining the man at the bar.

"What'll you 'ave to drink?"

"What do you have?"

"The usual. Beer, cask or bottle. Rum, wine and whisky."

"I'll have a whisky."

The man fetched a small glass, half-filled it with whisky and pushed it across the bar.

"That'll be a shillin'."

Joe found a coin and passed it over. "Busy night," he said.

"Always busy," said the man. "Travellers."

"Any coming back from the goldfields?"

"What's it to you?"

"Nothing. Just interested."

"Where're you goin?"

"West."

"Goldfields?"

"Maybe."

"Some of these other fellers are goin' there. See that table with the four fellers? They're 'avin' a drink, somethin' to eat and then sleepin' in their cart."

"I didn't see a cart."

"Probably too dark. It'll be out there somewhere. 'orses'll be in the paddock. Did you see 'em?"

"Didn't look."

One of the fellers got up from the table and came over to the bar.

"Four more," he said, his voice unsteady.

While the barman half-filled the glasses, the man turned to Joe.

"You goin' west?" he slurred.

Joe nodded.

The man looked poor. His clothes were ragged and torn, he looked dirty and smelled worse, but what bewildered Joe most of all was that he looked defeated. It struck Joe as odd that the man was heading to the gold fields without hope. *What was driving him?*

"So are we," said the man and waved an arm in the general direction of his companions. "Wudjer like to join us?"

Joe must have looked stunned, because the man laughed. It was a pleasant sound, more like a chuckle.

"No," said the man, shaking his head. "Not west. Just at the table. Bring your drink."

"When's supper?" Joe asked the barman.

"Whenever you like."

"I'll finish this first and then have supper," said Joe, picking up his whisky and turning to the man. "Yes, I would. Do you want help with those?"

"Nah," said the man, picking up two glasses in each hand and heading for the table. He stopped at the table, put the drinks down and turned back, waiting the moment or two it took for Joe to catch up. He stuck out his hand and said, "Dan."

Dan was young, although it was hard to see how young in the poor light from the candles. His hair was dark and short, as was his beard. His stood medium height and looked thin and starved. The semblance of defeat hung around him as though he had found the business of living beyond his capacity. And he was drunk. Very drunk.

Joe took his hand and said, "Joe."

"These're my friends. This'un is John," said Dan, pointing at a slightly older, grey-haired man.

John stood, shook Joe's hand with a firm grip, studied him intently, but said nothing.

"And these young fellers are Luke and Tim."

The evening was full of surprises. None of John, Luke or Tim seemed the worse for the drink. Joe wondered how Dan had managed to consume more than the others.

John was smiling. It suited him.

"We picked Dan up in Penrith," he said. "We'd arranged to meet him at Perry's Rose Inn. We were late leaving Windsor and Dan found someone to have a drink with, so he got a head start. It was nearly night by the time we got to here, so we decided to stop and try to catch up."

"Do you live in Penrith, Dan?" asked Joe.

"Nah. Mulgoa. Snot fer. Maybe a nour's ride from Penriff."

Dan stopped for a moment, as though struggling to find more useful information. He shook his head, stared at John and said, "I've 'ad nuff. Off to bed. See you in the mornin'." He stood up unsteadily, tried to walk and swayed against the wall behind him.

"Tim, Luke, help him to the cart," said John. "Roll him in a blanket and put him under it."

"What'll we do then?" asked Tim, looking crestfallen.

"Whatever you want. Come back if you want or stay there."

"What about Dan?"

"What do you mean?"

"If we come back?"

"He'll be all right. It's not as if it's the first time."

"C'mon, Tim," said Luke. "We've 'ad enough."

"There's still supper. We 'aven't 'ad supper."

"There's food in the cart. We'll boil the billy 'n' 'ave a cuppa."

"I was enjoyin' myself," said Tim, shaking his head sadly.

"There'll be a next time," said John.

"'Ope so."

The boys each took an arm, steadied Dan and headed for the door. No one in the room took any notice. Joe decided it must be a frequent occurrence.

John watched them go then turned to Joe.

"You haven't touched your drink."

"Hasn't been time," said Joe, picking it up and taking a sip.

"You been diggin' already?"

"How's that?"

"Your hands."

Joe looked at his hands. The knuckles were scraped, raw and bleeding. He laughed.

"No. Not yet. Scraped 'em earlier."

John produced a half-smile of disbelief.

"None of my business, anyway. Finish that and I'll get you another."

"I'd rather take my time."

"Up to you. I'm up for a drink and this is as good a place as any to have it. We'll just get our own. Will that be all right with you?"

"That's all right with me. I'd like a drink, but I'd like to take my time."

John got up and walked to the bar. Joe was glad of the few moments of respite. He was still unnerved by his encounter with the bushrangers, glad to be still alive and afraid that John might ask more questions. There was little to no chance he'd be associated with the two bodies. It was more likely that it would be deemed an accident, but he needed to be long gone before they were discovered and theories advanced as to the cause of the accident.

Returning from the bar, John slumped into his chair, took a large sip from his drink and sighed appreciatively.

"Where're you off to?" queried John.

"West."

"Gold?"

Joe nodded.

"So are we," said John.

"Dan said."

"I didn't hear him say anything about that," said John, squinting suspiciously.

"At the bar, when he invited me over."

"Ah! I suppose it's no secret, but I told 'em all the less said the better. There're bushrangers about."

"Why would a bushranger be interested in anyone going to the goldfields?"

"They know you need money for supplies. It's theirs if they rob you before you get there."

"If I was a bushranger, I'd rob people on the way back."

"You aren't, are you?"

"What?"

"A bushranger."

"No."

John laughed.

"As if you'd tell me. Anyway, you don't look like one."

"What do they look like?"

"Dan."

Not all of them, thought Joe.

"Why do they look like Dan?"

"Down on their luck. Not much money and less future."

"Is Dan a bushranger?"

John laughed.

"No, just looks like one."

"Maybe you and the others'll fix that."

"Dan doesn't think so."

"Why's that?"

"He's been digging in California. Didn't do any good there and thinks we'll do no better here."

"Then why're you going?"

"My idea. I like the idea of finding a fortune in the ground. I talked Dan into it."

"Why?"

"He knows what to do."

"It seems he may not."

"How's that?"

"He didn't do any good in California."

John laughed. Joe liked it. He could become friends with this man.

"There were other reasons for that. I'm hoping none of them will happen here."

"All right. You've got my interest. What happened to Dan in California?"

John looked around. Joe wondered if he was checking that Dan was not about. Others were, but no one paid them any mind. The room was warm making the atmosphere convivial and the chatter from other tables meant that no one else would hear John. A brief look about seemed to satisfy John that he wouldn't be breaking any confidence.

"Dan was married," he said, in a voice more serious than he had used before.

"In California?"

"No," said John, shaking his head. "Before I start, I'd like to get another whisky."

"I'll get one, too."

"Give me the money. I'll get it for you. You stay here. We don't want to lose the table."

John was right. More people had come in and most of the tables were now taken. Joe counted out the money, John left and was back in a few moments with two whiskeys.

"He wants to know when we plan to have supper," he said, jerking his thumb at the barman once he had put the glasses on the table.

"I'm hungry. Now would suit me. What is there?"

"He said boiled mutton with bread and cheese."

"All right with me."

"I'll tell him, and I'll be back."

John came back, settled in his chair.

"Tim won't be disappointed," he said.

"That he's missed supper?"

"That's right," he said, took a sip of his whisky and resumed the story.

21. CALIFORNIA

"She was such a pretty girl. Young, happy, and full of life. Dan met her a couple of years back on a property in Mulgoa Vale. She worked as a domestic servant for a wealthy farmer. He had cattle, sheep, vineyards, all manner of things.

"Dan went there to collect some wheat our da had bought. He had the idea to grow some like that in Windsor. I didn't know much about it, but he said it was better wheat."

"Are you and Dan brothers?"

"No. Well, maybe. I called Dan's father Da, but he wasn't my da. When Dan's da married my ma, I called him Da."

"But you're older than Dan."

"My ma was older than Dan's da. That's just how things work sometimes."

John took another sip of whisky and stared at Joe for a moment or so.

"I don't have to tell Dan's story. We can find other things to talk about if you like."

"I'll be quiet."

"Dan come home with the wheat and all he could talk about was this girl he'd seen on the farm in Mulgoa Vale. None of us knew what to make of it. Ma quizzed him, but he didn't even know her name. Hadn't even spoken to her.

"A week or so later, Dan was gone the whole day. Ma was worried and Da was furious. When he came home that evening, he said he'd been back to the farm. Now Ma was furious, too."

John laughed at the memory. Joe resisted the urge to ask more questions.

"We were sitting at the table over supper. Da told Dan he couldn't just go away like that. There were jobs to do and riding around the country didn't get anything done. Ma asked him what he thought he was doing. What would he gain by going there? Dan just sat there, eating his supper and ignoring the questions.

'Well,' said Ma.

'Well, what?' asked Dan.

I thought Da was going to hit him.

'You can't speak to your ma like that!' he thundered.

Dan pushed his chair back and stared at both of them.

"'Do you forget?' he asked. 'Do you forget what it's like? How did you feel when you first met each other?'"

John put his head back and laughed out loud. People at the tables nearby looked at him and shook their heads in annoyance.

"Of all the questions that Dan could ask, that was the one that stopped them both in their tracks. See, I was old enough to remember when they met. Dan wasn't. He was too young."

Despite being told to stay quiet, Joe couldn't help himself.

"Well? How did they meet?"

"It was arranged by the church. Dan's mother and my father died around the same time and the thoughtful neighbours and churchgoers thought our family needed a father and Dan's needed a mother, so they suggested the families come together. I suppose it seemed like a good idea at the time. There was no courtship, just a wedding and my ma and I moved into Dan's and his da's place. It was big enough and as far as I know, my ma and Dan's da have never shared a room or a bed."

John laughed again, even louder this time and again incurring cross looks from the tables nearby.

"So, you can see why Dan's asking how they felt when they met was the right question to ask."

John sat silently, lost in memories of the past while Joe reflected on the incongruity of sitting in an inn talking about the ironies of life having just fought a battle to the death. Australia was not a place for the faint of heart, or for people committed to niceties and protocol.

Joe wondered if he should ask John to resume the story when the barman arrived and put a plate of bread and a plate of cold mutton and cheese on the table.

"That'll be four shillin's," he said.

"Two each?" asked John.

"No. Four each."

They each counted out the money, the barman left and Joe and John sat staring at the plates.

"I suppose we use our hands," said Joe.

"What else?" said John, reaching out and folding some mutton and cheese between two slices of bread.

"I've 'ad worse," said John after taking and chewing several noisy mouthfuls. "Do you want to hear the rest of the story?"

Joe nodded, happy to divert his mind from recent events.

"It took a while the next morning to convince Dan that we should all go to Mulgoa Vale and meet the family. Da said he had things to do, Dan was worried that he'd be embarrassed because the girl wouldn't be interested, but Ma insisted. She said we owed it to Dan. After enough cups of tea to drown an ox, we all agreed and off we went. Da and Dan knew the way of course and Da knew the farmer, so we all agreed he'd do the talking.

"We got there late in the morning and the closer we got, the more excited we all became. It was something of an adventure for all of us except Dan and he just became more nervous. Pulling up outside the house, Da asked for the farmer who came out after a few minutes.

"'Patrick,' the farmer said, 'what brings you and your family here? Is there something wrong with the wheat?'

"'Nicholas,' said Da, 'it's a private matter. Do you mind if we talk?'

"'Private?' said Dan. 'How's it private?'

"'There, there Dan,' said Ma putting a hand on his shoulder, 'let yer da do the talkin'.'

"Da and the farmer walked off a little way. I could see Da doing all the talking and the farmer spent most of the time staring, listening and sometimes nodding. Eventually they came back to the cart, shook hands and Da climbed up.

"'Thank you, Nicholas,' he said, and we drove off.

"Several minutes passed before Dan asked, 'Well? What happened? Isn't she there?'

"Da looked at him and smiled.

"'Don't worry, lad, it's up to you now. We're comin' back for church on Sunday.'

"Dan went white."

"I'm getting another whisky," said John.

"Who said that?" asked Joe.

"Me," said John.

"I know, but who in the cart said it?"

John laughed.

"No one in the cart. It was me, just now. I feel like one more whisky. Want one, too?"

"Yes," said Joe and handed him a shilling.

John wasn't gone long, but while he was away, Joe noticed that a few people had already left and there were a few vacant tables, but the noise hadn't diminished. Perhaps alcohol was now playing its part. He also began to feel tired and worried that he wouldn't be able to hear the end of the story.

Returning with the whisky, John must have noticed Joe's fatigue, and he wasted no time continuing.

"Dan and Alice were introduced at church the next Sunday and contrary to Dan's fears, they were an instant match. It wasn't long before they were inseparable. They were keen to get married, but there was a problem. Alice was a convict, so she needed the Government's permission, and she hadn't completed her indenture with Nicholas, so she had to stay with him until she either got a ticket of leave or her certificate of freedom.

"Nicholas was a good man who wanted to do the best by Alice and Dan. He first got permission for Alice to marry and then had her re-indentured to Da. It took about a year to get all that done, so by the time Alice moved to our farm she and Dan had been married over six months and had not ever stayed together. We had to put another room on the house for them, and it was a wonderful day when she finally arrived. Dan left early in the morning to pick her up and when they came back to the house, I'd swear Ma and Da were jealous of their obvious love for each other."

Joe couldn't keep his eyes open and held up his hand.

"I'm sorry, John," he said, "I can't keep my eyes open. I'll have to hear the rest of the story another time."

"There probably won't be another time. I'm sure it doesn't matter. It's just one man's story and there are thousands like it."

"I doubt it. Thanks for your company and good luck with your search," said Joe, standing up.

"And the same to you," said John, still sitting.

Joe reached down, shook hands and went to the barman.

"About a room," he said.

"Yes. That'll be two shillings. You can have the last one. It's at the end. Out the door and turn right. There's a candle-lamp in the room. It should be lit."

Joe counted out the money, went out the door and found the room easily. The candle-lamp was another matter. It wasn't lit so he took off most of his clothes then lit a match, found the bed that looked dirty and smelled worse, crawled into it and passed out.

22. ALICE

Joe woke at dawn and took a few moments to remember where he was. It didn't take long to realise how awful the bed was, so despite the cold, he wasted no time getting out of it and getting dressed. Fortunately, there was a jug with water and a bowl on a nearby table, so he washed his face and hands and felt better for it.

Stepping outside, he was struck by the beauty of the dawn. Birds were tweeting and chattering all about, the early rays of the sun glistened off dew-laden spider webs in the trees nearby, dew sparkled on the ground and there wasn't the hint of a breeze. He admired it for a few moments before heading for the main room to see if he could get breakfast. The door was closed, so he opened it and peered in. There was no one there and no noise from the kitchen, so he decided he was too early, and little would be gained by hanging about. Perhaps it was a good thing, and he was better to hit the road right away.

As he turned away from the door, he smelled wood smoke. It wasn't hard to find the source. Without a breeze, the smoke hung lazily in the air. If he was lucky, someone would be making a brew, and he could at least get a cuppa before he set off.

Walking towards the thickest of the smoke, Joe saw a cart and a man sitting beside a fire. As he came closer, he could see the man was Dan. There were no horses and no sign of John, Tim and Luke. Joe's boots crackled on some twigs on the ground and Dan looked up.

"Mornin'," he said, without getting up, and poking at the fire with a stick.

"Mornin'. Any chance of a cuppa?"

Dan smiled. "We met last night, didn't we?"

"Briefly."

"Of course."

"Where are the others?"

"Sleepin'", said Dan, jerking his thumb towards the cart.

"Good for them."

"I suppose. I'd had enough sleep. I'm ready to get on with it. I thought I'd have a cuppa, fetch the horses, wake the others, have breakfast and take to the road."

Dan threw a handful of tea into the boiling billy, stirred it with the stick he was holding, pulled it from the tripod with the same stick and holding the metal handle, poured two pannikins.

"It's hot," he said, passing a pannikin to Joe.

"I'd be surprised if it wasn't."

"Sugar's here," said Dan, fetching two big spoonfuls of sugar from a half-empty bag at his side and passing the spoon to Joe.

"Thanks," said Joe and did the same.

The men sat in silence for a few minutes and Joe became aware of the noise from the other three men sleeping under the cart. They were surprisingly quiet, just the odd grunt, groan or snort.

"Good sleepers," said Joe.

"Too right. Don't know how they do it. I'd rather be up and about."

"Ready to get on with the gold search?"

"Ready to get it over and done with."

"How's that?"

"John tell you about California? He tells everybody. No secrets anymore."

"He started to. I fell asleep."

"Good for you."

Joe hesitated before saying, "I'd like to hear it. I'm awake and I've got time now. Better from the horse's mouth anyway."

Dan chuckled.

"There's not much to tell. John always makes more of it."

"Then I've definitely got the time."

Dan looked at Joe for a few moments, as though making up his mind.

"I was married." He looked at Joe as though to confirm that Joe at least knew part of the story.

Joe nodded and said, "John said."

"Where did John get to with the story?"

"You'd gone to fetch Alice home."

"Oh, that was a wonderful day."

Joe noticed that the lines and valleys on Dan's young face disappeared for a moment as he smiled softly with the memory. It was as though his mind had taken him back and he was again living the moment of bringing his wife to their home.

Joe said nothing. It was up to Dan now.

"We'd built a room for us. It wasn't much, but it was ours. I used to share a room with Da. It was a strange upbringin'."

Dan looked at Joe to see if he was still interested.

"Before Alice came, I shared a room with Da and John with his ma. Ma and Da never shared the same room, so when I brought Alice home, I shared with her, Da stayed on his own and John stayed with Ma. I never understood it. I didn't then and I still don't."

Dan looked at Joe again, as though to see if Joe had a possible explanation. Joe remained silent.

"We were there about a year. I suppose we were all surprised that Alice didn't get pregnant. I could see that Ma was the most surprised and I could tell she wanted to have a talk with me about it but couldn't find the words. Ma and Alice got on very well, sharin' the chores around the house. I'd always heard that two women under one roof could spell trouble, but it didn't under our roof.

"Then, I read about the gold rush in California. I became obsessed with it. I loved the idea that you could find a fortune, pick it up and it was yours. The farm was all hard work. Long hours, hot in the summer, cold in the winter, and disappointments every day. I suppose we did all right, but I couldn't ignore the idea you could make a fortune by findin' gold. I thought that was what I wanted.

"I talked it over with Alice and we decided to go. I had no money, of course. Da and Ma owned the farm, and all the money went to them. After followin' the papers carefully, I found that we'd need around ten pounds each for steerage to get there and some money for supplies and equipment. I read what I could about diggin' for gold and while there wasn't much, I had some idea.

"Eventually, I talked it over with Da. He was dead against it. Said we didn't have the money, he needed me on the farm, and he was sure it would be a waste of time and money. He said there's no such thing as a fortune in the ground, just there and waitin' for someone to come along. He said it reminded him of the fairy tales his mother used to tell him.

"Da couldn't read so I read him some of the things in the paper. He said I was makin' it up. John helped, read him the same things and reassured him that at least the paper said you could find gold and make a fortune.

"Finally, Ma talked him around. Said 'the young ones needed a chance and who were we to say it wouldn't work for them?'

"We had a good season that year and the farm did well. Da gave me thirty pounds and said that was all he could afford. Said if it wasn't enough, we couldn't go."

Joe said, "I like the sound of your da."

"He was a good man."

"Was?"

"That's another story. Let me finish this one."

"Of course."

"Da took us in the cart to Parramatta to book a passage to America and when the day came to leave, we all went to Parramatta for us to catch the ferry to Sydney. Da said it would be good practice at bein' on the water. He said he'd come on a sailin' ship from Ireland and it wasn't easy.

"We left Sydney on the *Regia*. It took us three months to get to California. I was seasick a lot of the time, but Alice loved it. Took to the water like a sailor. Said she'd become one if she could. She thought the sails magnificent, stretchin' white and tight against the blue of the sky and sea. She'd stand for hours at the bow, enjoyin' the spray and the motion of the ship. The captain became very fond of her and treated her like a daughter. I was so proud. Not everyone could have a wife like my Alice."

Dan's voice faltered. Joe didn't know what to do. He hadn't thought that Dan would become emotional. He preferred hearing the story from Dan but didn't know how to behave with another man showing emotion.

Dan looked at Joe for a few moments without speaking. Then he shook his head as though to clear it and went on.

"San Francisco was a surprise. It's a beautiful harbour, but the fog rolls in and it's as cold as a frog's hind leg. We were stuck on the ship overnight due to the fog. After that, we were stuck in San Francisco tryin' to find the way to the gold fields. I'd swear no man ever came less prepared for the task at hand. We had to discover everythin'. Everythin' was expensive, so a lot of the time was spent trampin' from place to place tryin' to get a better price. And hills! You've never seen hills like they have in San Francisco! Alice was bright and kept tellin' me not to worry. She said it'd be all right.

"Eventually we got on a schooner that took us to Sacramento. The skipper assured us it was the fastest, cheapest and best way to the gold fields. I think he was tellin' us the truth. He, like everyone else took a great likin' to Alice.

"After Sacramento, we managed to get a ride from a feller takin' supplies with a team of oxen to the stores in the gold fields. Once again, I found that Alice was a secret weapon.

"'I'll take 'er!' the big, burly driver called out and pointin' at Alice when we asked for a ride.

"'We'll pay you some money!' called Alice.

"'You can come for free!' shouted the man.

"'Then we'll go with someone else!'

"'We? Is it just you an' 'im?' shouted the man, pointing at me.

"'Yes.'

"'All right then. Get on. Both of you. I suppose the more the merrier. Do you know any songs?' he asked after we got on. I knew he wasn't talkin' to me.

"'A few my mother taught me,' said Alice.

"'They'll do,' he said and stuck out his hand to me. 'Name's Bull.'

"'That's it?' asked Alice. 'Just Bull?'

"'Not just Bull,' he laughed. 'All Bull!'

"I thought after a while that the oxen were so slow, we could just have well walked, but after an hour's singin', the man wouldn't let Alice out of his sight. He insisted she sing song after song and never cared that he'd heard them many times. I was sure that when I looked at him, there were tears on his cheeks.

"We camped overnight, and he insisted that we all sleep close to each other under the cart. He said there were grizzly bears and coyotes about, so we needed to be careful. We put Alice between us and I thought she'd be safer there. I was never sure if he made up the danger so he could have a woman sleepin' close by. I suppose it didn't matter. He was so gentle with her and treated her with such respect that I never once thought she was in danger.

"Once we got to the fields, the adventures started all over again. Where to dig and how to go about it? After a day or so we teamed up with some men who were happy to have Alice there to cook and wash and when they found she could sing, why we couldn't leave if we wanted to.

"I started to worry when I saw the danger and the violence. There were frequent fights over claims. There was no formal system. You just marked out an area and it was yours while ever you worked it. It was anyone else's as soon as you moved on. Sometimes, men would go to a town to get drunk and when they got back, someone else would be workin' their claim. There was no law or order, so people stood up for themselves and the only way to resolve anythin' was with fists or guns.

"Alice didn't care. She just laughed and told me that nothin' worth havin could be had easily. I'd been blind, of course. The real danger had been there all along, and I'd not even noticed it."

There was no noise coming from under the cart and Joe wondered if the others were awake and listening to the story. He had a moment's thought that he might not want to hear what was coming and it may be best to stop Dan. The thought passed, curiosity got the better of him and he remained silent. He looked at Dan and noticed that Dan seemed to be steeling himself for what he had to say next.

"We were diggin' for alluvial gold and the trick was to find an old riverbed where the river had once run but had now retreated. I didn't know this of course but learned it from the others. There was a lot of water over the winter months and the rivers would rise by many feet, scourin' the earth and releasin' the gold which would be left behind when the water retreated. We had two teams of three workin'. One man would dig, another carry and the third would use a rocker to separate the gold. It was back breakin' work, but it was the only way to get the gold. All three would dig away the surface dirt where no gold would ever be found as it was heavier and fell through to the bottom. At the bottom was a thing called a deadpan, and all the gold would be found in the dirt just above it.

"At first there wasn't a lot of people diggin' and we did well. As the year dragged on, many more people came, and it was harder to find places to claim and dig.

"Alice would come to help if she finished her chores. The men loved it when she did. There were so few women about that we were the envy of all the other men. She didn't do a lot. Bring us a drink of water, or maybe somethin' to eat. Then she heard the men talkin', sayin' it was harder to find good places to dig and she volunteered to spend time each day lookin' for new spots. She said she knew what to look for, she'd been watchin' us for a while and had a pretty good idea where to find the gold.

"I didn't like it at all and neither did the other men. We all thought it too dangerous. Men fightin' over claims that she might accidentally stumble on, local Indians who'd been pushed off their lands, men who hadn't seen a woman for months and would welcome findin' one walkin' alone."

Dan stopped and looked at Joe.

"Joe, there's not a day goes by that I can't believe how stupid we all were to allow her to do that job. Anyone of the rest of us could have done it, but we allowed her to convince us that she'd be all right and she was the most available to do it."

Dan stopped again, staring into the fire. His voice trembled when he continued his story.

"Life turns on the simple things, Joe. There're moments when you turn left or right, go forward or back and you have no idea what might come from what seems such a simple decision. It wasn't long after we'd all agreed she could have a go at it. I was workin' on a ridge above the river, not far from our camp. I was diggin' and I heard her call. I looked down and she waved, turned and headed up river, away from the camp. She looked so small in the distance, her blond hair tied back by a scarf, but even from the hill I could see her smile. It was radiant as always. The other men stopped and waved as well, but she'd already turned and was almost out of sight. That was the last time I ever saw her."

There was no sound, even the bush had gone quiet. No sound from Dan, from the others under the cart, or from Joe.

"What happened to her?" asked Joe, finally.

"I don't know," said Dan, shaking his head. "I looked for her for months, wanderin' all around, but no one had seen her. The others joined me for a few weeks, but eventually it was my problem and I alone had to solve it. They gave me some of the gold and I used that to live on while I searched. When the gold ran out, I had to give up. There was nothin' else for it. I could curl up behind a rock and die or come home."

"Couldn't you have gone back to the others, dug for more gold and continued the search?"

"I thought about that, but I decided that if I hadn't found her in the time I had, I was never goin' to. You see, there was only the miners and the people in the towns to ask. And I could only describe her. Most people weren't interested anyway. Who cared about a woman that disappeared? Certainly no one that I met in California. No Joe, I made a stupid mistake and I'm payin' the price. Every day I pay a little more, and I'll pay 'till the day I die. I thought about jumpin' off the ship on the way home, but I knew she wouldn't want that. As hard as it is, I have to live for both of us now."

"How did you get on a ship if you'd run out of money?"

"It was easy. So many men had jumped ship that it was easy to get a job as a sailor. They weren't too pleased when they found I suffered from seasickness."

"Do you think she's still alive?"

"I can't think that, Joe. If I thought that, I'd have to go back. I had to decide she wasn't alive before I came home, so I've already accepted that she's not."

Joe was silent. He wasn't sure what he'd do in Dan's place and was not inclined to find out.

"Well, I hope you find some gold," said Joe, standing up and stretching out his hand.

"You too," said Dan, shaking Joe's hand without standing.

Joe walked off, leaving Dan to his loss and loneliness and the others to their sleep.

"I'll come with you," said Dan, calling to Joe's back. "It's time I got the horses anyway."

It was only a short walk to the yard where the horses were kept. All the horses there came to the gate when Joe and Dan arrived. They walked past the yard to the stable where Joe got his bridle and Dan got some lead ropes.

Joe was about to head for the yard when Dan stopped him.

"I do know what happened to her, but no one else does," said Dan, "and I don't want them to find out."

"Why not?"

"I don't know if I did the right thing. What I did when I found her, I mean."

"Then why tell me?"

Dan smiled briefly. It was a sad, lonely smile with no humour in it.

"Because you don't matter. I can tell you and it doesn't matter what you think."

"I might tell them."

"I don't think so. Anyway, if you do then I've misjudged you."

"Why didn't you tell me at the camp?"

"The others were listenin'. They always listen. No one believes what I told them."

"I don't envy you, Dan. It must be hard to live with a secret."

"Most people do. We all make mistakes. Most of us don't want anyone to know. I think most people will lie to protect themselves if they think they can get away with it."

"And even if they don't."

Dan smiled again. It was warmer this time.

"The others helped with the search at first. We were all sure she'd fallen or been taken by a bear. I imagined her lyin' somewhere, unable to move, so I pushed myself and the others relentlessly, searchin' through creeks, rivers and valleys all around the camp. They started to give up one by one after a few weeks. They said she couldn't be alive and as sad as they were for me, they had to get on with diggin' for gold.

"I finally decided they were right, and she'd probably been taken. I had no idea where to look other than to travel all about the gold field to see if anyone had seen her. It was hard, Joe. I could only describe her, and most people weren't interested. It was a big area, and the Sierra Nevadas aren't easy to travel through. I bought a horse and lived and travelled rough. I looked bad and smelled worse, but I didn't care. I had to find Alice. That was all I thought about, all I cared about. It had been my idea to come, and I struggled with my failure as a husband.

"After months of hardship, I'd almost given up the search. I'd pretty much run out of money and ideas. That's when I heard her. It was almost dark when I rode into a town, and I heard her singin' in a saloon. You can imagine my disbelief. Singin'?! In a saloon?! It couldn't be her!

"I tied my horse to the hitchin' rail and pushed my way in. The place was crowded, but everyone was focused on the stage and there was Alice, wearin' next to nothin' and singin' some bawdy sea shanty. I just stood there, unable to move, unable to think.

"'She's good, in'she?' whispered a huge fellow standing beside me. I suppose he noticed my shock and misunderstood it.

"'Who is she?' I whispered back.

"'Dunno. She's new. But the best part is you can have her for five dollars when she stops singin'.'

"I don't know how I stood there. The relief of findin' her and then the shock of what I just heard crushed my ability to think or act. I knew enough about the gold fields to know that I couldn't go to the stage and demand my wife go with me. Someone would shoot me before I finished the sentence.

"'Who do I see to take a turn?' I whispered to the man beside me.

"'That fellow over there. See, the one near the stage.'

"He pointed and it was Bull. Bull looked towards us, but it didn't matter. No one would recognise me after the past few months. I stared back at him and knew then that I would have to kill him to get my wife back. Right at that moment, I'd never looked forward to somethin' as much in all my life."

"How did Bull get her?"

"I found out later that it was just one of those things. Alice saw him, trusted him and went to talk. He took her. It was a simple as that. Knocked her out and took her."

Dan was pale and visibly shaking.

"Shall we go back for another cuppa?" asked Joe.

"No," said Dan, "the others are there, and this is our secret. I'd like to finish, if you have the time. It's helpin' to talk about it, and I may not get the chance again."

Joe nodded and Dan went on.

"I waited until she stopped singin' and went up to Bull. I wasn't the only one.

"'How much?' asked the fellow closest to Bull.

"'Five dollars,' he said, 'and you have to hurry. There're others. Plenty of others.'

"He laughed. I walked off, I didn't have five dollars, but I had to get it. I had to see her, talk to her and come up with a plan. She'd be able to tell me when best to help her escape. As I left, I could see her bein' led upstairs by a man. I didn't think too much about what was happenin'. It's strange, Joe. I was just so glad to have found her alive. I knew I'd have my revenge in good time and my total focus was to help her escape.

"I went out and sat outside the saloon. The noise from inside was deafenin' with talkin', shoutin' and an out-of-tune piano.

"The only way to get five dollars was to steal it because I needed it right away. I wasn't going to wait until the next night to free Alice. Most of the fellers inside were drunk, so I could follow one when he went outside, knock him out and steal five dollars. I went back inside, bought a whisky with the little money I had left and sat by myself in a corner. It wasn't long before a man that had been drinkin' and shoutin' louder than the rest struggled to his feet and announced he was leavin'. He went out front and I followed. He fell through the doors and crashed onto the ground. It was wet and muddy. I hurried over and pulled him to his feet. I pretended to struggle with him and rifled through his pockets takin' everythin' that felt like money. No one took any notice of us. I pushed the money into a pocket, dragged him over and propped him against the saloon wall before goin' back inside.

"Returnin' to my whisky, I checked the money. I'd stolen over a hundred dollars. There was no one near Bull, so I counted out five dollars, finished my whisky in a single swallow and went over to him.

"'Five dollars, you said?'

"'Sorry. Lady's finished for the night. Don't want to work her too hard. Got to get my share as well,' he sniggered.

"If I'd had a gun, I would have shot him then.

"'Will you be back tomorrow night?' I asked, as calmly as I could.

"'Yep. Like every night.'

"'Can I go first?'

"'If you're here first.'

"'What time should I come? When do you get here?'

"'About sundown. We get here about sundown.'

"'See you then,' I said.

"All I had to do now was to get a gun and wait for Bull to leave."

Joe noticed the horses getting agitated in the yard. It reminded Joe that he needed to be gone before the bodies near the bridge were discovered. Two saddled horses would certainly lead someone to investigate and find the bodies.

"We need to get moving," said Joe.

"There's not much more," said Dan, sounding disappointed. "I've not ever told anyone and now that I've started, I want to tell it all."

"I'll ride with you for a while. We'll get another chance."

"Dan?" a voice called. "Where the devil have you got to? Breakfast is done. Where are the horses?"

It was John, emerging from the trees.

"We heard you both go. We didn't think it would take this long to fetch the horses. I decided to come and find you. We need to get going."

"Sorry," said Dan when John came close. "We got to talkin'."

"What about?" asked John suspicion in his voice.

"Nothin'."

"How can you spend so long talking about nothing?"

"We had to catch the horses," said Joe.

"I know that's rubbish. They're all standing by the gate, waiting. They're as keen as we are to get on with it. Anyway, if you don't want to tell me, that's up to you. But say your *good-byes* and let's get on with it."

"Joe's going to have breakfast with us and ride with us for a while."

"Is he now? Now, why would that be?"

"Turns out he knows about gold diggin'. He might be useful."

"Does he now? So, I thought you knew all we need to know. What does Joe know that you don't?"

"I think not much," said Joe, 'but two heads are better than one."

"We've got all the heads we need," said John tersely. "I don't know what you two fellers have been cooking up, nor why you're both lying to me, but I'm here to tell you. Joe's not having breakfast with us, nor is he travelling with us. This is my show and I'll be damned if you or anyone else is going to make the decisions."

"Sorry," said Dan. "I just thought …"

"Then stop. I'll do the thinking," said John.

"Then I'll be going," said Joe. "Nice to have met you and good luck in the gold fields. There's nothing sinister here, John. You're making more of it than you need to. Dan and I were just talking. That's all. Just talking. See you, Dan."

Joe waved at Dan and went to his horse by the gate. He quickly put the bridle on and walked his horse to the stable, where he fetched the saddle, put it on quickly, mounted and set off on the road west. There was no time for breakfast and part of him was glad that John had come along. He'd spent too much time talking and he knew as much as he wanted to hear the end of the story, stopping for breakfast would surely have been a mistake.

23. THE MOUNTAINS

It was pleasant riding west. The road wasn't all that bad and wasn't crowded, although there was plenty of other traffic, most heading west. Joe couldn't shake the feeling that the ride wouldn't be as pleasant for Dan. John seemed plenty riled up and would no doubt continue the interrogation to find out what Joe and Dan were discussing for so long.

The road wound its way along a ridge which was wide enough so that little was visible in the way of gullies on either side. A few times it narrowed, and he could see deep gullies, but thankfully there was enough room on both sides to continue confidently. He stopped around midday in a grassy area to brew a cuppa and eat some of his provisions. There was enough grass for his horse to graze and no need to hobble him. The meadow wasn't that big. He'd decided the weather would be favourable, so it was time to work out how to set up a camp. There was no way he wanted to try it in the dark, so he pushed his horse a little harder in the afternoon to make good time.

The ridge grew steeper as the afternoon went on, and the road at times was so narrow and the sides so steep that only a few vehicles or horses could use it at the same time. One part looked like logs pulled together to form a bridge over a large gap between huge rocky outcrops and he hoped there wouldn't be many of those. He was nervous as he crossed it and relieved to get to the other side. Someone told him later it was called 'Cox's Downfall' and he thought it an appropriate name.

Towards evening he saw fires winking in the distance and pulled up in an area where a few people were camping. There was an inn nearby as well, but he stuck to his original plan and camped. A few of the people were gathered around camp-fires and he was made welcome when he approached. They offered him some tea and he happily accepted, munching on a cheese and damper sandwich he had made. People mostly talked about finding gold, the weather and bushrangers. It wasn't long before Joe excused himself, hobbled his horse, fed him some oats and turned in for the night.

By morning he decided there was nothing to recommend sleeping out and he'd be thoroughly sick of it if it took too long to find his fortune.

He'd asked people the night before if he could reach Bathurst in the day and they told him that if he pushed hard, he'd do it.

"Be careful of Mount Victoria," someone had called when they heard the answer. "You can't go quickly down there."

"Oh," said Joe. "Why is that?"

"It's steep and it's dangerous. Just take your time. Let your horse work out where to go."

"Get off," said another. "You'll find it safer if you both walk."

Talk turned to accidents that people knew of and Joe thought Cox's Downfall might have been a small taste of what was to come.

Turned out he was right.

The first bad news was there was another toll gate, just before Mount Victoria. The man was pleasant enough and expressed sympathy when Joe showed outrage as he passed the money across.

"It's fer a good cause," said the man. "Fixin' roads and things like that."

"From what I've seen it's mostly been wasted," said Joe, unappeased by either the sympathy or the explanation.

The man seemed to take the criticism personally, so Joe apologised and pressed on.

After a few miles, the road seemed to disappear into thin air. It came to a cliff with a wonderful panorama west which Joe couldn't admire as he was too confused by what happened to the road. He got off his horse and walked to the edge. He gasped when he realised the road went over the edge and down into the valley.

"Jesus!" he muttered, conscious of the warning at the camp fire. The road followed along the cliff face, no more than ten or so yards wide and switching back and forth as it descended. He could see where carts had gone over the edge and bodies of horses and bullocks were to be seen where they'd been dragged over the edge by vehicles on the way down, or died in their exertions to pull vehicles up. Joe walked carefully holding his horse's reins and hoped it was the last he would ever see of Mount Victoria Pass. Several times he passed other people both going up and down, but no one had time for each other. They were totally focused on the task at hand. Most of the animals whether going up or down were sweating and terrified and the people weren't that much different.

When he reached the valley floor, he saw logs scattered about and understood why the vehicles coming down had logs tied to the back. It stopped them careering out of control. Not for the first time was he glad he was on horseback and glad that he hadn't stayed with Dan and the others.

He passed slower vehicles and walkers from time to time as he rode through a wide, open and beautiful valley. People were more jovial now, no doubt glad to have survived the Pass. There were gibes for people going the other way, but Joe didn't join in. He was keen to get to Bathurst before dark, so pushed his horse hard, not even stopping at midday.

The valley more or less continued, sometimes being wide and at other times narrow. The road crossed rivers and creeks, going up and down, but never more than a few hundred feet. At one time, after crossing a river, it climbed high up on the side of the valley to avoid a ravine, then came back down again to the river. It was hard going for both him and the horse. After a while there was more evidence of habitation and he hoped it meant he was approaching Bathurst.

It was close on dark when he rode into Bathurst. The river crossing just before town was sandy and difficult due to the previous passage of vehicles and he could imagine it would be impassable when flooded. There was a steep climb up the bank on the other side and the track zigged and zagged to enable carts and wagons to make the ascent. Once he reached the town, the streets were wide and there was a lot of traffic of all kinds. He could see lamps burning outside a hotel in the near distance, so he went to it and wearily dismounted. His horse was tired and stood dejectedly as he let the reins drop and went inside to see if he could get a room.

"Sorry," said the man. "We're full. Everyone comes here, 'cos we're the first pub you come to once you cross the river.

Try the next street along. There's more pubs in that street. You'll find somewhere and you look like you need it!"

"The next street along this street?"

"Continue on this one to the first cross street, go right and then go left."

"Thanks," muttered Joe, heading out into the dark, more tired than he'd ever been.

When he approached his horse, it looked at him as if to say, "Oh, no!"

"Sorry, old feller," he murmured, "I hope it's not far now."

He rode past several pubs not wanting another wasted stop and finally stopped at one that looked run down and quiet.

"Plenty of room," said the man and smiled, obviously grateful for another customer.

"And my horse?"

"Put 'im 'round back. Stables there. Cost you sixpence."

"And me?"

"You can stay in here. Rooms're upstairs. How many nights?"

"Just the one."

"Supper and breakfast?"

Joe nodded. He was too tired to forage for himself.

"That'll be five shillin's all up. Take your 'orse around the side to the stables. Put 'im in any empty stall. There's oats there, too, so he'll be a snug as a bug in a rug."

"And my room?"

"Upstairs. Any room with an open door. Privy's at the back. You'll see it when you tend to your 'orse."

"Supper?"

"Through that door," said the man pointing a nearby doorway

Joe counted out the money, went out front and took his horse around the back. In spite of his tiredness, he took a few extra moments to rub his horse down and make sure there was water and oats. There was a couple of lamps hanging from the roof which cast just enough light to see. More tired than he could ever remember, he used the privy, went upstairs and found a room with an open door, fell on the bed and went to sleep.

He woke to the pale light of an early sun and wasted no time before having breakfast, ravenously hungry after missing supper the night before. After collecting his horse, he set about finding stores that were open to replenish his supplies and buy what else he needed for the imminent task of looking for gold. Despite the early hour, there were plenty of shops open and people about. Clearly Bathurst was commercially alert and ready to serve the needs of a pliant public.

He asked about the road to the gold fields. The man just smiled and said, "Follow the river."

"What river?"

"Did you come from Sydney?"

"Yes."

"The river you crossed when you came into Bathurst."

"Back towards Sydney?"

"I thought you said you wanted to find the gold fields?"

"I did."

"Then why would you want to go back towards Sydney?"

"Which way do I go then?"

"The other way. Go back to where you crossed the river and follow the road away from Sydney."

Once Joe did as he was told, the road to the gold field was obvious. There were already people on it, their intent clearly demonstrated by what they carried. Joe joined the throng and walked his horse patiently with them. Every now and then he could see discarded items which were probably found to be too bulky or heavy. Sometimes people with a cart would stop and collect them.

The people with whom he shared the road were less friendly than those on the Blue Mountains road, but Joe didn't care. He was happy to keep to himself and found a good spot away from anyone else when he camped overnight. Once again, he was up and, on the road, early. He didn't need either directions or a map as there were enough people about and enough evidence of those that had gone before. The country was unlike anything he had seen so far, constantly changing from wooded to meadow and back again. They seemed to follow a creek, but sometimes it wasn't possible where it went through a ravine, so the road would veer away and climb a ridge. Joe thought it strange that when he climbed, he always had to go down again to re-join the river. There was the odd farm or building, and once he saw what looked like a church and at another time, a village. Late in the day, he climbed higher than he had before and from his vantage point, he could hear and see men digging down by the creek.

Well, at least I'm there. What next?

24. OPHIR

Standing beside the creek, Joe saw people were digging on both sides of the creek downstream, both near the water and on the sides of the hills. He and the other newcomers stopped at about the same spot to take in the view.

"Jesus. Where do I start?" said one man nearby.

Joe thought it a good question as he had no idea either.

"What're you fellers goin' to do?" asked the same man of others in the newly arrived group.

"None of your business," said someone, tersely.

"No need to lose yer shirt. I was just askin'. No harm in that, is there?"

He didn't wait for an answer, but sat on a stone beside the water and said bitterly, "I've come a long way. Feller offered to sell me a book on what to do, but I can't read. Now that I'm finally here, I don't know what to do."

Joe felt sorry for him. He looked around at the group. It was obvious no one knew what to do.

"Should have asked before you left," said Joe. "If you've come a long way and you don't know what to do, you'd better find out. Otherwise, it's a long way to go back and you'll have nothing to show for the journey."

Joe walked his horse away from the group. There was nothing to learn from them and their naivety would make it difficult to talk to anyone. He glanced at the sun. It would be a few hours before sunset, but no doubt it would be colder and darker sooner in the ravine. He hoped he could find somewhere to buy a drink and someone to talk to. All the things he'd learned from Margaret, Jacob and Dan would need to be investigated. He didn't doubt there'd be plenty of people ready to fleece the newcomers, so he'd need to be on his guard, too.

He didn't have to go far from the tents and buildings to find a good place to pitch his tent. There was evidence of a previous campfire, so someone had been there before and if he was lucky, they hadn't been moved on. He set up the tent, but left his horse saddled and everything of value either on him or on the horse. It didn't take long to get the fire going, make some tea and cook a simple meal. There'd be time enough to be more sophisticated later. When it began to get dark, he mentally marked some trees and buildings so he could find his way back in the dark and leading his horse by the reins, went in search of a drink.

It wasn't hard to find a place to drink. There was a sly grog shop only a few hundred yards away, but customers bought the drink and moved on. Joe had heard about people illegally selling grog in the gold fields. He hadn't expected to find a dealer so soon. Anyway, such an establishment was no good to him. He wanted someone to talk to.

"Where can I buy a whisky?" he asked the man standing in the doorway of the canvas tent. The tent looked like it backed onto a cart so the man could dismantle it and be gone in minutes.

"'Ere," was the curt reply.

"I want some company while I drink."

"Woman? Not many 'ere and none for what you want."

"No, I don't want a woman. I've just arrived. I want to find out what's doing."

"If you buy me a drink, I'll tell you what's doin'."

"Don't you sell it?"

"Doesn't mean I can't drink it."

"No one else is staying to talk."

"You're right. I don't want people hangin' 'round. Makes it easier fer the traps to find me, but I'm outta 'ere day after tomorrer. I need to get more supplies, so you can come in fer a chat if you like."

"I found you easy enough."

"Fair enough, but this is new for us, too. Still tryin' to work out how and when the traps'll come. Come on. Let's talk inside."

The man seemed friendly enough, so Joe followed the man through the doorway. As soon as he was inside, the man bent down, picked up a bottle and put it on a small table.

"That'll be a pound," he said. He pulled the cork and filled two glasses.

"Must be the good stuff," said Joe.

"'cos it's a pound?" asked the man, smiling.

"No. You're drinking it."

"I only sell the good stuff," said the man laughing. "I don't want my customers to end up dead."

He took Joe's pound, picked up his glass and sipped it, smacking his lips appreciatively.

"Nothing like a drink at the end of a long day," he said.

"You been digging?"

"Yes, I do a bit," nodded the man.

"Where's best to dig?"

"If I knew that, I wouldn't be sellin' grog."

"Where do you dig?"

"Down river. 'bout a mile from 'ere."

The man was interrupted by someone at the door, wanting to buy a bottle.

"Been busy tonight," he said when he came back.

"Why?"

"Sattidy. They take tomorrer off to nurse a sore head."

"How do you mark your claim?" asked Joe, trying to find out all he could before the man became too busy to be interested.

"It's not mine. I just work with some other fellers."

"How do they mark it?"

"You just pick a likely spot and start diggin'. There's talk you'll need a licence from the first of next month. You'll register your claim with the Commissioner and buy a licence."

"How much will the licence cost?"

"They say a shillin' a day."

"Only if you find gold?"

"Whether you find gold or not."

"Where's the Commissioner?"

"You come from Bathurst?"

Joe nodded.

"You would have ridden past his tent as you came down the hill to the ford."

The man re-filled the glasses. Joe was silent, thinking about what he had learned. Two more men appeared in the doorway wanting whisky.

"That it?" asked the man when he returned.

"Where can I camp?"

"Where are you now?"

"Over by the river."

"Make sure you boil the water. All sorts of things in it."

"Should I move?"

"Best to camp near your claim. If you don't, someone'll take it. The fellers I dig with are down river. People are tryin' to find new places. Less competition."

"Should I go down there?"

"Up to you. If you've got supplies for a few weeks, it's better to be away from anyone else. There's the licence too. Once that comes in, they'll be checkin' for it."

"Will everyone buy one?"

"Doubt it. It's a lot of money if you're not findin' anythin'."

"What will they do if you don't have one?"

"Story is you'll pay a fine or go to gaol. I think that's a good reason to get away. They'll 'ave to find you first."

Another man appeared in the doorway. As soon as he was served, two more appeared.

"I'll be going," said Joe when the man had finished serving.

"Take your whisky," said the man, "you bought it."

Joe went back to his tent and stoked the fire before taking the saddle and bridle from his horse. He put the saddle in the tent to use as a pillow, hobbled the horse and sat on a rock, watching the flames and sipping his whisky. He thought he'd follow the man's advice and go down river the next morning. There were supplies enough for a few weeks and that should be long enough to work out if his search would be successful.

He spent a fitful night, trying to get used to sleeping on the ground. There was noise from the diggers too, shouting, cheering, arguments and the occasional smash of a bottle. It was cold, so he was glad when light in the tent told him it was nearly dawn. Strangely enough, just as he was thinking about getting up, he fell into a deep sleep and was roused by people singing nearby. Peeking out of the tent he saw that the day was well advanced and that the singing was coming from a group near the river. It made no sense until he remembered it was Sunday.

After a breakfast of tea and damper, he packed up and headed down river. It was easy going and not hard to follow the track. He guessed the track was often used, but he didn't see anyone else. He thought it odd, then remembered that most diggers didn't work on a Sunday. As he rode, he thought about where to dig. He liked Jacob's idea of a sign that said *dig here*, but knew there was no such a thing. Jacob had said he thought the gold was leached out of the hills by water and so found its way to places by the creek. Whatever else this was going to be, it would be a learning exercise, so it might be good to do some trial and error. He doubted there would be many people with experience, so it wouldn't do just to follow others. Jacob had said the gold was caught by a mud or rocky bottom, so he studied the sides of the creek as he went along.

At last, he saw some men, sitting around a camp fire, undoubtedly enjoying some breakfast.

"Mornin'," Joe said as he rode up to them. "Can you spare a cuppa?"

The men all stared at him suspiciously and remained silent.

"I suppose that's a no," said Joe after a minute or so of silence. He turned his horse's head to continue his journey.

"What are ya doin' 'ere?" called one of the men.

Joe stopped and turned back.

"Looking for somewhere to dig."

"There's plenty of places upstream," said the man.

"That's what I hear, but I thought I'd look down this way."

Joe studied the men and the area carefully. They didn't look like trouble, but they did look resentful, so there was probably gold about. He couldn't see where they'd been digging, but there was a cradle by the creek and piles of rubble scattered nearby. There was no evidence of a tent or a hut either, but it couldn't be far away unless they walked down from Ophir and that wasn't logical as it was Sunday.

"Go further down, then. There's nothin' for you 'ere."

"Fair enough," said Joe and once again turned his horse to the track. It wasn't long before he entered a grove of trees and just before he did, he looked back to see that none of the men had moved and all were still watching him. Once hidden by the trees, Joe stopped his horse and dismounted.

"You be quiet and wait here, young feller," he said, tied the reins to a fallen log and walked back along the track being careful to remain hidden by the trees. The men were still sitting by the fire, no longer looking in his direction. Smoke from the fire drifted upwards and was borne away by a slight breeze. It wasn't long before the men all got up, picked up the cradle and hid it with the pannikins and whatever else they used for breakfast in some bushes nearby and started walking up the track towards Ophir. Joe was in a dilemma. He didn't want to leave hoof prints around the camp as the men might see them and come looking for him. Nor did he want to leave his horse behind and have it stolen, or wander off. Finally, he decided to ride. The loss of his horse would be much more serious than raising suspicion amongst the men. If they came to see him, he'd deny being near their camp.

Joe went back, got his horse and rode in the direction of the camp. He rode carefully, keeping a watchful eye on the track ahead to be sure the men hadn't guessed that he might return and be waiting for him. The track was a messy affair and there was no doubt the creek would flood and cover it from time to time. There were big boulders and fallen trees scattered about, so he trusted his horse to find the best way and kept his eyes on the track ahead.

He paused at the camp just long enough to spot a path leading off into the trees away from the camp. Taking the path which was muddy in places, he knew the men would know he'd been there as hoof prints would be easily discernible. There was little that could be done about it if he was to learn where the men found gold. It wasn't long before he saw a large tent and not far past it signs of where the men had been digging into the side of the hill.

Dismounting and holding the reins, he peered into the hole and saw that it wasn't deep, maybe only ten or fifteen feet. He looked around nervously. He didn't really want to go into the hole, but knew he had no choice if he wanted to see where the men found the gold. It didn't feel right, but he could see no other way to achieve his goal.

There were plenty of rocks nearby, so he put the reins on the ground and dropped a rock on them. If something happened to him, his horse would be able to get away, but would be unlikely to run away in the few minutes it would take to inspect the men's diggings. He crawled into the hole, as far as he could go and allowed his eyes to adjust to the darkness. There was a lamp there and it would make it easier to inspect the men's workings. He pulled it close, struck a match and got it going.

The diggings were nothing spectacular. The men were following what must have been an old creek bed, just as Jacob had told him. There was sand, gravel and rocks and he could see he was lying on bedrock, so the men had cleared down to it. Most of the area above him was probably removed so the men could dig into the side of the hill. The gold would be close to the bed rock. There was no timberwork, so the roof was holding in position, but could no doubt fall at any time. In the moment, he admired the men's bravery to be working in such a place. He was uncomfortable and would be glad to get out. There wasn't much more to see, so he extinguished the lamp and crawled out backwards. Despite the danger, at least he had a better idea of where to look for gold.

Emerging from the hole, he was about to push himself to his feet when a female voice announced, "That'll do, stranger. I'm holdin' a gun, so you just lie there for a while. I'm expectin' the men soon and they'll know what to do with you."

"I mean you no harm," Joe said, his face uncomfortably close to the ground.

"That right?"

"Do you mind if I sit up? We can talk easier that way."

"I don't want to talk. Save your talkin' for the men."

Joe knew he had to be gone before the men got back. He'd get short shrift from them.

"I'm going to sit up," he said. "If that means you shoot me, go right ahead."

It didn't matter if he rolled to the left or the right, she would shoot when he stopped moving. He tried to think of a way to roll over, jump at her and take the gun, but no useful thought came to mind. Her voice gave him some idea of where she was, but the prospect of rolling over, leaping to his feet and disarming her filled him with dread. Knowing it might be the last thing he ever did, he rolled over, sat up and looked in the direction of the voice.

The sight of her took his breath away.

She was blonde, small and exceptionally beautiful. Her clothes were drab and worn, but their lack of beauty only emphasised hers. She was holding a revolver with two hands, but it was way too big for her and the strain of holding it was evident.

"You didn't shoot me," he said.

"Thought about it."

"I'm glad you didn't."

"Gonna happen anyway. When the men get back. I'm not much good at shootin' people."

"Does that mean I can go?"

"I said I'm not much good at it. Doesn't mean I won't."

They sat staring at each other for a few moments. Joe decided he was wasting time.

"If you're going to stop me, you'll have to use that."

"What're you doin' 'ere anyway?"

Joe decided she didn't want to shoot and was playing for time.

"I made a mistake."

"You got lost?" she said, her voice dripping with sarcasm.

"No. I'm new at looking for gold. Been told a bit about it, but I wanted to see where to find it. I didn't expect anyone to be here, so I thought I'd have a look and go. You're here, so I made a mistake. Like I said, I mean you no harm."

"How do I know you won't come back later?"

"You don't, but I'm hoping you'll trust me."

"Trust you? Why would I trust you? Crawlin' around in our claim! I should shoot you, not wait for the men to get back."

"If you were going to shoot me, you'd have done it before now."

"Don't push me, mister. I know how to use this!"

If she looked uncomfortable holding the weapon earlier, she looked distressed now.

"I know there's men," Joe said, hoping to put her more at ease. She looked like she might shoot him just to get it over and done with. "I saw them earlier. That's why I came by. They acted unfriendly, so I figured they'd found something up here. I only wanted to check it out. Now that I've done that, I'll be on my way."

"There's men all right," said a male voice from the path. Joe hadn't noticed the men returning.

That's torn it!

"Well done, Becky," said the man and took the pistol from the woman. "Are you all right? Did he do anythin'?"

"No, Phil. I'm all right. He says he doesn't mean no harm."

Phil and Becky stood together, the man now holding the gun. The other three men stayed on the path as though to block Joe's escape.

"You the feller we saw earlier?" asked Phil.

"I am."

Joe knew all wasn't lost because he was still alive. His gun was in the saddle bags, so there was no hope that he could get to the bags, get the gun and hold it on them before he was shot himself. His only choice was to talk his way out of the situation. They may beat him up, but he might get away alive. The fact that the man hadn't shot him already was cause for hope.

"What do you want?" asked Phil.

"He says he just wanted to see what we was doin'," said Becky.

"He can answer," said Phil and waved the gun in Joe's direction.

"Like she said. I arrived yesterday. Thought I might learn from what you're doing."

"How many of you are there?"

"Just me."

"He's lyin'," shouted one of the men from the group on the path, "I heard about these fellers. Find a claim that's good, do away with the fellers that are diggin' and take it fer themselves." He took a step forward. "Ain't that so, mister? Shoot 'im, Phil. Yer wastin' time. Just shoot 'im. If you don't, I will." He walked up to Phil and took the gun, turned, walked over to Joe, pointed the weapon at him and pulled the trigger.

Nothing happened.

Everyone, including Joe looked at the man, disbelief on their faces.

"Misfire!" shouted the man and pulled the trigger again.

Nothing happened.

Joe leaped forward, grabbed the gun by the barrel from the man's grasp and belted him across the side of the head with it. The man collapsed on the ground. Phil and the others started towards Joe, but he waved the gun at them.

"Take it easy, now, fellers. No one else needs to get hurt. What I said was the truth, so I'll just go to my horse and be on my way."

Joe knew from the weight of the gun that it wasn't loaded, but knew he was the only one that had worked it out. He'd need to get his own gun and soon.

"You men," he said, waving the gun at the men on the path, "join Becky and Phil over there."

The men moved and stood beside Phil and Becky. The other man was still motionless on the ground. Joe backed away and reached his horse. He made as though to mount, but removed his own gun from the saddle bags.

"That's better," he said, now holding both weapons. "I know mine'll work. Don't know about this'n."

He threw the gun on the ground at the group's feet. No one moved.

"I think we should work a few things out," said Joe, "and now's as good a time as any. So, why don't you all sit and be comfortable?"

Everyone sat, still staring at Joe and his gun as though they only had moments to live.

"Like I said," continued Joe, taking the reins in his free hand and standing beside his horse. The horse snorted as though to add reinforcement to Joe's words. "I only wanted to see your workings. Nothing more, nothing less. I knew you wouldn't invite me, so I invited myself. I knew it was the wrong thing to do, I knew you wouldn't like it, but I hoped to get it done and be gone. Becky here kind of messed up that plan. She's a very brave girl."

He was rewarded with a brief smile from Becky.

"Now, we'll all be neighbours and I don't want this little fracas to come between us, so let me introduce myself. Name's Joe. I'm sorry about your friend there, but he gave me no choice. I expect the only damage I've done is that he'll wake with a headache. Now for the rest of you, take it easy and this'll be the end of it. I won't interfere with you or your claim.

Becky, please pick up that gun and don't let anyone touch it until I'm gone. You're the only one I trust with it."

Becky got up, picked up the gun and retreated to the group sitting on the ground. Despite what she'd said, Joe knew she wasn't used to guns and wouldn't know it wasn't loaded.

Mounting his horse, with his gun still trained on the group, Joe touched his horse with his heels and rode quickly down the path. He expected one of the men to wrestle the gun from Becky, and waste time shooting at him before they realised it wasn't loaded. He didn't think it would be Phil, more likely one of the other men.

He could hear cries of recrimination for him and the others as he rode away. They'd be mad at him for making them look foolish, but mad also at whomever had failed to load the gun. He'd had a lucky escape and resolved to be more careful in the future. There wasn't much of a chance the men would come looking for him. It was more likely they'd see him somewhere and decide to take revenge, so he'd need to be alert. It was a bad beginning, and he cursed his stupidity. Sure, he'd learned what he needed to know, but a little planning would have given him the same information without the risk.

25. DIGGING

He couldn't move quickly once he got back to the main track. It was too erratic, twisting around boulders and fallen trees. Perhaps if the men ran, they could catch him. It was better to take his time and get far enough away that even if they came looking, they wouldn't find him.

Other camps were visible as he rode along, and he did his best to avoid being seen. It helped that it was Sunday as there was little activity. Finally, he spied what he hoped was a good spot and crossed the creek to it. He'd be less visible there and if the men came looking, they would have to cross the creek too giving him some warning.

Joe dismounted and looked around. If this wasn't the most inhospitable place he'd ever been to, he wondered where that might be. The ridge towered above him, leaving some space between it and the creek, maybe twenty yards or so. There were some flat places and even some grass for his horse, but the terrain was rocky and torn up by the creek. Gum trees of all shapes and sizes littered the slopes and the ridge was scarred and torn by wind and water. Oaks grew along the creek, their spindly shapes testimony to their harsh treatment at the whim of the weather. If there was anything good about it, it was that it was unlikely other people would be coming through. He'd not always been good at solitude, but he realised he was about to get plenty of practice.

What to do with his horse? It would be a number of days before he would need him again, so it would be best simply to set him free to graze. The lack of grass would mean that he would wander off over time. Nor did Joe want to build a holding yard, as that would take time and mean that he would have to hand-feed. He'd need to think on the problem, so he hobbled the horse and set him free. He was sure the only threat the horse faced was being stolen, so the hobbles shouldn't put him in any other harm's way.

He found a spot to pitch his tent, as far above the water line as he could get, but not that far he'd have trouble carrying water for his daily needs. There was a spot away from his camp that in his opinion showed the least prospect for finding gold that he designated as a privy. Then he walked back and forth along the base of the ridge and tried to find a spot that looked most promising for gold. He took his time, not because he wanted to be sure, but because he didn't want to be hopelessly wrong.

At last, he decided on a spot and with some daylight left, he brought his bucket, pick and shovel to where he would start work.

Knowing he had to find bed rock first, he dug in and down, using his pick and shovel by turns. It was hard going, and he was soon a mass of perspiration and blisters. He'd been working for an hour when he realised he'd chosen a bad spot. He was down about four feet and hadn't found bed rock. Instinct told him the creek was on bed rock, so he decided to go down to the creek and try to chase the bed rock up the side of the ridge. Darkness wasn't far off, so he resolved to have some supper, turn in early and be up with the birds the next morning.

Joe spent the rest of the week working from dawn to dark, chasing bed rock, trying to emulate what he'd seen the others do. Every now and again he'd take a bucket of dirt to wash in the creek, but when he found nothing, he came to distrust his technique. Each day compounded the disappointment so that by the end of the week, he was ready to give it away. The blisters were gone and had been replaced by calluses, but that was small comfort. Listening to Jacob and exploring someone else's claim hadn't taught him a thing. As far as he could tell, it was Friday, so he thought he'd give it one more day and if he'd had no luck, he'd head back to Bathurst.

Sitting over another pannikin of tea at breakfast, he thought that rather than continuing with the same strategy, he'd think a little more about it. Birds flittered amongst the trees and huge white cockatoos screamed at each other from high in the branches. He felt like screaming too but reasoned it would be no help and he would have to nut the problem out for himself. If he hadn't had the confrontation with the other diggers, he might head into the town and try to hook up with someone else, but any trip to town would be dangerous.

Jacob had said the gold was washed out of the old creek beds. The fellers up-creek had dug in to the side of the ridge and found one of those old creek beds. It didn't mean they were everywhere and maybe the fellers had just been lucky. Maybe too they knew a lot more than he did and knew where to find them. Then it hit him. It was like he'd never thought about it. Of course! If the gold leached out, why wouldn't he find it on bed rock on the creek just below him?

He grabbed his pick, shovel and pan and headed down to the creek. Bed rock abounded, so he tried to find a spot where the gold might have been caught. He found a likely spot just above the water line, removed the surface dirt and using his pick and shovel, half-filled his pan. Still unsure of his technique with the pan he worked it slowly, removing dirt and rocks by pushing them out of the pan, then adding more water and swirling the contents. There was a small indentation about six inches long near to the edge of the pan on one side and he swirled the contents of the pan in the water at the edge of the creek with the indentation away from himself. Again and again, so less rubbish remained after each swirl.

As the dirt, stones and gravel floated out, he sat back stunned.

"Jesus!" he shouted to the trees and mindless of sitting on the wet ground.

Gone was any sense of doubt, the fatigue, the sense of hopelessness, of wasting his time. There, swirling in the pan was what he had come to find. Gold! It had been there all along. In the creek right below him. He'd allowed himself to overthink how it might be found. He'd tried to learn without being taught. He'd wanted to be smarter than them all and finished up being the dumbest gold hunter at Ophir. Until now.

Then he realised he didn't know what to do with it. He hadn't brought anything to carry it in. Should he dig a hole and bury it? Come back and get it later when he had something in which to carry it?

The cockatoos started yelling at him again, squawking and screeching. What had he done to upset them? Taking it as a timely reminder, he went and sat on a rock. Thinking had fixed where to look. Thinking might fix where to keep. He remembered one of the men buying whisky at Ophir had paid for it with gold he took from a piece of cloth. Of course! Put a piece of cloth in a depression on the ground and pour the contents of the pan into it. He undid his kerchief, scooped out a hole, put the kerchief into it and washed the contents of the pan onto the cloth. He had to do two washes before he got it all. It didn't look as much once it was out of the pan.

He spent the rest of the day, not stopping for lunch and digging all around the creek. It took a while, but by the end of the day he was successful at finding the good places that yielded the best gold. The excitement remained with him the whole time and even if the pan only showed a flash of colour, the excitement was undiminished.

It was nearly dark when he stopped and the kerchief was so full, he was afraid that if he lifted it, it might tear, and he would lose everything. The cloth was a good idea to empty the pan, but it was a bad idea for storage. Rather than tempt fate, he put a flat stone over what he'd found and resolved to solve the problem overnight and retrieve his gold in the morning.

A storm started that night and torrents of water fell on his tent. There was no way to keep it out and by morning, he and everything in the tent were soaked. Shivering and cold, he crawled out at dawn and could hear the creek now that the rain no longer hammered above him on the tent. It was much higher than the night before and he was glad he'd pitched his tent so far up the ridge. The thought had hardly formed when he wished he hadn't. If he'd been closer to the creek, he'd have heard it rising and might have been able to save his gold. Where he'd stored it was now under water and only a miracle would stop it being washed away.

Despite the disappointment, he burst out laughing.

"God giveth and God taketh away," his mother used to say. Wasn't that the truth? He knew where he'd left the gold, and he carefully marked the spot by lining up trees and rocks. If there was anything left, he'd find it when the water subsided. In the meantime, he was soaking wet, freezing cold and hungry. He crawled back inside the tent and did his best to keep the water out. At least it didn't fall on him like it did outside. The wind picked up now and he realised his tent would be no match for winter. Now that he'd worked out how to find gold, he had to work out how he'd store it safely and where he'd live. There was a lot to do, but he was on a better path now and hope and confidence had returned.

Nibbling on salted beef, he wished for a cuppa, but knew there was no hope of a fire. It would take time, but the best thing he could do would be to buy a bigger tent or use what he had to build a hut. He'd seen others on the journey but hadn't taken time to check the construction.

There was a part of Joe that enjoyed the challenges and another part that resented it. He supposed that when the resentment grew stronger than the enjoyment, he'd give it away and go home. The roar of the creek came to him every now and again and he knew it would be several days before he could get across even if he wanted to. He dozed off and on over the day and was glad when the next morning arrived with the storm gone and sunshine in its place.

It took him two days to build a hut of sorts. He put it higher up the ridge than the tent since he could always move the tent, but not the hut. It was a rude affair, made of poles, bark and the two tarpaulins he used to create the tent. The bark he stripped from trees with his axe, and it was back-breaking work. He used bark and one tarpaulin for the roof, bark for the walls and the other tarpaulin for the door. A fireplace posed a different problem, but he solved it finally by creating a lean-to at the front under which he could cook. It would mean there would be no source of heat inside the hut, but it wouldn't burn down either and he could cook even if it was raining. He built a bed of poles and bark about a foot high to keep him off the ground.

The water went down after two days, and he found his gold exactly where he'd left it. He couldn't believe his luck and resolved not to be so stupid again. Emptying one of his saddle bags, he stored the gold in it. It was only a temporary solution, but it would do for the moment. It was better than the kerchief and would be able to hold the weight.

By the end of the next week, he'd doubled the gold he had found and nearly consumed all his supplies. It was time to take the risky trip to Ophir.

26. A TRIP TO THE SHOP

Joe had lost all track of time. He thought it might be three weeks since he'd started digging as he'd brought supplies for three weeks and they were nearly exhausted. The trip to Ophir would be dangerous only if he ran into the fellers whose claim he'd invaded, and he had no idea if one day would be better than another to avoid them. He'd heard and seen quite a few other people from time to time, but he'd not ever seen anyone looking for him. One time his horse whinnied and another whinnied in response, but no one came to investigate.

He woke to a bitterly cold morning; the wind blew harder than he'd seen it so far and he thought there might be snow later. It didn't take long to decide that this was as good a day as any to sell his gold and buy more supplies. If he was to get snowed in, the least he could do would be to make sure he had food for himself and his horse.

His horse came quickly when he called him. It was as though he too wanted to make a change to the daily routine. There was a quick moment of satisfaction when he hoisted the saddle bags over the horse's rump, taking pride in the weight of gold. Mounted, he was about to cross the creek when he thought he might be able to get to Ophir using his side of the creek and cross at the ford he'd used on the day he arrived.

There was no discernible track and he had to dismount several times to bypass fallen trees and big rocks. He supposed the other side of the creek had looked like this before gold diggers had carved out the track. The wind howled through the trees above him, branches and leaves fell, only to be borne quickly away. He tried to take note of the terrain, thinking that there would probably be gold there as well. It would be more convenient to dig closer to the town, but there would likely be more people as well and that would make selecting places more difficult. He'd hardly had the thought when he came upon a group of diggers, working the creek for alluvial gold the same as himself.

"Morning," he called, loud enough to be heard above the wind.

"Jesus!" shouted one of the men, "you startled me! I've not ever seen anyone come from that direction."

"Sorry."

"No matter. What're you doin'?"

"Looking for gold. Like you."

"Never seen anyone do it from a horse before."

"Been looking further downstream."

"Anythin' there?"

"No. That's why I'm coming back."

"Didn't see you go through."

"Went down the other side."

"Where's your gear?" asked the man suspiciously. The other men gathered around, all eyeing him suspiciously.

"Yeah," said another, "where's your gear?"

"What's it to you?" asked Joe.

"Perhaps you aren't what you say you are."

"What would I be?"

What kind of a place is this? Everyone suspicious, and some looking for a fight.

"Let 'im pass," said a man who had been silent so far. "It's none of our business and there's enough of us to deal with 'im if he's up to no good."

"Thanks," said Joe to the man. "You fellers have nothing to fear from me. Good day to you."

He touched his horse's sides with his boots to get him moving. After a while he looked back and saw the group still standing together and still watching him. He thought they'd probably do that until he disappeared. Now there was trouble on both sides of the creek. The closer he got to Ophir, the more groups he encountered. He noticed men working the sides of the ridge, higher up and well away from the creek. No one paid him any mind and he was pleased to pass by without further trouble. A track became discernible, and he made better progress. Finally, he crossed the ford and went into Ophir.

The few weeks he'd been away had made a difference. There were more tents and buildings and a lot more activity upstream from the town. He decided it wouldn't be long before he'd have company where he was working.

Riding into the town, he stopped a man and asked where he could sell his gold.

"Doin' all right, are ya?" the man asked with a grin.

"Enough to sell some."

"Good fer you. Store is best, although you'll get more if you ride into Bathurst or Orange."

"Which is closest?"

"The store," said the man and pointed to a building made of canvas and wood nearby.

"No. Bathurst or Orange."

"Orange."

"Thanks," said Joe and rode to the store, pulling up outside, tying the reins to a wooden rail, pulling off his saddle bags and going inside. The store was a mess, goods stacked in piles all around, on shelves built from planks along the walls and in no apparent order, but it did have a wooden floor. There were a few people to serve, so Joe waited his turn and while he waited, he checked out the floor, thinking he might do the same.

"Help ya?" said the storekeeper finally. He was a big man with a shock of curly dark hair, a sallow face, bushy beard and a smile that would make the devil feel welcome. He was standing behind a bench made of rough-hewn planks.

"Do you buy gold?" asked Joe.

"Sure do."

"How much do you pay?"

"How much have you got?"

"This much," said Joe, putting the saddle bags on the bench.

"I can sell you some canvas bags," said the storekeeper, "they'll be much better than this."

He put a piece of canvas on the bench, opened the bags in turn and shook the contents on to the canvas. The locket fell out with the gold.

"That's nice," said the man, picking it up. "Do you want to sell that too?"

Joe had forgotten about it.

"No," he said. "It's a keepsake."

"Fair enough," said the man and passed it to Joe. Turning behind, he picked up a set of scales and put them on the bench. Then, using a scoop he filled a bowl on one side of the scales, put weights on the other and gradually weighed all the gold. He poured the bowl into another canvas bag as he weighed each one.

"I make that ninety-six ounces, seven pennyweights," he said finally. "Not bad at all. That's two hundred and eighty pounds and one shilling. I suppose you don't want to carry that money around with you?"

"I don't mind, but I have to get supplies, too, so we'll see what's left after I get them."

The man laughed. "You've come to the right place and yes, everything is expensive and there's little can be done about it. What do you want?"

"Tea, flour, sugar, dried meat, oats."

"I've got some fresh meat. Only mutton, but it might make a change. Got some tinned things and potatoes. Over there. Check 'em out. See what you think."

The man served other customers while Joe wandered around and made some selections from the tins of preserved fruit and vegetables. He added some tinned herrings, a bottle of golden syrup, a kerosene lamp and some kerosene deciding it would be good to have some light in his hut after the sun set. Once again, he waited his turn.

"I'll get your flour, tea, sugar and oats. Do you want some fresh meat?" said the man.

"Yes, but I don't want chops. Maybe some shoulder, loin or shank."

Once everything was stacked to go, Joe asked how much?

The man worked on a piece of paper for a while, double checking several times. Customers started to queue, some looking agitated. "Can you get a move on?" one of them called.

"Keep your shirt on," said the storekeeper. "There's only one of me."

He continued to tick off the goods and work from the paper.

"That's forty-five pounds, sixteen shillings and four pence," he said finally.

Joe was shocked and his face must have showed it.

"I told you it was expensive," the storekeeper said and looked hard at Joe. "Can you wait while I serve these people? I won't be long."

Joe nodded, unsure why he was asked to wait.

The man finished with the customers and one more who came in just before he got to Joe.

"Store's empty," he said when the last man left, stating the obvious. "I didn't want to give you your money while there were people here. I don't know most of 'em and I'm sure someone would be happy to murder you for what I was about to give you."

"Fair enough," said Joe. "I appreciate it."

The man worked on the paper again.

"I make it two hundred and forty-three pounds, four shillings and eight pence I owe you. Do you want to check?"

"No, that's what I worked out too."

"Good with numbers, eh? How much did I pay you for an ounce of gold?"

"Three pounds."

"Fair enough," said the man laughing. "Lot of fellers pretend. Do you want a hessian sack to carry your supplies? I won't charge you for that, if you want it."

The man counted out Joe's money, gave it to him and fetched a sack from a pile behind the counter. Joe put everything in, thanked the man and headed for the door.

"Just a minute," said the man. "You forgot the sacks for your gold. How many do you want?"

"How much are they?"

"A shilling."

"Give me four," Joe said and passed the man four shillings.

"Come back again," said the man.

"I might go to Bathurst the next time."

"Suit yourself," said the man, shaking his head. "Everyone says that, then they realise the time they take to get to Bathurst would be better spent digging. More people coming all the time, so the gold'll run out sooner or later. Better to dig for it while it's there."

"Makes sense," said Joe. "I'll think on it."

Joe fixed the saddle bags and the sack on his horse and walked over to the sly-grog seller's tent, but there was no one there. *Pity,* he thought. *I would have liked a whisky. No matter, though. I'll be back in a couple of weeks.*

Mounting, he pondered the problem of how to get back to his hut. He decided the best way was to stay on this side of the creek and hope he didn't bump into the fellers whose diggings he'd trespassed. In any event, there might only be one or two doing the washing and there'd be less trouble from them than the six or so on the other side.

He'd forgotten to ask the storekeeper what day it was but decided it must be Saturday judging by the number of people heading towards the town. Most people ignored him, but a few nodded. Everyone was rugged up against the cold and seemed to have little interest in anything but getting to their destination. Nobody asked why he was going the wrong way. Most people were walking, and he wondered why they didn't use their horses and decided there might be somewhere to leave them. He'd ask about that the next time he came to town. There were fewer people the further he went along the track. He passed the men's camp without incident and breathed a sigh of relief as he crossed the creek and rode up to his hut.

27. BECKY

The kerosene lamp made the hut more habitable, but lonelier too. There was nothing to do but stare at the lamp, so he sometimes didn't bother with it. He decided he'd be better to work out how to build a chimney and light a fire inside the hut. There was a danger it might burn down, so he put his money in a tin and buried it outside.

The weather stayed cold and windy and there were flurries of snow from time to time. He dug for gold from dawn to dark each day. One advantage of the lamp was that he didn't have to leave off digging to prepare his supper. It gave him another hour of digging each day and he put it to good use.

Towards the middle of his second week after the shopping expedition, three men came along the side of the creek carrying picks, shovels and pans. Joe was still working the creek banks and there was evidence of his searching everywhere. He saw the men before they saw him, alerted by their talking. He walked up to greet them.

"Morning," he said. They stopped, looking surprised.

"The Commissioner said there weren't many diggers down here," one said.

"The Commissioner? Who's the Commissioner?"

"The District Commissioner, Mr Hardy."

"What's a District Commissioner?"

"You don't know? Have you got a licence?"

Joe remembered Jacob and the grog seller talking about a licence.

"No. Should I?"

"Everyone digging must have a licence. If you don't have one, they take your gold, fine you and put you in gaol until you pay for one."

"When did that start?"

"First of June."

Joe wondered why the storekeeper hadn't mentioned it, but decided it was probably none of his business.

"How do they find out you don't have one?"

"Christ, mister. What is this? It has nothing to do with us. Go and talk to the Commissioner."

"Before they put you in gaol," laughed one of the men.

"You doin' all right here?" asked the man who hadn't spoken yet.

Joe looked at him. He was the oldest of the three with a bushy beard, battered hat, unkempt hair and well-worn clothes.

The question stunned Joe. He realised everything was about to change. If the Commissioner had told the men to come here, then he would tell others too. Joe's private gold field would soon be overwhelmed, and he would have to share what he'd been lucky enough to have for himself until the men arrived. Now he also understood what he'd encountered when he'd trespassed on the other men's diggings. Fewer people meant more gold, but secrets can't be hidden forever.

"Nothing to say?" asked the first man who had spoken.

"No," said Joe, "just wondering how to answer."

"Then it's *yes*," said the first man, smiling, "and if you don't have a licence, you don't have a claim and we do, so we can dig anywhere, and you can't do a thing about it."

"Hang on fellers," said the older man, "we need to give this man some time. He doesn't know about any of these changes. How would you feel if it was the other way around? He's here, minding his own business and we turn up and tell him what's his is ours? Just because they made a law and didn't tell everyone about it is no excuse for us to behave like a bunch of bushrangers."

Joe looked at the older man appreciatively. He still didn't know what to say or how to react. The wind continued to tear at them, and Joe was so cold now that he'd stopped working.

"C'mon," said the first man, "let's get set up and get to it. There're others coming and there's no time to waste."

"Others coming?" asked Joe.

"Yes," said the older man. "We heard the Commissioner telling others to come this way. Said there's enough already digging upstream."

"Tell me more about the licence," said Joe, looking at the older man.

"What do you want to know?"

"What area does it give you a right to dig?"

"Ten feet at the creek."

"Feet?"

"Yes, feet."

"I'd do that a half dozen times in a day!"

"You can do that so long as no one else is digging there. The area you are digging is yours while you are digging it. Same for other fellers."

"What does it cost?"

"Shilling a day. You get a licence for a month for thirty shillings."

"Does it start on the first of the month?"

"That's right."

"What if you get a licence after the first?"

"Still thirty shillings for part of the month. That way, all the licences expire on the same day."

"That's ridiculous! Everyone will try to renew their licence on the first."

"Commissioner comes along at the beginning of the month; finds you digging and sells you a licence or renews your old one. It's easier for them, I suppose. If the police ask for a licence, no one can say they're just about to get one. All the licences have to be current all the time."

"Police?"

"Yes, the police enforce it. There's a police camp near the Commissioner's Tent on the bluff."

"Bluff?"

"Yeah. The ridge above the ford."

"C'mon," said the first man again. "I've 'ad enough of this. Let's get to it."

"Where are you digging?" asked the older man of Joe.

"Along the creek. You can see where I've been."

"You working your way up or down?"

"Up."

"Then we'll go down."

"Fair enough," said Joe.

The older man stuck out his hand.

"I'm Alex. This is Bob and Pete."

"Bob," said the first man when they shook. "Sorry if I behaved ornery. Alex is right."

"Pete," said the other man, shaking Joe's hand enthusiastically. "Pleased to meet ya."

The men set off and Joe watched with sadness. His life was suddenly turned upside down. What was worse, he'd better get a licence. In the meantime, he'd bury most of his gold so it wouldn't be found if the police came looking.

He finished off his week, working his way upstream. He didn't see much of Alex, Bob and Pete. They kept to themselves, working down the creek. Joe had no idea if they were successful. For all he knew, they had the best of it.

After not knowing the day of the week, he'd taken to marking a tree for each day, so he knew it was Friday when more groups of men came down the creek. He avoided any contact and no one came near him. Doubtless there were more groups working up the creek and finding someone digging was no surprise. There'd been no sign of the police since he'd heard about the licence.

On Saturday morning, he was up early and had a quick breakfast of tea, damper and golden syrup. The fresh meat he'd eaten in the first few days, the dried meat, flour and golden syrup were nearly exhausted. He dug his gold from the ground and loaded the sacks into his saddle bags. The weather was a little better as the wind had dropped, but the sky looked dark with the threat of rain. He set out as the first rays of the sun peeped across the ridges, picking his way carefully upstream. The journey was only a few minutes old when he came across the first group of diggers. He marvelled that they'd been so close, and he hadn't heard them. Ignoring them, he rode on only to find many groups that he had to thread his way past. They were scattered along the creek, into the gullies and along the ridges above him. It would appear the Commissioner had done a good job of encouraging others to invade his domain.

When he reached the ford, he asked a man standing there where he'd find the Commissioner.

"In his tent," the man said, pointing up the road that Joe had ridden down on his first day. "It's up there. You can't miss it."

Joe rode up the hill and hadn't gone far when he saw a timber and canvas building on a cleared area off to the side of the road. There was a British flag flying on a pole nearby. If it wasn't the camp, then at least they'd know where to find it. A line of men stretched away from the building. Joe dismounted and walked to the end of the line.

"You after a licence?" Joe asked the last man.

The man nodded. He was immaculately dressed in hat, waistcoat, long corduroy pants, boots and smoking a pipe. His white beard was tobacco stained, so Joe guessed the pipe was a permanent fixture.

"For you?" asked Joe, intrigued. *What is this fellow doing getting a licence?*

The man nodded again, but still said nothing. Joe sighed. It was going to be a long wait.

At last, it was the man's turn and he stepped through the door. Unfortunately, Joe couldn't hear what went on inside, so he had to wait his turn to find out. The man came out with a piece of paper in his hand, nodded to Joe and walked off.

"Next!" a voice called. Joe turned to the man behind him, asked him to hold his horse's reins. The man nodded, took them and Joe stepped into the tent.

There was a man at a small desk with an open book on a table in front of him. He looked harassed and was hatless, but his uniform presented neatly.

"I'd like a licence," said Joe.

"Wouldn't be here otherwise," said the man, looking up without seeing and turning the page of his book at the same time.

"Name," said the man, bending over the fresh page.

"Joseph Stratton." He deliberately lied. He didn't want to leave any footprints leading to the events in Sydney.

"Where do you want to dig?"

"Down the creek."

"Which creek?"

"The one at the bottom of the hill."

"Anyone near to where you want to dig?"

"No."

The man looked up at Joe, this time taking some time and Joe could see that he made an entry in the book giving a rough description of the licence holder.

The man kept writing, signed the page, tore part of it from the book, passed it to Joe and said, "Can you read?"

"Yes."

"Good. Then I won't have to tell you what it says."

"No, you won't."

"That'll be thirty shillings."

Joe counted out the money and put it on the table.

"Next!" called the man. The man outside waited for Joe, passed him the reins and went inside. Joe held the reins and studied the paper.

The licence permitted him to dig in the district of Bathurst during July, 1851. It said it was non-transferable, but had only his name, so he guessed the man at the desk had noted Joe's appearance in the book. He must always carry the licence with him and must produce it when asked. If he failed to carry a licence and was found digging for gold, he'd be fined five pounds for a first offence, fifteen for a second and thirty for any subsequent offence. There was nothing about where he could dig in Ophir, about any gold he had already found, nor how much area he could claim for his own, only that the Commissioner could assign an area. So, what was Alex on about? He folded the licence, put it in his pocket, mounted his horse and headed down the hill to the store.

Leaving his horse outside, he took his now-empty hessian bag and went in. There were more people than when he'd last been here, so he busied himself collecting some of what he wanted from the piles.

"I didn't expect to see you here!" said a voice. He looked up to see Becky. He started and looked about quickly to see if any of her companions were nearby.

"Don't worry," said Becky laughing, "I'm here on my own."

Joe felt relieved and must have looked it.

"It's only George that wishes you ill. I think his head still hurts."

She put her head to one side and studied Joe who wondered what she was thinking.

"A penny," he said.

"They're worth more'n that," she said laughing, "but today they're free. We talked about it after you left. We agreed George was lucky the revolver wasn't loaded. It didn't seem right to kill a man who was only curious."

"Becky, I'm sorry I went on your claim. I knew it was wrong and knew it was a mistake, but I knew nothing about finding gold. As it turned out, I learned nothing and nearly paid for it with my life."

"You know my name. I don't remember yours."

"It's Joe," he said, tipping the brim of his hat.

"You said you didn't learn much. You've been here for over a month. That's a while longer than some of the others."

"What do you mean?"

"Lotta people gone to the Turon, 'specially when the rain started."

"Where's the Turon?"

"It's about thirty miles northeast of Bathurst. They found gold there too. Some say there's a lot more'n here. I haven't met anyone that's been there, so I don't know if it's true. Anyway, how come you're still here if you've learned nothin'?"

"I learned nothing from my investigation. I thought I had, tried to put it to use and found nothing. Then I figured it out."

"You should tell others. Lots have been tryin' to work that out."

Joe laughed. He liked this girl. Shame she was married.

"Where are the others?" he asked.

"Workin'," was all she said, as though that was enough.

"How come you've got the day off?"

"I came to get supplies."

"Will you carry them? I mean, I didn't see any horses the other day."

"Of course!" she stated firmly, laughing again. "I can't carry as much as the fellers, but I can carry enough. I can't do much to help at the diggins, but I can do these jobs. I can also do cookin', washin', cleanin' and chasin' off intruders!"

"You should get your husband to do it."

"Do what? Chasin' off intruders?"

"Fetching supplies," replied Joe, smiling.

Once again, she put her head to the side, smiled and then burst out laughing.

Joe was embarrassed and knew he looked it.

"What's wrong?" he stammered.

"What makes you think I've a husband?" she said, showing Joe her empty left, index finger.

"I'm sorry … I just thought … I mean, you're way too beautiful not to have a husband!"

"Aren't you the one?" she said, suddenly looking serious. "Did you think one of the fellers is my husband?"

Joe realised he wasn't out of the soup yet.

"Well. I did. I'm sorry. I didn't mean to offend."

"I'm not offended. They're my brothers. Anyway, no one has ever called me beautiful," she said, smiling shyly. "I like it."

Joe's mind raced. Imagine meeting someone like this on the gold fields! Who would have thought it? He was tongue tied and his usual confidence had gone.

"Oh, dear," said Becky, quietly, "I hope I haven't offended you."

"No," said Joe, hastily. "It's just that, well, I'd like to come calling, but I suspect your brothers wouldn't like that."

"You're right, they wouldn't, but it's not up to them. I say who calls on me, but I'm sorry to say we're off to the Turon day after tomorrow."

"Why? Aren't you doing well enough here?"

"Yes and no. We're not doin' much better than wages and we hear it's much better at the Turon. Besides, it's dangerous diggin' under the ridge. Part of the roof collapsed a few days ago. We got some wood and shored it up, but the boys don't like it, so we're on the move."

"How will you get there? I mean, if you don't have horses."

Joe didn't really care. He was stalling for time, anything to keep her talking while he worked out a way to see her again. The brothers, especially George would be a problem, but she was attractive enough to him that he'd manage that when the time came. Of course, she and her brothers going to the Turon changed everything. He wasn't prepared to leave yet, that was for sure.

"We've arranged to go with someone else. He's got a cart, so we'll go with him. Maybe you should think about it, too?" she said, hopefully.

Joe shook his head. "I'm not ready to go yet, but when I do, I'll go to the Turon. Through Bathurst, you say?"

"That's right. Couple of miles outside Bathurst off the Sydney road. Probably follow the crowd. I think there's quite a few goin'."

"If you're leaving, why are you buying supplies?"

"Trustin' sort of feller, aren't you?" she asked, smiling. "Don't you believe me? Do you think I'm givin' you the brush off?"

Joe really liked this girl. She had more spunk in her little finger than many people he had met had in their whole body.

"No," he said, shaking his head and laughing out loud. "Look, I'm going to get some supplies, too. Perhaps I can help you carry your supplies back to your camp?"

"There isn't much. There's what we want for tomorrow and what we need to get to Bathurst. And there's two more mouths to feed with the cart driver and his mate."

"That doesn't matter. You'll be safer with me anyhow."

"You might not be when George sees you."

"I'd like to help anyway. If you'd like me to, that is."

"Yes, I would," she said smiling shyly. Joe figured she had no idea how attractive that smile made her look.

"I've got some of the things already," said Joe, holding out the hessian bag with its bulging contents by way of evidence. "Perhaps if I also buy some whisky I may be welcomed by your brothers?"

"It's worth a try."

Becky browsed the store while Joe completed his purchases. While he waited in the queue Joe stole glances at her. He'd been in love before, so he knew what was happening. When his turn came, he again bought enough for two weeks and was surprised the price was less than the last time despite the addition of a bottle of whisky.

"Lotta people gone," said the storekeeper by way of explanation. "There's trouble diggin' with all the rain and they say there's better gold and more to be found other places."

Becky noticed that Joe's shopping was complete, so she joined him and was in time to hear the storekeeper's comment.

"We're off to the Turon day after tomorrow," she said.

"You might be back," said the storeowner, hopefully.

"Maybe," she said, looking at Joe, "if there was a reason."

Joe felt his heart miss a beat and couldn't wait to get out of the store and on the road to the camp where he could get to know her better.

Becky had a canvas bag, so they tied the bags together at the top with some rope and slung them either side of Joe's horse, across the saddle bags.

28. AN ACCIDENT

Joe felt the journey back to Becky's camp was over before it started. Walking side by side with Joe leading his horse, they talked about all sorts of things. Nevertheless, he was vague when she asked what he did before becoming a gold digger. He liked the anonymity of the gold fields, and how he could use the time to become someone else.

She said she and her brothers had come from a farm near Bathurst and the same man that was taking them to the Turon had brought them to Ophir. He had the next farm, so he had brought her and her brothers in exchange for her elderly parents keeping an eye on things while he was gone. It'd had been a difficult decision to come, but her parents had pushed hard. They couldn't leave the farm to all their sons, and they couldn't leave it to one, so they decided the best thing would be for them all to make enough money looking for gold to buy their own farms. Becky had to go too, they said to look after the boys. She didn't mind, but she worried about her parents all the time, so she was looking forward to calling in on them on the way to the Turon.

He was content to listen. She chatted on gaily, hardly stopping for breath. Joe decided she didn't get to talk much, and he was certainly a willing audience. Every now and again she'd ask a question, but Joe found she was so keen to talk that she hardly listened to the answer, so he could be vague if he wanted. When she asked where he was from, he just said Sydney and she has happy with that. Then she asked what he did before becoming a gold digger, he said he worked for the Government and she was happy with that, too.

Joe had expected to find some of her brothers at the camp beside the creek. In fact, he'd been hoping two or three would be there to reduce the number of opponents if the brothers wanted to continue the fight. However, none were there, although the cradle was almost full. Becky said he could go on his own way if he wanted. Joe thought about it but decided to accompany her to the claim. He'd need to get any confrontation out of the way, and he preferred to do it sooner rather than later, so they continued walking up the path together.

When they reached the tent, they both heard panicked shouts from the hole where her brothers had been digging. They exchanged fearful glances.

"Phil?" called Becky. "Phil? Is everythin' all right?"

Just then, Phil emerged from the hole.

"Oh, Becky!" he shouted. "Jesus! Look who's with you!"

Phil was so shocked, he stood still, gaping.

"Where are the others?" asked Becky, tensely.

"Oh, Becky. The bloody hole has collapsed. George is in there. We're tryin' to get 'im out, but we can't find 'im."

"Can't find him?" shouted Becky. "What do you mean you can't find him?"

"Charles was workin' the cradle; Fred and I carried the dirt. We came back to get some more and found the tunnel collapsed and no sign of George. We've been scrapin' away at the dirt and rocks trying to find 'im."

"Can I help?" asked Joe.

"There's not much room in there and it's dangerous. It could fall again."

"If I can help, I'd like to. I think I owe you one."

"All right," said Phil. "The most important thing right now is to find George."

"What can I do?" wailed Becky.

"Pray," said Phil. "And stay outa there. Pa'd never forgive me if anythin' happened to you."

"How long has he been in there?"

"I don't know. Maybe ten or twenty minutes. Fred's just got back after I sent him to get Charles."

Joe and Phil crept into the hole. Charles and Fred were frantically moving dirt and rocks with their hands. Neither of them looked at Joe, too focused on the task at hand. All four lay side by side, dragging at the dirt and rocks. There was barely enough room to lie beside each other and work.

"We should work in teams of two," said Joe. "If we lie close to the sides, we can pull the dirt and rocks down the middle and push it to our partner behind. It'll be faster that way. There'll be more light too. All of us jammed in the entrance is making it hard to see. Do you have another lamp?"

Joe and Phil were working on the sides, so the other brothers went behind and Joe heard one of them ask Becky to get a lamp. It wasn't long before one was passed in and Phil held it up.

"Shoulda thought of that before," he muttered as the light cast shadows from the stones when he moved it and highlighted the large pile of stones, gravel and clay that had fallen.

"Doesn't look like the wood we put in 'ere has done any good at all."

The planks across the uprights had fractured and the all the wood lay tangled and broken in the mess.

"Where would he work?" asked Joe. "Was anyplace better than any other?"

"Towards the back. He wanted to go deeper. That's why we shored it up."

There was enough space to crawl across the top of the pile, so Joe took the lamp and crawled deeper into the hole.

"I'll do that," said Phil. "He's my brother."

"I'm already on my way."

Joe thought he saw colour towards the back and started for it. He brushed the roof and more gravel fell.

"Careful," called Phil. "For God's sake, be careful."

Joe reached the colour, holding the lamp up and scraping away at the dirt with his spare hand. He found a shirt. He could only guess that the head was closer to the wall. Moving across the dirt as carefully as he could, he scraped away dirt and stones and found George's head. Against his every instinct that told him to hurry, he worked slowly as he moved earth away from George's mouth. George didn't move and Joe feared the worst. Then he heard a slight cough. He put his hand on George's face. It still felt warm, but he supposed that would be normal. Then, he felt a slight movement as George coughed again.

"He's alive!" called Joe. "I've found him and he's alive!"

"Can you get him out?"

"Not easily, but at least he's breathing. He's lying around the middle of the fall, so we're going to have to move a lot of it to get his legs and pull him out. I think he's been knocked out, so he can't help. Dig towards the lamp. I'll stay with him and keep everything away from his mouth."

"Fred, you dig with me at the front," said Phil. "We'll pass the dirt back to Charles. C'mon boys! Work like the devil!"

"Can you get me some water?" called Joe, "if I can wake him up and he isn't hurt, it'll be much easier to get him out."

"Becky! Becky! Bring some water, quick!" called Phil. "Hurry!"

Within moments Phil crawled up beside Joe and passed him a billy with some water.

Joe struggled to get close enough to George to use the water. Finally, he just leant across him and poured some water on his face. It washed some of the dirt into George's mouth, but George didn't wake or move.

"It didn't work," called Joe. "He might be hurt."

Joe could feel the other three working furiously behind him. More dirt fell from the roof onto George's face. Joe tried to brush it away, but it mixed with the water, turned to mud and flowed into George's mouth. George coughed again and started to moan. Joe tried to get closer, but only succeeded in dislodging more dirt from the roof. A lot more this time, so Joe decided the only way to get George out was to pull him by the feet and do it as quickly as possible to minimise any chance of blocking his airways with dirt.

"Here's the billy," called Joe, passing it back. "I can't wake him."

Phil took it and threw it out of the hole. Joe moved back and to the side and tried to pull dirt off George. There was more ceiling room and less chance he would dislodge more dirt. He worked furiously, but it was several minutes before he'd moved enough dirt to expose George's legs.

"Help me here, Phil. I've found his legs!"

There was enough room for Phil and Joe to work on the digging and they pushed all the dirt and rocks back to Fred and Charles. There was a big rock lying across George's legs and it took both Joe and Phil a lot of effort to move it back for Fred and Charles to pull it clear.

"Jesus!" yelled Fred. "Did that fall on him?"

No one answered, too busy digging to even think about the what ifs. Finally, they'd moved enough earth for Fred and Phil to get a good hold on George's legs. Joe crawled back towards the end of the hole to try to keep dirt away from George's face, but there wasn't enough room for him to lie there and not be in the way as the others pulled.

"Get some rope," said Joe to the others. "We'll tie it to his legs and all pull from the outside. It'll be quicker that way and he'll be less likely to get dirt in his mouth."

They tied the rope to George's legs.

"Stay with him Phil. I'll use the horse if I can. But get out as soon as he's clear. I think there's more ready to fall and there might be a lot of it."

Joe crawled out, made a loop from the rope and passed it across the horse's chest.

"There, there. Take it easy old feller," he said to the horse to quieten him. "I know you're not used to this, and you don't like it, but it's not going to hurt, I promise you."

His horse settled down.

"Ready?" called Joe.

"Ready!" came a muffled voice from inside the hole.

"C'mon boy. Let's do our bit for Becky's family."

He eased the horse slowly forward. The rope tightened.

Becky, Charles and Fred all pulled on the rope at the entrance.

"I hope we don't pull his legs off," muttered Joe to the horse.

The horse started to move slowly forward.

"Well, old feller. Either he's coming out, or we've pulled his legs off."

"He's comin' out!" yelled Becky. "He's comin' out! Keep goin'! He's nearly out! That's it! That's it! You can stop now!"

Joe stopped his horse and gently removed the rope. "Good boy," he said, "well done."

"Tell Phil to get out! Quickly!" called Joe to the others.

Joe didn't know why, but he felt a premonition that the roof would collapse soon. He hurried to the entrance, saw Phil's head and shoulders coming into the light.

"The lamp," said Phil. "I forgot the lamp!"

"Damn the lamp!" yelled Joe. "Get the hell out of that hole!"

He grabbed Phil's arm and dragged him out of the hole.

"Lamp's cost money," said Phil, but Joe could see he was smiling.

"I'd rather have you than the lamp," said Becky. "Thanks Joe. For everythin'."

"I can't find anythin' broken," said Fred, kneeling beside George. "I suppose we have to wake him up before we really know if he's hurt."

"Let's take him inside and clean him up. Poor George. I hope he's all right," said Becky.

"Anyway," said Phil, "you were wrong about the hole, Joe. It's ready for us to go back in."

"Over my dead body!" shouted Becky. "No one from this family is going near the hole again. I don't care how much gold is in there!"

There was a sudden *crump!* and the front of the hole collapsed. A much bigger fall than before.

"You were saying, Phil?" asked Joe.

"If George was under that, we'd never have found him," said Charles. "I don't know who you are mister, but we sure are grateful."

"He's Joe," said Becky. "His name's Joe."

"Isn't Joe the feller that hit George with the gun?" asked Charles.

"Same one," said Phil.

"C'mon, everybody. Enough of the chatter. Let's see to George," said Becky. "We can sort everythin' out once we know George is all right."

George lay still on the ground, the rope tied to his legs and covered in dirt.

"Poor George," said Becky, untying the rope and brushing the dirt away. "He looks so helpless. Help me, fellers."

Phil bent down and picked George up, one arm under his shoulders and the other under his knees. Joe was impressed as George wasn't a small man. Everybody followed Phil into the tent. There was plenty of room inside and there were beds made of saplings and bark and covered with blankets.

"Put him here," said Becky, indicating a bed just inside the entrance. She ladled some water from a bucket into a bowl and washed George's face with a towel and the water.

"I thought he'd wake," said Joe. "He groaned a couple of times earlier."

As if on cue, George groaned.

"George?" said Becky, wiping his face constantly. "Can you hear me?"

George groaned but didn't wake.

"Should we get a doctor?" asked Fred.

"There's none in Ophir," said Becky. "At least as far as I know, there's none."

"We could take him to the Commissioner's tent", said Charles who hadn't said much so far.

"Is he a doctor?" asked Joe.

"I don't think so," said Charles, "but if there's one in Ophir, the Commissioner would know."

"Take off his clothes, Phil. Let's see if there's any wounds."

"Take off his clothes? Then he'd be naked!" said Phil.

"Good grief!" exclaimed Becky. "Do you think I haven't seen a naked man?"

George groaned and muttered, "Where am I? What happened?"

Joe mentally breathed a sigh of relief; glad they didn't have to remove George's clothing. Becky might have seen a naked man, but Joe had only ever seen naked cadavers and had no interest in seeing a naked George.

"The roof of the tunnel fell on you," said Phil, taking the cloth from Becky and wiping it around George's mouth where some dirt had gathered.

"Tunnel? What tunnel?"

"Where you were diggin'."

"Oh," said George. "Can I have a drink of water? Do you have some water?"

Becky gave George a drink of water from a pannikin.

"That's better," said George.

"Are you hurt?" asked Becky. "You've been knocked out."

"Knocked out?"

"Yes. You've been unconscious for a good while."

George saw Joe for the first time. His eyes widened.

"Jesus!" he almost shouted. "Did that feller hit me with the gun again?"

"No, no," said Phil, "he helped save you. He and his horse pulled you out of the hole."

"Are you hurt?" asked Becky, again. "Is anything broken?"

"I think I'm all right. Can I have some more water? There's dirt in my mouth."

"There's dirt everywhere," said Charles. "And you're on my bed."

"Leave him be, Charles," said Becky. "Who cares whose bed he's on?"

"What's he doin' 'ere?" queried George, nodding towards Joe. "How come he helped?"

"It's a long story, George," said Phil, "if you're all right and nothin's broken, why don't you take it easy for a while? Let us worry about why he's here."

"What about the diggin'?" said George. "I think I was onto some good gold."

"You can forget about that hole," said Phil. "It's way too dangerous now. You're lucky to escape with your life. Joe here told us to get out and lucky he did. Anyway, we'll all leave you to it. Take it easy. Lord knows, you've earned a rest. C'mon everyone. Let's leave George in peace for a while."

Joe looked back from the door and saw that George was already asleep, or perhaps pretending so. Becky put another blanket over him.

The men gathered a short distance from the tent. Phil turned to Joe and put out his hand. "I'd like to thank you for helpin' us. Not sure we could have done it without you. I suppose you've done this before?"

"I brought a bottle of whisky", said Joe, avoiding the question. "I'm sure we could all do with one after all the excitement." Joe walked over to his horse and fetched the bottle.

"We're better to gather around the fire. Let's leave George to sleep it off," said Phil, looking at the sky. "It'll be dark in a couple of hours, so we'll need to start supper soon. Will you stay for supper, Joe?"

"That's all right by me," said Joe.

"We'll have to use pannikins for the whisky," said Charles. "Glasses are in the tent."

"Nothin' wrong with whisky out of a pannikin," said Fred who had mostly been silent, "but why did you want to see us? What do you want? And why did you bring whisky?"

Fred, Charles and Phil stood in a half circle on the other side of the fire from Joe. No one had moved to get pannikins, and no one had done anything about the fire. The thought crossed Joe's mind that he shouldn't have come. Wanting to clear the air and bringing the whisky had been impulse, just as the things he did to save George, but now Becky's brothers had reverted to form and were again suspicious. Even Phil had changed perhaps because Joe had failed to answer his question about doing such a thing before. In a matter of moments, everything he had done for George was forgotten and he was the same trespasser they had found earlier on their claim.

"I'm ashamed of you!" shouted Becky, coming out of the tent. "You've got a brother in that tent that wouldn't be alive if this man hadn't helped! And all you can think to do is question him. About what? He brings a bottle of whisky and offers to share it with you and the best you can do is wonder what he's after! I know what pa would do. He'd lay the belt across the lot of you!"

"Now, Becky," started Fred. "I was just askin'."

"Don't you 'now Becky' me, you sorry excuse for a brother! I asked Joe to come here. Met him in the store. He offered to help me carry the supplies. I agreed and suggested he get some whisky to make things right with George. I told him we agreed after he left the other day that a man doesn't deserve to be shot for bein' curious and George was lucky the gun wasn't loaded, but here you are, wantin' to start the fight all over again. If I was bigger, I'd fetch that belt myself!

"What did any of you do to help George? Scamperin' about like a bunch of nitwits. Joe here took control, found George, got his horse and pulled 'im out! George'd be dead if it wasn't for Joe! Then when he tells you the tunnel is about to collapse, you tell him it isn't! So don't any of you 'now Becky' me!"

She stormed over to Joe.

"Give me that bottle!" she shouted.

Joe was stunned. He'd never been afraid of a woman before, but Becky in full flight was a sight to behold.

"Well?" she demanded again. "Give it to me!"

"What are you going to do?" stammered Joe.

"Break it over someone's head!"

"Whose?" was all Joe could think to say.

"The first brother I can catch!"

"I'd rather drink it," said Joe, but couldn't help laughing. The thought of Becky chasing her brothers about to break a bottle of whisky of one of their heads had come to mind. "They deserve to have it broken on their heads, but we all deserve a drink more."

"I'm sorry, Joe," said Phil, smiling. Joe supposed he could see the same image. "Becky's right. We've been stupid. All a bit worked up, I suppose. We didn't expect to see you again. Thought you'd be long gone. Who you are and what you do is none of our business and we do have you to thank for our brother. C'mon, lads, let's shake the man's hand and be done with the nonsense."

"That's better," said Becky, the anger gone from her voice and nodding as the men shook hands. "Fred, you fetch some wood and get that fire goin'. Charles, you get the pannikins and I'll organise some supper. While I do that, you can all enjoy some of Joe's whisky."

Fred put more wood on than was needed and the fire became too big to cook supper. They all decided they'd have to drink more whisky while they waited for it to die down. Becky encouraged Joe to talk about his digging. He explained that he'd found a place on the other side, a mile or so further downstream, tried to use their method of digging into the ridge and that it had failed. Phil explained that they'd found the gold by accident and there was nothing special about their approach, but they did think it funny when Joe confirmed that all he wanted when he checked out their claim was to see how it was done.

"If it failed," said Phil, "why are you still here?"

"Well, that approach failed," said Joe, "but I thought about it and now I'm digging where I think the gold might be and that's working. Well enough, anyway that I'm not ready to give it away yet."

The evening was well advanced when they finished supper and Joe's bottle of whisky. He was grateful there was a moon for him to find his way back to his camp. They wished him well with his digging, shook his hand and sent him on his way agreeing they might all catch up in the Turon one day. Joe had hoped he might have some final words with Becky, but it didn't happen.

29. A DRINK AND A SWIM

Joe woke the next morning with a slight hangover and decided the best cure would be to continue to dig for gold. He was aware that it was Sunday, but Sunday had never meant much to him, and he'd wasted the day before going to the store, helping with George and drinking with the brothers. Then there was Becky. He thought a lot about Becky and had to resist the urge to go visiting. She was a very fine woman, but she was going to the Turon, and he still had unfinished business with the gold in Ophir.

It was late in the morning, and he'd been surprised that he'd seen nothing of Alex and his mates. Perhaps they'd gone into Ophir, moved on or maybe took the day off for the Sabbath. It didn't matter. He had the area where he was digging to himself, and he was grateful for it.

He worked without stopping as was his custom and the pile of gold steadily grew. Later in the day, he thought he heard someone calling Joe! It was coming from upstream and sounded like Phil's voice.

"Phil!" he called back. "Are you looking for me?"

There was a muffled reply, and it was some minutes before Phil appeared on the opposite bank.

"What's wrong?" called Joe. "Is there something wrong?"

"I'll come over. I won't be long."

When he arrived, wet to the knees from the creek, Phil looked very serious.

"Becky asked me to come," said Phil. "She said I had to tell you."

"Tell me what? Is she all right?"

"Yes, she's all right, but George is not," said Phil, his voice breaking. "He died last night. We don't know when. He was dead this mornin'. Becky said she checked on him in the night and he was all right."

"Oh, Phil. I don't know what to say."

"Becky said to tell you. After you helped to save him and all."

"Shall I come back with you? Is there anything I can do?"

"No, that's all right. We'll take him back to Bathurst tomorrow. Bury him there. It'll be sad for Ma and Pa. I'll have to tell them. Can't ask anyone else to do it."

"Will you still go to the Turon?"

"Of course. Reason for diggin' is still there. Won't be the same without George, though. He was the youngest in the family. Becky said only the good die young. Me, I don't know. I figure we all have to die sooner or later. Some's young and some's old. That's just how it is."

"Would you like a cuppa? I don't have any whisky."

"No, I'll head back. Turned out you're farther down the creek than we thought, so it took longer to find you. Thanks again for your help. You did your best."

"Please tell Becky that I'm sad for her loss. Sad for all you, of course."

"She knows that. It's why she asked me to come. I think she likes you, Joe. She sure stuck up for you. Haven't seen her do that before. She's like Ma, you see. We're lucky to have her. Becky, that is. Well, both of 'em. Her and Ma."

Phil stuck out his hand. "Thanks, Joe. Might see you around." He walked off, crossing the creek, wading through the water without care. Joe watched him go, watched him until he was out of sight. It was all Joe could do not to chase after him and walk back to see Becky. He sighed. If that's what Becky wanted, Phil would have told him. Perhaps they would meet up again. Who knew? Who knew about such things?

Joe went back to his digging, glad to have something to do.

Towards dusk, the clouds rolled in, the wind freshened, and rain began to fall. Joe gathered his things and climbed the hill to his hut, glad to get out of the rain, but already soaked. He didn't have much to show for a hard day's digging, the fire was hard to light, and he was beset by a feeling of sadness. Perhaps he too should think of moving on. It didn't take long to realise that to do so would be foolish. He'd only dug in a small area and there was plenty of creek further downstream to explore.

By the morning, the rain had reduced to showers, so he set off downstream to explore for other suitable places to dig. The creek was up, running strongly and making a lot more noise than usual. There was plenty of evidence of others searching and he presumed them to be Alex and his two mates. He stayed well away from anywhere that they had dug but didn't find more than colour. After several hours, he'd gone about a mile downstream, hadn't found any good areas and hadn't seen anyone. He thought all the gold must be upstream and despite a nagging feeling he was wasting time, pressed on further down the creek.

Spot checking as he went and finding little, he rounded a bend in the creek and was shocked to see men working on his side of the creek. There were too many to have come past his camp, as he would certainly have heard such a number coming and going. The number said this was likely a better place than where he was working, so he pressed on to investigate if only to find how they came and went. As he came closer to the men, he reckoned on about fifty or sixty. He'd had little success meeting people at Ophir, so he wondered how he might ask how they were doing and how they came and went. To his immense relief, he spotted Alex and Bob so the need to introduce himself became irrelevant. The ground was rough where it had been dug over with sand, shale, rocks and dirt scattered about in piles.

"Alex," he said, walking up to the men. He could see that Pete was working in a pit, digging and passing buckets of dirt up to Alex and Bob who walked a short distance to the creek and tipped them into a cradle.

"Hello Joe," said Alex, smiling broadly, "what brings you down this way?"

"Gold," said Joe, bemused by how pleased he was to see the men.

"Run out up your way?" asked Alex, laughing.

"Just looking. How long have you been here?"

"We didn't find much up your way, so we kept coming. Found some good gold here and have been working it ever since."

"When did the others arrive?"

"Been building steadily. There's a lot more around the corner. You can't see them because of the ridge," said Alex, nodding his head at the next bend in the creek.

"How many?"

"Couple hundred, I guess. Might be more, might be less. There's a town there with shops and someone said there'd be an inn soon."

"I hear some are going to the Turon."

"I hear that, too."

"I haven't seen you coming and going."

"No, we go along the ridge there," said Alex, pointing to the other side of the creek. "The road goes to Orange and Bathurst. That's how most of the diggers get here."

Joe glanced briefly at the other two. Both had stopped working and neither pushed Alex to stop talking and get back to work. Joe decided they were probably glad to take a rest.

"You get a licence?" asked Alex.

Joe nodded.

"You see the Commissioner yet?"

"When I got the licence."

"He's been here a few times. Might only have time to go where most of the diggers are. You haven't seen him where you're working?"

"No."

"They say he's busy. Might have been someone else you saw to get your licence. I hear they'll sell you a licence at the tent if you ask for one, but they need to know where you're digging. Mostly, the Commissioner goes around the diggings all the time, issuing new licences and renewing old ones. They say most of the diggers are above the ford and around here, so I suppose we get all the attention."

"I might be digging in the wrong spot."

"No such thing as a wrong spot," said Alex laughing. "Nothing wrong with any spot if you find gold."

"How did you know where to dig?"

"Just kept trying."

"But you're down about six feet! How do you keep digging holes like that?"

"We dug a lot of holes six feet deep," said Pete, "and not all of 'em had gold!"

"People don't like to talk about what they do, Joe," said Alex. "If you tell someone how to be successful, they'll be getting the gold instead of you. I will tell you that we mostly find the gold around here above a level of clay. It's at different depths. I don't know why. We dig until we find the clay and if there's no gold, we move on."

"I thought the Commissioner allocated you an area to dig."

"He does. That's why he needs to see where you're digging. He calls it a claim. He allocates an area along the creek. We can go back as far as we like, but the clay runs out once you get some way from the creek."

"What do you do then?"

"Find another place along the creek. No one seems to mind if you have a licence and you're not using someone else's claim."

"I saw some fellers high up, on the ridge," said Joe.

"They're reef mining," said Alex. "Looking for quartz. It's harder work and you have to bash the gold out of the quartz. We might do that eventually, but we're doing all right now."

"How much are you gettin' where you are?" asked Pete.

"Don't answer that if you don't want to," said Alex, looking at Pete reproachfully. "It's none of our business, Pete. You know that."

"I don't mind," said Joe. "If we don't tell each other, we won't know where's best."

"I'd rather you didn't," said Alex. "You see Pete here wants to move. Wants to go further up Lucas Gully. Says that's where most of the whooping and hollering comes from. Isn't that right, Pete?"

"I suppose," said Pete, casting his eyes down.

"Why don't you move?" asked Joe.

"We bought the story that all we had to do was come here to be rich. Gold for the taking, they told us. Well, we found that isn't true. It's not easy to find and it's back breaking work. I figure that if we find some gold, there'll be more there, and we should stick with what we know. Otherwise, we'll be running about, always changing places, finding nothing and learning nothing."

"Doesn't make you right," said Pete, sullenly.

"No, it doesn't, but we elected me leader and as leader, that's what I say we do. You want to be leader, we'll do what you say."

"I'm all right with what you say, Alex," said Bob. "Be nice to know how we're doin', though. What about it, Joe? How much're you makin'?"

"I suppose a few pounds a day. Some days are better than others."

"That's about the same as us," said Alex. "I figure you're making a little more than you say, but that's what the fellers around the corner say. Not much better than wages and a lot of hard work."

"There's some fellers getting nuggets up near Ophir," said Pete, unable to keep the rancour from his voice.

"That's not Lucas Gully," said Bob, hotly. "One minute it's Lucas Gully, the next it's Ophir."

"Don't you start," said Pete, turning and glaring at Bob. "I've a good mind to do like Joe here. Just be on my own. Be leader. Of myself."

"C'mon, Pete," said Alex softly. "I don't pretend to know everything, but I think we're doing all right and I know we're better off with each other."

"What makes you think that? Joe here is doin' all right. He's on his own."

Joe just shrugged. There was nothing more to do here and Alex clearly had his problems. Joe wasn't helping and couldn't help, so he'd be better to leave the three men to their debate.

"I'll be off," said Joe. "Been good to catch up. I wish you well."

"Come see us some Saturday night. We sometimes go into Ophir, or maybe get some whisky from the store in the town around the corner and drink it by the creek. They call it Newtown. You can look for us in Ophir and if we're not there, come to Newtown. You can ride up the hill from Ophir and come back down along the ridge."

"On the other side?"

"Yep. We cross over here and go up the ridge," said Alex, pointing at the creek. "Might be a bit hard today with the water up like that, but it'll be down by Saturday. It's a bit of a walk up the ridge but creates a thirst."

"I don't need to go walkin' to create a thirst," said Pete, dejectedly. "This diggin' for gold is not what they told us it would be."

"Not much ever is," said Joe, smiling.

"That's the truth if ever I've 'eard it," said Bob.

Joe turned and headed back upstream, glad to be on his own.

It was nearly dark by the time he got back to his hut and the rain had started again. Light, misty, soaking rain. He'd never been so grateful to see his hut. Unfortunately, there was no sign of his horse, so he must have strayed upstream looking for fodder. Joe had not ever been away for a whole day before and he wondered if the horse might have gone looking for him. It was too dark and too wet to look for him that evening, so wherever the horse was he'd have to stay there until morning.

Joe spent a miserable night in the hut, unable to get either dry or warm. He decided it might be time to add a chimney so that he could have a fire in the hut. There had seemed little point up to now as he would move as soon as the gold ran out and anything he did to the hut would be a waste of time. He felt badly about the horse too. He'd be in trouble if he was lost or stolen and resolved to leave him in an enclosure if he was again to be gone for the whole day.

At first light, he was up and looking. The rain had stopped, and it made it easier knowing the horse would be on his side of the creek and upstream. He'd only been looking for ten or so minutes when he heard the horse snicker and saw him still hobbled and standing under a tree.

"Good boy," said Joe walking up, removing the hobbles and fitting a lead. "Sorry for leaving you all day. Can't promise it won't happen again, but I can promise to take better care of you. Let's get back to camp and I'll give you some oats."

Joe spent the next two weeks working the area around his hut. Rain fell every day and working was miserable. One day, towards the end of the second week, he decided to dig a pit, like he had seen Alex and the others do. He thought for a while before starting the dig, checking the ridge for signs of a clay layer where it had been eroded by the weather. Perhaps the gold he found had come from higher on the ridge and been washed out of the clay layer by the elements. It wasn't as though digging along the creek wasn't producing results, it was just that he'd like to find a big deposit of gold, or even a nugget like he'd heard others had done.

Eventually he selected a spot and started the dig. He was a few feet down when he realised, he didn't have a cradle! How did he think he'd separate the gold? He didn't know enough to build one, nor was there anyone nearby from whom he could borrow one. Not that anyone would lend him one! He laughed at himself. The idea that he could borrow a cradle from another digger! That was about as silly as it gets. No. His pan would have to do. It meant he'd have to bucket what he thought would be useful dirt to the creek and throw away the large stuff before using the pan.

It was a long, hard day and he was exhausted by the end of it. He'd found nothing resembling a clay layer, and by way of checking, had taken many buckets to the creek to wash. It would be easier if he knew what he was doing, but he only knew what he'd learned so far from his own experience and from what others had told him. Perhaps he should find someone that had experience and work with them for a while. He pondered it over supper that night but had not decided before going back to finish the hole the next morning.

Once again it had rained off and on overnight and there was a foot or so of water in the hole. He was confused that it simply hadn't soaked away as he was well up on the side of the ridge. It didn't take long to get rid of it with the bucket and he set to, deciding that he wouldn't dig deeper than another one or two feet. The hole was about four feet deep, and he reckoned that anything deeper than six feet would be dangerous. He wasn't sure why, he just felt that way.

He filled the bucket with dirt. It seemed coarser, with sand and small rocks dominating. It looked a different colour too, more orange, but that might have been caused by the water in the hole.

When he washed the bucket, he couldn't believe his eyes! He now knew what a lot of gold looked like. He swirled it in the pan. It was a dull yellow, almost orange colour. The pieces were in many sizes, from as big as a pea to nothing more than a fleck. He sat back, mindless of the cold ground to marvel at what he'd found. It was hard to find, but Lord! When you found it, it was certainly worth the trouble. Looking up guiltily, he checked to make sure no one was watching. In a moment he understood what Alex had said about not telling anyone anything. This was not a secret he was about to share. Nothing about it. Neither where it was, nor what he'd done to find it. Yet, Alex had told him. Just that little piece of information. A gem! Dig a hole and look for the clay layer. The result was there, but the solution wasn't complete. He didn't know what the clay layer looked like, just that the water had been trapped in the hole and there appeared to be a reddish, gravelly sand. How would he find that when he didn't know what he was looking for?

He was torn between going back to the hole and digging for more to reassure himself and going for a cuppa. Instinct told him to go for a cuppa. Thinking had proved valuable before and might do so again.

It was only a few minutes to restart the fire and put the billy on to boil. He could see the hole from his hut and tried to remember why he'd chosen that spot. It stood to reason that there was a layer of gold along the side of the ridge, and it was washed down to the creek by erosion. The gold he found along the creek was only there because of water and gravity.

If he could find the layer along the ridge, he could dig all of it and get all the gold for himself. He'd need to be careful and find several people to sell it to in Ophir, maybe even keep some and take it to Bathurst every so often.

Sipping his tea, he thought how lucky he was that maybe he'd be someone that struck it rich in the gold fields. He'd need to be careful about that, too. He didn't want any publicity finding its way to Sydney. That would be a certain way to bring himself undone. He'd need to find out what had happened about the shooting after he left Sydney, but there'd be plenty of time for that. Why, he'd only been gone a month or so. Police business didn't go all that fast.

He'd just about finished his pannikin when he heard a *cooee! Joe!*

Looking towards the creek, he saw Alex coming up the hill towards him. He looked around quickly to make sure there was no evidence of his recent find. Luckily, he'd brought his canvas bag back and put it in the hut. There was nothing to give away his recent success.

"Alex!" Joe called, "up here!"

Alex came up the hill, using the path that Joe used. It was now well worn despite Joe's efforts to conceal it.

"I'm just finishing a cuppa. Will you have one? There's plenty there."

"Yes. I'd like that," said Alex and after looking around, added, "so this his home? Not bad."

"It works. What can I do for you?"

Joe passed Alex his spare pannikin and left Alex to add sugar. Joe kept it in a golden syrup bottle where the ants couldn't find it.

"I wondered if you want to join us," said Alex.

"Us?"

"Bob and me."

"Where's Pete?"

"Gone off on his own. I knew he would. It was only a matter of time."

Joe just nodded. He hadn't thought this would happen and now it had, he had no idea what to do about it. Alex watched him, saying nothing. Both men sipped their tea from time to time.

"You taking a rest?" asked Alex finally.

Joe nodded. "It's miserable. Been raining off and on all morning, but you know that."

"Not doing so well?"

"I'm still doing all right," said Joe, guardedly.

Alex squinted, looking at Joe in a different way.

"I think better than all right," said Alex after a few minutes. "Like I said the other day, most people don't tell the truth."

"I'm not most people. Anyway, why do you need me? Can't you and Bob work on your own?"

"It's a job for three people. I like you, Joe. Like the cut of your cloth. I didn't think you were most people either, but just then, well you looked like you might have not been telling the whole truth."

"Does it matter?"

"No, I suppose not, but there's something about the truth. Sometimes people don't want to hear it, but mostly we're grateful for it."

"Where did Pete go?"

Alex shook his head. "Dunno. He didn't take anything, so he's got nothing to dig with. He might have gone to join someone else. Might have met someone at Morkill's."

"What's Morkills?"

"Store in Newtown."

Alex finished his tea and stood up. "Doesn't sound like you want to join us."

"I'm a loner, Alex. I work better on my own. If there's other people with you, you need to make decisions that suit them. I only have to suit myself. I like it that way."

"Fair enough," said Alex. "Bob'll be disappointed. Like me, he was hoping you'd say yes."

"Pete might come back."

"There's always that. See you around. Come up to see us one Saturday. If you come, we can talk some more."

"I might do that."

Joe watched Alex walk away, his shoulders hunched against the drizzle. His stride was quick, and he handled the uneven path with ease. Joe had to be more careful. Alex had noticed something and if Joe was to keep his secret, he'd have to get better at hiding it.

The sky was still dark and held the threat of even more rain. He spent the rest of the day in the hole, and it wasn't until darkness fell that the gold, he pulled from the hole with each bucket began to diminish. The canvas bag was full, and Joe reckoned on three- or four-pounds weight. That's over one hundred and fifty pounds sterling! And he'd dug it all from one hole!

Over supper that night, Joe pondered his dilemma. If he kept the find to himself, he could only dig so much. When others found out about it, they'd be crawling all over the area between the creek and the ridge. He could pretend that no one would ever hear of it, but he knew he was only fooling himself. Alex was already suspicious, and Joe wouldn't be in the least surprised to see Alex and Bob searching his area of the creek the next day.

The best thing he could do would be to get busy digging. He'd kept all the hessian sacks, so he could use those to keep the gold, provided he didn't put too much in them. There was no way they'd handle the same amount as the canvas bags. Then he could transfer it to the canvas bags from time to time to transport and sell it.

His supplies were about to run out, as was his licence. If the Commissioner didn't come looking for him, he'd have to find the Commissioner. It wouldn't do to be caught without a licence and have his gold confiscated.

He rose early, checking both his date tree and his supplies. Both tasks took no more than a few moments. It didn't take long to decide that he'd spend that day which he knew to be Friday digging, then head into town the next day, buy supplies and sell his gold. He knew he'd get away with it this time as a few pounds weight of gold wouldn't raise too many eyebrows, but if he was that successful every day for two weeks, then his secret would be known.

The drizzle continued and made for miserable digging. He stayed with the same hole, widening more than deepening it. He cursed the rain. It made it so much harder to understand what made up the sides of the hole. He had to be able to recognise the clay layer and the rain made that impossible. The water still puddled in the bottom of the hole, and he had to bucket it out from time to time. Late in the day he saw some people pass by on the track below, heading away from Ophir, but they didn't stop. He reckoned that he'd added about a pound's weight of gold to his haul. That was no cause for disappointment, but he still didn't understand where best to dig, or how far to go down.

Not knowing how long it would take to renew his licence, he was up early the next morning and saddled his horse for the trip to Ophir. He noticed the leather of the saddle was mouldy and supposed that he probably stank after several weeks without a bath and probably looked every bit as mouldy as the saddle. Nobody smelled as much in the winter, but he resolved to clean himself up a little before going to Ophir the next time.

The licence was easy. There weren't many people in the queue and a different man served him. He asked for Joe's current licence, stared at it and stared at Joe.

"There's nothing wrong with this one," the man said. It's good until the end of the month. That's another two weeks."

"Sorry. I lost track of time."

"Don't worry. Lot of people do. Lot of people don't know the time, either."

Joe left, slightly embarrassed and headed for the store. As he rode down the hill, he noticed a lot more activity above the creek in the hills and ridges on the other side. The sound of digging and talking came to him clearly on the morning air. Ophir was becoming busier. *Doesn't matter,* he thought. *So long as they all stay up this way and leave me alone.*

The water at the ford was higher, but not dangerous so it was easy to cross, and it wasn't long before he rode up to the store. He noticed there were less tents in the village.

It was the same storekeeper, but he didn't recognise Joe who didn't mind. Not being noticed was a good thing.

He sold all his gold, and the man didn't raise an eyebrow. He gave Joe the change after he deducted the cost of the supplies.

"Your mates'll be pleased with the money, but I'll bet they'll complain that you didn't buy enough supplies!" said the storekeeper when he handed Joe the money.

"One of the fellers brings the rest from Orange. I'm just topping up."

"You could sell your gold there," said the man. "Might get a better price."

"We're happy with your price."

"Fair enough. Not tryin' to rob you."

"That's what we think. I noticed there were less tents about outside."

"Some have moved to the Turon. Sick of the rain and not findin' much. Folk say they might come back when it stops rainin' if they don't like the Turon."

Other customers came into the store and Joe took the chance to leave. He would have liked to stay and chat, finding out more about what was happening. The rain made it harder to dig, but it was no more than a nuisance.

There was a boy outside the store, throwing stones at a tree.

"Maybe it's moving," said Joe.

"What do you mean, mister?" asked the boy. He looked no more than ten, had a shock of red hair and was shoeless.

"The tree. Maybe it's moving."

"Trees don't move!" said the boy proudly as though informing Joe of recent news. "What makes you think it's movin'?"

"Well, it seems you can't hit it."

"Can too!" shouted the boy. "Watch!"

He threw several more stones, none of which hit their mark.

"Must be moving," said Joe. "You look like a pretty good shot to me. Anyway, where's Newtown?"

"Newtown?"

Joe nodded.

"Down river."

"How do I get there?"

"Two ways. One is up the hill there," said the boy pointing. "That's the best way. You need to be careful. You can miss the turn off and finish up in Orange. The other way is to foller the creek. Track's difficult that way. Pa always goes up the hill. Says it's longer, but easier."

"You been there?"

"No," said the boy. "I live down here. I go to school over there." He pointed down Lewis Ponds Creek.

"The creek?" asked Joe, pretending to be confused.

"No. To the side of the creek. They wouldn't put a school in the creek. That'd be silly."

"No, it wouldn't. Haven't you heard of a school of fish?"

"No. What's a school of fish? Is that in a creek?"

The boy then broke into a huge grin.

"You're fun mister. You're funnin' me, aren't ya?"

"No. Ask your teacher. I didn't know there's a school here."

"It's not really a school. One of the mothers does the teachin'. She's all right."

"I have to go," said Joe.

"Where are you goin'?"

"Down the creek a mile or so. Might even go to Newtown."

"Why don't ya go up the hill?"

"If I go this way, I can go to my claim, or go to Newtown. I don't care if the track is difficult. Horse'll do most of the work."

"Can I walk with you for a bit? I'm going to school, so I'm goin' that way."

"You can ride if you like. I'll walk."

"Oh mister! That would be a treat!"

"Here you go then," said Joe, picking the boy up and dropping him on the horse. "I'll take the reins and you hold the saddle."

"It's pretty high," said the boy, doubtfully.

"Haven't you been on a horse before?"

"No. I've only ever been in a cart."

"Where are you from?"

"Sydney."

"Sydney's a big place," said Joe, idly wondering where in Sydney.

"I think so too. Do you mind if I walk? I don't like it up here."

"Don't you think you should at least try for a while? You won't get any better if you don't try."

"I suppose. Some of the children ride to school. They come from a long way, but I don't know how far."

"Then they must know how to ride. It might be too far to walk."

"I'm glad I live close."

"How long have you been here?"

"A month. Pa's got a blacksmith's shop."

"Is he in the town?"

"Yes. We all live there. He says he's busy and he's glad he came."

"What were you doing at the store?"

"I walked there with Ma. She wanted to do some shoppin'. She left me outside. I don't like it in there. He hasn't got any treats."

"Won't your ma worry about you?"

"Why?"

"Won't she expect you to be there when she comes out?"

"No. She went shoppin' and I was goin' to school."

"How come you were throwing stones at the tree?"

"I'm not allowed to do it at school."

"Where in Sydney are you from?"

"Redfern."

"Which is better? Redfern or Ophir?"

"That's a silly question."

"Why?"

"We live in a house in Redfern. Here it's only a tent. Pa's the only one that likes it here. Everybody else wants to go home."

"If he's busy, then he's making money."

"That's what he says."

"I might come and see him if my horse's shoes need fixing."

"You can if you want. I have to get off here." The boy sounded relieved.

"Why?"

"The school's just there" said the boy, pointing at a canvas and timber structure.

"Don't forget to ask your teacher about the school of fish," said Joe, helping the boy off his horse.

"She might laugh at me."

"She won't."

"See ya," said the boy and walked to the tent.

Leaving Ophir behind, Joe followed the track along the side of the creek. He was familiar with it now and walked his horse easily and unhurriedly. Going past the point where he'd seen Becky's brothers cradling for gold, he thought about them and hoped they were doing well. The day was not far advanced when he reached the point to cross the creek to his hut, so he crossed, left his supplies at the hut and returned to the other side of the creek.

The track followed the creek and every now and again he had to cross smaller creeks running into it. The recent rain was still evident and all the creeks he crossed were flowing, contributing to the main creek. There were more men working, some along the creek and others along the ridges. He sometimes saw horses fending for themselves and no evidence of digging or diggers. Perhaps they were strays and perhaps they were hobbled.

He thought about his decision to explore several times, but decided he needed company. It would be good to find Alex who might doubt his motives, but the need to share a drink and conversation drove him on. Besides, he wanted to find out what was at Newtown.

From time to time the ridges beside him were steep, winding their way upwards amongst the trees. The eucalypts grew thickly on the ridges above him, sometimes so thickly that he knew he wouldn't see diggers even if they were there.

He rounded a sharp bend in the creek not far from where he had seen Alex and the others working the other side of the creek, but there was no sign of them now. Other men were working the same area, some digging, some carrying dirt and others using cradles. Perhaps he should get a cradle. It looked like they made washing a lot easier.

The ridge to his left came down to meet the creek and he was aware of a road and some traffic. Not much, a few men, horses and a cart. He must be nearing Newtown, and this must be the road that Alex talked about that enabled carts to bring supplies from Bathurst and Orange.

Finally, he could see quite a few tents and a few buildings in the distance. He guessed that to be Newtown. It didn't matter. If it wasn't someone there would know where to find it. He saw a building made mostly of canvas, but with some timber and a chimney. It all looked very new, maybe even a few days old and Joe rode up to it. He had to ride around some trees and rocks at the bend and climb a little up a hill. All the tents and buildings were far enough up the hill to avoid water if the creek flooded.

Several saddled horses and a cart with two horses still in harness were standing out front. Some chickens pecked at things on the ground and glanced at Joe without interest as he rode up.

There were three steps leading up to a platform at the front and a man in his shirtsleeves with a hammer looked to be doing some work on them.

Joe rode up and pulled up beside him.

The man looked up and wiped his brow with the back of his hand holding the hammer.

"This Newtown?" asked Joe.

The man nodded.

Joe looked around briefly again before dismounting.

"Hot work?" he asked, raising an eyebrow.

"Is there any other?" asked the man, smiling. "Be done soon, anyway. Still got plenty to do. What're you looking for?"

"Whisky."

"We've got that. You're new to the diggins?"

"Sort of. Been here a month or so. I thought to meet a couple of fellers here for a drink."

The man shook his head. "You can't drink here," he said. "I can sell you a bottle of whisky, but you can't drink it here. Maybe you're meant to meet your mates somewhere else?"

"Is there somewhere else?"

"There's always somewhere else."

"You're not being much help."

"Mister, I'm a storekeeper. You want to buy something, I'm your man. You want help to find your friends, you'll need to talk to someone else. Anyway, I don't have time to talk. I've got to finish this and go back inside."

"Is there another store?"

"Do you want the whisky or not?"

"Is there another store where I can buy the whisky and drink it there?"

"Do you mean an Inn?" asked the man, smiling.

"I suppose."

"Not yet. Might be one day, but not yet."

Joe suddenly remembered. "Is this Morkills?" he asked.

"No," said the man, still smiling.

"Sorry to trouble you," said Joe, mounted and rode off, sorely embarrassed.

There was a man riding slowly down the road, not far away. Joe rode up to him.

"Do you know where I can find Morkills?"

"The store?"

Joe nodded.

"Follow the road around. He's a bit further along. You'll find him easy enough."

"Some friends said I can have a drink with them there."

"You can't drink there. Fellers buy whisky and drink it by the creek. If it's cold they light a fire, sit around it, drink whisky and tell stories. Sometimes there's a feller that sings."

"Where by the creek?"

"Just below the store. That way, if they run out of whisky, they can buy some more."

"Do you go there?"

"Sometimes. Depends on the weather. Been rainin' too much. There'll be no one there yet. Mostly they meet around sunset. Get a good day's diggin' in first."

"Where are you going?"

"Now?"

Joe nodded.

"Back to my camp. Why?"

"Just wondering. I thought you might be going for a whisky."

The man laughed.

"Like I said, too early. I've been in Orange. Rode there to sell my gold and get some supplies. Just gettin' back."

"Why don't you sell your gold and buy your supplies here? There're at least two stores."

"Well, supplies are cheaper, and I get a better price for the gold in Orange. The new store might change that, but we'll see."

The man looked at Joe sharply. "You've got a lot of questions," he said.

"Sorry," said Joe. "I suppose I'm killing time."

"How's that?"

"Waiting to meet my friends. They said to meet them at Morkills."

"Be a few hours yet," said the man, looking at the sky. "What're your friends' names?"

"I only know their first names. Alex and Bob."

"Don't sound familiar, but there's lots of fellers and they come and go."

"Thanks for your help," said Joe. "Might see you later."

"Sure," said the man and kneed his horse to get him moving.

Joe rode back to the store.

"You again?" said the man, looking up from his exertions. "I thought you were off to Morkills'?"

"Thought I'd buy the whisky from you."

"If you wish. I won't be long if you want to wait. Unless you want to help me, that is."

"I can do that. What do you want me to do?"

"Just hold the step. It's come loose. Customer fell off it. Lucky, they didn't hurt themselves. Been trying to nail it back on."

The man was trying to hit a small nail with a large hammer.

"I think you need a smaller hammer, or a bigger nail."

"You're right. Just being lazy. Back in a few seconds. Just gotta go to the cart."

"I'll come with you."

"It's just there. Anyway, do you think the nail needs to be that big it'll take both of us to carry it?"

"All right," said Joe laughing, "I'll wait here."

He cautioned several people coming and going from the store to be careful of the step. The day was cool with little wind and the rain still held off. The sun came and went as clouds rolled by. He thought he could spend a few minutes waiting in worse places.

The man came back and held up the nail to show Joe.

"There you are," he said, "and managed to carry the damned thing myself."

"Good for you!"

It took no time to finish the job. The man dropped the hammer to the ground and said, "Let's go!"

"I've got time if you want to put the hammer away," said Joe, nodding at it.

"It'll still be there later. I can do it then. There's no rush. Let's get you that whisky."

The door into the store was made of canvas and wood. Once inside, the man walked to a corner and picked up a bottle of whisky from some crates. Goods were stacked about in haphazard fashion and Joe marvelled that the man knew where to find anything.

"That'll be ten shillings," said the man, putting it on a table that Joe guessed acted as a counter.

Joe didn't argue about the price. He knew things were more expensive at the diggins. He counted out the money and passed it to the man who put it in a tin.

"See you again," said the man, smiling.

"Maybe," said Joe.

"Why did you come back?"

"I didn't feel right about not buying the whisky from you."

The man just nodded. Joe picked up his whisky and left the store.

Once outside, he glanced at the sky. The wind had picked up and the sun played hide and seek behind dark clouds. It looked like rain and Joe was torn between waiting the hour or so for men to arrive by the creek or heading home and not bothering to catch up with Alex and Bob. *That's if they are even coming*, he thought. Thinking it would take up some time to check their claim, he rode back around the corner and gazed into the middle distance. No one that looked like them was digging where he thought they might be, nor on closer inspection did they seem to be anywhere along the creek.

Despite the impending rain, he rode back along the creek to Morkills and then down to the creek where he could see the remains of a large fire with rocks and logs gathered around it. He supposed that's where the diggers would gather and the need for company overcame a sense of wasting time to wait for anyone to turn up.

He found a spot with a little grass nearby and with the bottle under his arm, left his horse to graze and went back, sat on a rock, took a glass from his pocket, poured a whisky and sipped it, enjoying the little warmth he received from the feeble rays of the setting sun.

It wasn't long before he saw a rider crossing the creek in front of him and recognised him as the digger he'd met earlier. The creek flowed swiftly, the water reaching up to the man's feet. Despite the depth, the horse walked steadily as though accustomed to the crossing. The man pulled up nearby, fixed a nose bag to his horse, pulled a bottle of whisky from his saddle bags and joined Joe. He took a glass from his pocket and poured himself a whisky.

"Should get the fire goin'," he said as he clinked his glass against Joe's.

"I suppose," said Joe. "I thought you said it was too early."

"Saw you sittin' 'ere. Thought I'd join you. Too late for diggin'."

Then he looked up at the sky. "Might rain soon too, so there'll be no chance of getting' together if that 'appens. Might as well get started."

"Where do we get the wood for the fire?"

"Around. Mostly from the side of the creek or in the bush behind us," he said, sticking a thumb over his shoulder.

"When do you want to do that?"

"I don't want to do it at all. Mostly I wait for other fellers to do it. I usually come a bit later. You mucked things up a bit."

Joe looked at him, wondering if he should take offence. He stuck out his hand. The man took it and said, "Tinker, but everyone calls me Tink."

"Mine's Joe."

"Pleased to meetcha, I'm sure. Haven't seen you before."

"No. I work a bit further up the creek."

"Where do your friends work?"

"Little bit up the creek, too. But not too far. Just around the corner."

"Some of those fellers have gone up past me."

"Where's that?"

"Lucas Gully. They're findin' alluvial gold there."

"The fellers were talking about it."

"Everybody's talkin' about it. I wish they'd shut up."

Tink drained his glass and put it and his whisky bottle beside the rock where he was sitting. "Be dark soon," he said. "Best get some wood while we can still see."

They spent the next fifteen minutes dragging some wood to where the fire had previously been.

"It's all a bit wet," said Tink. "I'll get some dry stuff to get things started. Back in a minute."

Joe could hear him amongst the trees away from the creek, stumbling and cursing in the near dark. He came back and stuffed some leaves, twigs and sticks under the wood pile. Joe struck a match, and it wasn't long before the fire had started and they resumed their drinking, sitting quietly watching the fire take hold.

"Should be some others here soon," said Tink. "Fellers in the tents nearby won't worry about the rain."

They filled their glasses, sipped their whisky and sat in silence. The evening was nothing like Joe had expected and he regretted his rash decision to stay. He'd expected more company and worried his only company would be Tink.

Joe looked up at the stars. Those he could see twinkled brightly and looked close enough to touch. Despite the stars the night was pitch black and if it wasn't for the fire, Joe wouldn't be able to see his hand in front of his face. He hadn't thought about the journey back to his hut and realised he might have to camp out. There'd be no way he could go back along the creek, and he didn't fancy the long ride over the Orange road.

"Worryin' about gettin' 'ome?" asked Tink. Joe couldn't see his face, but he was sure Tink was smiling.

"No," said Joe, but knew there was no conviction in his voice.

"If your friends come, you can stay with them."

"They're not expecting me."

"If you don't want to stay, horse'll know the way."

"How's that?"

"He'll be able to see. Let him 'ave 'is 'ead. He'll get you 'ome."

"Maybe," said Joe, unconvinced.

Some other men turned up and it wasn't long before the whole mood of the evening changed. There were stories, songs and poems. Everyone had brought a bottle of whisky and while most people poured the first few drinks from their own bottle, it wasn't long before drinks were poured from any bottle into any glass. Some of the men introduced themselves, but Joe forgot the names almost as soon as he heard them. It didn't matter. Names weren't necessary to listen to the stories, the poems or to enjoy the singing. Now the evening was everything he had hoped for and throwing caution away, he settled into enjoying himself and before long he lost all track of time and how much he'd drunk.

At one stage Joe thought he might have been talking to Alex but wasn't sure. More wood was brought, and the fire became too hot to sit near. Having moved away from the fire, Joe could no longer find his bottle, but it didn't matter. As soon as his glass was empty, it was filled again.

"Here comes the rain!" someone called out and large drops fell into the fire, causing it to hiss and crackle.

"I'm off!" called someone else and the crowd began to disperse.

Joe was vaguely aware that Tink was talking to him. "Will you be all right?" he thought Tink said. "Do you want to stay with me? It'll be cramped, but who cares?"

"I'll be all right," mumbled Joe. "Where's my horse?"

The rain fell heavily and Joe tried to peer into the dark, hoping to see his horse. Tink was gone and he couldn't see him either.

"Tink?" he called. "Are you there?"

He had trouble with the words and even to him they didn't sound right.

A man stood beside him.

"Joe. It's Alex. Where's Tink?"

"Tryin' to find my horse," mumbled Joe.

"He won't find it in the dark," said Alex with authority.

Tink came up to them.

"I can't find my horse either," he said. "Hope no one's nicked 'em. We'll have to get 'em in the mornin'. Alex, can Joe stay with you?"

"If we can get him across the creek."

Joe was only vaguely aware of the conversation about him.

"Can't go without my horse," said Joe.

"No choice," said Tink. "Don't worry, we'll find 'im in the mornin'. C'mon Alex. Let's get Joe outa the rain."

They took an arm each and headed for the creek, supporting Joe under the armpits. Joe had trouble walking, so he leant on the men heavily.

"He's heavy," said Alex. "Why don't we leave him? Find a tree and put him under it?"

"C'mon Alex. Just put your mind to it. You wouldn't like it if we left you," said Tink.

They got to the creek. As drunk as he was, Joe could see the water was definitely up and probably more so since earlier.

"I don't like the looks of it," said Alex.

"Rubbish," said Tink. "Anyway, I'll bet you can't really see it."

"That might be true, but I can hear it!"

Joe was aware of the conversation and aware he was being carried if not dragged to the creek.

"Don' wanna. Jush let me stay. Let me schleep," said Joe.

"Not you too, Joe," said Tink. "It's too wet to stay out tonight. You'll catch your death. C'mon Alex. Let's get it done."

"All right," Alex muttered, "but I don't like it at all."

Joe was aware of being dragged into the water. He could hear it roaring, feel it bashing against his legs and getting deeper as they waded out.

"Jesus," said Tink. "It feels stronger than when I came over earlier. Let's get back."

They tried to turn around, but Joe slipped from their grasp.

"Christ! I've lost him!" shouted Alex.

"Me too!" shouted Tink.

Joe could feel himself being dragged under by the fast-flowing water. The cold and the effect of the whisky meant that he was completely disoriented. He tried to stand up, but his feet didn't reach the bottom. The water dragged him under, and he gasped in fright, filling his lungs with water. In that moment, he knew that he was drowning, knew that his life was over. He tried to think of one good thing that he'd done, one good memory someone might have of him. Nothing came to mind and in that moment, he knew that he'd wasted his life. It made no sense that he'd been put on the earth and if it hadn't been for a reason, then why was he there? He thought he saw his mother reaching out to him to help him. As he tried to reach back, he felt a blow to his head, and everything became black.

30. SPARROW

When his consciousness returned, he wondered if he was in heaven. In his church-going days he was told that heaven was a wonderful place with happy people and comfortable beyond anything he could imagine. There was a pretty, young face not a foot from his, staring at him intently. A girl, he decided, a pretty, young girl. Her blonde hair was pulled back from her face, her eyes round and inquisitive. He couldn't see her teeth as her serious expression prevented their exposure, but he'd be willing to bet they'd be perfect.

"Hello," he said and smiled.

"Da! Da!" the girl screamed. "He's awake!"

She was so close and the scream so loud that it hurt his ears, leading him to the conclusion that it may not be heaven after all. But then, if it was hell, everything he'd been told about hell might be wrong too as he wasn't hot at all.

A large face with a black beard and a smile loomed close to his, replacing the girl's.

"We thought we'd lost you," the voice said, softness and warmth in it.

"Where am I?" asked Joe.

"Lewis Ponds Creek," said the man, "downstream from Newtown."

"How far down?"

"A mile or so."

"How did I get here?"

"Sparrow found you."

"Who's Sparrow?"

"That's me," said the girl's face, now leaning close as well. Joe's vision was filled with the two faces.

"I'm Jim," said the bearded face. "Are you hurt?"

"Where did Sparrow find me?"

"By the creek. You were caught up in the branches of a tree that had fallen into the water at the edge. We decided you must have fallen into the creek too. Sparrow was woken by our dog barking and went to investigate. Found you and raised the alarm."

"Dog?"

"Brownie," said Jim. There was a brief yelp in response to the name and an extra face was added to Joe's vision. Joe guessed the face belonged to Brownie. It was cocked to one side and studying him inquisitively.

"Are you hurt?" asked Jim again.

"My head hurts," said Joe.

"I saw the bruise there," said Jim. "You probably did that when you fell in the river. Where are you from?"

"Ophir," said Joe.

"My goodness!" a female voice exclaimed. Joe immediately knew there was yet another face to add to his collection, but the new one did no more than talk at this stage.

"Ma took your clothes off," said Sparrow.

"What!" exclaimed Joe.

"Don't worry," said Jim. "Susie was a nurse in Sydney, so there's nothing to be embarrassed about."

"What's your name?" asked Sparrow.

"I'm Joe," said Joe, glad to have something else to think about. He was terribly embarrassed that someone had removed his clothes.

"I can't believe you've fallen into the creek at Ophir, been swept all the way down here and you're still alive," said Susie. "If you have then it's a miracle."

"No, I was at Newtown last night. I suppose I fell in there."

"Suppose?" asked Sparrow. "Don't you know where you fell in?"

"Now, now, Sparrow," said Susie, "you leave Joe alone for a few moments until he collects his wits. He's lucky to be alive. Jim, you and Sparrow organise a cuppa. I'll check Joe out and make sure he's all right."

"But!" exclaimed Joe. "I'm all right. Can't I just get dressed?"

"Goodness me," said Susie, "what's with you men? What part of a naked man do you think I haven't seen before?"

"Can I stay?" asked Sparrow. "I haven't seen a naked man before."

Jim laughed, a nice, gentle belly laugh that sounded more like a chuckle.

"Not this time, our little bird," whispered Jim, "there's plenty of time later for that."

"Oh, Pa!" exclaimed Sparrow as she and Jim left.

Susie wordlessly moved to somewhere else in the room and Joe tried to work out where he was. He was on a bed that felt like the standard bark and pole construction and as far as he could see, he was in a canvas and timber hut. Susie stood by the bed. She was a bigger version of Sparrow as far as face and hair were concerned, but she was big of body and bosom. *Every bit a nurse*, thought Joe and resigned himself to his fate.

"Your clothes aren't quite dry yet," said Susie, "but I'm sure they're dry enough to satisfy your modesty. I'll leave them here, you put them on and when you're dressed call me and I'll come and check you out."

"How long have I been here?" asked Joe.

"Three, maybe four hours," said Susie. "You were as cold as charity when Jim brought you in. It took me almost all that time to warm you up."

"How did you do that?" asked Joe, almost afraid of the answer.

"Hot rocks wrapped in cloth. I'm surprised you can't feel 'em in the bed. There are so many there, Jim was worried the bed would collapse."

"Whose bed is it?"

"Sparrow's."

"Poor Sparrow."

"It's no such thing. She was so excited to find you. Anyone would think you'd come from the moon! Anyway, let's get you dressed and checked out. I must admit, I don't think we'll find anything too wrong, but I'd rather be sure than sorry."

Susie left, Joe pulled the covers away and sat on the side of the bed. The ground was covered in a tarpaulin and cold to the touch of his feet. He sat for a moment before getting up and putting on his damp clothes. His boots were far from dry, and he pulled them on with difficulty. Emerging from the hut, he saw Jim, Susie and Sparrow seated near to a fire on pieces of a log that were cut to about a foot long and standing on their ends.

"I'm ready to be checked out."

Susie got up, took his arm and led him back inside.

"How do you feel? Is anything broken?"

"I don't think so. Nothing hurt when I got up and walked."

"You've a nasty bump on your head. You might have a headache for a day or so, but I think you're one lucky feller. Let's join the others."

"Here he is," said Susie, stepping outside. "Here take this log close to the fire. We've had breakfast, but I can get you a cuppa and some damper if you would like."

"We'll all have a cuppa and keep you company," said Jim.

Susie busied herself with dough and water and had a damper cooking in a metal dish in no time. She poured four pannikins of tea and gave Joe his first. Sparrow gave him a spoon and held a small bag of sugar while Joe put three spoonsful into his tea. When he had finished, Sparrow didn't move but stood looking at him intently.

"How did you fall in the creek?" she asked.

"It was an accident," said Joe, "I didn't mean to."

"Accidents happen," said Jim. "Do you remember the time you fell while you were chasing the lizard?"

"That was the lizard's fault!" said Sparrow defiantly. "I wouldn't have fallen if he didn't try to get away!" She went back to her seat, her question forgotten.

"Well, it doesn't matter," said Susie, "the main thing is that Joe is alive. And doesn't appear to be hurt. You look cold, Joe. Jim, fetch one of your coats. The poor man will freeze to death out here. Perhaps we should sit inside?"

"I like the fire," said Joe, "let's stay out here."

Jim came out with a coat and Joe put it on gratefully.

"The weather's been awful," said Jim. "So much rain and looks like we might get some more today."

"Where's your claim?" asked Susie.

"Close to Ophir," said Joe. "Maybe a mile downstream from there."

"Are you doing all right?" asked Jim.

"I'm finding some."

"Maybe more than some," said Jim, smiling.

"Where's your claim?"

"Lucas Gully. Just over the way there. It's not far. Quite a few fellers digging there."

"You doing all right?" asked Joe, smiling.

"I'm finding some," said Jim, also smiling.

Susie took the dish from the fire, cut the damper into pieces and smothered them all with golden syrup.

"Are we having some too?" asked Sparrow, hopefully.

"If you like."

"I would, but just to keep Joe company," said Sparrow smiling impishly.

Susie put the pieces on a plate and passed them around.

Joe hadn't realised how hungry he was until he took his first bite. His piece disappeared in seconds.

"I think we'd better leave the rest for Joe," said Susie, laughing. "That piece sure didn't last long!"

"Sorry," said Joe, gratefully accepting another piece. He finished his tea and stood up.

"I'd better be off," he said. "No doubt my friends will be wondering what's become of me."

"Of course!" said Jim, standing. "I'd forgotten. They would be worried."

"They might be looking for you," said Sparrow.

"Yes, they might. What's the best way back to Newtown?"

"Go up the hill behind us there. There's a track of sorts. People bring goods from Orange. When you get to the top of the ridge, go left down the hill and you'll find Newtown at the bottom."

"Thanks, Jim. Thanks to you all. I don't know how to thank you. Especially you, Sparrow. If you hadn't found me, I might be dead."

Sparrow just smiled and Joe got up, gave the coat back to Jim and set off towards the ridge. The sun poked through the clouds from time to time and he was glad of the warmth when it did. It didn't take long to reach the top and it was a steady walk down the ridge to Newtown. When he reached the bottom and came near Morkill's, he saw Alex standing on a rock with his back to him, talking to a group of men. There was a man sitting on the wooden platform at the front of the store.

"What's going on?" Joe asked the man, nervously.

"Feller's lost in the creek. They're organising some men to go lookin' for 'im."

"Alex! Alex!" shouted Joe.

"Shh!" said the man. "He's tryin' to talk to those fellers."

"Alex!" Joe shouted even louder, ignoring the man.

Alex looked around and his face broke into a huge grin.

"Joe! Oh, Joe! How good it is to see you!"

He jumped down and ran over, shouting as he did.

"This is the feller! He's all right! We don't need to look for him!"

"This is him?" asked someone, disappointment in his voice. "Now I'll have to join the family in Sunday prayers."

"You can stay here," said another man. "I've got some whisky. We could have a drink to celebrate."

"Good idea," said the first man.

"Where did you get to?" asked Alex of Joe. "We've been looking all morning. I came back to organise some more men. Tink and Bob are still looking for you."

"I was knocked out. Some people pulled me out of the creek and looked after me until I came to."

"C'mon. Let's find Tink and Bob and give them the good news. Tink will be relieved. He thinks we killed you."

"Has Tink got his horse?"

"Dunno. I don't think so. He didn't use it this morning. Why?"

"I don't see mine."

"Maybe Tink's got them both somewhere. Let's go and see what's doing."

Joe and Alex headed off down the creek. There was very little evidence of any digging and large rocks and tree trunks made the going very difficult.

"We've been fighting with this stuff since first light. It's made it very difficult to look for you. We thought you might be jammed under a rock, so we've been taking our time."

It was about thirty minutes before they came on Tink and Bob. They had to come up close before getting their attention. The water in the creek was tumbling amongst the rocks making it hard to hear.

"Joe!" shouted Tink when he saw that Joe as alive. "I thought I'd killed you! Thank God you're alive. Where did you get to? We've been lookin' for you all mornin'! How did you get upstream?"

Both men were soaking wet from searching in the creek.

"Some people pulled me out of the creek about a half mile downstream. I walked up the ridge and came down into New-town from up there," said Joe, pointing up at the ridge line.

"Be easier than walkin' through this stuff," said Bob. "It's been a lot of hard work."

"Have you seen my horse?" Joe asked Tink.

"No. He might be in the trees somewhere near Morkill's. Let's go back up the ridge like you did. Be much easier to go back that way. It's funny no one's been diggin' anywhere along here."

"No gold, I suppose," said Bob.

"How would they know if they haven't looked?"

"Beats me."

The four men clambered up the ridge. It was hard work without a track, tree branches and bushes tore at their clothes, and they slipped frequently on stones and pebbles.

"I don't know which was worse," said Bob when they reached the top. "But at least I'm not cold anymore."

"I'm sorry about you wasting your time searching," said Joe as they walked along side by side down the ridge to Morkill's. "But I was knocked out, so I couldn't get back earlier."

"Don't worry about it, said Alex. "I'm just glad you're alive. We tried looking for you last night, but it was a waste of time in the dark. To be honest, I only expected to find your body this morning. Tink didn't give up hope though. He was out and about with the dawn, searching the creek."

"Thanks, Tink. You too, Bob."

They arrived back at Morkill's and each chose a direction to look.

"He won't have gone far," said Tink. "Mine was in the trees there. I didn't look for yours. I was too busy lookin' fer you."

They didn't look for long. There weren't many places to look.

"I hope he's not stolen," said Bob when they all gathered back near Morkill's.

"Me too," said Joe, feeling stupid for getting so drunk, falling in the creek and failing to look after his horse.

"What'll you do?" asked Alex.

"I'll go to the police in Ophir tomorrow. Someone might have turned him in."

"Good idea."

"I'll go home now," said Joe. "I'm beat."

"Will you come back for a whisky next Saturday?" asked Alex.

"I might never drink again," said Joe, "but I might have to come back."

"How's that?"

"There's a lot of people went out of their way for me this morning and I should buy them a whisky to say thanks."

"You don't owe us anythin'," said Tink, "but I wouldn't say no to a whisky."

"We've all got to cross the creek, so let's go together," said Alex, smiling. "Don't want any more accidents."

They crossed easily where the ford had been built up.

"Should have crossed there last night," said Joe.

"Too hard to see in the dark. Anyway, it doesn't matter. There's been no harm done."

"Except for my horse," said Joe, bitterly. "See you Saturday."

Joe's boots were still wet and chafed his feet as he walked. He was sure he'd have blisters like walnuts before long. It took Joe an hour to walk back to his hut and it was nearing dusk when he arrived. All the way he cursed himself for his stupidity and carelessness. He'd heard the ancient Christians had flogged themselves as penance and he understood why as his feet hurt more and more. There was some satisfaction in the self-inflicted pain. As he started walking up the ridge to his hut, he was startled to see a shape move in the shadows and he whooped for joy when he heard a brief snicker of recognition. He ran the last hundred yards and startled his horse by putting his arms around his neck. Joe felt overwhelmed with gratitude and struggled to control his emotions.

31. THE PRESENT

Joe spent the next hour tending to his horse. The saddle and cloth were still wet from the rain the night before. He stripped the tack and put it in the hut. There's be time enough to dry it later. He rubbed his horse down with hessian sacks, talking all the while, apologising and promising to take better care of him. Once he was done, he hobbled the horse and gave him extra oats in a nose bag. The horse stayed close to the hut as though he too was glad to be reunited.

"He could have headed off at any time last night," Joe muttered to himself. He'd taken so little notice of his horse while drinking whisky.

Joe cooked himself a bigger than usual supper and turned in early. His sleep was troubled by dreams of drowning, and he was glad when early light filtered into his hut, and he could get on with the job of digging. A quick breakfast of tea and damper and he went back to the hole he'd been digging.

There was about a foot of water in the hole, and he had to bail it out before taking some mud to the creek to wash. He continued to get good gold all day, scraping at the sides of the hole, but knew by the end of the day it was spent.

Joe spent an hour the next morning trying to find another place to dig. If the layer of reddish clay held the gold and rain and weathering leached out the gold which was then washed down to the river, it stood to reason that the clay was at some angle to the ridge. Perhaps it ran along it or was at right angles to it. It was impossible to tell, but Joe would eventually have to work out how to keep finding it if he was to be successful in hunting for gold.

Eventually he decided to just enlarge the hole he'd already been working on. If he could chase the clay layer, all the better. The rain and the water in the hole made it difficult to distinguish any features, so he reluctantly started on another hole nearby. He hadn't been digging long when he heard a *cooee!* from the track below. He looked down to see a young policeman astride a horse.

"Yes?" called Joe.

"You got a licence?"

"Yes."

"Then bring it down and show me." The policeman's voice was young and uncertain. He sounded like he wasn't used to giving orders.

Joe went down the slope, scrambling over rocks and pushing aside ferns. He always tried to use a different path so people wouldn't easily see where he'd been digging. Well, that's what he tried to do. Alex had no trouble finding the path he used, he admonished himself. Joe waited until the man crossed the creek, then pulled his licence from his shirt pocket and gave it to him. As he did, he studied him. He looked young, maybe early thirties. His uniform was new and the standard issue like Joe used to wear. Joe had heard that there was some trouble with the country police force where they preferred to wear their own clothing, but it looked like this young man was proud of his. He was blonde and clean shaven under his cap. His face wore an earnest expression, as though he took his job very seriously.

"I suppose you think this is a joke," he said to Joe, turning the licence in his hands.

"Why?" queried Joe, taken aback by the question.

The policeman passed the licence back.

Joe looked at it. It was blank. He'd forgotten that it had been for a swim and had spent several hours in his wet pocket. The writing had all been soaked off.

"It's a valid licence," said Joe. "It's been in the water. I fell in the creek."

"It's not a valid licence if I can't read it."

"It's valid I tell you."

"Where did you get it?"

"At the Commissioner's tent."

"You can't get a licence at the Commissioner's tent," said the policeman, but with a little uncertainty in his voice as though he wasn't sure. "Anyway, it doesn't matter. It's not a valid licence if I can't read it."

"Have you got the book?"

"What book?"

"The book you use to issue licences."

"Why?"

"Well, I can show you where my licence was issued."

"All right," said the policeman, dismounted and took the book from a saddle bag.

"When was yours issued?"

"End of last month."

The policeman looked in the book and Joe looked over his shoulder.

"This book starts on the fifth of July," said the policeman triumphantly.

"Then it's in another book."

"I can't help that."

"Give me a replacement."

"A replacement?"

"Yes, write out another licence for me for this month."

"I will if you give me thirty shillings."

"Why would I give you thirty shillings?"

"That's the price of a licence."

"I've already paid for it. I don't want to pay again."

"But I have to give the Commissioner thirty shillings for every licence I issue."

"Didn't they tell you how to replace a licence that's been ruined?"

"No one mentioned it."

"Look," said Joe, "I know it's your job and they should have told you, but I've got a valid licence. See? It's the same shape as the ones in the book."

"But it doesn't have any writing!"

"Doesn't mean it's invalid. You could be in a lot of trouble if this goes to court, and they ask you why you didn't accept a valid licence."

"Trouble? Court?"

"How about I go to Ophir and get another at the Commissioner's tent? They'll have the original book where it was issued."

"Yes, do that," said the policeman sounding relieved. "I don't know anything about replacement licences. I'm new and Mr Green, the Assistant Commissioner told me to check on people's licences and issue them to people that didn't have one. He told me he'd expect me to have thirty shillings for every licence I issue."

"Where are most of the people digging now?"

"Most of them seem to be upstream of the Bluff at Ophir. There's no one along here. You're the only person I've seen."

"What about Newtown?"

"That's where I was going when I saw you. I don't know how many people are down there."

The policeman looked around as though seeing the area for the first time.

"Perhaps you should move? Go where the other people are? This can't be a good place if there's no one else here?"

"I found some gold down by the creek when I first came here, but nothing since. You might be right. Perhaps I should move. Where are people mostly finding it?"

"I don't know. Like I say I'm new. You could ask at the Commissioner's tent when you get your licence. I'm sure they'd know. But if I was you, I'd move."

The policeman mounted and was about to ride off.

"What will I do if someone else comes along?" asked Joe.

"They said they usually go around at the beginning of the month, so I doubt you'll see anyone before then. Besides, I'm only going through here on the way to Newtown. One of the fellers said they usually go west up the hill and around the ridge. Mr Green said to come this way to see if anyone was digging, but apart from you I haven't seen anyone this far down."

"Is there anyone closer to Ophir?"

"Yes, on the flat downstream of the town."

"Thanks," said Joe and waved. The policeman waved back, crossed the creek and rode on.

Joe worked for the rest of the week, starting early and finishing late. The new hole proved a success, and his collection
of gold steadily grew. He tried to work by using several buckets to collect material for washing. He never left his pan close
to the creek and tried to throw rocks and dirt out into the
creek so he wouldn't leave obvious tailings. He always checked
to make sure no one was on the track before he went to pan.
He didn't always manage to avoid people, but no one ever
bothered him even if he was panning by the creek. Everyone
seemed to think he was in the wrong spot as did the young
policeman.

Sometimes he heard people moving on the track below and
one time a horse whinnied and his did the same in response,
but no one came looking for him. One day it rained hard all
day, and he spent a miserable time in his hut waiting for the
rain to stop.

The following Saturday morning he was up early and
headed for Ophir. He had to wait before the Commissioner's tent was open, then argued with the man on duty about
replacing a licence. Eventually, they found the right book and
Joe's entry and the man reluctantly wrote out a replacement
licence. Like the young policeman, he'd not previously had
such a request, but came to see the logic of it. He agreed that
a digger shouldn't have to pay for a licence twice.

Armed with his new licence Joe rode down the hill, across
the ford and into Ophir. He went to a store that he hadn't
used before. There were two women talking in the doorway
and he thought to ask them for help. Dismounting, he went
over to them. He went to take off a hat that he wasn't wearing and stood looking foolish with a hand hovering near to
his head.

"I wonder if you'd help me?" he asked, dropping his hand by his side. The women were about the same age, but one looked friendly and the other didn't.

"Is it your head, dear? Is something the matter with it?" asked the friendly one.

"No, not at all. No, my head is all right. It's just that I want to buy a present for a young girl and I haven't done such a thing before. I don't know what to get."

The unfriendly one looked even more unfriendly as though she doubted Joe's motives.

"You might need to go into Bathurst," said the friendly one.

"Go to Bathurst?" demanded a loud voice. "Who wants to go to Bathurst?" The storekeeper approached. He was a big man with a shock of white hair, a red face and a belly that stretched the apron he wore to what looked like its limit.

"Ah, Samuel," said the friendly one, "this man is looking to buy a present for a young girl. I said I thought he might have to go to Bathurst."

"Dolls," said the unfriendly one. "Girls like dolls."

"I don't have any dolls. Why would I have dolls? Diggers got no use for dolls."

"I was just suggesting," said the unfriendly one. "I thought it might help."

Joe wished he'd gone somewhere else. It looked like he'd stirred a hornet's nest.

"Now Samuel, you must have something. Betty was just trying to help. Weren't you, Betty?"

Betty looked at her friend gratefully as though pleased to be a part of the discussion again.

"How old is she?" demanded Samuel.

"I don't know. Perhaps ten."

"Perhaps you could get her a bonnet?" suggested Betty.

"I've got some sweets. Does she like sweets?" said Samuel.

"Everybody likes sweets," said the friendly one.

"Come and have a look," said Samuel to Joe. "They're back here."

He walked behind some stacked boxes and reached to a shelf that held some jars, taking one and putting it nearby on the stack of boxes.

"These are acid drops," he said, taking the top off the jar and letting Joe have a whiff of the contents.

"I think they're too sour," said Betty. "I don't like them."

"What about you, Grace? Do you like them?" asked Samuel.

"I do," said Grace. Betty looked crushed as though she was again deserted by her friend.

"Can I try one?" asked Joe.

"If you pay for it."

"That's all right. Perhaps the ladies can try one too?"

Samuel reached into the jar and pulled out an acid drop for each of them in turn.

Joe tried it and grimaced.

"That's what I think, too," said Betty, triumphantly.

"You'll get used to it," said Grace, laughing. "You have to have a few, then you'll like them a lot."

"I never will," said Betty, seeming to try to stand taller as though getting ready for an imminent fight.

"Is that all you've got?" asked Joe.

"I've got some lolly sticks."

"Oh, they're my favourite!" exclaimed Betty.

"Can we all try one of them, too?" asked Joe.

"If you pay for it," said Samuel, reaching for another jar on the shelf.

Joe nodded and Samuel reached into the jar, pulled out three lolly sticks and gave them one each.

"You chew pieces off," said Grace. "Little bites are best, like this."

She bit off a piece and Joe did the same.

"What do you think?" asked Betty. "They're better, aren't they?

"Yes, I think they are," said Joe, enjoying the sweetness of the treat. "How much are they?"

"A penny each."

"I'll take a dozen of each."

The ladies went to move away and Joe once again went to touch a non-existent hat.

"You should buy a hat, too," said Grace.

"I will! Thank you both for your help."

"I hope the little girl likes them," said Betty.

"I'm sure she will. Good day to you both."

The men watched the ladies leave and Joe turned to Samuel.

"I need a hat."

"Over there," said Samuel waving at a shelf with only one type of hat. "Those ones are popular."

Joe didn't think he needed to mention that there was only one type of hat there. He tried several before he found one that fitted well enough to buy. He went back to the counter and waited while Samuel served another customer.

"How much?" he asked.

"What else do you want?"

"I don't need anything else."

"Where do you get your supplies? I haven't seen you before."

"The other stores."

"Why did you come here?"

"The women were standing out front. I needed their help."

"I'll offer you a better price. Come here the next time."

"I might. How much for what I bought?"

"I've wrapped the sweets for you," said Samuel, pushing a parcel across the counter. "That's two shillings for what you've got there, a sixpence for what you and the ladies have had already and ten shilling for the hat."

Joe counted out the money and went to leave.

"Remember?" called Samuel. "Don't forget!"

"I won't," said Joe, thinking he might. However, if the treats were a success, he might be back for more.

He left the store, put the parcel in a saddle bag, mounted and rode down the creek towards Newtown. It was about mid-morning and a typical mountain winter's day. A brisk wind blew, grey clouds flitted across the sky and the air smelled like more rain might be coming. He's never been in a place that rained so much. Riding past where he'd met Becky's brothers, he thought of them all, but especially of Becky. Since his adventure in the creek, he thought more about Becky and regretted not finding out more about where she lived so he could find her. He was developing a plan that he could have a future with her, but it would mean he'd have to build his nest egg and his search for gold was now more important.

Around the middle of the day, he rode past Morkill's and up the ridge, turning off when he reached the track down to Jim's.

He came out of the trees and crossed the grassy area, pulling up outside Jim's hut. He had a better chance to look it over this time and was impressed with what he saw. Jim had done a good job. It was a sound structure of timber and canvas, but not that permanent that it couldn't be pulled down and moved. Pulling up outside and dismounting, he called out, "Hello? Anyone home?"

There was no answer.

A man cutting wood nearby stopped working and called, "You lookin' fer Jim?"

"I am."

"Why do you want him?"

"I've a present for Sparrow."

"She'll like that."

"I hope so," said Joe, smiling.

"They're up the gully," said the man, pointing. "That one there. They're not too far, although I haven't been to his claim."

"Thanks for your help," said Joe, getting back on his horse.

"No trouble. I needed a spell anyway. It's hot work."

"Good on a day like this," said Joe, waving an arm in the air.

"If it wasn't fer a day like this, I wouldn't be doin' it."

"Fair enough," said Joe and rode through the creek where he now knew the ford to be.

He rode up the gully the man had indicated. It was wide at the bottom with grass on both sides of the creek which was flowing briskly. Men worked on both sides, some digging and others cradling. The cradles were placed regularly along the side of the creek with men bringing buckets of earth to them. No one took any notice of Joe, who rode carefully between the cradles and the hill, taking what he assumed was the usual track.

There was a man standing watching two others working a cradle.

"This Lucas Gully?" he asked the man.

"No, it's Black Springs Gully."

Joe was confused. Her thought Jim had told him that he was working in Lucas Gully.

"Do you know Sparrow?" he asked.

"Everyone knows Sparrow," the man replied.

"Do you know where I can find her father's claim?"

"Now, why would you want to find that?"

"I assume Sparrow will be there and I want to see her."

The man looked at Joe suspiciously and remained silent.

"I've got a present for her."

"A present? What kind of a present?"

Joe was getting a little annoyed and was about to ride off.

"You the feller that fell in the creek? The one Sparrow found?"

"I am," said Joe. "I bought her a present to thank her. I reckon Sparrow might have saved my life."

"I think that's probably true. They're just up the ways a bit. You can't miss them. She'll be pleased to see you. Talks about you all the time."

"Thanks," said Joe and continued walking his horse up the gully. Like the man said, he'd only gone about another hundred yards, and he saw Jim digging not far from the creek. The hole wasn't deep, so Joe thought he might have just started it. Susie and Sparrow fussed over a cradle beside the creek, their backs to him.

"Hello, the digger," called Joe as he came close, admiring Jim's strength and effortless use of the pick.

"Well, look who the cat's dragged in!" shouted Jim, looking up from his digging.

"Joe! Joe!" called Sparrow. "You've got a horse! I didn't know you own a horse!"

Joe dismounted near the cradle and Jim joined them.

"Good to see you!" Jim said, shaking Joe's hand furiously. "What brings you up this way?"

"I nearly got lost. I thought you were digging in Lucas Gully?"

"Moved the other day. It's better here."

"I'd like to have a horse," said Sparrow, wistfully.

"She's always liked horses," said Susie.

"When we strike it rich," said Jim.

"Did you strike it rich, Joe?" asked Sparrow.

"Not yet."

"See Daddy? You don't have to strike it rich to get a horse! Can we get one? Please?"

"We'll see," said Jim.

"That means no," said Sparrow.

"Maybe," said Susie. "Like Jim says, what brings you up this way?"

"I brought a present for Sparrow."

"For me? The horse? Oh, thank you Joe!"

"Steady on, young lady," said Jim. "Let's ask Joe what he brought for you."

"I brought this," said Joe and pulled the parcel from the saddle bag.

"Oh, Joe. Thank you. What is it?"

"Open it and see," said Susie and sat on a stump. "Here beside me on the grass. You don't want whatever is in there to spill out."

Sparrow knelt beside Susie and opened the parcel so slowly and carefully that Joe wondered if she thought he'd brought her some eggs.

"What are they?" she asked in wonder when the contents were visible.

"Sweets," said Joe. "I brought you some sweets."

"What do you do with them?" asked Sparrow.

"Why you eat them!" announced Susie. She seemed just as surprised as Joe that Sparrow had never seen a sweet.

"There're two kinds there. One's a lolly stick and the others are acid drops."

"Which one should I try first?"

"I think these ones, the acid drops," said Joe, pointing. "They're not as sweet, but the man says you'll like them after you have one or two."

Sparrow picked up one and put it in her mouth. She grimaced like Joe had earlier. When she had finished, she tried a lolly stick and proclaimed them to be the best.

"Would you all like one?" she asked, a small frown on her face as though dreading that everyone would.

"No, they're your present," said Susie. "Besides, if we try your acid drops, you won't have enough left and the man said you had to try a few before you'll like them."

Sparrow wrapped the parcel as carefully as she had unwrapped it.

"Thank you, Joe. It's a wonderful present."

"Why, it's to say thanks for saving my life. I think I'd be shaking hands with the devil if it wasn't for you."

"The devil? Do you know the devil?" said Sparrow with a small look of fear on her face. "They said at school that he's not very nice."

"No, I don't," laughed Joe "and I don't want to!"

"Will you stay for supper, Joe?" asked Susie. "I can put some more water in the stew."

"No, I won't. I promised a whisky to the fellers that looked for me last Sunday. Will you join us, Jim? I'd be pleased if you would."

"I don't drink whisky, Joe. Did once, not anymore."

"I'll be heading back then," said Joe.

"We'll come with you," said Susie. "Jim has started a new dig and we can't do much at the moment. We were just fooling around when you got here. That all right with you, Jim? I can start supper so it'll be ready when you finish here."

"Of course, off you go."

"Would you like to ride, Sparrow? Would that be all right, Susie?" said Joe.

Susie looked at Jim who nodded.

Joe took the parcel, put it in a saddle bag, picked up Sparrow and popped her onto the saddle.

"Is it all right up there?" he asked, but the smile on Sparrow's face told him it was more than all right.

"You hold the saddle at the front and I'll lead him so we can take it easy."

"Look at me, Daddy! Oh, will you look at me! Oh Joe, thank you."

Joe took the headstall on one side and Susie walked beside him on the other as they set off slowly and carefully down the track. Joe looked at Sparrow from time to time to make sure she was all right, but Sparrow waved at the diggers, calling excitedly, "Look! Oh, will you look!"

"I think you've made someone very happy," said Susie, laughing.

Most of the diggers stopped working and waved, some calling encouragement.

"I take it she hasn't been on a horse before?" asked Joe.

"I don't know. She's always loved horses, but Jim hasn't ever told me why."

Joe looked at her quizzically. The answer made no sense to him.

Susie looked at Sparrow to see if she was listening, but she was too busy calling to the diggers, replying to their encouragement.

"Sparrow's not my child. I'm Jim's second wife."

"She calls you ma."

"And I like it."

"Do you have any of your own?"

"We haven't been married long and being in the diggins doesn't permit what's needed to allow that to happen."

Joe was embarrassed. He hadn't expected the conversation to take such a turn.

"I'm sorry, Joe. I didn't mean offence. I'm a nurse, so I'm happy to talk openly about it. If you're not, we can talk about something' else. What about you? Tell me about you?"

"There's not much to tell."

"Oh, you men! You'd rather be tortured than talk about yourselves! I feel foolish asking such a stupid question!"

"It's not stupid."

"You said there's only you. Has there been anyone else?"

"No," Joe said, but Susie looked at him sharply.

"There is someone, isn't there?"

"Possibly."

"Is she here?"

"She was, but she left."

"Where did she go?"

"The Turon."

"Jim says we might go when there's nothing left here."

"Where will we go?" asked Sparrow.

"Nowhere for busy bodies," said Susie laughing. They'd arrived at the ford and crossed easily. Joe lifted Sparrow down and she hugged him fiercely.

"Oh, Joe! You're such a good friend!" she exclaimed. "The best one any girl ever had! Will you come again? Soon? Please?"

"You can still change your mind about supper," said Susie, her head to one side and smiling broadly. "I think Sparrow would like you to stay. I think she's afraid you might be breaking other hearts all over the diggins!"

"No, I'll be going," said Joe, looking at the sky. "I think we're in for more rain, so I'd like to get there, buy a whisky and get home."

"As you wish. Thank you for coming and for making our little one so happy."

"Please come soon!" called Sparrow as he rode away.

He stopped briefly before heading up into the trees and was delighted to see Sparrow and Susie still watching him. He waved and they waved back. Joe couldn't remember another time in his life when he'd enjoyed himself so much. Such a simple gift and Sparrow was so grateful.

It didn't take long to get to Morkill's where he hobbled his horse and set him up with a nose bag. He went and bought two bottles of whisky and spent the next half hour collecting wood and dumping it in the fireplace. Checking the nose bag showed his horse had finished, so he took the bag off and left him to graze.

Alex and Tink came around sunset, and both were delighted to discover Joe had found his horse. Joe poured a drink into their glasses, and they all laughed about the events of the previous Sunday. When other men arrived, he poured them a drink too. The drink did the trick, and no one teased him about falling in the creek.

As soon as his two bottles were empty, he took his leave amidst protest and headed home across the creek. It started drizzling on the way and he pulled his coat tighter around his shoulders. He thought if the gold didn't play out soon, he'd have to build a chimney on his hut so he could be warm inside and an enclosure with protection for his horse. Then, if he did, he would only draw unwanted attention to himself.

32. BATHURST

Joe spent the next few months following a familiar pattern. He was never able to work out how the clay layer was positioned in relation to the ridge. If there wasn't too much rain, he was able to find the layer and track it, scraping at it and filling his buckets. It was only ever a few inches deep, so if it rained the layer became mingled with the dirt and he couldn't distinguish it. He would always find good gold at the bottom of the hole he dug even after heavy rain, so he never abandoned a hole before he'd find very little in a pan.

The layer seemed to meander, so he decided finally it was an old creek bed. Sometimes he would find it when he dug a hole and sometimes, he didn't. When he didn't, he had to do several holes until he found it again. The layer wasn't continuous, so what he found was pockets of gold in some indeterminate pattern.

When he exhausted his supplies, he would head into Ophir to sell his gold and to buy more supplies. He often thought he'd come home via Newtown and catch up with Alex, Bob and Tink and perhaps even see Sparrow, but he never did. His focus was now on finding all the gold he could before someone else came and took a claim near to him.

Each time he went into Ophir, there seemed to be fewer people and one time one of the stores was gone. The store-keeper that he used told him that the Turon was proving to be more successful, so many people had gone there meaning there were less customers. Joe thought that when his gold ran out or he faced digging competition, it might be time for him to go there too.

Then there was the matter of Becky. She was never far from his thoughts, but he consoled himself that he was build-ing his store of gold for both of them. He sometimes feared that she may not be as excited about a future together but would put the fears aside since his memory of her liking him remained clear. He'd never really resolved how he would find her. She told him a little about herself and he knew at least the first names of her brothers and that one of her brothers had died in Ophir.

There came a day when he'd gathered sufficient money that he was no longer content to leave it in a tin in the ground. A trip to Bathurst was inevitable where he'd open an account in a bank and leave his money there. He only supposed there'd be a bank there, but if there wasn't then there had to be some-where that he could safely put his money. Of course, Orange was closer, but Becky came from Bathurst.

As he dug for gold, he planned the trip. There were two main goals. The first was to put his money in a safe place, the second was to make inquiries about Becky. He thought that if he moved quickly enough, he'd be able to get there in one day and return the next. His hut on the side of the ridge wasn't all that visible, but he didn't like the idea of being away too long and coming back to find someone in residence. Neither of those days could be a Sunday as nothing would be open for him to achieve his goals. No, the best idea would be to go on a Friday and come back the next day. He hoped he'd get there in time to at least put his money in a bank, but if he didn't, he could do it the next morning. It wouldn't matter what time he got back on the Saturday night, although he knew it would be hard to navigate the track from Ophir to his hut if there wasn't a moon.

Then there was the matter of how much money he would carry. He'd heard talk of people being able to pool their gold with the Commissioner for safe transport to Bathurst, but he'd heard nothing about the same facility for money. There could well be robbers on the road, and he could only hope that they had also gone to the Turon. After pondering the problem for some time, he resolved to be armed, ready and vigilant.

Before dark on the next Thursday, he cleaned, loaded and fired his revolver. There'd be no room for error if he was attacked and it wouldn't do if his weapon failed. He doubted anyone would be close enough to check on the recent shot and would likely ignore it thinking someone had bagged a kangaroo.

He got up at dawn the next morning, had a quick breakfast, put some biscuits in his coat pocket and set out for Bathurst. The thought crossed his mind that such was the change in the weather, he'd gone to sleep in Ophir and woken up somewhere else. There was little breeze, the sky was blue, the air crisp and he had a wonderful feeling that it was good to be alive. The foliage was wet from the night and his legs were soaked before he reached the hill that he would have to climb past the police camp and the Commissioner's tent. There was no one about as he rode by, but there didn't need to be. He had no business at either place.

There was no one else on the road, although as he rode up the hill, he passed a few tents at some of which fires were lit and people stirring. No one took any notice of him. The hill was steep, and his horse worked hard despite being fresh. He didn't recognise anything from his journey to reach Ophir until he came out of the trees and into the more open fields. There was nothing specific, just the sense that he remembered the road and the surrounding area.

Hour after hour his horse plodded on, and the oncoming traffic increased as the morning went on. There was no shortage of water in the creeks they crossed as he had hoped. It was mid-afternoon before he approached Bathurst from the west. The country was rolling green hills despite being winter. The Macquarie River was to his left and came close to the road from time to time. He could see where people had camped, no doubt using the river as a convenient place to stay on the journey to Ophir.

Bathurst seemed to stay forever on the horizon as he crossed the rolling hills. He'd been fretting for the last hour or so that he wouldn't get to a bank that day and would have to hang on to his money overnight. Despite his decision that he could do all his business on the Saturday morning, the prospect of spending the night with a large amount of money in his possession filled him with dread.

Finally, he could see that the town was close, and he stopped a man as he rode across a creek not far from the town and asked him where he'd find a bank.

"There's one," the man said pointing, "and it's new. You have to stay on this road."

"Is it on this road?"

"No, it's on William Street. Goes off this one"

"How far?"

"I don't know. Don't know much about distances."

"How long?"

The man shrugged. Joe guessed he didn't know much about time either, so he continued his way.

"If you reach a bridge, you've gone too far!" called the man to his back.

"Bridge?" asked Joe, stopping his horse and turning in the saddle.

"The new bridge over Vale Creek."

"So, if I see something that looks like a bridge, I've gone too far?"

The man just nodded, so Joe turned his horse around and moved quickly along the road towards the town. The Macquarie was to his left, so he continued until he saw the ford he'd used to come into the town when he'd first arrived.

Once more he stopped and asked a man walking along the road about the new bank.

"That street there," said the man with a heavy foreign accent, pointing to a street running uphill, away from the Macquarie. "Take that one. Bank's up there. New building. You can't miss it."

"Which side?" asked Joe.

"Dunno," said the man. "Don't know what a side is. But it's near the gaol."

Sighing with frustration, Joe headed up the street. There were several new buildings, but they luckily displayed signs to alert passers-by as to their purpose. Joe was once again fretting that he was running out of time when he saw a new building declaring it to be The Union Bank of Australia opposite a building so forbidding it had to be a gaol.

People were still moving inside the building, so taking his saddle bags and feeling greatly relieved he headed towards the front door. It was a two-storey stone building with shuttered windows and an elegant entrance where it struck Joe that you might stand out of the rain to raise or lower your umbrella. There was a white picket fence to the side with a gate and Joe decided that the building was probably both a bank and a residence. Just as he got to the front entrance, two people came out and a well-dressed man inside looked to be about to lock the door. Joe tried to push it open, and the man resisted.

"We're about to close," he said.

"Can I deposit some money?" asked Joe.

The man looked inside and called to another man, "Man wants to deposit some money!"

"Let him in," a muffled voice responded.

"I've come from Ophir," Joe said to the man holding the door open. The man just shrugged, pointed towards the other man and said, "Over there."

A young man stepped forward. He was very smartly dressed with a friendly, intelligent look.

"May I help you?" he asked, crossing the room to meet Joe. "Mr Kennedy," he said, shaking Joe's hand firmly. "I'm the manager. Did I hear you say you're from Ophir?"

The man's appearance, neatness and friendliness compelled Joe to be ashamed of his own appearance. He no doubt smelled and looked like a homeless vagabond and in that moment, Joe regretted not going to a hotel first and putting his money in the bank the next morning.

"You did," mumbled Joe.

"Oh, dear. I hope I haven't offended you?"

"No, I know I must look and smell like I came from Ophir."

The man surprised Joe by smiling.

"I suspect you're like every other digger and more interested in putting their money in a safe place than how they appear," he said.

"Mr Kennedy, I just hadn't thought about it before, but I did when I stepped into your beautiful building."

"Don't let it worry you. I'm sure you have worries enough. Do you want to open an account, or do you want to send your money to another bank?"

"Open an account."

"Good, good. Come and sit down."

The manger directed Joe into an office and said to his staff, "You may all go now, I'll handle this," before joining Joe and closing the door behind him.

"I'm grateful for your kindness," said Joe. "I must admit I didn't want to have the money with me one minute more than was necessary."

"That's all right. We'll get this done and you can be on your way. How much do you want to deposit?"

"This much," said Joe and pulled the money from a saddle bag.

"Goodness me, you've done well. How much is there?"

"I haven't counted it."

"All right. I'll do that. It won't take long."

The manger busied himself for several minutes, first separating the notes and the cash and then creating piles of money in like denominations. Then, making notes, he counted the piles and looked at Joe with a smile.

"There's seven hundred and forty-nine pounds two shillings and sixpence here!" he almost shouted. "How long have you been at Ophir?"

"A few months."

"Well, I've known others that haven't done so well. Do you want to deposit all of it?"

"Yes," said Joe. He'd kept some to cover his expenses in Bathurst.

Once again when asked he used the name Joe Stratton, and it wasn't long before the transaction was complete, and the manager gave him a receipt.

He stood up and on impulse said, "I met a family at Ophir who come from Bathurst, and I thought I might catch up with then while I'm here."

The manger looked at him strangely and said, "In what way can I be of assistance?"

"I don't know where they live."

"What's their name?"

"I don't know their surname," said Joe shaking his head. "There's four brothers and a sister. One of the brothers, George was killed in a mine collapse in Ophir. The other brothers are Phil, Charles and Fred. The sister is Becky. Becky said her parents have a farm in Bathurst."

Joe was grateful the manager didn't ask any more about Becky.

"I don't know anyone like that, but it's not surprising. Perhaps the father does all the dealings and doesn't mention his family. You could ask at the watch-house. They might know them. One of the boys might have been in trouble at some time. It's hard without the surname, though."

"Where's the watch-house? Is it at the gaol?"

The manager nodded. "Just across the road," he said with a smile. "You can't miss it."

As he was leaving, he asked the manager to suggest a hotel for the night.

"The Shepherd's Inn," the manager said. "It's not far and it's in this street. Go down the hill and you'll see it on the right. I'm sure you'll like it. Mary Carmen runs it. Everyone likes her. Tell her I sent you."

"Thanks," said Joe, shaking the man's hand and relieved to be no longer carrying so much money.

The Shepherd's Inn turned out to be all a man could want, although he didn't get to meet Mary. Joe stabled his horse, checked in and soaked in a bath for a half hour, then realised with dismay he hadn't brought a change of clothing and would have to dress again in the dirty ones he'd worn to town. They looked and smelled so offensive now that he was clean that he'd pay any money for a fresh set but knew nothing was open. Despite that, after a good meal, a good night's sleep and a huge breakfast, he went to the watch-house.

There was small risk someone would recognise him. His appearance and demeanour were considerably different to what they'd been in Sydney, so the risk was small, and he thought worth it.

"I don't know anyone like that," said the young policeman after Joe had explained what he wanted. "One of the others might know them. I'm the only one here now. Perhaps you could come back later?"

"It doesn't matter," said Joe, trying hard to hide his disappointment. He hadn't realised how much he looked forward to seeing Becky until it became obvious, he'd need more than first names.

"You'd be better if you had the surname," said the helpful young policeman. "When you've only got the first names someone has to know them well."

Joe turned and headed out.

"You could check the courthouse or the lands office. They're near to here," the policeman called to his back.

"Thanks," replied Joe waving and trying to be friendly.

He mounted and rode back the way he had come. Down William until he reached Durham, then left and followed the road from there. Disappointment gnawed at him. It was more than disappointment; it was a sense of loss and failure. Ever since the accident in the river, Becky had never been far from his mind and now there was no way to find her. He didn't even know why he thought the police in Bathurst might be able to help. What if someone else had come from Sydney and he'd been recognised? He'd taken a risk, and it hadn't paid off and now he was annoyed with himself for taking a pointless risk.

His horse plodded along steadily, ignoring other traffic on the road. There wasn't as much as he'd encountered when he first came. He supposed that more were now going elsewhere and maybe even some of the other travellers were returning like him. It would be easy to find out – he had only to ask, but he couldn't be bothered and continued on his private journey, wrapped in his own hurt.

At least the weather was better, and the journey wasn't anywhere near as miserable as he had previously endured.

Stopping at the Commissioner's tent on the way down the hill into Ophir, he renewed his licence. It was a new clerk who had no interest in him. He copied the details from the old licence, wrote out a new one and tore it from the book.

He crossed the ford, bought some more supplies and thought of going for a whisky, but decided against it. It'd had been a long day and no doubt his horse was just as tired as him. It was nearly dark when he arrived back at the river where he crossed to go up to his camp. He had to blink several times to make sure his eyes weren't deceiving him. There was a light glowing at his hut. It seemed his fear that someone would take up residence might have eventuated. Just to be safe, he took his revolver out and checked it before crossing the river after which he stopped and dismounted. There'd be less noise if he walked, leading his horse by the reins and he'd be able to carry the weapon, ready to use it if need be.

The sounds of men talking reached him when he came close to the hut, but he couldn't tell how many there were from the sound. There was also the risk that not all the men were in the hut, and someone could be watching him even now. He looked around quickly, but there were no shadows out of place. Approaching cautiously, the weapon in one hand and the reins in the other, he peered into the hut.

There'd never been much order to the hut, as there didn't need to be. There was only ever the bed, a small table and some shelves he'd built from saplings and bark, but everything that had been on shelves was now on the floor.

Two men searched, checking everything carefully, both with their backs to him. One was digging in the ground, the other checking the tins and jars from the shelves. The lamp that he'd bought was lit and it was that light he'd seen from the river.

"It must be here somewhere," said one of the men.

"We'd better hurry before he gets back," said the other.

They both looked like unsuccessful diggers. Torn and dirty clothes and since his bath, Joe could smell them both from where he stood.

"Too late," said Joe. "He's back."

Startled, the men stood and turned to face him. They weren't young, possibly middle aged and looked even harder up than Joe had originally thought. One was tall, the other short. No one moved, the men focused on Joe and him on them.

A small smile appeared on the short man's face. It didn't make his face look any better. It was still mean and shifty.

"Evenin'," he said. The smile disappeared when Joe pushed his right hand out front, showing him the revolver.

"This is my place," said Joe. "I don't remember inviting you in."

"We met you at Morkill's," said the tall man. "You bought us a whisky. We helped to look for you."

"What're you doing here?" asked Joe. He was still nervous there could be a third man, so he kept his hand on the reins hoping his horse would shy if someone tried to reach him from behind.

The men looked at each other. Joe supposed each was hoping the other would come up with a good reason.

"We came lookin' fer you," said the short man.

"That's right," said the other. "No one had seen you for a while, so we came to be sure you're all right."

"Did you think I might be hiding on the shelves, or maybe in the ground?" said Joe, indicating the mess with his weapon.

Both men were silent for a few moments, both looking at the revolver nervously.

"Sorry," said the short man. "We knocked it over in the dark. We was just tryin' to fix everythin'."

"It looked like it," said Joe and the tall one looked relieved.

Joe's voice was calm, but inwardly he tried to assess what to do. The men posed a threat. Cornered men always posed a threat. No doubt they'd been looking for gold or money or both and nothing had happened to convince them there was none to be had, so they'd still be on the lookout for an opportunity. It would come if Joe failed to cover them both properly, or left the men with any thought that failure this time could be followed up with success the next.

Sighing with resignation, Joe let the reins go and stepped into the hut. Both men looked apprehensive, especially the tall one who had thought a few moments ago that Joe had bought their story.

"What're you goin' to do?" they both asked at the same time.

"You won't like it," said Joe, nothing but resignation in his voice.

"We won't?" asked the men, still at the same time. Joe wanted to smile. In other circumstances, it would be funny, but this situation was anything but funny. He had to make sure that when he let the men go, they would neither hang around, nor ever come back. The men had to be hurt, but able to walk away. Hurt enough to be afraid, but not hurt enough to seek revenge.

"Just like I didn't like you both coming in here with some cock and bull story about checking up on me. And look at this mess. I don't like that either."

"We didn't mean any harm, mister! Honest!" said the tall one.

"That's right! We were only wantin' to help. That's what diggers do! We help each other!"

The thought crossed Joe's mind that it would be better if he had a bigger hut. It would be hard to do what he must in such a small room, but first he had to move so the men could get away. However, as soon as he moved, the men would be looking for a way out. Even now they'd be thinking each man for himself, so neither of them would care if only the other was injured. As Joe thought about the problem, he came up with a solution.

"I want you to face each other," said Joe.

"What do you mean?" asked the short one. Joe took the chance to take two steps to his right, so he was now only one step from where he wanted to be. The men were focused on the instruction, not thinking about what Joe did. They both studied Joe, fear and apprehension on their faces. The lamp was to Joe's right, so he still had a clear view of the men.

He'd found long ago that if you gave someone an order that didn't make sense, they forgot about everything else. Facing each other was such a simple order, just inexplicable that Joe would ask them to do it.

"I think you know what I mean. Don't face me, face each other." As the men turned, Joe took the one more step that he needed. He was now less than an arm's length away from them, too close if they decided to rush him. There was no time to lose.

"Now, that wasn't too hard, was it?" Joe asked as the men turned their bodies to face each other but kept looking at Joe.

"This is the part you won't like. I want you to punch each other as hard as you can on the nose. Remember, it's the nose you've got to punch. Are you looking at the nose?"

Reluctantly, the men turned their faces and looked at each other. Both were clearly suspicious something else was in the plan. They'd hardly looked at each other when they looked back at Joe again, thinking he was the real threat.

"When I count to three, punch each other as hard as you can on the nose. I should tell you that you shouldn't hold off. Be serious. Really serious. If you just make a light punch, we'll get to do it again, even if your mate gets a good one away. So, focus on your mate's nose."

The men faced each other. Joe worried about the tall one. He didn't look committed.

"Remember. Do it properly."

The men settled into a boxing position, each squatting slightly, right arm ready.

"One..." said Joe and the men tensed, making sure their opponent didn't steal a march.

Joe stepped forward and brought his gun down hard on the nose of the short man. He was the greater threat, so best to deal with him first. The tall man stared at the short man for a moment too long, bewildered by what had happened. Joe brought the gun down hard on his nose, too. Both men fell to the floor, screaming in agony.

"Christ! That hurts!" screamed the short man. The other man just lay on the floor, both hands holding his nose. Joe could see blood on their faces which would be a mess for a month or so.

Joe waited until the men could do nothing but whimper how much it hurt.

"Get out," he said softly. "Get out before I change my mind and kill you."

The men got up as quickly as they could and pushing past Joe's horse, headed off into the darkness. Joe didn't envy them. They probably couldn't see well at that moment, and it probably wouldn't be long before they couldn't see at all. There'd be no further problem from them that night as neither of them would be able to see him to exact any revenge. They wouldn't be able to get far that night in their injured condition and by the morning, he hoped they'd only wish to be further away.

Once the noise of the men cursing and stumbling disappeared into the night, Joe sat on a rough bush stool and looked at the mess. It wouldn't be hard to clear up, but Joe was getting sick of the way of life. The money was good, but living was primitive and lonely. There'd be a point where the money would no longer be enough. Perhaps he was at that point now, but it wasn't the right time to make such an important decision. Sighing heavily, he got to his feet, stripped his horse and put him nearby with some oats. The horse might alert him to unwelcome company. One day, he'd get a dog. He contented himself with damper and tea for supper and rolled into bed exhausted.

The next morning, he felt much better and was glad he'd delayed any decision to quit. Ignoring the local rules related to a Sunday, he was back at work early, trying to find another wash along the side of the hill. He'd learned that the orange, sandy clay was the best place to find gold, so it was a matter of working his way along, checking different depths as he went. Skipping lunch, he worked for the whole day and having found nothing, returned to his hut as darkness fell, dispirited and miserable.

One more day, he thought when he woke the next morning. *I'll need to find something to warrant my returning to Ophir.*

As he approached his last attempt, he realised that he'd always moved north along the ridge. What was wrong with trying south of the first place he'd dug?

Sure enough, as he approached the depth where he'd found gold before, the sandy, reddish layer of clay appeared, and he was once more finding gold. It was easier this time as there was no water in the hole and he could easily see the layer in the darker dirt. It meant that he could pursue the layer through the dirt, easily find where it was thicker and make sure he followed it towards the ridge.

He had a very successful day, but that night it rained again, the hole filled with water and the next day he could no longer see the layer clearly in the darker dirt. Still, he knew roughly how deep it was and where it was going, so most of the buckets of wash he took to the river contained gold.

By the end of the week, he'd run out of patience and gold. If there was more gold on the Turon, then digging would be more productive and he might even find Becky. It was time to leave Ophir.

33. THE BANKER'S WIFE

It was easy to pack up and move on. He put his lamp and digging kit in hessian sacks and draped them both in front and behind him on the horse. The horse seemed a bit uncertain at first, but they hadn't gone far when he no longer seemed to notice. Perhaps he too was pleased to be on the move. There was enough gold in the saddle bags to justify his return to Ophir from Bathurst, but not enough to justify him staying. Setting off for Bathurst, he was content with his decision. The contentment didn't last long. When he got to Bathurst, he realised it was Saturday evening and the bank was closed. He had planned to drop the gold off, stay overnight and ride on the next morning, but such a plan was now useless.

Sitting on his horse outside the bank, he tried to come up with another plan. There were only two options. Camp by the river or stay at an inn. Even as he had the idea, the rain started, and it made the river option no longer possible. It was too dark to find the river and to set up. No, it had to be an inn and probably best to go to the Shepherd's again.

He rode to the Shepherd's Inn, cursing himself roundly the whole way. He'd ridden past the inn on the way to the bank. He could simply have gone there in the first place. The only thing for it was to ask the publican if she could keep the gold somewhere safe until the Monday. Of course, he might as well walk into the bar carrying a sign, *Gold Digger with Gold*. He sighed. He'd been dealt a difficult hand by his own stupidity and his only choice was to play it.

Dismounting, he pulled off his saddle bags and walked into the inn. He doubted anyone would try to take his kit or supplies. There were enough people in the street to deter any would-be thieves. When he reached the door, he was met by a wall of noise. He walked up to the bar and asked for the publican.

"Can I help? She's busy," said the man.

"I'd rather see her."

"All right. Wait a minute."

He came back several minutes later with a woman in her mid-thirties, average height, red hair and with a face that looked like it had already seen too much life. She put one hand on her hip, the other extended and said, "Mary" and even in the single word established her heritage as Irish.

"Joe," said Joe, shaking the hand firmly. "Can we talk in private?"

"Thanks, Bill," said Mary, sending the man away with a wave of her free hand.

"Do you have an office?" asked Joe.

"No. Won't this do? No one will hear."

"Perhaps somewhere more private?"

"I'm busy," said Mary, "and I don't have anywhere more private."

"It's just that I have something in the saddle bags that I'd rather put somewhere safe."

"Ah, I see. Bank'd be the best place for that."

"Bank's shut."

"Doesn't have to be. Which bank?"

"Union."

"Manager lives with his family beside it. Knock on his door."

Joe had never known anyone that ran a business that was happy to be disturbed outside business hours, least of all a manger who worked for someone else. Besides, Mary had a half smile, so Joe wondered if she was just having fun.

"It's raining."

Mary put her head back and laughed. "You can't be a digger in this part of the world and be bothered by the rain."

"Might be so, but I've had enough. For a while, anyhow."

"All right," said Mary. "How much is in there?"

"A few pounds."

"Weight or sterling?"

"Weight. Maybe a hundred pounds sterling."

"At the moment, people would presume you're negotiating for a room. If you give me the bags down here, people will know what it's all about and I'll be putting my family at risk."

"Risk?"

"Yes, if someone decides they want your bags, they'll come to my rooms looking for them."

"I can't allow that to happen."

"What do you want to do then? If you get me to hold the bags, I have nowhere else to put them."

"I'll brave the rain and see the bank manager."

"That's what I think you should do anyway. Do you want me to hold a room for you?"

Joe nodded, turned and headed out the door into the rain.

"Do you have a gun?" called Mary to his back.

"Do you think I'll need one?"

"You never know. Dark night, digger with saddle bags. Plenty of fellers would rather take what you've got than find it for themselves."

"I'll be careful," said Joe, before going outside, putting the bags across his horse, mounting and riding back to the bank.

Mary was right, though. It was dark, especially up near the bank where the imposing building of the gaol and courthouse on the opposite side threw little light onto the street. He was aware of people watching him as he rode past hotels and buildings but shrugged off any concern. There were enough people about that someone would investigate if there was a commotion.

He pulled up outside the bank and was relieved to see lights in the windows at the rear. Hating the idea of disturbing the manager after hours, he nevertheless pulled the bags off his horse, slung them over his left shoulder, pushed open the gate and walked along a narrow path between the bank and the grounds of a nearby church.

As he walked, he had a sensation that he was being watched. He stopped and looked around carefully. It was darker back here and certainly a good place for someone to attack him, but he couldn't see anyone in the shadows. The only noise he could hear was the gentle pattering of the rain and the sound of wind in the trees in the churchyard. Once again, he shrugged off feelings of disquiet, walked to the door and knocked.

The door opened revealing a young woman with a child on her hip. She stood partly behind the door, probably using it as protection. The door being opened by a young woman only made Joe feel worse about disturbing the family.

"Evening," said Joe, touching the brim of his hat.

"Can I help you?" asked the woman. She looked fearful as though unaccustomed to answering the door at night.

"I'm looking for the bank's manager," said Joe. "Does he live here?"

"He does," said the woman. "But he's not..."

She didn't get to finish the sentence before Joe was pushed roughly from behind into the room. It was all he could do to avoid colliding with the woman and her child. However, in the act of avoiding the woman Joe lost his balance and fell heavily to the floor which was wooden, and he landed on a floor-rug, sliding along until it reached the opposite wall. He heard the door slam shut and tried to look back to see what had happened but was roughly forced down by a push in his back.

"Sorry, missus," said a voice. "I don't mean you any 'arm. Just have some business with this feller 'ere."

"Please don't hurt my baby," said the woman falling more than sitting into a lounge chair nearby, clutching her baby in her arms.

"Yer baby's all right," said the voice. "I mean you and it no 'arm."

Lying on the floor, Joe took in as much of the room as he could which was difficult given his head was almost against a wall. It was sparsely furnished to the point of utility. Clearly the owners could ill-afford anything else. The woman was in a two-seater lounge to his right and there was a table with two chairs to his left. The only light in the room was furnished by two lamps on small tables in opposite corners. He couldn't decide about the pressure on his back but thought it might be a booted foot.

"You, mister," said the voice. "Stay on the floor, face down, but let go of the saddle bags."

"I can't move," said Joe.

There was silence for a few moments, as though the owner of the foot was trying to work out what it meant.

"How's that?"

"I think my arm's broken," said Joe, his voice strained with pain. "The one under the bags. I can't move it."

"Sorry, mate, but I suppose accidents do happen."

Joe felt the foot move from his back and sensed more than saw a figure leaning over him. Then someone was pulling at the bags, trying to pull them from under his left side.

"Oh, stop!" shouted Joe. "That hurts!" He tried to put all his weight on his left side to pin the bags to the floor.

"Christ!" said the man, "I thought you'd be tougher, bein' a digger an' all."

He tried to move Joe with one hand and pull the bags with the other. The task proved too difficult, so he knelt beside Joe, leaned over him and rolled Joe to his right. Joe groaned loudly, causing the man to hesitate. Joe reached up with his left hand, grabbed the man's shirt and pulled hard, slamming the man's head as hard as he could into the wall. There was a thud, the man fell and lay still.

"Is he dead?" the woman whispered, as though fearful if she spoke loudly, she might wake him if he wasn't dead.

"I don't think so," said Joe, "but he might be soon."

"What are you going to do?" whispered the woman, fear in her voice.

"This," said Joe, getting onto his knees and gripping the man's shoulders, slammed his head into the wall again.

"Do you have some rope?" he asked.

"No."

"A clothesline?"

"Yes. There's one out the back."

"Can I borrow one of your lamps?"

"Why?"

"I'll need it to find the clothesline."

"Why do you want the clothesline?"

"To tie him up."

"Oh."

Without waiting for an answer about the lamp, Joe took one and headed out back to get the clothesline. He opened the door, and he left it that way so that if the man woke, he would escape rather than causing trouble for the woman and the baby. It was easy to find the clothesline and Joe was back inside in a matter of minutes. The woman was clearly relieved to see him back, although the man still lay motionless on the floor.

Using the rope line, Joe tied the man's hands and feet.

"Are there police at the gaol?" he asked the woman while he worked.

"Of course," she replied, nodding.

"I'm sorry about this."

"It's not your fault."

"Will I go for the police, or would you prefer to go?"

"I'd rather go. It's not far and I don't want to be here with him. He might wake up."

Joe nodded. The woman stood, put the baby on her hip and headed for the open door. She stopped when she got there.

"It's raining," she said.

"It is," Joe agreed.

"I don't want to take the baby out into the rain."

"You can't leave him here."

"You go."

"What about him?" said Joe, nodding at the inert man.

"Did you tie him well?"

"I did."

"Then I'll be all right."

"I'll be as quick as I can."

"Please."

The woman sat down again, and Joe headed for the door. He stopped when he got there.

"Mine's Joe," he said, looking at the woman seated in a chair.

"I'm Lettie. Please be quick."

Joe hurried across to the gaol through the drizzle, going past his horse. Joe had to bully the policemen into helping, telling them the manager's wife was at risk. Two police and Joe hurried back, the police cursing the rain and the dark. Arriving at the door, which was still open, Joe was pleased to see the man still lying in the same position on the floor.

"Thank you for coming," said Lettie to the policemen, smiling. "My husband will be grateful."

"Is he dead?" asked one of the policemen. "I thought you said he was dangerous. Doesn't look too dangerous to me."

"It's hard to be dangerous when you're unconscious, but he might wake soon," said Lettie, stiffly, "and I don't think he's dead."

"What do you want to do?" asked Joe of the police.

"I suppose we'll have to carry him," said the one that had already spoken.

"Drag him out into the rain," said Joe. "That'll wake him up and then he'll walk, and you won't have to carry him."

"Good idea," said the policeman. "Help me."

Joe went forward, but the policeman said, "Not you. Him," and nodded at his mate.

The policemen rolled the man over onto his back so they could hold him under the arms and by the legs. There were cuts and marks on his forehead that would certainly bruise later.

"You did a good job of knockin' 'im out," said the policeman. "He might be dead."

"No, he's not dead," said his mate. "See, his chest is movin'."

"All right," said the policeman. "I don't want to carry 'im and I can't be bothered waitin' for 'im to wake. You go back to the gaol and get a pushcart. We'll take 'im in that."

"Good idea," said the other, hurrying away.

"You all right, missus?" asked the policeman of Lettie.

"I was a bystander. Anyway, it didn't last long. Joe was clever and pretended to be hurt. It caught this feller off guard."

As if on cue, the prisoner groaned.

"Looks like you won't need the cart after all," said Joe. "But I wouldn't untie his feet until your mate gets back."

"I wasn't plannin' to."

All three stood watching the prisoner who continued to groan.

"Oh, oh," he said when he opened his eyes and saw the policeman. He moved his head and eyes around, taking in the room and its occupants. He tried to move and realised that his feet and hands were tied.

"What're you doin'?" he asked.

"Bein' sure," said the policeman.

"What're you goin' to do?"

"Take you to gaol."

"I haven't done anythin'."

"What about attempted robbery?" said Joe.

"What do you mean?"

"You tried to take my saddle bags."

"No, I didn't. I was tryin' to protect the lady. I figured you was up to no good. You all right missus? He hasn't hurt you or nothin'?"

"I'm all right," said Lettie, smiling.

"That's good. Anyway, the police are here now, so he can't do nothin'. If you'll untie me, I'll be on my way."

"You might need to see a doctor," said Joe. "Your head is a bit of a mess."

"Did I fall over?"

"Something like that," said Joe.

"Well, I can't see a doctor if I'm all tied up."

The sound of a wheel squeaking and rolling over stone came from the outside and the other policeman appeared in the doorway.

"Got it," he said.

"Don't need it now," said the policeman, "prisoner's awake."

"What's that for," asked the prisoner.

"Might as well still use it," said the policeman that had brought the cart. "He can't run away without his legs."

"Good point," said the other. "Let's load 'im in."

They loaded the protesting prisoner into the cart, on his back with his legs dangling over the end.

"You'll need to come with us," said the policeman to Joe. "You'll need to give us a statement and lodge a complaint."

"Can I do that in the morning?" asked Joe, knowing full well that he wouldn't.

"That'll be all right," said the policeman. "There'll be someone there to 'elp you."

"Good-o," said Joe, relieved the man hadn't asked his full name.

The sound of the strident complaints from the prisoner and the trundling wheel disappeared along the path and Joe looked at Lettie, still standing in the centre of the room. She looked both tired and relieved. She had put her baby on the lounge earlier and he slept soundly.

"He's a good baby," said Joe.

"You know about babies?"

"Not a lot, but I've worked out quiet is good."

"Why did you want to see my husband?"

"I've some gold in the bags. I was hoping he would put it somewhere safe for me until Monday."

"He's in Sydney. I'm afraid there's no one here now that can help you."

"All right," said Joe, resignation in his voice. "I suppose I'll spend the rest of the weekend beating off fellers like that."

"I'm sorry."

"It's not your fault. I'm glad you and your family weren't hurt. I'm sorry for what happened. Good night."

Joe turned to leave, but Lettie called, "Would you like a cuppa? I could use one. I'm sure you could too. It's the least I can do, since I can't help with your gold."

Joe looked back, thinking she was just being nice, but the look on her face was open and welcoming.

"I'd like that," said Joe.

"I won't be a moment then," said Lettie and disappeared down a hall to the back.

"Can I help?" called Joe, hoping she could hear.

She was back in seconds.

"No, it's all right," she said quietly. "I have another son sleeping upstairs. I'm surprised he hasn't woken with the noise. You just sit at the table there and I won't be a moment."

Joe sat at the table, rolling his hat in his hands, thinking about what had just happened. The man must have seen him heading into the bank with the saddle bags over his shoulder and guessed his motives. He felt very lucky to have escaped so easily. It might not have gone so well if the man had an accomplice, so no doubt it was a spur of the moment thing.

Lettie swept back into the room with a tray laden with cups, a pot of tea wrapped in a woollen cosy, a bowl of sugar, spoons and some scones.

"The scones are fresh. I made them this afternoon. Would you like milk with your tea?"

"No thanks," said Joe. "A cup of tea and a scone will do nicely."

"There's some lovely plum jam. I like it, I hope you do too."

"I'm sure I will."

"Where have you been digging?"

"Ophir."

"I'm sure you've done well, since you have some gold in the bags."

"I've done all right. I've been to the bank before. I suppose that's why I thought your husband wouldn't mind me disturbing him. Me being a customer, that is."

"I'm sure it would have been all right, but he's in Sydney for some meetings. I don't like it when he goes away. I worry that someone might try to rob the bank."

"I think they'll only try to do that when the bank is open. It's people like me they rob outside hours."

Lettie laughed. It was a nice sound, soft and feminine.

"You make it sound like a job for them," she said.

"I suppose it is," said Joe, sipping his tea. Lettie had looked surprised when he put four spoons of sugar into his cup. His first sip told him why. It was way too sweet. He tried not to show it.

"It might be too sweet," said Lettie. "These cups probably aren't as big as you're used to."

"Don't' worry, it'll be all right. Can I hear an accent?"

"Scots."

"How long have you been here?"

"A few years."

"Do you like it?"

"I miss Scotland, but this is home now. Where are you from?"

"Born here."

"Do you like it?"

"I suppose so," said Joe, laughing.

"Who's here, mummy?" called a young voice from the hallway.

"It's a customer," said Lettie. "He's come to see your daddy."

"But he's away!"

"The man didn't know that."

"Why is he still here?"

"I thought he might like a cup of tea."

"I'd like one."

"But you don't drink tea!"

"Warm milk then."

"You sit with the man, I'll get your milk and then it's off to bed with you."

The boy sat at the table with Joe, eyeing him intently.

"How old are you?" asked Joe.

"I'm five," said the boy, shyly.

"Do you go to school yet?"

"Next year."

"Do you want to go?"

"No. I'd rather stay home."

"You'll like it when you go. You learn lots of things and meet other children."

"Did you like school?"

"I did."

Joe wondered what else to talk about but didn't have to wonder long as Lettie swept back into the room with a glass of milk.

"Here you are," she said. "Be quick now. Then off to bed."

"But mummy. I'd like to stay!"

"I'm sorry, little man. It's off to bed with you."

The boy drank his milk, stood up and said, "Goodnight," before walking down the hall.

"Is he all right by himself?" queried Joe, wonder in his voice.

"Yes, he always does that. He's never wanted a story or to be tucked in."

They sipped their tea in silence for a few minutes.

"Do you have a family?" asked Lettie.

Joe shook his head as Lettie poured some more tea for him.

"It's nice to talk," she said. "My family lives out of town, and I don't see them much. My husband is away a lot."

"Would he mind me being here?" Joe thought Lettie's husband may not like him being there, at night drinking tea with his wife. What would the neighbours think?

"I don't think so. The robber might have come because of you, but my husband would be grateful that thanks to you, his family came to no harm."

Joe just nodded. He was feeling tired now and thought he should go soon.

"I'm surprised you're not married," said Lettie.

"Why is that?"

"Most people are by the time they reach your age."

"I suppose so," said Joe and hesitated before continuing. For a moment, he thought he'd look stupid talking about Becky, but decided on impulse to do so. "I did meet someone at Ophir. She lives somewhere near Bathurst. I tried to find her the last time I came to town, but it was a waste of time."

"A waste of time?"

"Yes," Joe nodded. "I know so little about her, I just looked foolish."

"How did you meet her?"

"In a store at Ophir."

"What was she doing there? In the store I mean. Working?"

"No. She and her brothers had a claim nearby. She was buying some supplies."

"That's all? A spark from an encounter in a store?"

"No. I walked her back to her claim. When we got there, we found there'd been a rock fall and her brother was buried. I helped to save him."

"How many brothers?" said Lettie, suddenly showing interest.

Joe noticed the change in tone and looked at her, intrigued.

"Four brothers."

"Did the brother that was buried survive?"

"No, he didn't."

"I know that family. They bank with us. The father blamed himself for the son's death. Said if he hadn't insisted, they go to Ophir, his son wouldn't have died."

"Do you know where they live?"

"The parents have a farm on the Vale Rd."

"Becky said they were going to the Turon."

"That's right. The daughter's name is Becky and yes, as far as I know, they've gone to the Turon. They could be back now, of course. It's been a while since I've heard talk of them."

"Do you know the surname?"

"I think it's Shepherd, but I don't really know. My husband would know."

"When's he due back?"

"About another week. He only left yesterday on the stage. He'll spend the week in Sydney. I'm not sure which day he'll be back. There're a few companies running stages between Sydney and Bathurst. I suppose he'll catch the first one he can when he finishes his meetings."

"Do you know where the farm is?"

"Only that it's on the Vale Rd. I'm sure if you asked around you could find it."

Joe sat in silence, exhilarated and disappointed all at once. Exhilarated because he now had a chance to find Becky, but disappointed because he didn't know everything and wouldn't for at least a week. Still, he could ride to the Vale Rd tomorrow and see if he could find the parents. That would be a good start.

"Where's the Vale Rd?"

"You ride south out of Bathurst."

Joe finished his tea and stood up.

"Thank you for the tea and your hospitality."

"Make sure you stop by when you next come to town," said Lettie, also standing.

Joe picked up the saddlebags from the floor, draped them once again over his left shoulder, put on his hat and headed for the door.

"'Night," he said, nodding at Lettie, opened the door and headed out into the rain.

34. THE SEARCH BEGINS

Joe was soaking wet and beyond exhaustion when he arrived at the Shepherd's Inn. He put his horse in the stables, had a quick supper and went to his room. He was disappointed to not have at least a whisky in the bar, but way too tired to enjoy it. Rummaging in his bag, he found the night shirt that he hadn't used for some time and put it on once he removed all his clothes. After a few moments of indecision, he put his saddle bags in the bed, climbed in with them and was asleep in seconds. He knew nothing until the next morning.

It was way past dawn when he woke, and he was relieved to find the saddle bags exactly where he'd put them the night before. Daylight was his friend, so he took advantage of it by picking up his bag with his clothing and the saddle bags and heading to the bathroom. He knew where it was after his last visit and was pleased to find it vacant. Then, it would be unusual if it wasn't. Most travellers didn't bother with a bath.

He put some water in the tub, picked out the best of his clothing, threw the rest in the tub and climbed in with them. Once he'd given the clothes and himself a good scrub, he dressed, put his wet clothes in a basket and carried his saddle bags and the basket into the yard. It was a warm day with a good wind blowing, so it was what his mother called "a drying day". He draped the clothes as best he could on the line using the pegs that were already there, then went back and got his bag. He'd decided that if his bag was stolen, so be it, but the saddle bags would stay with him until he sold the gold.

Once he'd put his bag back in his room, he went for breakfast. He felt stupid carrying the saddle bags, but had no other choice.

Sitting at a table on his own, he ignored everyone else until someone stood beside him. It was Mary.

"No luck?" asked Mary.

"No. No luck."

"I heard there was some trouble at the bank last night."

"Where did you hear that?"

"Mind if I sit?"

"Not at all."

"Some of the fellers in the bar talked about it. They work at the gaol and come here at the end of their shift. Anything to do with you?"

"No. Nothing to do with me."

"What did the manager say?"

"He wasn't there, so I came back."

"I didn't see you come back."

"Does it matter?"

"No. Anyway, I can buy it from you."

"Why didn't you do that last night?"

"Because today I can sell it to someone, so I won't have to hang onto it."

"Can't I sell it to someone?"

"If you like. Do you know anyone that might buy it?"

Joe looked at Mary. She was smiling.

What was she up to? Was she just having fun?

"I don't understand," said Joe, eventually.

"Do you think I'm trying to cheat you?"

Joe shrugged.

"I'm not," said Mary, shaking her head. "I'm just trying to help. I'll buy it for the going price and sell it for the same amount. Besides, you'll find it easier to hide the money than the gold."

"How will you weigh it?"

"I've some scales. Fellers get me to weigh their gold sometimes before they go to sell it to be sure they aren't cheated. I also take gold if a customer doesn't have money."

"All right," said Joe. "I'll be glad to stop carrying the bags around."

"They're a bit of a give-away. I'm glad it wasn't you last night. I thought as you left that anyone looking at you would easily guess why you carried the bags away from here. It wouldn't have surprised me if you had trouble. Finish your breakfast, find me and we'll get it done."

"Thanks, Mary."

When the deal was completed later, Joe asked Mary if she knew the Shepherd's farm on the Vale Rd.

"Same name as the Inn?" asked Mary.

"As far as I know."

"No," said Mary, shaking her head. "But that's not surprising. Anyone from there would be unlikely to come here for a drink. Plenty of other places closer."

"I heard this was the best place."

"I think so and so do many others," said Mary laughing, "but you have to come here to find out."

"How do I get to the Vale Rd?"

"Head south. Vale Rd is not easy to find, so head along the street out front and up the hill until you can see a road heading south. If you get lost, ask someone."

"Thanks Mary. I'm grateful for your interest."

Joe went to the stables, got his horse and eventually found the Vale Rd after several detours and frustrating forays into streets that led nowhere. Still, it wasn't a bad day for riding being cloudy and warm and it was a welcome relief to have a day without rain. That was as far as the day's enjoyment went. The road was dreadful being nothing more than a succession of mud pools and he felt nothing but sympathy for people manoeuvring carts and other vehicles.

There were many small farms and properties along the road, and it didn't matter where he went, no one knew of the Shepherds. He eventually decided that Lettie had given him the wrong name and all he was doing was wasting time, so he turned back for Bathurst. Many of the people he met were of advanced years, and for all he knew, he'd met Becky's parents and didn't know it. Several times it crossed his mind to ask for Becky rather than the Shepherds but was reluctant to bring her specifically into his search. It just didn't seem right somehow. He also thought people would be less likely to acknowledge that they knew someone if he said he was looking for a woman.

Dispirited and hungry, he arrived back at the Shepherd's Inn late in the day and knew his horse was as grateful as he was that the day was done. He hadn't wasted the day as he had to wait until the Monday to deposit the money he'd received for his gold, so at least he'd made the effort to find Becky's farm even if it had been unsuccessful.

After stabling his horse, he went to the bar and got himself a whisky. Sitting alone at a table, he thought about what to do after he deposited the money the next morning and the decision was easy to make. He'd go to the Turon. The fact that Becky was possibly there, and the gold was better than Ophir made it an easy decision.

He heard footsteps and Mary approached his table accompanied by a man.

"Mary," said Joe, pleased to see her. She reminded him of Margaret who he'd met in Parramatta.

"Hello, Joe. Let me introduce Robert. He's the man that bought your gold. He's staying tonight too, so I thought you fellers should meet."

"Do you mind if I sit?" asked Robert.

"Please. Will you stay too, Mary?" asked Joe.

"I'm busy, but I'm sure you two will find plenty to talk about."

"Would you get me a whisky, Mary, and another for Joe?" asked Robert.

"Of course," said Mary. "This one's on me."

"She always does that," said Robert with a half-smile.

Joe didn't like the comment. He thought it petty to mock another person's generosity. Then, Robert knew Mary better that he did, so perhaps there was a reason.

"Do you live in Bathurst?" asked Joe.

"No. I live in Sydney. I go around the gold fields buying gold from the diggers. Haven't been doing it long though and I'm still getting used to it."

"I expect it's not easy. Dangerous, too."

"Ophir and the others aren't too bad, but Sofala is the worst. It seems that every criminal in NSW has gone there."

"Why?"

"Too much gold. There's lots more there than anywhere else. There's ten times the amount comes out of there. What about you, Joe? Where're you from?"

Maybe he's not bad after all, thought Joe. *He seems friendly enough now that we're chatting.*

"I've been digging at Ophir."

"I know. Mary told me. Before then?"

"Oh, I'm from Sydney," said Joe, hoping to sound vague. "How did you get into the gold buying business? Are you with one of the banks?"

"No, nothing to do with the banks. It was my father-in-law's idea. He set up a gold buying business in King Street. He buys gold in Sydney, and I buy it in the gold fields and send it back."

"How do you send it back?"

"There's a police escort. It costs money, but it's worth it."

"I've been selling my gold in Ophir."

"Oh? To other buyers?"

"No, to the stores. They seem to give a good price."

"We give the best price. Because we deal in volume, we can give the best price. We're the biggest buyer." The last was said with a hint of pride.

"I can't imagine that what you do is safe. Everyone knows who you are, you'll take money to the diggins and gold back. You can get robbed in both directions."

Robert laughed. It wasn't a pleasant sound and didn't reflect mirth. Joe thought it sounded derisive.

"I don't need to carry much money. Some people want money for small amounts, but mostly I give them cheques and promissory notes. Besides, I disguise myself and never ride alone to and from the diggins. Sometimes I go on the stage. I try to be unpredictable."

"Is your family in Sydney?" said Joe, deliberately changing the subject. There'd been enough talk of robbery.

"Just my wife. I don't have any children."

Nothing was said for a few moments, then Robert consulted a flashy fob watch and announced it was time to retire.

"Good night," he said, standing. "Look for me the next time you have gold to sell. You'll do better if you do." He walked off without shaking hands.

Joe sat there, sipping his whisky and thinking what a strange encounter. He'd expected Robert to be more personable, the type of man whose company one would enjoy. There was something else too, but he couldn't decide what.

"Has Robert gone to bed?" asked Mary, standing at the table.

"He has," said Joe, nodding.

"Can I buy you another whisky?" asked Mary, sitting down.

"You've already bought me one."

"I wasn't aware there's a law saying I can't buy you two," said Mary, smiling. "Is there?" She didn't wait for an answer and signalled the bar for two whiskeys.

"I'm honoured."

"Don't be. I just wanted to let you know to be careful with Robert."

"How's that?" replied Joe, warily.

"Some people say you can't trust his weights."

"But you do?"

Mary laughed.

Now, that's a laugh to be proud of, thought Joe. The laugh was more of a chuckle that started light and breezy, like water running over rocks and finished deep and throaty like her whole body was involved.

"I don't need to," said Mary. "I've got weights too, so we always double weigh the gold. He doesn't like it, says it means I don't trust him, but he wants the gold, so we always do it."

"Why did you introduce me?"

"You'll come across him sooner or later. He's the biggest buyer, so most people have dealings with him."

"He said he's the biggest."

"His father-in-law has the shop in King Street in Sydney, just across George Street from the Union Bank. He takes whatever gold he buys during the day to the bank in a wheelbarrow before it closes at the end of the day."

"If he does that every day, you'd think he'd be robbed every day!"

Mary laughed again and Joe laughed too, without knowing why. The fun was infections.

"I don't think so," Mary said. "An employee pushes the barrow and Bill walks beside it with a loaded pistol, ready to shoot anyone that shows interest in the gold. It isn't far and it'd be a brave man that took him on."

"Or desperate," said Joe, seriously.

"I'll grant you that," said Mary, also suddenly serious, "but it hasn't happened yet, so maybe the prospect of taking him on is too formidable."

Joe signalled for another two whiskies.

"I'll make this the last," he said. "I'm off to bed soon, too."

"One more is fine with me. I only ever have two a day and then towards the end. What about your supper? Or did you have it somewhere else?"

"I'm too tired to bother."

"Are you going back to Ophir?"

"No," said Joe, shaking his head. "I'm going to try the Turon."

"It's worth it. There's a lot more gold there."

"Robert said that. I don't know why that would be so."

"There's dry diggins at the Turon, so the diggers can work even when the river is flooded."

"I haven't heard of dry diggins," said Joe, suddenly awake and interested. "What are they?"

"Places on the sides or the tops of the hills away from the creeks and the river. They have to take the dirt to water for cradling, but they can dig even when there's floods or it's just raining. There's lots of places like that, so digging is continuous, and more gold is found."

"I've been digging in places like that. I suppose I've been working dry diggins and didn't know it!"

Mary just smiled.

"How long have you had the pub?" asked Joe, after a few minutes. He didn't really care, just wanted to make small talk as they finished their whisky.

Mary looked at him carefully before answering, so much so that Joe was embarrassed.

"I'm sorry to offend," he said.

"I'm not offended, I just wondered if you're really interested."

"I wouldn't have asked otherwise."

"You asked like a man filling in time," said Mary, way too seriously for Joe's liking. He was about to learn something he wouldn't like but had the sense to stay silent and wait.

"My husband died a few months ago. We worked it together for a few years, now I do it on my own. I've two children as well, so it's not easy."

"I don't know what to say. I feel so foolish."

"It's all right," said Mary, shaking her head. "You couldn't have known. Besides, it gives me something to do and there's money coming in. I suppose I was lucky I worked it with him, so I know what to do. I miss him, though. He was a good man."

"You haven't touched your whisky," said Joe.

"Talking too much," she said and took a sip. "What about you, Joe? You married? Do you have a family?"

"No," said Joe, shaking his head. "Not yet."

"But you'd like to."

"I think I would. Other people seem to do it and it works."

"Not always."

"No, not always."

"Have you left a girl somewhere that you'll go back to with your fortune?"

"My fortune?"

"I think you must be doing all right."

"How's that?"

"Judging by what I sold to Robert."

"A swallow does not a spring make, nor a bag of gold a fortune."

Mary looked at Joe in astonishment, then once again gave him the benefit of her chuckle.

"That's worth drinking a whisky with you, Joe!" she exclaimed.

"Don't you like whisky?"

"Not much, but I like to drink it with some customers. I've added you to the list."

"What list?"

"The list of customers I'll have a drink with."

"How long's the list?"

"Now wouldn't you like to know? Anyhow, I want to hear more about this girl who'll share your fortune."

"How do you know there's a girl?" Joe really liked talking to Mary, she was fun and interesting.

"If I wasn't sure before, I am now. C'mon mister, out with it!" For whatever reason, Mary was intrigued, her cheeks flushed and her eyes sparkling.

Don't flatter yourself, thought Joe. *It's probably the whisky.*

"I met someone in Ophir," said Joe, and knew to continue so that Mary would have the whole story. He told her about the tunnel collapse and the death of Becky's brother.

"I think I heard something about that. Did the family come from Bathurst?"

Joe was about to blurt out that he'd been told as much by Lettie but stopped himself just in time.

"That's what she said."

"She?"

"Her name's Becky."

"What's her second name?"

"I asked you about it this morning. I think it's Shepherd."

"Ah! The family on the Vale Road! You could have told me this morning and I might have thought harder."

"Think harder now."

"I'm not sure I want to," said Mary, looking serious.

"Why is that?" asked Joe, intrigued.

"I might want you for myself."

Joe was shocked and his face must have shown it.

"Don't worry, Joe, you're safe," said Mary, smiling. "I just get lonely sometimes and you look and sound like a good man."

"I'm not that good. I've done things I'm not proud of."

"What sort of things?"

"They don't matter. Things that are better left in the past."

"Perhaps meeting Becky has changed you?"

"Meeting Becky was only one of them. Besides, Becky has no idea I'm looking for her."

"She doesn't know how you feel?"

Joe was suddenly uncomfortable. The conversation had suddenly become very serious, and he had no idea how it had come to pass. He wasn't in the habit of discussing feelings with strangers.

"I'm sorry, Joe," said Becky, "I went a step too far. It's your business and none of mine. I remember the incident, but not the names of the people. If I hear anything, though I'll tell you the next time we catch up. I hope there'll be a next time. I enjoyed talking with you and I'm sorry if I got too personal."

She stood up and lightly touched his shoulder.

"Take care, Joe. Perhaps I'll see you around. Good luck in Sofala."

"You haven't finished your whisky."

"I've had enough. You can leave it or finish it. Good night."

She walked away to the bar where she helped the staff with some cleaning duties. Joe couldn't shake a feeling that he'd somehow ruined the encounter, or perhaps even upset her. He went to his room, donned his night shirt, put the saddle bags with the money in the bed and reflected, as he drifted off the sleep that the boy-girl thing was in no way straightforward.

35. JOURNEY TO THE TURON

Joe had a hurried breakfast and went and waited outside the bank until it opened. He deposited most of his money but kept some for the supplies that he'd need to take to the Turon. He was relieved he didn't see either Mary or Lettie as he'd already shared enough of his feelings.

He asked at the store where he bought supplies about the route to the Turon. The man was dismissive and simply told him to take the "Sydney road and follow the crowd". It turned out to be that easy. There were plenty of people coming and going from the Turon, so he was on the right road in no time at all.

Arriving at the village of Peel around the middle of the day, he stopped at a bush inn where some of the patrons looked like they were making a long day of it. The inn was called the Shearers Arms and Joe wondered at the title. The building was not far from a creek, long and low with a small bar and a post veranda all along the front. It looked more like it had been thrown together rather than being built, as though its whole purpose was to take advantage of the diggers and other travellers to the gold fields and had probably never been graced by a shearer. The veranda was crowded with lively drinkers, none of whom took any notice of him and once he stepped into the bar, it took a while for his eyes to become accustomed to the darkness. The room was very small with the only natural light provided by the open door. A couple of lamps on the walls struggled to have any effect.

"What'll you have?" called a voice from behind the bar.

"Do you have any cool beer?"

The barman nodded at the end of the bar where a tub stood covered with some wet hessian sacks.

"What is it?"

"Porter."

"What's it cost?"

"Five shillin's."

"I'll have a whisky."

"Thought you might. Most do. Man's wastin' 'is time even puttin' the beer in the tub."

"Then why do you do it?"

"New chums like it."

The man poured the whisky and pushed the glass towards Joe.

"That'll be a shillin'."

Joe gave him the money. Two more men came in so Joe left and stood on the veranda out front. It was a pretty, warm spring day and trees around the pub provided welcome shade. Saddled horses stood around, looking bored. A group nearby was talking excitedly about recent gold finds at Tarshish on the Abercrombie. A man nearby scoffed at them and told them quartz with gold had been found behind the pub a couple of weeks ago and at the nearby village of Brucedale on a tributary of the Winburndale Creek.

Another group of obviously would-be diggers affirmed by their new clothes expressed interest that they wouldn't need to go to the Turon at all but could find all they wanted in the local area. Joe watched an old man seated on a bush chair nearby smoking contentedly on a pipe, wordlessly smile and shake his head.

Pushing through the other groups who continued to argue the merits of various finds, Joe stood beside the old man who simply looked up and nodded.

"'Day," he said.

"Not a bad one," replied Joe.

"I've seen worse."

"You from around here?"

"What's it look like?"

"Lot of people going through."

"You don't know the half of it. All the time. No end to 'em."

"All after gold?"

"Most of 'em. Not all 'em find it, though. Lots been comin' back headin' for other places. Some goin' back to Ophir, some even goin' to Victoria. I suppose that feller there'll go to Abercrombie," indicating with the stem of his pipe the man who had spoken earlier.

"Is it true they found some behind the pub?"

The man chuckled and shook his head as though in wonderment.

"They did, but somebody might've put it there. Doesn't matter, though. There's gold everywhere, just not as much as on the Turon. If I was younger, that's where I'd go."

"Can I buy you a whisky?" asked Joe.

"Don't mind if you do, but only if you're 'avin' one. Feller doesn't like to drink on his own when another feller buys."

Joe went and got the drinks, came back and sat on the floor beside the old man's chair.

"Been here long?" asked Joe.

"I come every day. Listenin' to these fellers is better'n readin' a book. I'm guessin' of course. I can't read. Wish I could, but there was no school about here when I grew up. Ma and Pa settled the area. The whole family came out from Windsor. It's good country, but the black fellers wasn't too sure about us. Still, we shared what we grew and a sheep every now and again and we got on all right. Not like now. There's robbers and thieves and bushrangers about. Man's not safe in his own bed."

The man re-lit his pipe and tapped Joe on his shoulder to get his attention.

"You goin' to the Turon?"

Joe nodded.

"Wish I could go," said the man. "Too old, now. A few years ago, nothing would have stopped me. I can't recommend this gettin' old business. My ma and pa left us when they was only young, but me? Why do I 'ave to put up with gettin' old? It's not fair if you ask me."

The man tapped Joe on the shoulder again.

"Do you want to know where to dig on the Turon?"

"Do you know?"

"Sure do," said the man, pride in his voice. "I listen to all the fellers on their way through. Them's that find gold are so pleased with themselves they can't wait to tell someone."

He chuckled and coughed, a nasty, rattling cough that started deep in his lungs and sounded like he'd cough up parts of his body before he'd finish. Joe thought he might get his wish and join his parents soon.

"Stay with the dry diggins," he continued. "Up on the hills, away from the water. Too many fellers take a claim in the river, or in the bed of nearby creeks. They all think the gold has found its way there and it has, but it's come from places above the water and there's plenty still there. There's too much rain, so it's hard to work a claim in the water 'cos it's always too wet."

"Why don't they dam the water?"

"There's talk of it, but they'd have to divert the water, 'cos people need it downstream. You can't please all the people all of the time, young feller."

"Tell me more about the Turon."

"What do yer wanna know?"

"Why do they call it the Turon?"

"It's the river. The Turon River. It's a giant gold field. There's gold all the way from Jew's Creek where the Turon waters come from on the Mudgee Road to where the Turon meets the Macquarie. That's nearly a hundred miles. You can dig anywhere you like, and you'll find gold."

"Anywhere?" said Joe, incredulous.

"Well," replied the man, chuckling and coughing again. "Some places are better'n others, but they tell me anywhere."

"How far to the Turon?"

"You ridin'?"

"Yes."

"If you left now, you'd get there about nightfall."

"Then I'd better get moving."

"As you wish. Nice talkin' to you. Thanks, fer the drink. Good luck," said the man, knocking his pipe out on the leg of his chair and refilling it.

Joe mounted his horse and continued riding north. There was plenty of traffic of all kinds, walkers, riders, carts and wagons. Some people spoke, but most kept to themselves, quietly pursuing their goal.

36. SOFALA

Towards nightfall, Joe sat astride his horse on the hill over-looking Sofala. Earlier, after he'd left Peel, there'd been cultivated fields and crops, but later he'd ridden though scrubby country, sometimes cleared but mostly covered in gullies and gums, although the closer he got to Sofala, the steeper the ridges and hills became. It was unwelcoming country, not unlike what he'd crossed to get to Ophir. Some distance from Sofala, he'd climbed a steep hill, so steep it was sometimes prudent to dismount and walk. Then he crossed some flat country where he could see tents pitched about the place and evidence of digging. He could even see tents pitched on the distant hills that looked steep and dangerous. Perhaps the old man had been right and there was gold aplenty. He continued through the flat country, above the surrounding area before he reached the descent to the town.

Sofala was an impressive sight. It was nestled in a much prettier, wider valley than Ophir, with high hills on all sides. Joe guessed it was the Turon River running along the base of the hills, but it was the town that took his breath. He had no idea what the buildings were, but they were significant and impressive and there were quite a few of them, some bearing flags even at this late hour, not all of which he recognised. In his mind's eye, he had pictured something like Ophir, but the only similarity was that he rode down a hill into the town. However, this descent enabled him a view not unlike a relief map, with everything spread out before him.

To the left of the buildings, nestled amongst still standing trees and on slightly higher ground were what looked like the Commissioner's tents and the police barracks. It was like what he had seen in Ophir. All along the river, both up and downstream from the town were hundreds of tents, some timber and bark huts and even some rude gunyahs. There might be more gold coming from the Turon because there were a lot more people looking for it. Joining the other travellers, he rode down into the town feeling as unsure as he had when he rode into Ophir.

The town was even more impressive as he rode into it. There were places of entertainment, accommodation, pubs, churches and stores. It didn't feel like rain, and he'd had some practice at detecting its arrival, but a cool breeze blew, and he didn't fancy the prospect of finding somewhere to camp so late in the evening. He'd kept money enough, so he decided to pull up outside the first pub he came to and thought it would be good to have a whisky, some supper and a proper bed before working out where to dig the next day. The road forked, angling left and right and without thinking, Joe rode down the left fork and pulled up at what was obviously a pub. It was an impressive timber building. There was plenty of noise coming from inside and quite a few patrons spilled out onto the street.

Joe dismounted, dropped the reins, stepped up onto the wooden veranda and pushed through the crowd. No one paid him any mind. It was clear that a stranger on a horse was no novelty in Sofala. The bar ran the full depth of the hotel and many patrons not only stood at it, but along the walls opposite. It was hot and uncomfortable, but no one seemed to care.

"What'll you have?" asked the barman as Joe approached.

"I'd like to organise a room."

"Sorry. Pub's full."

"Is there somewhere else?"

"What do you think I am? The town guide?" The man turned and walked off, leaving Joe speechless. He pushed back through the crowd, picked up the reins and walked his horse, too angry for words. As he walked, he realised there was no shortage of pubs, although some looked ready to fall. There were plenty of lamps along the street, most designating a pub, but some outside stores that were still open. It was easy enough to tell the pubs as they were the buildings with lamps and people drinking on the road outside.

He stopped outside the next pub, dropped the reins and pushed through into the bar. It was only small with a few tables and chairs. Some people ate what looked like bread and cheese and Joe realised how hungry he was. With hindsight, he should have stayed in Peel overnight and ridden on to Sofala the next day. The barman wore a huge smile above his black beard and below an unruly shock of curls.

"Drink?" he said, and Joe could only just her him above the din.

"Room."

"Sorry," said the man, shaking his head and still smiling. "We only have a couple and they're taken."

"Where else should I try?" asked Joe, readying himself for rejection.

"Go further through the town," said the man. "Everyone calls in at the first place they come to. There's plenty of places, pubs and rooming houses, too, so you'll find something easily enough."

"How far?"

"One or two hundred yards should do it."

Joe went back out, took the reins and continued walking. The noise from some places was deafening, so he decided to avoid them. They were likely drinking only, so there'd be no peace before the patrons were asked to leave at closing time. Eventually he came to a single storey, bark and slab building with only a few people drinking out front. He went in and asked for a room.

"Of course," said the barman. "Anything else?"

"Something to eat and a stable for my horse."

"Stables are around back. Just walk your horse down the side. I can organise supper and a drink if you'd like one."

The man was thin, old and friendly. There weren't many customers and Joe had a passing thought that maybe the food, or the room may not pass muster.

"How much?" he asked, guardedly.

"For you and the horse? Six shillings."

It sounded way too reasonable, so Joe was even more wary.

"Can I see the room?"

"Of course. Doors to the rooms're out back. Take one of the lamps, go through that door there and find any one of the three you like. They're all empty now. Privy's out back."

"Somewhere to wash?"

All the patrons looked at Joe like he'd arrived from outer space.

"There's a jug and basin on the stand beside the bed," said the barman smiling.

Joe took a lamp from the end of the bar, lit it with a match and went through the back door. He could hear the river nearby. Holding the lamp in front of him, he peered into the first room and could barely contain his dismay. The room was clean and neat with a quilted single bed, a low boy and a bed-side table with a jug and bowl. Stepping out of the room and holding up the lamp, he saw the privy and the empty stables at back. He had a feeling he should apologise to the barman.

"Everything all right?" asked the barman, smiling as Joe stepped back into the room.

"Yes," said Joe. "Can I take the lamp and stable my horse?"

The barman just nodded and responded to a call from a table to provide more drinks. Joe went out and stabled his horse, pleased to see the stables were also clean and tidy and there was not only water and oats, but a small, grassed yard where his horse could roam. He found some brushes and cloths, rubbed his horse down and thanked him for a job well done. After a little searching, he found a place where he hoped his saddle, kit and supplies would be safe. He picked up his bag, walked to his room, put it under the bed, had a brief wash in the basin, threw the water into the yard and walked back to the bar through the back door.

The half dozen customers still sat quietly at the same tables. Most of the noise and conversation came from outside.

"Drink?" asked the barman.

"Whisky," said Joe, nodding.

"You still want supper?"

Joe nodded.

"Lamb, cheese and bread is what we got. That do you?"

"Good enough."

"Now?"

Joe nodded.

The man walked out the back door and came back within a few minutes with a plate full of food.

"How much?" asked Joe.

"Still six shillings for the room, stabling and supper and a shilling and threepence for the whisky."

Joe counted out the money.

"Sit anywhere you like," said the man, waving an arm at the room. Joe chose a table on his own and ate ravenously. He was nearly finished when he felt a presence. Looking up, he saw a man standing at his table.

"Mind if I sit?" asked the man.

"Suit yourself."

The man sat. He wore typical digger's clothes, checked shirt, long pants, boots and a well-grown beard. Joe thought him to be about thirty

"You new?" asked the man, putting a glass of whisky on the table as Joe pushed his plate to one side.

"Depends."

"Depends?"

"Yes," said Joe, "depends."

"On what?"

"On what you are wondering I'm new at."

"Oh. Diggin'."

"No."

"New to the Turon?"

"Yes."

The man sat back in his chair and studied Joe for a few moments. Neither man said anything. The man looked like he was about to leave, but then a short smile played around his lips.

"Sam," he said, putting out his hand to shake Joe's

"Mine's Joe."

"Where've you bin diggin'?"

"Ophir."

"Do any good?"

"I suppose."

"Do you know how to dig?"

"I use a pick and shovel."

Sam studied Joe for a few moments, then put his head back and laughed out loud. His whole body shook.

"I like that," he said. "Hadn't heard that before. I'm lookin' fer somebody."

"To do what?"

"Dig."

"You got a claim?"

"I do."

"Why don't you work it?"

"Too much for just one. I need someone to help."

"Why me?"

"Saw you come in and thought you might be interested. No harm if you're not."

"How long have you had the claim?"

"About a month."

"Been working it on your own all that time?"

"No. I had a partner."

"What happened? He leave?"

"I suppose he did. Bit by a snake. Died."

"Christ! When?"

"Three days ago. Buried 'im yesterday."

"Where's your claim?"

"Not far from here. Big Oakey Creek, but there's not much water in the creek, so I've got to drag all the dirt down to the Turon for cradlin'. Can't do it on my own."

"I thought there'd been a lot of water."

"In the river. Not in the creek."

Joe sat thinking. One man's misfortune was another man's luck.

"What do you think?" asked Sam, breaking into Joe's thoughts.

"Let's talk awhile. What if we don't get on? Have you asked anyone else?"

"Have you worked with anyone before?"

"No," said Joe, shaking his head.

"You worked on your own?" queried Sam, dismay in his voice.

"What's wrong with that?"

"Nothin'," said Sam, "but you don't hear it too much. Most fellers work in teams of two or three, but thinkin' on it, I s'pose it'd be better on yer own. Less arguin'."

"Where were you when you saw me come in?"

"Over there, at that table with the two men." He pointed and the men waved.

"Who are they?"

"Friends. Got a claim near to mine."

"Why don't you partner with them?"

"They're all right," said Sam, shaking his head. "So was I until my partner died, so best just to replace 'im. Anyway, come over and meet 'em. If nothin' else, you might learn somethin' about the Turon."

"All right," said Joe, picking up what was left of his whisky and following Sam to the other table.

"This is Joe," said Sam, sitting on an empty chair while Joe sat on another. "This is Alan and Bert."

The men shook hands and looked at Joe, as though assessing him for suitability.

"You hear about Mac?" asked Alan. He was the older of the two men, maybe ten years older than Sam and seemed the more interested of the two. Bert studied his glass as though he preferred to be somewhere else.

"Who's Mac?" asked Joe, wondering what he'd missed.

"Feller that got bit," said Alan. "Terrible business."

"How was he bitten?"

"Went to get some wood from a pile near our camp," said Sam. "Cried out when he got bit. Yelled for me to 'elp. I hurried over. He was shakin' and scared. I told 'im it may not be deadly."

"Did he see the snake?"

"Said he did. Said it was a long, brown one, but I didn't see it 'cos it was gone when I got there."

"They don't 'ang about," said Alan. "I think they're as scared of you as you are of them."

"I doubt it," said Joe. "I don't like 'em and I'm plenty scared of 'em. Besides, unlike them I don't bite."

The other three men laughed, then Alan became serious.

"Sam ran down and called us to help, but we didn't know what to do. We tried to walk 'im to town to see the doctor, but it didn't take long before he was too crook. Couldn't walk properly and had trouble breathin'. I hurried back and got a pushcart, but it took me a while. It's not as though there's a proper path or track. We loaded 'im into the cart. Bert 'ere ran ahead to make sure the doctor was there, but Mac was dead by the time we got to town."

"I didn't think a snake would kill someone that quickly," said Joe, nervously. "I suppose I don't know much about it."

"Well, I'd stay away from 'em if I was you," said Bert.

"I plan to," said Joe. "Shall we have another whisky? I'm up for it after all this talk of snakes." The others nodded and Joe signalled for more whisky and paid when it arrived.

The talk turned to gold digging and the differences between Ophir and the Turon. There were more diggers at the Turon and the town was more like a town, but the digging seemed the same. More luck than planning and more disappointment than success.

Bert had been silent during the conversation. Joe judged him to be someone who preferred listening to talking. Alan and Sam were more animated, more interested and more involved.

"What did you do before you became a digger?" queried Bert, unexpectedly.

Joe was shocked, both by the question and where it came from. He should have anticipated the question and been ready for it with a credible answer. The conversation had been enjoyable, so much so that he'd dropped his guard.

Lacking a response, Joe just stared at Bert.

"What's up?" asked Bert, looking concerned. "None of my business, I suppose."

"That's right," said Alan, "it's none of our business."

"It's mine," snapped Sam. "I want to know if he's to be my partner."

Joe looked at each of them in turn, playing for time.

"It's all right, Bert," he said. "It's nothing to hide, but I'd rather not talk about it."

"That's not good enough," said Sam, firmly. "I want to know."

Joe had only ever been a policeman. It was all he knew, but it would be a mistake to tell anyone he'd been in the force with the police being generally unpopular. He had to keep it a secret and provide an acceptable alternative answer.

"You can know, Sam, but if I tell you, I won't join you. So, it's up to you. I'm not your man if you can't control your curiosity."

"Are you in, then, if I let it go?"

"I'm in."

"Then we have to discuss the money."

"What money?"

"The money you owe me for your share in the claim."

"How much did you pay for it?"

"I didn't. Mac and I registered it."

"Then, why do I owe you anything? Wouldn't we work it and share in what we find?"

Sam thought for a while, his pleasant demeanour completely gone. While he waited, Joe looked at the others. He thought Bert looked distressed, as though his question had ruined an otherwise pleasant encounter. Alan looked bemused, as though the turn of events was more fun than serious.

"Doesn't seem right," said Sam eventually.

"What's not right?" asked Joe.

"I found it. Gotta be worth somethin' to you. You don't have to go lookin' or anythin'."

"Perhaps I should pay Mac? After all, it's his share."

"That'll be 'ard," said Alan, still looking bemused.

"Did he have a wife?" asked Joe.

"Might've 'ad, but I don't know about any wife," said Sam, still looking unsettled.

"Why're you askin' for money, Sam?" asked Alan. "Joe doesn't know if it's any good. He's only got your word for it, so maybe he pays you and gets nothin'."

"Whose side are you on?" demanded Sam. "This is none of your business, anyway. It's between Joe and me. As far as I'm concerned, if Joe wants in then it'll cost 'im."

"Sam let's just take things quietly for a moment," said Joe. "You're right that without you I have to find my own claim, and you said you can't work the claim on your own, so we both have a problem to solve. Let me buy another whisky and let's talk some more. Are you willing to do that?"

Sam nodded.

"I'll get the whisky," said Alan. "You got the last one and I'll not abuse a man's generosity." He waved at the barman and paid when the whisky arrived.

"How many ounces a day do you get?" asked Joe of Sam when he thought it would be all right to get started again. He was of two minds about the offer. Sam might not be worth the trouble.

"Around thirty, I suppose. Sometimes more, but mostly around that."

"About a hundred pounds a day."

"That's about right."

"Well, I'll tell you what. We share everything equally. The cost of whatever we need and the sale of whatever we find. If at the end of the first week, we average thirty ounces of gold a day, I'll pay you two hundred pounds for my share. And if we ever sell the claim, we take half each."

"It's not good enough," said Sam, shaking his head. "I want five hundred pounds."

"Then, let me make another offer. We share everything equally. The cost of whatever we need and the sale of whatever we find, but it's your claim. If you ever sell it, whatever you get is yours."

"What about my five hundred pounds?"

"What's with the damned five hundred pounds!" exclaimed Alan. "I've never heard such nonsense! You've found someone to work with you, who sounds like he knows his way around a gold field and all you can think about is five hundred pounds! I've never heard of such nonsense!"

"It's nothin' to do with you, Alan. Mind your own damned business!"

"Mind my own damned business? You tell me to mind my own damned business! We've just helped you bury your partner and now I have to mind my own damned business?"

"All right, all right," said Sam, regret in his voice. "I didn't mean that. I'm sorry I said it."

"He's right, you know," said Bert.

"Christ, Bert! Just because I let Alan tell me what to do, it doesn't mean you can too. What's goin' on here? Is it three against one?"

"Sam, I'm not against anyone," said Joe. "We've talked about a couple of ways that this might work, but it doesn't matter to me. I'm just as happy to go my own way."

"All right, all right," said Sam, resignation in his voice. "I'm sorry I got so het up. I suppose two hundred is better than nothin', so let's go with your first offer."

"Good idea," said Alan. "Now, let's finish the drinks and go. I'm worn out by all of this."

"How will I find you tomorrow?" asked Joe.

"Aren't you comin' with us?" exclaimed Sam, as though dismayed by Joe's question.

"No, I'll stay here tonight and join you in the morning. I've paid for a room, stabled my horse and like Alan, I'm ready for bed."

"What about my two hundred pounds?"

"I want to see the claim first."

"You didn't mention anythin' about that!"

"What's bothering you, Sam!" exclaimed Alan. "Have you ever heard of anybody buyin' something without seein' it? For God's sake, I'm tired of this."

"All right, all right," muttered Sam, turning to Joe. "Head up-river outa town and go about a mile along the river. You'll come to the second creek on this side of the river and then follow it about a mile up the ridge," said Sam tersely, as though disappointed that Joe would not go with them and would not give him the money.

"Don't be fooled by the gullies, Joe. There's a few before you get to the Big Oakey. There'll be plenty of people to ask if you're not sure," said Alan.

Joe nodded his thanks to Alan and ignored the slight from Sam, shook hands with the three men and went out to his room.

37. THE TURON DIGGINS

Joe was up with the birds the next morning and was disappointed to discover there was no breakfast at the inn. The problem was easily solved and after a quick breakfast at a nearby eating house, he rode out of town. The road followed the river closely for a mile or so and there were plenty of tents and huts about with smoke from fires where the miners were also making an early start. Dogs marked his passing with aggressive barking, and he was careful to avoid any confrontation. As he rode, he was shocked by how much the ground was torn up on both sides of the river.

The river was on the left side of the floor of the valley through which he rode. The hills on both sides were about the same height, but the river being to the left meant that there was a lot more of the valley floor to his right and the diggers had made good use of it. It looked like the valley narrowed in the distance, but even there he could see many tents scattered about. There were still some oaks along the river, but many of the trees on the lower parts of the hill were gone. The whole place was a credit to man's enterprise as the effort expended to move all the earth was almost unimaginable. He knew he was looking at the results of the work of thousands of people, but he was still awed by the sight.

Finally, he came upon the promised creek and followed a track away from the road. The creek wound its way up into the hills with diggers already working hard, digging on both sides and in the creek itself. Like Sam had said, there wasn't much water, but some of the diggers had put their cradles near pools that looked like they held more mud than water. No one took any notice of Joe as he rode, climbing all the time, although dogs continued to mark his progress. He'd been looking out for Sam and the others since he left the river and the higher he went, the thicker became the trees and shrubs so just when he thought it might be time to ask about them, he saw Alan and Bert working the left side of the creek, about twenty feet from its bottom. Of Sam there was no sign.

Joe stopped his horse, dismounted and looked around. He knew that gold was where you found it, but no one in their right mind would want to find gold here. Tents were pitched all about, dogs kept up an incessant warning, the clatter of picks and shovels filled the air and the smell of many people living closely together hung on the gentle morning breeze. It was nothing like where he'd been digging at Ophir, and he marvelled that anyone could endure it.

Alan saw him, stopped digging and came over, stretching out his hand. Joe took it.

"Bert thought you may not come," Alan said.

"How's that?"

"Thought Sam's behaviour might have put you off."

"It's neither here nor there," said Joe. "The business of getting on with people is not always straight forward."

Alan just nodded, as though Joe had observed nothing out of the ordinary.

"Where's Sam?" asked Joe.

"His claim's higher up the hill and a bit further over. I'll walk you up if you like," said Alan, pointing.

Joe looked at where Alan pointed and could see other men working amongst the trees and the tents, but couldn't see Sam. The ground was just as torn up as it was down nearer to the town. He thought getting on with the country might be harder than getting on with Sam.

"C'mon," said Alan. "I'll show you. There's a track, but it'll be quicker if I show you." He turned and called his intention to Bert who simply waved and went back to the digging.

"Where's your tent?" asked Joe.

"Just there," replied Alan, pointing to near to where Bert worked.

"Where do you get your water?"

"The river. There's a feller that sells it too, but he doesn't come up this high. Can't get his cart up 'ere."

They walked together up and across the ridge, Joe leading his horse by the reins, following a track that wound around the trees that still stood, holes that were left, the piles of rubble from them and tents scattered about. Joe could see a few horses, but there was little in the way for grazing for them.

"What about the horses?" he asked Alan.

"What about the horses?" replied Alan, smiling.

"What do they eat?"

"You've got one. Ask him."

Joe wasn't sure if he should be annoyed. Alan was clearly having fun with him. He decided to ignore it. It might just be part of being on a gold field.

"I mean up here. I see horses, but I don't see much grass."

"Oats, mostly," said Alan, the smile gone. "There're fellers down along the river that will take care of them for money, but the ones around here are used for transport and it's a nuisance to fetch 'em when they're needed. They keep 'em here and feed 'em on oats. Poor bloody things. It's not much of a life."

"What should I do?"

"About what?"

"My horse," replied Joe, unable to keep the exasperation out of his voice.

"Ask Sam. It's nothin' to do with me."

They continued the journey in silence while Joe pondered Alan's disinterest in idle chatter.

As they went up the ridge Joe could see more of the valley stretched out below them and couldn't resist stopping from time to time to take in the view.

"How far is it?" Joe asked, eventually.

"Why, he's just there," said Alan, pointing at a tent.

The tent was a combination of hut, tent and gunyah. Sam and Mac must have cobbled it together over time as they found things to use, or the inclination to improve their habitat. It was tall enough to stand in, the walls were both bark and canvas and the roof was all bark. There was a fireplace nearby with a still smouldering fire, a tripod above it to hang a billy, a bucket that probably held water and pots and pans stacked nearby. It looked like Sam wasn't preoccupied with domestic duties.

"I don't see him," said Joe, scanning the diggers scattered about.

"He'll be down in the creek, workin' his claim. Come on, let's find 'im."

They continued for another twenty or thirty yards up the ridge line until they reached Sam's tent.

"Leave your horse here," said Alan and continued walking, but away from the ridge line and towards the creek along a well-formed track.

Joe dropped the reins and followed Alan who stopped when he reached the edge of the creek. The creek was about fifteen yards wide and when he reached the edge, Joe could see that it was about ten feet deep, deep enough to hide Sam who Alan said was working the side of the creek nearest to Alan and Joe.

"Hello in the creek," called Alan, loud enough to be heard above the sounds of the picks and shovels used by the diggers who were scattered both along the creek bottom and along its sides.

Joe peered over the edge, but still couldn't see Sam.

"We'll have to go down there," said Alan. "He's further in than the last time I was here."

Alan scrambled down the side of the creek, still following the track and supporting himself by using rocks and tree roots sticking out from the side of the creek. Joe followed, wondering if he'd made a mistake offering to be Sam's partner. The sides were steep and torn about by water and diggers. The bed of the creek was a jumble of discarded dirt, rocks and bushes. There were a few shallow pools, around which was the detritus of panning.

When they reached the bed of the creek, Alan walked a few yards uphill, knelt and peered into the darkness of a tunnel dug into the side. Joe joined him and was relieved to see Sam working by the light of a lamp only five to six feet away in the tunnel that was about five feet wide and four feet high.

"I've got Joe with me," called Alan.

Sam stopped work and stared back at them in surprise, before dropping his pick and crawling the short distance to join them.

"Hello Joe," said Sam, his face beaming with pleasure. "I'm sure glad to see you. I thought you might have changed your mind."

It was a different Sam to the uncertain one Joe had left the previous evening.

"Thanks for bringin' 'im," said Sam to Alan.

"I'm glad I did," said Alan. "I don't think he would have found you. Might have given up and left."

"Let's go up and 'ave a cuppa. I'm about ready for one."

"I won't join you," said Alan, shaking his head. "Best get back to Bert before he wonders where I've got to. Anyway, probably better if I leave you fellers to it. You've got a bit to talk about if I'm a judge."

He shook Joe's hand, smiling once again. Joe realised he couldn't have answered any of Joe's questions as Sam might have a different way to deal with matters and any answers from Alan may just complicate things.

They all climbed out of the creek and Alan headed off down the track with a wave of his hand.

"He's a good mate," said Joe.

"None better," replied Sam.

Joe's horse whinnied as they neared the camp and peered out from behind the tent where Joe had left him.

"Good, good," said Sam. "You brought your horse. I hoped you would."

"You could have told me to bring him," said Joe.

"No, I couldn't. One man can't tell another what to do with his horse."

"That might be true," said Joe, "but a partner can agree to what's necessary. He's part of the deal if he's useful."

"Real useful. Like I said, we've got to take the dirt to the river for cradlin', so he'll be right handy for that. Mac used to do it with bags on a pole across his shoulders, but now we can dig and carry more."

"Might take a while for him to get used to it. He's only ever been a saddle horse."

"Well, like Mac I suppose you'll carry the dirt if he doesn't," said Sam roaring with laughter. "Then I bet 'e'll get used to it soon enough!"

Joe liked this new Sam, the one that was quick to laugh and to find the humorous side of things.

"Where can he graze?" asked Joe, pretending ignorance.

"There's not much up 'ere. We'll need to get 'im some oats or corn. I'll borrow some until we get to town. There're other fellers 'ere with 'orses, so we'll buy some from them. We need to take care, too that nobody steals 'im. Plenty of that goin' on."

"I've got some oats. I always carry some. It might be enough for a few days," said Joe.

"Let's see how we go."

Sam busied himself getting the fire going and set the billy on to boil.

"Can I help?" asked Joe, feeling useless. He wasn't used to someone else doing the work.

"Not yet. Let's 'ave our cuppa and then I'll show you around. There's plenty of daylight left, so we can do a bit of diggin' and take the dirt to the river. I'll show you where to find the cradle."

"Do you hide it?"

"Nah. It's on some other fellers' claim down by the river. They don't mind. We'd buy 'em a whisky every now and again, so I hope you're all right with that."

"I am."

Sam filled their pannikins with scalding black tea, put four spoons of sugar in his own and looked at Joe quizzically and put three in Joe's when he held up three fingers.

"Do you want some damper?" asked Sam. "I've still some left from breakfast."

"Not for me."

"Or me, now that I think of it."

They sat side by side on a log and sipped their tea, slurping it to avoid burning their lips.

"Do you know many of the other diggers?" asked Joe, waving a hand in the general direction of the other men working around them.

"Some by name and others by sight. They come and go. Lot of fellers don't have the patience for diggin'. There's a lot of gold about, but it's still hard to find. It seems to be in pockets. You can find a pocket and a feller twenty feet away will find nothin'."

"How do you find it? The gold, I mean."

"Just dig in a likely place. As I say it's in pockets. It's good along the creek, in the sides and in the bottom, but fellers find it along the ridge too. It's not always at the same depth, either, but it's always in layers of sand and mud. If you find some, then you can dig nearby following the layer and find more."

"What's a likely place?"

"Anywhere from the top of the hill above us to the river below. I like the creeks, of course. Most of the people diggin' around the creeks do well."

"Do you need supports in the tunnel? I don't think I saw any."

"Dunno. I haven't thought about it. Why?"

"Tunnel collapsed over at Ophir and killed a feller."

"Happens here, too, but I didn't think I was in far enough to worry."

Joe was torn. He knew it was dangerous but was reluctant to tell Sam so. He thought he might come across as a know-all.

The men sat without speaking until they finished their tea.

"Let's go and have a look," said Sam as he threw out the last of his tea. Joe did the same and they climbed back down into the creek.

They knelt on the ground in front of the tunnel, both peering into the semi-darkness. Sam had left the lamp burning, but it didn't cast enough light to see anything from the entrance.

"See? It's not too deep," said Sam.

"What are you digging in there?"

"There's a layer with sand, gravel and gold. I'm diggin' into the end of the tunnel and fillin' bags with what I think might contain gold. I dig a bit higher and lower than the layer. It's easy to see, so it's easy to follow. There're some bags there that need to be cradled. We could put more in 'em now that we have your horse."

"Have there been any falls?"

"There's been a few from the sides, but not from the top. I've only been diggin' this hole a few weeks. I did the diggin' and Mac did the cradlin'. He didn't like the tunnel."

"I don't blame him."

"We can do the same, if you like," said Sam, laughing. "The tunnel doesn't bother me."

Joe thought Sam more foolish than brave but didn't say anything.

"You think it's dangerous, don't you?" said Sam after a few minutes of silence while the men stared into the semi-darkness.

"I do, but it's not my job to tell someone what they can and can't do. We all assess and take our own risks in life. If I take a turn digging in there, I'll want to put some supports under the roof."

"Diggin'll take much longer. We'll have to find some timber, cut it to size and wedge it in place. It's not easy to find. Lots of diggers are usin' it for huts and fires as well as for supports."

"If others are using supports it only says that we should be doing it too. I've no wish to die in a hole in the side of a creek in Sofala."

"Fair enough. I reckon havin' a partner says he'll do half the work and half the thinkin' as well, so I'd be silly not to listen. Let's take the bags for cradlin' so I can show you where it is and we'll try to find some timber for supports. Once we do the cradlin' you'll see there's still enough gold to make it worth our while to keep diggin'."

Sam dragged the four canvas bags of wash-dirt from the tunnel and together they hauled them to the top of the creek and lashed them with rope across the horse's saddle, two on either side before setting out down the hill to the river.

Joe wasn't surprised they took the same general direction as he had followed up the hill to find Sam. They passed Alan and Bert on the way, but the sight of two men and a horse with bags lashed across it required no more than a wave of recognition. There was a constant view of the valley and the sounds of digging from the hundreds of diggers scattered along the river, the ridges and the valley below. Evidence of enterprise was everywhere, and Joe marvelled at how different it all was to Ophir.

They eventually reached an area near the river not far from Sofala and Sam introduced Joe to three men working a claim that Sam called Second Golden Point. The men dug their claim and carried the wash-dirt not far to the river where their cradle was lined up with many others. Sam pointed to a cradle nearby and declared it belonged to them. There were a few moments of embarrassment when Joe had to confess that he'd never used a cradle, but Sam seemed not to care and took pleasure in showing Joe how to wash the dirt. There was about a pannikin of gold in the four bags and Joe was shocked when Sam said he thought it would be worth over five hundred pounds! Joe had never used a pannikin to store gold and had no idea that it could hold so much. In any event, he no longer had any concern about paying Sam two hundred pounds.

Joe wanted to take the gold into Sofala and sell it, but Sam wanted to find some wood for supports, get the tunnel reinforced and start digging again. He said he'd thought about it and Joe was right. Thinking about it had made him realise that if it rained water would get into the tunnel, cause it to collapse and any gold they might get would be lost.

"Where will we get some wood?" asked Joe.

"Maybe an abandoned hut, or where we climb from the valley up the ridge where there's still some trees standing."

"Did you bring an axe?"

"Not me," said Sam, stopping to look at Joe. "Have you put supports in a tunnel before?"

"No," said Joe, "but I've seen it done."

"How big do the pieces need to be?"

"They put a patchwork of flat pieces against the dirt on the roof and force logs under them to hold them and the dirt in place."

"Flat pieces on the roof?"

"If we can."

"That'll be hard to find. Can you use bark?"

"Probably, if the pieces are big enough, but we'll still need a patchwork of pieces under the bark."

They spent the next few hours scouring along the ridge finding fallen trees, bark and logs that they thought might do the job. After experimenting, they managed to build a frame on poles tied to the saddle and dragged behind the horse on which they could load everything. It meant it was easier to leave the horse in one place and bring the timber from where they found it. None of the other diggers took any notice of them and Joe decided that such activity was not unusual in the wooded areas of the gold field.

When they eventually arrived back at the camp it was late afternoon and Sam announced that he'd had enough for the day. Joe disagreed and convinced Sam that they should spend the remaining hours of the day putting supports under the roof. He argued that since neither of them had done the job before, they would need to work out best how to do it and the sooner it was done the better. Sam reluctantly agreed and threw himself willingly into the task. The hole wasn't deep, so the amount of wood and bark needed for the roof and supports wasn't great and they not only found they'd brought enough, but the job also didn't take as long as Sam had expected, and they finished nearly on dark by the light of the still burning lamp.

Two very tired men said little over supper which consisted of chops, bread and copious tea. They shared the tent and Joe spread his blankets over the low wooded frame recently vacated by Mac and despite the noise from the nearby camps, was asleep in seconds.

38. SAM'S WIFE

The next morning Joe broached the matter of the two hundred pounds nervously expecting Sam to say the gold they cradled the previous day had been found by Sam, but he did no such thing. They agreed Joe would pay Sam the two hundred pounds when he next went to Sofala.

They spent the following two weeks digging and finding about the same amount of gold each time they cradled the wash-dirt. Joe was more than pleased with the arrangement and judging by Sam's attitude, so was he. On the Friday at the end of the first week, Joe rode into Sofala to sell their gold and to buy more supplies. They certainly needed more oats as there was little foraging for the horse. Once Joe's supply had run out, they'd managed to buy a bag from a digger on the promise that they'd replace the bag for the same amount of money when they next went to Sofala. Sam didn't hesitate to give Joe all the gold they had and agreed that through the bank's agent, Joe would open an account for Sam at the bank in Bathurst and put half the money plus Joe's two hundred pounds for Sam in it for safekeeping.

Joe rode into Sofala bemused by Sam's total trust in him. He could have sold the gold and ridden out of the valley. If he did so, then Sam would never hear of Joe and his gold again. Joe thought how far he'd come in being trustworthy in just a few months. He had to admit to himself that he liked being trusted and liked the feeling that Sam found him reliable.

On the way back to the camp, he stopped to chat with Alan and Bert. They said they were doing well and suggested they get together on the Saturday evening in a week's time to enjoy a drink in Sofala. Joe readily agreed that he'd talk it over with Sam and he'd let them know the next time he went to the cradle.

Sam welcomed the idea of a drink in Sofala when they discussed the matter over supper that night. Joe confirmed that all the money had been deposited with the bank's agent. Sam expressed regret that he hadn't got Joe to deposit all his money there too. He said that he and Mac had simply hidden it in the tent.

"Never had much time for banks," said Sam.

"Why not?" asked Joe, intrigued.

"Well, for one thing I heard the bushrangers take your money and the bank doesn't replace it."

"That might have been the case once or twice, but bush-rangers mostly steal from coaches."

"That's not what I heard. Anyway, we figured ours was safer in the tent."

"Is Mac's still there?" asked Joe, staring at his partner in disbelief. Joe always hid his money until he could get to a bank but would never do it as a matter of course.

"As far as I know," said Sam. "To be honest, I'd forgotten about it."

"How much do you think is there?"

"Be the same as mine. Be a few hundred pounds."

"Hundreds of pounds? A few hundred pounds!"

"What's wrong?" asked Sam, looking bewildered.

"What if we hadn't talked about it? What if we moved on before you thought about it, and it was left here?"

"Joe, I don't know what you're so upset about. It's Mac's money. Anyway, I'm sure I'd remember about it if we decided to move."

"I know it's Mac's money, but he doesn't need it anymore. If there's no family for us to give it to, I'll bet he'd rather you have it."

"I suppose so. Like I said, I just hadn't thought about it."

"Do you think you could find it?"

"Why?"

"You can't just leave it! It's way too hard to come by. If you don't want it, we'll find someone to give it to. Anyway, if you find it, you can work out what to do with it."

"It's in the tent somewhere."

"I don't understand this, Sam. You and Mac were partners, but you didn't trust each other enough to hide your money in the same place."

"It wasn't like that," said Sam in an offended tone. "I told Mac that I hid mine under my bed."

"So, you told him where you hid yours, but he didn't tell you where he hid his?"

"I never asked him!" in a tone that showed Joe he was now irritated.

Joe thought he had to take a risk. They couldn't just waste the money. To do so was unthinkable for Joe, even if it involved an argument with Sam.

"Perhaps Mac hid his under his bed?"

"Maybe. Do you want to look?"

"I'll tell you what. Look under my bed in the same place you hide yours under your bed. I'll wait here until you get back."

Same came back minutes later with two small, cloth bundles.

"This is both of 'em," he said gruffly and passed both bundles to Joe.

"Sam, I only wanted to find Mac's so we wouldn't waste it. You didn't need to get yours, too!"

"I decided you might as well put it all in the bank. We can talk with Alan and Bert about what to do with Mac's. He was their friend, too."

"Do you want to count it?"

"Better we don't. We hid it so people wouldn't know we had it. It's a lot of money, so best you put it away quickly. Some fellers'd murder their mother for that."

"I'll take any wash-dirt you've gathered to the cradle in the morning and take the money to Sofala on the same trip. It'll be safer there."

Sam just nodded. He looked tired in the light of the fire. Sad, too. Joe wondered if his thoughts had turned to his time with Mac. Maybe Mac was a better partner than Joe.

"Did you keep some pounds for buying drinks?" Joe asked.

"Can't I get 'em from the bank when I need 'em?"

"Agent has to be there and he's not always. You're best to keep some."

"What's the good of the bank then if you can't get your money when you need it?" Joe thought it odd that he couldn't tell if the look on Sam's face was disappointment, or triumph. Perhaps it was neither.

"Safekeeping. People mostly put their money in the bank to keep it safe."

Sam didn't reply, sipped his tea and stared into the fire.

"Do you have a wife, Joe? Family? Do you have a family? I should have asked before."

"No, I don't."

Sam continued to stare into the fire.

"Sorry I sounded angry about the money," said Sam.

"You didn't sound angry. Not that I noticed, anyway."

"My wife's family lost everything to a bank," said Sam in a soft whisper that sounded like it came from a painful memory.

"You have a wife?" asked Joe, astonished. "I didn't know. You haven't mentioned her before."

"I don't anymore," said Sam, shaking his head and still speaking in the soft voice. "She's dead now. Well, I think so. Haven't heard of her for a while."

Joe was torn. His curiosity was overwhelming, but he knew it was none of his business and he couldn't ask about Sam's wife.

Sam looked up from his reverie and studied Joe as though they'd just met.

"Don't you want to know what happened?"

"I suppose I do, but it's none of my business unless you want to make it so."

"Her name was Becky."

Joe couldn't help his sudden intake of breath and sharp look at Sam. If Sam noticed anything, he didn't acknowledge or comment.

Becky? Her name was Becky? Was this a coincidence, or was Sam playing a trick?

"We lived in Goulburn. Have you been to Goulburn?"

Sam asked the question but didn't wait for an answer.

"My ma and da had come from England, but not together. They met in Cow Pastures, a few miles south and west of Sydney. He worked around the district, mostly as a shepherd. I know, what's a shepherd doing in Cow Pastures? I suppose Cow Pastures was a better name than Sheep Pastures."

Sam looked at Joe and smiled. There was a part of Joe that was glad it wouldn't be a sad story.

"My ma was a housemaid when they met. They decided not to stay in Cow Pastures a few years after they were married and answered an ad in the paper for a job for a family as shepherds in Goulburn."

"Why did the ad want a family?"

"Families are better. It's a lonely job, living in a hut out in the bush, so families stick it out. Not so good when I got older though, schools were too far away, so we had to move again. It's beautiful country and there are lots of sheep and cattle stations there, so it wasn't hard to find another place to work. Becky's father owned a cattle station, and Ma and Pa worked for him when I was about twelve."

"I thought you said you worked with sheep?"

"We did. There were sheep on the cattle station, too. Fink was a good man with a good family, but only one child and that child was a daughter."

"Fink?"

"Everyone called him Fink. Dunno what it meant," said Sam smiling.

Joe inwardly sighed with relief. It wasn't his Becky that Sam had married.

"Working on his station meant we had a lot to do with each other," continued Sam. "I suppose I became the son, and it was inevitable that his daughter Becky and I would marry. Once we married, as far as Fink was concerned, he had both a son and a daughter."

"How did your own ma and da take that?"

"Not too well. Oh, the wedding was a grand success. People came from all around and the party went on for days, but in the months after, Becky's father took more and more of my time to go over plans and ideas. It was flatterin' at first, but tiresome after a while. I knew nothin' about cattle and as much as he tried to teach me, I was terrified of the things. There's a big difference in size between a bull and a ram, or a cow and a ewe for that matter. Knowin' my da thought he'd lost his son, I took every chance to work with him and the sheep, so I was torn between what I wanted to do and what my father-in-law wanted me to do."

"What about Becky? What did she think about you taking her place?"

Sam laughed. Joe hadn't expected it and stared at Sam.

"Sorry," said Sam, "maybe it's not funny, but she didn't like it either. So here I am, caught in the middle of a battle of wills between my father and my father-in-law and my wife and my father-in-law. There was more pull and push goin' on than I'd ever seen workin' with the sheep.

"The other funny thing was that Becky and I might have got on all right, but we didn't love each other. We got married because everyone thought we would. After we married, I moved into the fine stone house and shared her bedroom, but that made it easier for her father to talk with me about his plans. I think Becky wished me back living with my parents again."

"What happened?"

"Somethin' had to give." said Sam, smiling, "Like many things in life, it's not one thing, but enough things added together causes change.

"Fink worried that I was a coward. He hated how I feared the cattle and he would walk away when I tried to do anythin' with them. At first, he tried to help, but later he was just embarrassed. I wasn't too bad if I was on a horse, but when we'd work with them in the yards, I'd spend most of the time runnin' and hoppin' up onto the fences. His other men thought it funny and most of the time I could handle their fun at my expense, but one day it got too much.

"We'd brought a wild bunch in for brandin' and one of the bulls was a problem from the start. Dartin' to and fro, this way and that and it took a lot of time to keep 'im in check. I was hopin' the other fellers would do the hard work when it came to the brandin' yard, but no such luck. When we got to the yard and it was obvious they wanted me to catch 'im, I wondered if they'd been stirrin' 'im up so he'd be a handful."

"Why was he so big and hadn't been branded yet?"

"Fink's station was a few thousand acres and some of the cattle wouldn't be found for a few years in which time they'd grow big. I used to try to avoid musterin' them, but it didn't always work. Many a time I wished I'd married a woman whose father raised chooks!"

"I'm not too sure about that. We had chooks and I had to get the eggs. The hens always attacked and pecked me. I hated it."

Sam smiled and continued. "Anyway, I'm in the yard with this beast whose otherwise pleasant life had been disrupted, tryin' to work out how to control it while my work mates sat along the fence hopin' to see me make a fool of myself.

"There was a lot of shoutin' and false encouragement and to make matters worse, Becky and Fink had come down from the house to see what the excitement was about.

"I don't know if you've ever confronted an angry bull, but they pound the earth, blow their nostrils and make false moves to frighten you. In my case, it worked more than the bull could have imagined. I was scared to death, but at the same time I knew my courage was facin' a test. To be honest, if I'd had a gun, I would simply have shot it. As far as I could tell, everyone was on the bull's side.

"'Grab 'im by the horns!' shouted one of the spectators gleefully.

"'Why don't you bastards get off the fence and help?' I yelled back. 'No one is supposed to do this alone!'

"'I'll grant you that!' yelled Blackie, another spectator, 'I'll help!'

"He jumped down from the fence and my initial relief turned to dismay when all he did was run up beside me and start yellin' at the bull, much to the amusement of everyone else!

"The bull charged and to the sound of laughter from the onlookers, Blackie and I ran for the fence. We got there just in time, leapin' onto the fence, but the bull had forgotten about the fence and in its rage to get us, it ploughed into the fence and knocked the pair of us onto the ground on the other side. Luckily the fence held."

Joe shook his head at the dangerous antics of the men. He knew enough about cattle to know you didn't trifle with them. Any big animal only ever deserved respect.

"I was as angry as I'd ever been," said Sam, continuing his story. "Before Blackie could get to his feet, I was on mine and charged him. I hit him in the shoulders and drove him against the fence. The bull thought we were havin' a go at him and charged the fence again. Once more the fence held, but now Blackie was mad, got to his feet and pulled me up too.

"'What's the matter with you?' he yelled. 'We were only havin' fun!'

"'Have fun with someone else!' I shouted. 'I'm sick of you havin' fun!'

"Blackie was about twenty years older than me and had probably been in more fights than a circus boxer, so when I took another swing at him, he avoided me easily and pushed me onto my back. I looked pathetic and that only made me madder.

"'Take it easy, lad,' said Blackie quietly, pulling me to my feet and holding my head at arm's length while I tried to grab his arm with one hand and swung at him with the other. 'We don't mean you any 'arm.'

"I suddenly realised there was no noise from the spectators, so I stopped and looked around. Some were still on the fence, but Becky, Fink and the rest were all standin' nearby lookin' at me disapprovingly. I'd made the mistake of fightin' back but doin' it badly. You could fight back, but you had to make a decent showin'. Besides, it didn't matter that Blackie had run from the bull too. I was the coward that had refused to deal with the bull in the first place."

"What did you do?"

"Got my horse and went to see my pa and ma. It wasn't far away. I told them what had happened. They understood I'd had enough. Ma said every now and again you have to say *enough*. I rode off the next mornin'. Haven't been back since."

"Didn't Becky come to see you in the evening?"

"No. I supposed she figured I'd come home sooner or later, or maybe she was glad I didn't come back."

"What about your ma and pa? Don't you want to see them?"

"It's all right. I finished up in Carcoar and worked for a farmer there. They joined me when I wrote to them and told them where I was."

"What happened to Becky?"

"I met Blackie in the pub a year or so ago. Fink always wanted to make his station bigger, and Blackie said after I left, Fink borrowed money from a bank and bought some more acres. Things didn't go so well, he couldn't pay the money back, so they took the cattle station and everything he owned and sold it all out from under him for less than it was worth just to get their money back. Blackie said it hit Fink and Becky hard. The fine house, the good livin' and all their friends were gone. He said he'd heard they'd moved to Sydney and Becky'd been crook."

"I suppose it wasn't easy being married to someone you didn't love."

"There were good times and bad times. Ma asked me once about not being married anymore. I told her that being married was like being single. Half the time I wished I wasn't!"

"You haven't thought to get married again?"

"Haven't thought to be chased by a bull again, either!"

The more Joe got to know Sam, the more he liked him.

Joe took the wash-dirt to the cradle the next morning, sold the gold to a buyer and took the money to the bank's agent. The agent wasn't always there even though he assured Joe he'd be there every Friday. There were other ways to manage the gold. He'd agreed with Sam that if the agent wasn't around, then he'd either put the gold on the armed escort for Sydney or the coach for Bathurst. On the way back, he stopped to tell Alan and Bert that they would all get together the next week in Sofala and he and Sam would call by on the way.

They dug, washed and did well with gold in the week before they went to Sofala. Judging from the periodic shouts around them, they weren't the only ones finding gold. Still, Joe was excited when the Saturday arrived, and they stopped working in the late afternoon to fetch Alan and Bert for the much-anticipated trip to Sofala.

Sofala was heaving when they got there. Every other digger must have had the same idea. There was music, singing, laughter and shouts from the town as they walked up the street, Joe leading his horse. He'd decided not to leave him behind in case they stayed in town overnight. However, judging from the crowd Joe thought it might be hard to find a bed anyway.

They went back to the pub where they'd first met and despite it being crowded, they found some places to sit outside. Joe hurried away and stabled his horse. He returned to find the others engaged in conversation with other diggers. All the talk was of the recent petition to the government relating to the diggers' grievances and of a group of men some eleven in number who were doing well on the Louisa but were keeping the location of the finds to themselves. Such behaviour was considered dishonourable by most diggers, and many were angry. There was talk that some had set off, trying to find the locations of the scoundrels' success.

Whisky flowed freely as the men discussed digging conditions and more local successes. There was hope that a renewed enthusiasm for building public houses would mean there would be more competition and fewer sly grog shops.

"You bin to the new marquee of Brant and Jones?" asked a man nearby of Joe's group, proudly pronouncing the word *markee*.

"What's that?" asked Alan, his interest piqued.

"It's on the way into town," said the man. "Nearly finished, too. Had a look at it this mornin'. It's somethin' to see and that's fur sure."

"What is it? What's a *markee?*" asked Bert nervously, seemingly afraid that he might be the only one that didn't know.

"It's a big tent," replied the man. "I only peered in, but it looks like there's a saloon and places where people can sleep. Cloth hangin' down all over the place. Someone said they'd seen something like it in Egypt or Africa or one of those places."

"Have you been to those places?" asked Alan, smiling.

"Didn't say I had," said the man testily, "only said that someone else had. Anyway, I didn't go in. Probably only rich people can afford it."

The man turned back to his group.

"Shall we have a look at it?" asked Bert. "I think I've seen it but haven't thought much about it."

"Not this time," said Alan. "It's nearly dark, so it'll be hard to find and we'll probably only waste time. Better to stay here and enjoy ourselves."

"There's somethin' to talk about, too," said Sam.

The others looked at him expectantly.

"Mac," said Sam finally.

"What about Mac?" asked Alan.

"I'd forgotten about it, but he left his money in the tent. Joe's put it in the bank, but we have to work out what to do with it."

"What are you thinkin?" asked Alan.

"He didn't have a family, did he?" said Joe.

"Not as far as I know," said Sam. "Do you know of any, Alan? Bert?"

They both shook their heads.

Darkness had fallen. Moths flitted and darted around the lamps that lit the area and patrons slapped at a few early, late-winter mosquitoes that relished the warmth and the exposed flesh.

"Your shout, Bert," said Alan, "and check to see if we can get inside. Too many mozzies out here."

"All right," said Bert, collecting their empty glasses and walking into the inn.

"Might be lucky," said Joe, "but I haven't seen anyone leave."

"Doesn't do any 'arm to check," said Alan, "and I've already 'ad my share of mozzies to last me a lifetime."

They sat in silence while they waited for Bert. The people around them became noisier under the influence of drink.

"Might have to leave soon anyway," said Sam. "These fellers are making it hard for a feller to think."

Bert came back with the drinks. "There's some standin' room inside, but it's pretty noisy. Might be better to say here."

"Here's all right with me," said Joe and the others nodded their agreement.

"What about Mac's money?" said Alan, bluntly. Joe thought he sounded like the topic was unpleasant.

"What'll we do with it?" asked Sam.

"Only two things we can do with it. Keep it or give it away. Anyway, how much is there? Might not be worth worryin' about," said Alan

"It's a few hundred pounds."

"What's a few?"

Sam looked at Joe.

"Two hundred and fifty-four pounds, three shillings and four pence."

Alan looked at each member of the group as though assessing their reaction to the amount. No one said anything.

"You keep it, Sam. You were his partner. He'd want you to have it. That's what I think, anyhow," said Alan. "I don't want any of it."

"That goes for me, too," said Bert.

"And me," said Joe.

Sam nodded briefly.

"I put it in your account when I put it with the bank's agent," said Joe, smiling. "I thought that's what we'd decide."

"We could spend some of it on a wake, couldn't we?" said Sam, smiling broadly.

"Already done that. The wake I mean," said Alan. "You keep it all, Sam. Besides, we should agree what should happen to our money if anythin' happens to us."

"Good idea," said Joe. "I'd want anything from the claim to go to Sam."

"What about your family?" asked Alan.

"Don't have one," said Joe, shaking his head.

"Young, good lookin' feller like you?" said Alan. "Doesn't make sense."

"Just the way it is," said Joe.

"I'll bet there was someone," said Sam. "You fellers should have seen the way Joe reacted when I told him about Becky."

"Who's Becky?" asked Bert.

"You know. Sam's wife," said Alan.

"Ah, sorry, I'd forgotten," said Bert.

"Good idea," said Sam, laughing. "I've been tryin' hard enough."

"So, what about it, Joe? Was there someone?" asked Alan.

"It's a long story," said Joe, uncertain about the conversation.

"Doesn't matter," said Alan. "We all like stories and we all 'ave time. Lots of it."

"It might take a couple of drinks," said Joe.

"That's my kind of story," said Sam, "but if you don't want to tell it, you don't have to. Man's life is his own business. Probably shouldn't have said anythin' to the fellers in the first place."

"You think on it Joe," said Alan, "while I get another round."

Alan left and Bert took the opportunity to ask Sam something about his Becky, so Joe took the chance to think on it. He was unaccustomed to sharing his thoughts and feelings, but he did come to Sofala looking for Becky, so he had to tell Sam about it sooner or later. It didn't feel right to tell all three at the same time, but that might be a good thing. At least he'd only have to tell the story once.

When Alan returned, Joe announced that he'd thought about it and he was ready.

Looking at the expectant faces, it occurred to Joe that stories such as his were the only entertainment available to men like the diggers. They could go to the pubs and have a drink and sometimes see a show, sing some songs or tell some made-up stories, but stories like Joe's were real and familiar. Taking a deep breath, he told them about meeting Becky, helping her and her family and following her to Sofala.

"So, it was the name!" exclaimed Sam when he'd finished. "That was why you looked surprised!"

"I didn't think you'd noticed," said Joe.

"Just didn't think I should let you see I had!"

"What's she look like?" asked Alan, thoughtfully as though looking to match someone to the description.

"Blonde, small and beautiful. Feisty too. Can hold her own. Bit of a chatterbox."

"There's a few women here," said Bert. "Gold goes miles up and down river from Sofala. Even if she's here, you'll have trouble finding her."

Joe couldn't help feeling disappointed. His memories were sharpened, and his hopes raised just by talking about her.

"Did 'er brothers come with 'er?" asked Alan, suddenly.

"I think so. Can't be sure though."

"I think I've seen 'er. She was in a store. Kind of woman you describe, givin' the storekeeper what for because she thought he'd charged too much. Got 'im to redo the numbers and she was right. As if the storekeeper wasn't embarrassed! Made a right fool of 'im, she did," said Alan laughing out loud at the memory. "Describe the brothers."

Joe did so, excited like he hadn't been in a long time. A chance to find Becky!

"Could be 'er, but it's 'ard to tell. Look, I'll tell you where to find the store and you can ask there the next time you come to town."

Joe must have looked crestfallen.

"Don't worry, Joe," said Sam. "The good news is that she's not the Becky I married, and you might have found her! Besides, it's my shout, so give me those and I'll get 'em refilled."

They surrendered their glasses to Sam and Joe lost all interest in those around him. All he could think of was Becky and cursed the fact that they hadn't come earlier in the day, and he could have taken some time to check with the store. No, it was worse than that! He cursed the fact that he hadn't told his digging partners about her before, and he'd wasted weeks where he could have been searching.

39. THE SEARCH CONTINUES

Despite his hangover, Joe was up early Sunday and after a quick breakfast, went to the claim and worked so that he'd have wash-dirt to cradle and could go to Sofala on Monday to trade the gold he found. He knew he couldn't justify a trip to Sofala to talk to the storekeeper unless he had gold to trade. Sam laughed when he came to see what Joe was doing. Very few diggers worked on a Sunday. Most went to church and those that didn't saw to simple chores around the camp or found friends for idle chatter over tea or whisky. Sam assured Joe that he could go to Sofala whenever he wanted, but Joe insisted that theirs was an equal partnership and there was no time for slacking. Sam insisted that he couldn't work with a hangover and left Joe to it.

Joe was awake most of the night unable to control his excitement. He was up as soon as dawn broke, had tea and damper for breakfast, loaded his horse with the dirt and headed for the river. He stopped to confirm the store with a still-sleeping Alan who expressed surprise to see any one up and about so early. It was about mid-morning when he finished cradling and with a satisfactory amount of gold for trade, he headed into Sofala with mixed feelings of apprehension and excitement.

After arranging the gold to go on the coach to Bathurst, Joe found Alan's directions were good and the store was easy to find. It was a ramshackle affair made of wood and canvas. There were no customers in the store and Joe was disconcerted to find a woman in charge. Alan had said the storekeeper was a man. Joe hesitated in the doorway, thinking he must have come to the wrong store.

"May I help you?" the woman called to him. She was tall, nearly as tall as Joe, about his age, with brown hair, a full face and a welcoming smile.

"Is the storekeeper a man?" asked Joe.

"No," she said, continuing to smile. "I'm a woman."

"It's not what I meant," said Joe, excruciatingly embarrassed.

"Then, what did you mean?"

"A friend told me a man runs this store."

"He does."

"Is he here?"

"No, he's gone to Bathurst for the day."

"Perhaps you can help me."

"That's why I'm here."

"I'm looking for someone."

"I'm someone. Will I do?"

"I'm sorry," said Joe. "I'm making a mess of this."

"Why don't you explain what you want, and I'll see if I can help you," said the woman, laughing out loud. "I'm Hannah and it's my husband's store."

Despite his embarrassment, Joe liked Hannah and felt he could trust her. He introduced himself and told Hannah about Becky.

"Do you know her surname?" asked Hannah when he'd finished.

"No, I don't," said Joe, shaking his head. "As silly as it sounds, I never asked, but I did meet someone who thought it might be Shepherd."

"We let some customers buy on credit, so we have a list of their names. Anyway, I think I've seen your Becky, but I've not met her, so she's not one of those customers."

"You've seen her? Here at the store?"

"Yes, I think it was her," said Hannah, nodding. "She was in here not long ago. I was packing some shelves and heard her laughing. She gave my husband what for. He told me later he'd made a mistake with the bill. Like you say, she's noticeable."

"Not long ago! That probably means she's still in the diggins!"

"I think it does. I think they're working down near Wallaby Rocks. Most diggers that come here work the Lower Turon. You must be working up-river since I haven't seen you before."

"I've heard of the Wallaby Rocks. How far to there?"

"About five miles. There's a track of course, but there's a lot of people working there. It might be easier if you tell me where your claim is, and I can tell her you're looking for her and where to find you."

"I'm up on Big Oakey. But it doesn't matter. I'll go looking for her now and come back this way if I don't find her."

"She comes in with a feller."

"That'll be one of her brothers."

"If you say so," said Hannah, but looked doubtful. Joe was about to ask her why when a customer came in.

"Good luck, Joe!" called Hannah as she hurried away. She left too quickly for Joe's liking, but there was nothing more to be done, so he left the store. He stood by his horse for a few moments and contemplated the wisdom of looking for Becky. He'd told Sam he was going to Sofala, so Sam would expect him back about midday. It would take him an hour to get to the Wallaby Rocks even if he hurried and an unknown amount of time to search. There could be any number of reasons why he'd take more time and he could only hope Sam would guess the right one.

He hurried his horse along, cantering where he could. There was a track, but it was rough, close to the river and constantly crossed by creeks where he had to pick his way through boulders and debris. It was obvious the track was used by carts, but it was also obvious they wouldn't have an easy time of it. The terrain was reasonably flat at first, but quickly became hilly and rose and fell across steep ridges. Stubby gums and scrub grew beside the track and along the hills amongst rocky outcrops and it became difficult to see where he was going, much less where he'd been. Despite the recent rain, the ground looked hard and dry and all the bush had the appearance of struggling to survive. He stopped several times and confirmed with diggers along the river that he was on the right track.

"You'll need to keep your wits about you, young feller," said one digger. "You're on the Hill End Road and if you're not careful, you'll finish up in Hill End!"

"How's that?"

"Well, it's rough country where you're going. It's only a few miles from here, but the hills are steeper and higher the further you go and the river winds its way aimlessly through them. It mostly goes west, but it'll take off north and then south if the hills are in the way. If you follow the river, it'll take you hours and if you don't, you'll probably get lost. Round about Bradshaw's Flat, the road leaves the Turon, and you should leave the road, or you'll finish up in Hill End."

"How will I know when I get to Bradshaw's Flat?"

"It's near where the road crosses the river. You can't miss it."

"What do I do then?"

"Problem is, there's digging all about so there's tracks aplenty to follow and no way to know if you're following the right one."

"You're making this sound hard," said Joe, testily.

"You're not the first feller that's said that" said the man laughing. "Lots of people stop and ask for directions on where to dig. Hard to tell them that, too!"

"Sorry," said Joe. "I shouldn't ask for directions and get testy because it's too hard to explain."

"Young feller out here, no pan, pick or shovel. What're you looking for at Wallaby Rocks? Do you know someone there?"

"I do," said Joe, grateful to leave the difficult task of directions for the moment. "A girl. Woman. Name of Becky. Do you know her?"

"I might. What's she look like?"

"Young, blonde, feisty."

"I don't know her, but I'd like to. What's she to you?"

"A friend."

"I wonder if she'd say she's a friend. Is she a runaway wife or something like that?" asked the man suspiciously.

"If you don't know her, it doesn't matter," said Joe, turning back to the track and urging his horse forward.

"Steady on, young feller," called the digger to his back. "I didn't mean offence, but everyone's got a right to privacy, especially the women. There aren't too many here, so what's here we need to look after. I don't know your friend, but I'd like to help you, if you've a mind to accept it."

Joe came back to the man feeling slightly embarrassed at his own behaviour.

"Sorry," said Joe. "I'm keen to find her. I met her in Ophir, and I'd like to find her again."

"Where'd you ride from today?"

"I've a claim on Big Oakey Creek."

"You'll need time and supplies, young feller and by the look of things you don't have either. You'll need to scout the area, find where things are, get to know your way around and it'll take a few days. People come here looking for gold, so it doesn't matter to them how long it takes to get about, or how lost they get. Best to go back to your claim, get some supplies and come looking another day."

Joe couldn't help his look of disappointment.

"I suppose that's bad news. On the other hand, you could keep going and accept charity from other diggers, but you don't look to me like that kind of feller."

"Thanks for your help," said Joe after a few moments, hope and expectation crushed. "I'd be foolish not to listen."

"It's only my opinion. Ask some of the others. Someone might tell you different."

"No, I'll head back."

"Stop and see me when you come back. That's if I'm here of course. Been thinking of going to the Meroo. Talk is lots of fellers are going there. You do all right at Oakey?"

"Good enough."

"I might go there."

"Lot of fellers there already."

"Wouldn't matter. Water is the problem here. Too much rain and most of the gold is along the river. Can't get to it most of the time."

"Don't have that problem on Oakey. Not enough water and have to take the dirt to the river."

"Your horse'd be handy."

"He is. I'll be off. See you," said Joe, reaching down and shaking the man's hand. "I appreciate your help."

The man nodded in reply, Joe turned his horse and headed back to Sofala. All the way back, he wondered if he'd made the right decision. He could just as easily have continued, asking diggers as he went and maybe even reached the Wallaby Rocks. Eventually, he convinced himself the digger was right that without supplies, he would depend on charity and few diggers took adequate supplies, much less enough to give some to strangers.

Hannah was working on stacking goods when he entered the store.

"Ah!" she called out as he entered the store. "Perhaps returneth the vanquished hero?"

"Does that mean I didn't find her?"

"Well? Did you?"

"No."

"Then it does. You look a bit down. How far did you get?"

"Dunno. A few miles."

"Faint heart never won fair lady."

"What's that mean?"

"Why did you turn back?"

"Feller said it's rough country that will take time and sup-plies to search," replied Joe defensively.

"Becky might say you don't care enough."

"Whose side are you on?"

"I'm a storekeeper. Always impartial."

Joe shook his head sadly, not sure if he had the stomach or patience for banter.

"Have you been there?" asked Joe, more tersely than he'd intended.

"No. I'm a storekeeper. People come to me." Hannah put her head to one side and studied him. "You've had a hard and disappointing day, I can see."

"I have."

"Don't worry, Joe. It'll work out if it's meant to."

"I came to tell you where she can find my claim."

"I think you should go looking for her. I think you need to know one way or the other."

"Why did you think the feller she came with wasn't her brother?"

"I didn't say that" Hannah replied, anxiously and shaking her head.

"I thought you did."

"I'm sorry, Joe. They didn't behave like brother and sister."

"How do they behave?"

"You know. Brothers and sisters usually get on well, but there's no touching."

"Were they touching? Anyway, what do you mean by *touching*?"

"Joe, it doesn't matter. Find her and find out, is what I'm suggesting. Besides, you're back from a disappointing day. I could see how excited you were this morning, so you'll be better once you decide."

"Thanks, Hannah. Thanks for your help. Our claim is on the ridge above Big Oakey Creek. Follow the creek up. That's where I'll be. Drinking a whisky and forming a plan," he said, smiling ruefully.

"Do you drink a whisky?"

"I do. Do you have one here?"

"My husband has some. I can't sell you one of course, but I'll get you one on one condition."

"What's that?"

"You buy the supplies from me when you go looking for Becky."

"That's a deal," said Joe, laughing. He liked Hannah. She reminded him of Becky.

It was late afternoon when he arrived back at the camp. Sam was nowhere to be seen, so Joe presumed he was at the claim. He settled his horse with oats and water before looking for Sam.

"Sam?" called Joe at the entrance to the tunnel. He could see the light of the lamp in the darkness, so he knew Sam was digging. The light moved towards him as Sam came to the entrance.

"I was thinkin' to go looking for you," said Sam, emerging into the daylight.

"Why?" asked Joe, irritable with himself for being gone most of the day with little to show for it.

"Thought someone might have knocked you on the head for the gold you carried."

"No, I'm all right."

"I can see that. Did you find out about Becky? Was Alan, right?"

"Storekeeper thought she knew her. Thought she was digging near Wallaby Rocks."

"She?"

"Yes," said Joe. "Becky's a she."

"No. The storekeeper. Alan said a man."

"He was away. His wife was minding the store."

"So, what'd you do? Go lookin' at Wallaby Rocks?"

"Tried to. Gave up. Turns out to be harder than I first thought."

"What was hard about it? I've known fellers that worked there."

"It's difficult to explain. Be easier after supper. You done here?"

"I'm ready to quit. Alan came up about midday wonderin' why he hadn't seen you come back. Did you see him?"

"Didn't stop and didn't see him."

"Go back and see him. He was worried that he'd been wrong and had sent you off on a wild goose chase. Expected you'd check with the store and leave it at that. I told him if you thought you could find her, you'd keep goin'. Anyway, I'll get the supper while you see Alan."

Supper was ready when Joe got back, and he tried to think how to tell Sam that he'd need to take several days to go looking for Becky.

"So, what was hard about findin' Wallaby Rocks?" asked Sam when they finished eating. It was always a race to eat as the flies settled on their food requiring constant harassment to chase them away, so there was little opportunity to discuss anything over a meal.

They sat at their makeshift table, sipping their tea. The sun wasn't far off setting and the smell of fires and cooking came to them on the evening breeze.

"I talked to a digger. He said there were lots of trails and it would be easy to take the wrong one. Said even once I found Wallaby Rocks, it might take some time, so I'd be better to go with supplies and time. He observed correctly that I had neither."

"He's right. I hadn't thought of that."

"I'm gonna need more time, Sam."

"She's important to you, isn't she?"

"She is and more so now from a comment made by Hannah."

"Hannah?"

"The storekeeper."

"Oh? What was that?"

"She was with a feller."

Now, the thought was formed. Joe could feel a hollowness inside that was made worse by the look of sympathy from Sam. He'd been avoiding even thinking about it, but would have to confront it now that he'd told Sam.

"That's a shame," said Sam, shrugging his shoulders. "I suppose it's likely to happen in these places. Lot of men and not too many women."

They sat in silence for a few moments. Joe wasn't sure he could talk even if he had something to say.

"Do you know for sure?" said Sam. "I mean, it could have been one of her brothers."

"Hannah said they didn't behave like brother and sister."

"Then, it mightn't be her. Might be someone else."

Joe could have kissed him. He hadn't thought of that! Of course! He'd convinced himself that it was Becky, and she was lost to him. But what if it wasn't Becky?

"That's the first smile I've seen on your face since you got back," said Sam, smiling himself.

"I'd convinced myself it was Becky, and she was lost to me. I hadn't realised how much she meant to me until I thought she was gone. I shouldn't have let her go in the first place. Been a fool, really."

"Will you still look for her?"

"Can I take a few days? Will you be all right here?"

"Of course. I think it'll only take a couple of days anyway. The Rocks are easy to find despite what the digger told you. Keep askin' as you go along. Most diggers are happy to help especially if you tell 'em you're not lookin' for somewhere to dig! Once you get near to where she's diggin', someone will know her. I reckon your biggest problem will be that if you don't find her, you won't know when to stop lookin'."

"I hadn't thought of that. How many diggers do you figure are at the Rocks?"

"Maybe a couple of hundred. Who knows? It depends on whether they're workin' the river. People on the river have trouble with water, so they move on when there's too much rain."

"That's what the digger said."

"What digger?"

"The one that suggested I turn back."

"Might know somethin' after all. When will you go?"

"Tomorrow morning."

"What will you do if you find her?"

"What do you mean?"

"Will you stay with her? Maybe even bring her back?"

"I'll have to find her first. If she's got a feller, then I suppose all I can do is say hello. If she's still free, then it will depend on what she thinks about me. I might be all wound up over nothing. She may not even want me."

"You're a good man, Joe and I like workin' with you, but it seems to me you have to sort this out before we can get back to work. I don't think it's her. If you think about it, most of the women in the gold fields are young and feisty. They have to be to live and survive in places like this. There's the odd one or two that are wives of ministers or bankers, but the diggers' women are a breed apart. Anyway, you might find this one and you might like her better than your Becky, so it might work out all right in the end."

Joe couldn't help laughing. Trust Sam to find something positive!

40. THE SEARCH ENDS

Joe was up at dawn the next morning and walked his horse away from camp after a quick breakfast. Sam wasn't awake and there was no point in saying goodbye. He stopped just after leaving camp and it didn't take long to find the locket in his saddle bags. It was as safe a place as any. He unwrapped it from its cloth and studied it in the dawn light. It was a beautiful piece of jewellery, and he hoped Becky would like it. The idea to give it to her as a present had long been formed. It wasn't as good as a ring, but better than nothing and its value was obvious. A man wouldn't give such a thing to a woman about whom he didn't care. He re-wrapped it and pushed it deep into a trouser pocket.

He walked quietly down the trail, leading his horse past the tents and encampments of other diggers. There was no one up and about at Alan's camp either and that didn't bother Joe. He was in a hurry to find his quarry and the sooner he knew where he stood, the better.

True to his arrangement, he stopped at Hannah's to buy supplies. The store wasn't open yet, so he sat on a box out front and ate some damper that he'd brought for just this eventuality. There were a few people moving about the town, mostly attending to duties associated with work demanding an early start. Some people nodded to him, but most ignored him, intent on their own pursuits.

Finally, when the sun was too warm and he was thinking about finding some shade, he heard the store open behind him. He stood to see a man in the doorway.

"You must be Hannah's husband," said Joe.

"I am and to whom am I speaking?"

"My name is Joe. I'm here for some supplies."

"Ah, Joe. Hannah told me about you. Come on in and I'll get you sorted. I'll tell Hannah you're here. I know she'll want to say hello."

"Hannah? Hannah?" the man called loudly. "Joe's here!"

The man turned back to Joe.

"Mine's Pat," he said, holding out his hand. "You made quite the impression on my wife. She'll be pleased you're here because it means you're looking for your lady."

"Hello, Joe!" called Hannah, hurrying through a door at the back. "We weren't expecting anyone this early and here's me still a mess."

She might be a mess in her eyes, but not in mine, thought Joe. *Pat's a lucky man.*

"Not to worry," said Joe. "I'm here for the supplies as I promised."

"I didn't expect you quite so soon. I thought it would take a few days to get organised."

"I'm keen to find out what's happening. I'd rather know where I stand."

"I hope you're not acting hastily because of anything I said!"

"Yes and no," said Joe. "It bothers me that she might have found someone."

"I'm sorry, Joe. I shouldn't have said anything."

"How many days' supplies will you need? What do you want to take?" asked Pat.

"Maybe three or four. The usual stuff. Flour, tea, sugar, dried meat and oats for my horse. I won't bother with any fresh meat. I expect I'll be in the sun most of the time."

"I'll get it together for you," said Pat, nodding at Hannah.

Pat hurried away, collecting items as he went and stacking them on the counter. He overtly paid no attention to Hannah and Joe as though he was expecting them to talk about something not for his ears.

"Joe," said Hannah. "I want to say something to you."

"It's all right, Hannah. I understand."

"You may not," said Hannah, shaking her head. "I want to say that the woman I saw may not be your Becky. Just because I saw a woman with a man doesn't mean your Becky is lost to you. I talked it over with Pat who served her and he's not sure either. I might be sending you off on a fool's errand. I'm sorry if I am. I only meant to help."

"It's all right, Hannah. We're all making more of this than is necessary. I thought last night that because I find her attractive, doesn't mean she will find me the same. We've not ever talked about it and here I am, heading off to places I've never been trying to find her. This is all my idea and neither you nor Pat needs to apologise for my actions. Thank you for your concern, but it's not necessary."

"All right, Joe. Good luck with your search and I hope everything finishes up all right."

Pat stood beside them both and handed Joe a hessian sack.

"Here's your supplies," he said.

"How much do I owe you?"

"Two pounds, four shillings."

Joe counted out the money, took the sack and started towards the door.

"Just a minute, Joe," said Pat. "I'd like to tell you about the woman I served."

"I'd like to hear it," said Joe, turning back. "I thought you were avoiding me so you wouldn't have to."

"Just wanted to give Hannah a chance to talk to you. I know she wanted to. I'll come outside with you. That way, we won't be disturbed if anyone comes in."

They walked out together, and Joe saw Hannah fussing with her hair before a mirror hanging from the wall.

"Always wants to look her best," said Pat, noticing.

Once outside, they stopped in the shade of a small overhang above the doorway.

"It's not much, but it does the job," said Pat, waving a hand at the overhang. "This won't take long. There's not much to tell, but I thought I should describe her, so you'll know who you're looking for. She was young, about middle-twenties, sparkling eyes and a laugh I'd only expect to hear in heaven."

Joe's heart sank. It sounded exactly like Becky.

"And the feller?" asked Joe, trying to control his emotions.

"That's the funny part. The part I really wanted to tell you and not while Hannah was listening. She told me she told you they didn't act like brother and sister. He didn't say anything at all. She did all the talking and fast, like they didn't have enough time. Like they needed to get their supplies and get back to their claim. Most people like to have a chat, get the news and pass the time of day. Hard to get rid of 'em sometimes."

"What did he look like?"

"Why?"

"I expect when I find them, I'll find them together."

"Joe, that's what I'm trying to tell you. They didn't act like they were together."

"Hannah said they were touching."

"I know that's what she said, but to me it looked like she wanted to touch him, but he didn't want to be touched while anyone was looking. Maybe they'd only just met, or maybe they didn't know each other well. Do you know, it was more like she was his mother?"

"His mother?"

"I know that sounds odd because they looked to be about the same age, but you know how mothers behave. Guiding him, protecting him."

"What did he look like?" asked Joe again.

"Young feller. Scruffy. Probably sounds silly since most diggers are scruffy, but he looked don't-care scruffy. Dark beard. Didn't say much."

"Well, I suppose I won't understand any of it until I find them, but if I wasn't before, I sure am intrigued now. Have either of them been here more than that one time?"

"No. Anyway, they said there was a few of 'em working a claim down by Wallaby Rocks. Said they'd only been there a few days. Might have moved on, too. There's talk some of the folk there have gone to the Meroo."

"Thanks, Pat," said Joe, stretching out his hand. "I suppose every little bit helps."

"Glad to help, Joe," said Pat, gripping his hand warmly. "Hannah says you like a whisky. Call by for one on your way back. We'd sure like to know what happens."

Joe nodded, went and tied the sack behind his saddle, mounted his horse and headed down river.

He passed the point where he'd met the digger without seeing him and continued to the crossing. The water was a few feet deep and flowing quickly, but easily crossed. Joe stopped on the other side and looked around, hoping to see some diggers. He wanted to be sure to take the right track as there were a few heading off in different directions. Steep hills surrounded him and as the digger had said, the river ran around them and where he crossed, the river appeared to be flowing south. Some of the area was open and it looked like there's been digging camps at some point. The track he'd been on was heading roughly north and he knew from the digger it would go to Hill End, so he took a track that roughly followed the river. The track went up the side of a steep hill, winding through the trees and rocks. It was hot work in the blazing sun. He'd gone about a half mile when the track came back down to the river, and he saw some diggers working on the other side.

The men were intent on their cradling and didn't notice him at first. There was nowhere to cross, and he didn't like the look of what he could see of the rocky bottom of the river.

"Hello, the diggers!" he called. The men looked up.

"Is this the Wallaby Rocks?" he called. The men stared at him blankly. He wondered if they heard him above the noise of the river, the cicadas and the birds.

"No, it's not," replied one of the men.

"How do I get there?"

"On your horse!" replied the same man. The others laughed.

"I mean, which track do I take?"

"Hard to explain, but I wouldn't take the one you're on."

"Which one would you take?"

"Take it easy fellers," he heard an older man say. "No harm in helpin' 'im."

"He might be a trap," Joe heard one of the other men say.

"If he is, he's not interested in us. Wants to go to the Rocks," was the older man's terse reply.

The man walked away from the group and waded a little into the river.

"Sorry," the man said. "The boys are just havin' a bit of fun."

"I don't mind, but I'd like to find the Rocks."

"The country gets pretty rough, and the hills crowd the river further down on your side. You're better to get to the Rocks from this side where there's a bit more open space or go back to the Hill End Road."

"Which way would you go?"

"Fastest way is from this side. It's only about a mile as the crow flies. Go along a bit further and find somewhere to cross. Won't be easy as the river's up, but it's a lot quicker if you can find somewhere. It's real hard goin', but stay close to the river and you'll see the Rocks stickin' up on your left. You can't miss 'em."

"How did you get across?"

"River wasn't so high a few weeks back."

"And if I can't find somewhere to cross?"

"Go back to the Hill End Road and follow it. Keep your eyes on the river and when you see it swing north-west, go down to it and follow it. It's hard going and it's about three or four miles, so this side is best if you can get across."

"Thanks. I appreciate your help."

"Why the Rocks?"

"Looking for someone."

"Lot of diggers gone from there. Too much water in the river."

"Where do they dig when they're there?"

"Mostly along the river, but some have had some luck in the hills."

"You doing all right here?"

"No. We were over at the Crudine until a few weeks back," said the man, pointing his finger across the river behind Joe. "Might go back there. You a digger?"

"Other side of Sofala. On the ridge above Big Oakey," said Joe nodding his head.

"Do all right? Some fellers left here a few weeks back to go somewhere near there. Didn't come back, so maybe it's good there."

"We do all right, but there's a lot of dirt mixed with it."

"Good luck with the river. Take it easy. Don't want to read about you in the paper."

Joe waved goodbye and headed off downriver, looking for a place to cross. It was hard going through the rocks and trees, and it wasn't long before he had to dismount. He was just about to turn back when he saw what looked like a good crossing place. The bottom looked sandy, the river wider and the water not too deep. He led his horse across, making sure of the bottom before taking a step. The water came above his knees, but fortunately didn't reach the sack tied to his saddle. It wouldn't do to ruin his supplies.

Once on the other side, it was easier going for a while and then the hills closed in on the river again and he was once more leading his horse over broken ground. She-oaks grew thickly along the river and the riverbed and sides were scattered with fallen trees and large boulders. Then, suddenly to his left appeared a high, rocky outcrop that he presumed to be the Wallaby Rocks. As he came out of the trees, he could hear men digging and saw tents pitched in clear areas. He was sure he'd finally found the Wallaby Rocks and he hoped, Becky.

The ground was all torn up and the evidence of digging was everywhere. There'd been a lot of effort expended in the area, but Joe could only see about fifteen or twenty men working, digging and cradling. He approached the first group. There were five men, two cradling, two digging and one bringing the dirt to the cradle, although he only guessed the diggers were part of the group as the single man was bringing a wheelbarrow of dirt from the diggers to the cradlers.

One man paused from cradling, but the other kept working. He stared at Joe, fear and worry on his face. "What do you want?" he asked brusquely.

"Looking for someone," said Joe, hoping that his smile showed his intentions weren't sinister. The other man stopped working and the man with the wheelbarrow stopped his approach and watched. It was as though they were about to take flight.

"Oh?" said the man who had first paused. He moved so he was on the other side of the cradle from Joe.

"I'm not with the police," said Joe, still smiling.

"Wouldn't matter if you are," said the man. "We've got nothin' to hide."

Joe thought the look on his face said otherwise. He knew unlicensed diggers worked places the licensing police would find hard to access.

"I'm looking for someone," repeated Joe.

"There're diggers here, some more in the hills and others along the road to Bathurst on Box Ridge Creek. Unless you know where they are, you'll need to do a fair bit of lookin'."

"The road to Bathurst? You can get here from Bathurst?"

The man shrugged.

"I'm looking for a woman. Young, about my age, not too tall, blonde and feisty."

"What's she to you? She your wife or somethin'?"

Joe should have known the question would come and should have prepared an answer.

"My sister," he said and hoped it sounded convincing.

"Don't think I've seen her. What about you, Bob?"

The man standing beside him shook his head and said, "No."

Joe thought they were both lying but didn't know how to call them out. In a previous life, he would have threatened to march them to the cells, but he was no longer a policeman and there weren't any cells.

"All right," said Joe. "Thanks for your help."

He started his horse towards the next group.

"Why you lookin' fer your sister?" called Bob to his back.

Joe turned his horse back and studied Bob. He hadn't really looked at him before other than a casual glance when he answered his partner's question.

Bob was tall, not too old with an unkempt mop of hair that stuck out from under his hat and a beard that needed attention. His face was dark brown despite his hat. He had the appearance of an honest man. His clothes were wet and muddy from the cradling.

"Not my sister," said Joe. "I just said that. I met her at Ophir. I'd like to meet her again. Maybe, join her and her brothers and do some digging."

Bob just nodded, clearly assessing Joe and his answer.

"None of our business, Bob," said his partner, quietly but loud enough for Joe to hear.

"She's got brothers. They'll handle him if he's trouble."

"Still none of our business."

"Why'd you lie to us?" asked Bob. "Might've helped if you'd told us the truth in the first place."

Joe dismounted and holding the reins, walked over to Bob and his partner. Bob's face exhibited curiosity, his partner's animosity.

"Bugger off," said the partner, "you're not welcome here."

"Take it easy, Dave. Let the man answer the question."

"I don't care whether he answers it or not. He's not welcome here and that's the end of it."

Ah! thought Joe. *Looks like I'm in a queue for Becky's affections!*

Ignoring Dave, Joe looked at Bob.

"Name's Joe," he said, but didn't try to shake hands. "I first met Becky in Ophir. Helped pull a brother out of a tunnel collapse."

Bob and Dave looked at each other quickly at the mention of Becky.

"How's he now?" asked Bob, facing Joe.

"No good. He died not long after."

Bob looked at Dave as though to say, "I told you so!"

"What happened then?" asked Dave, defensively.

"They left to come here to the Turon."

"Who left?" asked Dave.

"Becky and her brothers. Phil, Charles and Fred."

"Was there anyone else with 'em?" queried Dave, obstinately as though trying to catch Joe out.

"Not that I know of. Might've been though. I didn't see them leave."

"How'd you know they left then?"

"Dave, I don't know what you're getting at," snapped Joe. "Phil came to see me to tell me they were leaving. I didn't see them go."

"You haven't answered Bob's question. Why'd you lie to us?"

Some other men had gathered around and looked from one to the other as the men spoke. It reminded Joe of when he was little, and his mother and father would argue. He would look from one to the other as they each had their say. The exchange was probably as bewildering to these men now as it was to him when he was young. A contest of wills was as old as humanity.

"Does it matter? I don't know. Probably thought you'd more likely tell me what I wanted to know. I'm sorry, if that helps."

"We knowed you wasn't a brother," snapped Dave. "All her brothers are with her!"

"Are they now?" said Joe, quietly.

Unexpectedly, Bob burst out laughing.

"Would you believe us if we told you we don't know her?" he said.

"Doubt it," said Joe, smiling again. He liked Bob who didn't seem to have the same interest in Becky as Dave.

"They're further down the river," said Bob. "About a mile. Near the road to Bathurst."

"They don't need any more diggers," said Dave, as though that might dissuade Joe from continuing the search.

"I don't think that's why Joe wants to catch up, Dave. Might be more to it. Anyway, Joe, we've work to do so I wish you well and don't tell 'em we sent you!"

"I won't," said Joe, laughing and mounting his horse. "About a mile you say?"

"Stay on this side. Ground's a bit tore up in places, but the goin's easy. No problem for your horse. You can't miss the road to Bathurst, and you won't need to go far along it. They're diggin' on the surface, so you can't miss 'em."

"Are there any others there?"

"A few, but Becky's the only woman."

"Thank you, gentlemen. I'm obliged," said Joe, riding off, excited to have found where Becky was working and afraid of what he might find when he got there.

As Bob had said, the riding was easy, much easier than it had been earlier, and he found a river crossing with a road leading away from it that likely went to Bathurst. He saw diggers from time to time, all of whom regarded him suspiciously, but he didn't stop or ask anyone for directions. No doubt anyone riding a horse from Sofala would be deemed licensing police.

He stayed on the road as he rode away from the river. He stopped and passed the time of day with several groups before he found Becky. They were working the bottom of a small creek, all intent on their tasks and Joe was on them before they saw him. Joe's heart skipped a beat on seeing Becky. She was as beautiful as he remembered. She fussed with something on the ground near to a large tent. He guessed that once again they all shared the accommodation. Stepping down from his horse, he recognised Phil and Charles. There was no sign of Fred, nor, he noted with relief, anyone else.

"Becky?" he said quietly.

She looked up, startled to hear a voice. As he thought, she hadn't heard him approach.

"Oh, Joe!" she shouted and threw herself into his arms.

It was a reception he'd hoped for but hadn't expected.

There's no one else, he thought with relief.

"Oh Joe! It's so good to see you! Phil, Charles, look who's here!" shouted Becky.

Phil and Charles dropped their digging tools and hurried over, gripping Joe's hand excitedly when he was able to disengage himself from Becky.

"You old son of a gun!" shouted Phil. "We didn't expect to see you again! This is so good, Joe!"

"Oh, Joe! What brings you here?" asked Becky, standing a step away and eyeing him up and down. "You look good! Oh, you look so good!"

"Did you think I wouldn't?" asked Joe, laughing.

"Well, what brings you here?" asked Becky again, still smiling.

"You," said Joe, softly, seriously, all the laughter gone from his voice, "and to give you this." He took the locket from his pocket, unwrapped it and gave it to her.

"Oh, no," said Becky. "Oh Joe, it's beautiful, but why?"

She turned the locket over in her hands, gazing at it with wonder. She pressed the clip and it popped open.

"Who's William? Are you William?"

"I found it," Joe lied, too embarrassed to tell Becky the truth. He would never be able to tell her the truth. "I kept it for you."

"For me? You kept it for me?"

Phil and Charles looked at each other uncomfortably, looking like they didn't want to be there.

Everything had gone from excitement and laughter to uncomfortable in such a short space of time.

"I'm sorry," said Joe, annoyed at himself for the honest answer and for giving her the locket before he understood her circumstances. "If I could take back the words, I would. I meant I came here to see you all. That's what I should have said. And the locket didn't cost anything. I thought you might like it. That's all."

"That's good, Joe," said Phil. "I knew that's what you meant."

Becky continued to stare at Joe. Try hard as he might, Joe couldn't understand the look. Why was she so serious? What was wrong with him saying he'd come looking for her? What was wrong with giving her the locket? She'd gone from excited to see him to glum and sad in moments.

"Are you still in Ophir?" asked Charles, obviously wanting to change the conversation to mundane matters.

"No, I'm working on the Turon too. Other side of Sofala."

"You come from there today?" said Charles.

Joe nodded.

"Is it good up there?" asked Phil.

"I've a partner. We do all right. You do all right down here?"

"Good enough. Not as good as some, better'n others. You know how it is."

"Where's Fred? Is he with you?" asked Joe.

The three looked at each other before Phil answered, "He's taken some dirt to the cradle. It's down by the river. I'm surprised you didn't see 'im."

"He goes downstream of the road," said Becky. "Joe wouldn't have seen them if they were at the cradle."

"Them?" said Joe, hating the question and dreading the answer.

"Dan's with him," said Becky, quietly.

"Dan? Who's Dan? Is he a brother I haven't met?" asked Joe, trying to make the question sound light. He couldn't, as the question sounded hard and tense.

"He says he knows you," said Phil, matter-of-factly.

"Dan? I don't know any Dan."

The excitement at meeting Becky and his wonderful reception seemed so far in the past, it was like it happened to someone else. He no longer wanted to be there, he wanted only to get on his horse and ride away. Something had happened and he knew he was not going to like it.

"Says he met you on the road at Lapstone. Said you spent about an hour talkin' in the morning," said Becky.

Joe looked at her, his heart heavy, his throat constricted and almost unable to speak. He'd never known such hurt. It wasn't humiliation, it was the pain of loss. A dream had been shattered and had become a nightmare.

"Yes, I remember," said Joe, struggling to form the words. "He was with some other fellers. They were going to Ophir."

"They came here."

"Where are they others?"

"They left when Dan joined us," said Phil.

"Can you stay for a while, Joe? I'd like to talk if you can stay," said Becky, putting a hand on his arm. He resisted the urge to snatch the arm away.

"Charles and I have a bit of diggin' to do," said Phil. "We'll get back to it."

"Yes," said Charles, nodding. "Be good if you could stay a while. Be good to catch up. We've some whisky, so we could all enjoy a drink."

"Be like old times," said Phil.

Joe looked at him and nodded, but in his heart knew it could never be old times again. The pain of loss threatened to overwhelm him and the urge to flee surfaced again and it was only with a tremendous effort of will, he controlled it and replied, "Yes. It would."

"You can stay tonight, if you like," said Becky. "There's plenty of room in the tent."

Joe wanted to reply that there wouldn't never be a tent big enough, but kept his thoughts to himself.

"I have some supplies," said Joe. "But I don't have any whisky."

"Don't worry. We have enough," said Phil. "We'll be off, you two catch up and we'll be back long before nightfall."

No, thought Joe. *However much whisky you have, it won't be enough.*

The others left and though they didn't have to go far, they'd be out of hearing.

"Would you like a cuppa?" asked Becky after a few moments, still clutching the locket.

"I'd best be getting back."

"How did you know I was here?"

"Feller saw you in the store in Sofala. Told me, so I came looking."

"We usually go to Bathurst. It's a chance to catch up with Ma and Pa. Dan wanted to go to Sofala, so we went there. It's too hard along the river, so Bathurst is better. There's talk there'll be a store here, soon so we won't have to go anywhere."

Joe looked at her, so much that she turned away, embarrassed.

"I'm sorry, Joe," she said, her voice wavering and she looked near to tears.

"Why did you make me so welcome when you have someone else in your life?" he asked, unable to keep the bitterness out of his voice.

"I missed you so when we left Ophir. I know I hardly knew you, but I asked Phil to tell you we were leaving. I was hoping you'd follow. I dreamed about you, prayed every night that you'd come to me."

"You should have told me."

"I thought you'd think less of me. I asked Phil to tell you I'd miss you."

"He hardly did that."

"Oh, Joe. What a mess. It was such a thrill to see you and you look so good. Here, take the locket back. It's a wonderful thought, but you should keep it for someone else."

"No, it's yours. You keep it. What about that cuppa?"

"I thought you were leaving."

"I'll stay for a cuppa." Joe wanted to leave, but wanted to understand how she could become involved with someone else, although he'd never told her how he felt.

They sat at the rough camp table, made from split wood and rope. The seats were covered in hessian to restrict the splinters, but seating still had to be done with care. It was still hot, the sun didn't affect them so much being blocked by the gums, but the clatter of cicadas and the sound of diggers came to them on the breeze.

"What happened, Becky? I won't pretend I'm all right. I thought you'd wait."

"Dan and the others came here. They were digging just over the way there. Most of us around the Wallaby Rocks get together every so often to tell stories, sing and for the men to drink a whisky. There aren't many women around, so I was always like the belle of the ball. All the men wanted to talk, but Dan was different. He seemed so sad, so out of place. I tried to find out about him, but his partners didn't ever say much."

"Why'd you want to find out about him?"

"I suppose I thought I might be able to help."

"Help?"

"Sounds silly, doesn't it? Phil told me to leave well enough alone. 'Just another lonely feller on the gold field,' he said. 'Leave him be.'"

"He said his wife died. I suppose that'd make a feller sad," said Joe, failing to keep the bitterness from his voice.

"I know. He told me one night when we sat together. Most of the men had gone back to their tents, but we stayed on talking late into the night. Phil was furious the next morning. Told me to take better care of myself. Anyway, Dan then comes by for a cuppa, whisky or supper most nights and one thing led to another. He's been through a lot for such a young man."

"Are you married?" asked Joe, stiffly.

"Not yet. He's asked me, though and I said yes. I'll take him to meet Ma and Pa the next time we go to Bathurst, and we'll be married."

"Will you come back to the diggins?"

"No. We'll stay with Ma and Pa and work the farm."

"Why did you say yes?"

"To getting married?"

Joe nodded.

"I don't know. I suppose I felt sorry for him, thought I could make him happy."

"What about you? Don't you want to be happy?"

Becky sat so still; she looked like a painting. Her hair was tied back and her shoulders square, but her chest was heaving, and huge tears rolled down her face.

"Oh, Joe. It's such a mess. Why didn't you come sooner?"

"You don't have to marry him."

"I've told him I would."

"That doesn't mean anything."

"It does to me, and I know it does to him. My word has to be worth something."

Joe was defeated. It was the one card he couldn't beat. "I know," he said, sadly. "Sometimes I think it's all we ever have that's worth anything."

"Hello, the camp!" called a voice from the road.

"It's Dan and Fred," said Becky, softly. "What we said is between us, all right? You can't say anything to Dan about this."

"I won't," said Joe, putting on his best, happy face.

Two men came up the road, close to the camp, leading a horse and walking slowly and tiredly. Both were covered in mud and sweat.

"Hello, Fred!" Joe called.

"Hello, stranger! What brings you?"

"I was down this way. Thought I'd drop in."

"Joe, do you remember Dan?" asked Becky.

"I do," said Joe, shaking hands first with Dan and then with Fred.

Joe couldn't help assessing Dan as competition. He knew the war was lost, but instinct took over and Joe wondered at the man that had taken the prize. Dan was expressionless.

"Why aren't the others here?" asked Fred, waving at Phil and Charles.

"I expect they'll come now that you're back," said Becky.

Dan stood to one side, as though the reunion of these friends was nothing to do with him. After a few minutes, he took his horse over to a small roped-off area, gave him some oats in a nose bag. When it was done, he set him loose to graze on what was left of the grass. Joe watched with interest. It was as though Dan wasn't part of anything.

"C'mon you fellers!" shouted Fred. "Look who's here!"

Phil and Charles acknowledged with a wave and set about stacking their tools and bagging the wash-dirt.

"It's so good to see you, Joe!" exclaimed Fred. "Are you staying for supper? We could have a whisky. Catch up. You know, it'd be like old times!"

"Joe said he has to get back," said Becky. "But perhaps you can persuade him to stay for supper."

Joe was in a quandary. He didn't want to stay, was still feeling battered by his conversation with Becky, but couldn't dismiss a flicker of hope. In his heart he knew that hope was a waste of time and the sooner he got over Becky the better, but what if? What if....?

Phil and Charles arrived back, full of merriment and excitement. It was as though they wanted to over-compensate for the sombre appearance of Becky and Joe.

"I don't know if you've heard Joe, but you're stayin' the night. It's so good to see you. We've all missed you and can't thank you enough for what you did for George," said Phil.

"I'm sorry about George," said Joe. "I thought he'd be all right."

"Not your fault," said Phil. "We wouldn't have got him out without your help. What happened then was no fault of yours."

"I think Joe wants to get back," said Becky.

"Nonsense! I won't hear of it. Joe's stayin' and that's that," replied Phil.

"Isn't it up to Joe?" asked Becky.

"No, it's not and that's the end of it. We'll have a whisky, talk a little and then have some supper."

"There won't be enough beds," said Fred. "Joe can have mine."

"If I stay, I'm not taking anyone's bed. I came ready to camp out and that's what I'll do," said Joe.

"Then it's settled! Becky, you get the glasses, I'll get the whisky and the rest of you settle yourselves at the table!"

It didn't take long before Joe was enjoying himself. There was still a deep-down hurt and sense of disbelief at what had happened, but the men were fun and full of stories about life in the gold fields. Dan didn't join in, just sat quietly sipping his whisky. Similarly, Becky just sipped countless cups of tea.

Phil said he heard there were still meetings between the diggers and the authorities about the cost of a digging licence and he hoped the diggers would win in the end. Charles and Fred talked less than Phil but matched him drink for drink. Becky took it upon herself to get the supper and Joe contributed some of his supplies. Dan helped Becky when she needed something carried or the fire stoked. Joe saw no sign of affection between them. It was as though they were partners, simply helping each other to cope in the process of daily living.

Joe took it easy with the whisky. He wanted to be sure to keep his emotions in check. It wouldn't do to let anyone other than Becky see his true feelings.

Fred was the first to go to bed, no doubt tired after a long day and too much whisky. He was followed soon after by

Charles, Dan and Becky. Joe was comforted by the knowledge that the others would be in the tent with Becky and Dan. The thought of them being alone in the tent was too much for him.

Finally, it was only Phil and Joe left by the fire. They'd long abandoned the table and benches, moving to cut-off logs that surround the smouldering blaze. Phil was the worse for wear but was still remarkably lucid. The smoke from the fire moved with the night wind, carrying the welcome smoke to stave off the mozzies. They had all worn as much clothing as necessary to restrict access to bare flesh, despite the warmth of the evening.

"I'm sorry, Joe," said Phil, slightly slurring the words.

Joe knew what he meant but didn't know how to answer.

"She's makin' a mistake, you know," said Phil. "I told her to wait, told her you'd be by. I don't know what got into her. One minute she would only talk about you and the next it was Dan. It doesn't matter, does it? I hope it doesn't. You're a good-lookin' young feller. Plenty of fish in the sea for you."

Joe didn't know what to say, but in the end, he was guided by his father who told him once that if he didn't know what to say, he should say nothing.

"Anyway, don't forget about us, Joe. I'll never forget how you helped and the risks you took. Lot of fellers wouldn't have done that. Good night. Hope you'll be all right sleepin' in the open."

"I'll be all right. I'm a digger, remember?"

"I remember you used to drink more than you did tonight. If things change, I'll find a way to let you know."

"No, Phil. I can't spend the rest of my life living in the past. What's done is done. We all make our choices and have to live with them. I could have come sooner, I didn't. Becky could have waited, she didn't."

"Fair enough. See you in the mornin'."

They shook hands and Joe poured himself another whisky, content to sit by the fire and reflect on the past. Despite what he'd just told Phil, he wanted to sit and think about Becky and what he'd missed. It seemed appropriate to do so while she slept a few feet away.

The whisky was nice, but he really didn't appreciate it. What he'd lost gnawed at him, left him with such a feeling of helplessness. Hannah had told him that maybe he hadn't tried hard enough. She was sure right about tonight. He'd agreed without hesitation to keep the conversation between himself and Becky private. A better man would come out swinging.

There was movement beside him and he looked up in surprise, instantly fearing that it could be a bushranger.

"Hello, Joe," said Dan. "Mind if I join you in a whisky?"

Joe would have preferred a bushranger. He had nothing to say to Dan and he was about to tell Dan that he was off to bed when he thought that nothing that happened was Dan's fault. It would be rude and churlish to refuse to join him in a whisky.

"Just the one," said Joe and failed to keep his voice friendly. "I'll be off to bed soon."

"One's fine with me. I don't drink that much these days."

Joe poured a whisky into an empty glass and passed it to Dan.

"How're you been? Doin' all right? You find some gold?" asked Dan.

"I've done all right. Did all right at Ophir, then came here."

"Becky told me about you and how you helped in Ophir. You made a big impression on her."

"That right?"

"We're goin' to be married."

"That right?"

"I think she'd rather marry you."

Joe looked up, startled and unable to keep the astonishment off his face.

"Didn't expect that, did you?" said Dan, chuckling. The smoke and the fire gave his face an impish look in keeping with what he'd just said.

"No, you've got me there. Last thing I expected, in fact."

"I think we've got a problem and I'd like to talk about it."

"What problem's that?"

Dan laughed and stopped quickly.

"I need to be careful," he said. "Don't want to wake anyone. I want to take the chance to have a chat and work out what to do."

"What to do?"

"Christ, Joe. You just pretendin' to be thick? You're not makin' this easy for a feller. You see, I knew you'd come. Becky told me about you, but I remembered you from Lapstone. I was hopin' to be married before you got here, but when I saw you and Becky sittin' together this afternoon, I knew it would be up to you and me to solve the problem."

"And what problem is that?"

"Becky's agreed to marry me and now she doesn't want to."

"Then, the right thing to do would be to let her go. Any reasonable feller would do that."

"I suppose that's what you think?"

"That's what I just said, didn't I?"

Joe sensed there was hope and like the drowning man he once was, he was prepared to grab it with both hands.

Dan chuckled again.

"You forgotten I was married once?"

"What's that got to do with it?"

"Everythin'. It's got everythin' to do with it."

"You'll have to explain that to me, 'cause I sure can't see it."

"Do you remember me tellin' you about my wife? Do you remember me describin' her?"

"I remember you telling me she disappeared in the California gold fields and you found her, but you didn't finish the story. Anyhow, what that got to do with Becky?"

"Don't you want to hear the end of my story?"

Joe couldn't tell by the light of the fire, but he'd swear Dan was smiling. They were talking about Joe's future and Dan had the gall to think it funny!

"Dan, I'll tell you straight. I don't care about you, your wife or your story! All I really care about is Becky!"

"If you care about Becky, you'll need to hear the end of my story. You see, it involves her."

"I don't have a choice, do I?"

"I suppose not. Here, I'll top up the whiskies and you make yourself comfortable. There's not much left."

"Of the whisky?"

"No, the story."

Joe laughed and this time he could see Dan smile.

"I found Alice with Bull. He was usin' and abusin' her, sellin' her for five dollars a time."

The memory of the story came back to Joe, how Dan had searched and searched and finally found Alice in a town with Bull. He'd robbed a miner to get some money, pretending to take a turn, but missing out because Alice's night was done.

He'd decided to get a gun, follow Bull and rescue Alice. Joe was once again engaged with the story.

"I had to get a gun, you see," Dan continued. "Bull was too big and too strong for me to get the better of him. I didn't care about any noise from the gun if I got a chance to kill 'im. People fired guns all the time in the gold fields. Anyway, gettin' a gun was easy. There were plenty of drunk miners and plenty of guns. I went out front of the saloon and pretended to be drunk. I lay down beside a couple of drunk miners, waited until no one was walkin' by, took a gun from the nearest drunk and crawled off into the night.

"Next problem was to wait for Bull. I didn't know whether he'd come out the back or the front of the saloon but guessed it would be the front. Of course, if he came out and got onto a horse or into a buggy, I wouldn't be able to follow, so I hoped he'd come out the front and be walkin'. He did both.

"Alice came out with him. She was sayin' somethin' to him softly, it sounded like she was pleadin', but I couldn't hear. It was all I could do not to rush and shoot him there and then and take off with Alice. There were too many people about, so I followed them, stayin' well back and makin' sure not to look like I was followin' them.

"Towards the end of the town, they came to a hut. It was a sturdy lookin' thing with glass in the windows, but rubbish strewn about. There was nothin' homely about it, so I figured Bull rented it while in the town. Perhaps he took Alice all about and this was just one of many towns. They went in and shortly after the light of a lamp appeared in the window.

"Bull had said he'd take a turn when they got home, and I thought it would be to my advantage. He'd be preoccupied and unlikely to have a gun in his hand.

"We all make mistakes, Joe.

"After about five minutes, takin' the gun in my hand, I pushed the door open and stepped inside, holdin' the gun in front of me. It took no time to get used to the light of the lamp and to see Alice sittin' on the end of a bed, facin' me. At the time, I didn't think she recognised me, just sat there starin'. I looked around but couldn't see Bull.

"'Where's Bull?' I asked.

"'Here,' said a rough voice and I was hit hard on the head.

"When I came to, I wasn't tied up, just sittin' on the floor at the end of the bed where Alice still sat. It was a bigger room inside than it looked from the outside. There was the bed behind me, a table and some chairs and a fireplace where a log fire burned brightly. There was nothin' homely about the outside, but everythin' homely about the inside. There was even a coloured tablecloth on the table and curtains on the windows. Bull sat in a chair a few feet away, holdin' my gun and staring at me intently.

"'Do I know you?' he asked in a voice that was more conversational than confrontational."

Joe marvelled at Dan's choice of words. They implied an education, but he didn't speak like an educated man.

"I realised that Bull wasn't in the least bit nervous or afraid. I suppose that comes with bein' a big man. There's not much to be afraid of when you're big."

'No,' I said. You don't know me.'"

"But you did know him!" exclaimed Joe.

"I thought it'd put 'im on guard if I told 'im I was Alice's husband. I didn't think he'd recognise me, or at least I hoped he wouldn't.

"'Then, why're you followin' me? Why'd you come in 'ere with a gun?'

"'I came to take somethin' from you.'

"'You're a robber? Is that all?'

"'In a manner of speakin' I am. I came to take 'er,' I said and nodded at Alice.

"'I know you!' Bull exclaimed. 'You came to take a turn, went away and got some money and took too long to get back. I thought you said you'd come back tomorrow. Couldn't you wait?" Bull burst into laughter at his own wit.

"I took the moment to look at Alice. She was lookin' at us like Bull and me was in a Punch and Judy show. You know, interested but not involved. I didn't understand it at all. I thought she would at least have recognised me by now.

"'There's no law to deal with you, so I'll have to deal with you myself,' said Bull. 'On your feet, stranger!'

"'What do you want me to do?' asked Alice. 'Does he want me now? I'm tired, Bull. Can't I have a rest? You said I could have a rest after we did it. Is it going to be him, you or both of you?'

"'Well, this feller has made a mess of our plans, darlin'. I'll have to deal with 'im first. You go to bed. You can have a rest. No more tonight. We won't be gone long. He will, but I won't,' Bull sniggered. It sounded childish from such a big man.

"'Can I have some laudanum before you go? Just a little. I know I'll need it before you get back.'

"Of course! Bull kept my wife in his hold with opium. That's why she didn't try to get away and why she put up with her miserable life. I had no idea what he intended to do with me, but now I knew he couldn't do it in the hut and I might get a chance to fight back once we went outside. Perhaps I could turn his lack of fear to my advantage."

Joe was mesmerised. The fact that Dan was there made the story much more exciting as Joe knew in advance that Dan had got the better of Bull. But how?

"Weren't you frightened? If not for you, for Alice?"

Dan looked at Joe and smiled, perhaps because he realised Joe was interested at last.

"I didn't give a damn about me. At that point I would have willingly given my life to see Alice out of the mess. She was so far gone on opium that she didn't even know who I was. My anger was growin' about what Bull had done. I hadn't thought about it until he sniggered. Up to that point, all I'd wanted was to get Alice out of there, but now I knew that even if I did, she'd probably never recover. No, now I wanted to kill Bull even if he killed me in the process."

"What about Alice? What would happen to her with you both dead?"

"Too logical Joe. There's no logic to what an angry man thinks.

"'I'll give you some when I get back, darlin'. C'mon you, let's go!' Bull barked at me.

"I started to get up but fell before I could get to my feet. I suppose the blow on the head, the realisation that Alice was gone forever, and I might soon be dead was too much for me.

"'C'mon you, stop bluffin'. We don't have time for your nonsense. Get up,' roared Bull and kicked me hard in the leg. As he did, he slightly lost balance and as he tried to recover, I kicked him in the leg. It didn't seem to hurt him, but it did make him angry.

"'You goddam bastard!' he shouted, pointed the gun at me and pulled the trigger. Nothin' happened. It wasn't loaded. I'd stolen an empty gun. He threw it at me, more in disgust than to hurt me. I think he thought me stupid to go after him with an empty gun.

"Bull bellowed, a roar that sounded more like his namesake. The noise was shockin' in the room and Alice screamed. It wasn't a scream of fear, but one of terror. Perhaps Bull got angry with her sometimes and when he did, he roared like he did now. Anyway, she jumped up from the bed and tried to crawl under it. As she did, she knocked the lamp off the table onto the floor, near to the curtains. It broke open, the oil burst into flames and the curtains caught alight immediately.

"'You stupid bitch!' bellowed Bull again. 'Now look what you've done!'

"He seemed torn between doin' somethin' about the fire and doin' somethin' to Alice. As far as I could tell, he'd forgotten about me. He reached under the bed and grabbed Alice by the hair and started to pull her out.

"'No Bull!' she screamed. 'Please don't hurt me! I'll do whatever you want! I'll be good, I promise! You and the feller go and do what you must! I'll wait until you get back!'

"'Other feller?' shouted Bull. He had forgotten about me and now Alice reminded him. He was bent over near me, still holding Alice's hair. There was no time to waste, so I quickly picked up the gun and holdin' it by the barrel, brought it down on Bull's head as hard as I could. I might as well have hit him with a toothpick.

"He let go of Alice and turned to me.

"'This is all your fault,' he said in a voice that was unexpectedly calm. I'd just hit the man on the head with a gun and it was only Alice that bothered him. He should have been worried about the fire. It had taken hold and most of the wall and part of the roof were ablaze. I could feel the heat of it as he bent down, grabbed me by the shoulders and threw me against the door. He took no more trouble or effort than he would with a bag of sugar.

"The door wasn't all that strong, it broke, and I fell to the ground outside. After a few moments, I got onto my hands and knees and looked back into the room. Bull was once again tryin' to drag Alice from under the bed, but she ignored the danger of the fire and clung desperately to the frame, kickin' at Bull at the same time.

"'C'mon you stupid, bitch! Do you want to burn to death? We have to get out of here!'

"'Alice!' I screamed from the doorway. 'Get out! For God's sake get out!'

"Bull looked up at my shout, lettin' go of Alice. 'I know you! You're 'er 'usband! I'll deal with you as soon as we get out of 'ere!' He turned back to Alice, but she'd retreated further under the bed. I started to get up to help him, but it was too late.

"The burnin' roof crashed onto the bed and that was the end of Bull and Alice. I sat back and stared at the flames. It wasn't long before other people came to help. They threw buckets of water on the flames, but I suppose the hut being made from pine meant it would burn such that nothin' would stop the fire until it burnt itself out.

"I watched it burn, sat there on the ground and watched it burn. It was daylight before there was nothin' but smokin' embers.

"I told anyone that asked that I'd seen the flames and tried to help. No one asked who I was, why I was there or why I stayed. One man asked if it was the woman that I mourned. He said it was a shame that the woman was dead and told me she'd been very popular since Bull had found her, knocked her out and brought her to sing and service the miners.

"Some men picked through the embers once the heat died down. They pulled the bodies out and took them away."

"Didn't you claim your wife's body?"

"What was the point? What would I do with it?"

"Bury her properly, I suppose. At least, you'd know where she was buried."

"What would be the point of knowin' that?"

"You could visit her."

Dan laughed, a hard bitter laugh.

"Go back to California? I don't think so."

"Why don't you tell people what happened?"

Dan looked at Joe and smiled. A smile without humour, an enigmatic smile, but one that also showed shame and bitterness.

"That's the question, Joe. That's the right question."

Dan stared at the fire for a few moments before refilling their glasses.

"Mostly shame, Joe. God had sent me a wonderful, beautiful woman and I'd failed to take care of her. I let her be kidnapped into a life of abuse, fear and drugs. I know I should have taken better care of her. Better that people think she disappeared. That way, they don't know how careless, useless and irresponsible I was."

"I think you're being too hard on yourself. No one would have guessed what happened and most wouldn't have kept looking for her."

"I regret lookin' for her. I wish I'd never found her." Dan spat the words out one by one as if each left a bad taste in his mouth.

"We all have regrets, Dan. Things we did or didn't do. It seems you're no different and I'd be surprised to find you are. I'm not sure anything matters that much that we have to spend our whole life regretting it."

"That's a fine sentiment, Joe and easy for someone who hasn't taken for granted a gift from God."

"How do you know I haven't?"

"You look like a man that knows where he's been and where he's goin'."

It was Joe's turn to laugh.

The fire crackled and sparks flew as a log collapsed into the fire under its own weight.

"Which brings us to now," said Joe. "What's all this got to do with Becky?"

"She's Alice, Joe. It's like they made two of 'em. I couldn't believe it when I saw her. It's like Alice didn't die in the fire and found her way here to Sofala."

"You're pulling my leg! That's it? She reminds you of Alice and you think you'll get another chance? A way to make things right? You think if you look after Becky, God will forgive you for not looking after Alice?"

"What's wrong with that?" stammered Dan, clearly taken aback.

"Everything's wrong with that! What about Becky? It's her life too! She's not here to help you make things right. It's a ludicrous notion and you know it!"

"Take it easy, Joe. There's no need to get your dander up."

"No need to get my dander up? No need to get my dander up! My dander's up all right and I've a good mind to knock your stupid head against a tree!"

"What good will that do?"

"I'll feel better, and it might knock some sense into you!"

"We're just talkin' here, Joe. Just talkin', that's all."

"You have to tell Becky the truth, Dan. You have to tell her what you just told me. She's got to know everything and when she does, there's no way she'll want to marry you."

"You think so?"

"I know so!"

"Well, I've got bad news for you. She knows everythin'. I told her she had to know before I asked her to marry me. So, I told her, then asked her and she said yes."

"I don't believe you!"

"Joe, it's of little concern to me whether you believe me or not. I'm tellin' you the truth so you'll know why Becky wants to marry you but will marry me."

"Why? I don't understand why?"

"It's simple. She's a woman of her word and I intend to hold her to it."

Joe drained his glass and stood up. He wanted to hurt Dan, hit him as hard as he could. Yet he knew it wouldn't help, wouldn't change anything, and would only make him feel better for a few moments before he felt a lot worse.

"It's a terrible thing you're doing, Dan. Nothing good will come of it and I have another regret now."

"What's that?"

"I regret you told me."

"I had to, Joe. I don't want you hangin' around. It'll be harder to get Becky to love me if you hang around. I knew you'd come and I'm glad you have because now I know you won't be back."

"Why won't I be back?"

"Because Becky will be married, and you know you'll only be wastin' your time. She needs to be free of you, Joe. In a month or so, I'll tell her you're married. I'll tell her you had a girlfriend all along and only came to see her to make sure you'd marry the right one."

"She'll know that for the lie it is."

"Maybe," said Dan, shrugging his shoulders and still sitting by the fire. "Like I said, you're wastin' your time and you'd be better to move on."

"I can stay, make a fuss, and tell Becky she's making a mistake."

"You can do all that, but if you love Becky, you won't. I'll look after her Joe; she'll have a good life with me. You won't have to worry about her at all. It's up to you of course, but I know what I'd do if I were you."

"And what's that?"

"I'd leave now."

"It's dark."

"Won't be the first time you've ridden in the dark, I'll warrant. Leave, Joe. There's no place for you here."

Joe stood still, his mind a jumble. He should fight, fight like he'd never fought before. He could probably even kill Dan, but what would that gain? It wasn't Dan he had to fight; it was Becky. Dan's mind was made up, so fighting him would only make things worse. She was the one to convince, but he didn't know any argument that might work. Her word was her bond, and she wasn't about to go against it.

"All right," Joe muttered, turned and walked to his horse, guided only by the light of the fire. The sky above was a blanket of twinkling stars, each one mocking him because it was a source of light that showed him nothing of the path in front. His trip to find Becky was more than a total failure, he'd found her, yet she was way beyond his grasp. It wasn't like digging for gold. The treasure might be an inch or a mile away, but diggers always had hope that it was an inch. Becky was way beyond a mile, she was up there with the stars, so far beyond his reach she might as well be in another universe. He'd found her and lost all hope. He was crushed. Dan was more than his match. He'd manipulated Becky for his own ends, and she knew it and was prepared to go along with it. The thought crossed his mind that she might be a fool, but he quickly put the thought aside and put her back on the pedestal. She was a person of her word, and they were rare enough.

He saddled his horse in the darkness. It wasn't hard. He'd left everything in place to sleep out, so everything he needed was near at hand. He didn't ride out of the camp, just led his horse by the reins. The road was easy to find and once on it, he mounted and rode towards the river. He looked back and saw Dan still seated near the fire. There was a brief surge of anger against Dan, then he let it go. It wasn't hard to imagine Dan as the devil, sitting in his fiery lair, plotting hate and malice against him.

Riding slowly in the darkness, he let his horse find the river and once there, he stopped and camped the night resolving to be up early enough in the morning as to be gone before Becky or her brothers could find him. There would be no simple explanation for his early departure.

41. THE TOFF

He was up at dawn, hardly slept during the night and was glad to be moving, to have something to do. Some diggers waved as he rode by and he waved back, but never stopped. People seemed friendlier to riders heading towards Sofala than those heading the other way. He didn't stop and see Hannah, or Alan and Bert and was back at the camp around the middle of the day. "Couldn't find her," he said briefly to Sam when he arrived back at camp.

"Fair enough," said Sam, "but you'll need a better response when we catch up with Alan and Bert."

"I'll work on it. Let's make up for lost time. Do you have any dirt for cradling?"

"I don't know how to break this news Joe, but you've only been gone a day and a half. I didn't expect you back so soon, so I've been taking it easy."

"All right. I'll help you dig and when we have enough, I'll take it to the river."

"It's good that you're back and more than ready to get to work, but I'd like to live to enjoy what we've found. Let's take it slowly at first. You're actin' like a man that's wantin' to forget."

"All right, all right. You've made your point, so let's get on with it."

Sam knocked off later in the day and went to start the supper. Joe continued to dig, slamming his tools into the earth, dragging out the dirt and separating the likely dirt with frenzied effort. He wanted to be so tired come bedtime that he'd find it easy to sleep. After he curled up in his bunk, he knew there'd be no such luck. He tossed and turned all night, his thoughts crowded with images of Dan and Becky, one pleading for him to go and the other for him to stay. His face burned with the memory of his humiliation by Dan. He thought of hundreds of better responses to Dan than the ones he'd made, but such reflection only caused him to stay awake and to relive the pain.

It was in the early hours that he thought he'd been rude to Sam, a good man who deserved better. It least that would be easy to remedy.

"Sorry I was sharp," he said to Sam over tea and damper.

"Nothing to worry about, but there's something on your mind. You shouted in your sleep last night. First time you've ever done that."

"I didn't think I got any sleep at all."

"Well, you shouted while you were awake," said Sam with a smile.

It was early and the sun peeped over the ridges at the end of the valley. Other diggers were up and about, accompanied by the sounds of tools, horses and the smell of cooking.

"You want to go into town tonight? We could have a whisky. Alan and Bert might join us."

"Tomorrow's Saturday. I can wait a day."

"Up to you."

"I'll take the dirt and cradle first thing. There's plenty there, then I'll take the gold to Sofala."

"How much longer do you think the claim'll last?"

"Dunno. We're still getting good gold. I think we should put in some more supports, though. We're getting deeper all the time. I didn't like the feel of it when I dug yesterday. I've done a bit of digging lately, so I'm now aware of what should be done."

"All right. Can you fetch some timber when you go cradlin'?"

"I might be all day if I do."

Sam nodded, threw out the rest of his tea and headed for the claim. Joe saddled his horse, tied the bags of dirt behind the saddle and led the horse down the track. Other diggers were about, finishing breakfast, gathering tools or setting to work. It had rained overnight and more looked to be on the way. The rain had cleaned the air, and it was fresh and crisp, although the objectionable smells of the gold field occasionally assaulted his nostrils.

As he neared the bottom of the ridge, he could see a small crowd gathered around a small girl standing on a tree stump and singing. She had a beautiful voice and as he came close, she finished what sounded like an Irish melody and the crowd showed their appreciation. There were shouts of encouragement and pleas for more.

Joe dismounted and walked to the back of the crowd. He guessed there to be forty or fifty people, mostly men and all were enchanted by the performance. It wasn't possible to get closer due to the press of everyone also trying to get close, so Joe remounted to get a better view.

As he mounted and looked to the front, the singing stopped and a young voice called out, "Joe! Joe! It's me! Sparrow!"

It was Sparrow, sure enough and the crowd turned to stare at the man who had stopped the performance.

"Don't worry about him!" someone shouted. "Keep singin'!"

"All right, I will," called Sparrow and resumed her singing.

Joe dismounted, not wanting to cause further disturbance.

"She's an angel," whispered a man beside. "A beautiful voice and straight from Heaven."

Joe noticed some of the other men brushing away tears. No doubt the nearness of Christmas and a child singing made many a man long for his home and family.

When Sparrow finished her song, she called out, "I can't see you, Joe! Don't go until we catch up! Please tell me you won't go!"

"I won't!" called Joe, "but you keep singing! These people might murder me if you stop again!"

A murmur of appreciative laughter rippled through the crowd.

Sparrow sang two more songs and Joe listened mesmerised by Sparrow's voice and her ability to sing fearlessly in front of people she didn't know.

Finally, Joe heard Jim's voice call, "That's it, everyone! Sparrow's done for today!"

"Oh, c'mon," called a man's voice. "Just one more!"

"Give the wee lassie a break," called another. "Ah! Ye've a treasure there and that's for sure. Thank you, lassie, and come again, soon!"

The crowd dispersed and Joe was able to join Jim, Susie and Sparrow.

"Oh, Joe! It's so good to see you!" said Sparrow and hugged Joe's waist, having to reach up to do so. "I thought we'd never see you again!"

"Well, aren't you the one!" said Joe. "And I didn't even know you can sing!"

"Oh, I'm not that good," said Sparrow, but beamed with pleasure at the compliment.

"I think you're very good," said Joe, and Sparrow's smile became even broader.

"We all think she's good," said Susie, laughing and hugging Sparrow.

"I want to be on the stage," exclaimed Sparrow.

"We'll see about that," said Jim and he wasn't smiling.

"How are you, Sparrow?" asked Joe, squatting down to her level. "It's been too long since I've seen you. What brings you to Sofala?"

"We've come for the gold," said Jim. "We're doing better here than at Ophir. You here too, Joe?"

Sparrow looked at Jim crossly and Joe thought she probably wanted to answer Joe's question herself.

Joe, still squatting looked at Sparrow.

"I'm good, Joe," she said. "How are you?"

"I'm good too," said Joe and smiled. Sparrow startled Joe by reaching out and hugging him again, but this time around the neck.

After she released him, Joe held her by the shoulders and asked, "And how come I find you standing on a stump singing for the benefit of all the diggers?"

Jim looked about to answer, but Susie put her hand on his arm.

"I do it sometimes. It's fun," said Sparrow, trying to hug Joe again.

"How long have you been here?" he asked her.

"We came about a month ago. I like it here."

Joe stood up, this time addressing Jim.

"Are you going to Sofala?"

"Yes, we're going in to get some supplies. Sparrow has some friends near to here and they always ask her to sing when we go to town."

"How do they know you're going by?"

"We always stop to see them," said Sparrow.

"Where are you off to?" asked Susie.

"Going to the river to cradle some dirt," said Joe, waving at his horse.

"Then you're digging here too?"

"Yes. Big Oakey Creek," this time waving at the ridge behind them.

"We're further along," said Jim. "We've got a claim on Nuggety Creek."

"You doing all right?" queried Joe.

"So far it's good."

"Will you come see us, Joe? I think Sparrow would like that," asked Susie.

"Of course. I'd love to catch up with you all."

"Where will you cradle?" asked Sparrow. "You said at the river?"

"Just down there," said Joe pointing to a spot on the river not far away.

"Can I go with Joe? Please?" said Sparrow, looking from Jim to Susie in turn.

"Well... Wouldn't it be better if you come with us?" said Jim, frowning.

"Joe will take good care of me, won't you Joe?"

"Joe may not want you. He might be too busy," said Susie.

"Not want me!" said Sparrow, indignantly. "Of course, he wants me! You do, don't you Joe?"

"Well, if it's all right with Jim and Susie. I'm sure you'll be able to help, and they can pick you up on the way back."

"How long will it take to cradle what you have?"

"About an hour."

"And can I ride your horse, Joe? I asked Daddy to get one, but he still says we can't afford it."

"Yes, you can ride. So long as Jim doesn't mind."

"Then, it's settled!" said Sparrow triumphantly, as though instrumental in a breakthrough on behalf of all children in the world.

"You will take care, won't you Joe?" asked Susie, a serious look on her face.

"Of course. There are others around too. We leave our cradle on some other fellers' claim and they'll be nearby."

"We won't be too long," said Jim. Putting his hand on Joe's shoulder. "You should know our little girl has a claim on the man whose life she saved."

"And I'm not little!" exclaimed Sparrow, hotly.

"All right, all right," said Jim. "I'm sorry. We'll be back within the hour."

Joe swung Sparrow up into the saddle and his horse looked back at his rider as though to say, "You don't have to worry. You're safe with me."

Joe walked off slowly, holding the reins while Sparrow kept up an incessant chatter about what they'd been doing since they'd last seen each other. It wasn't a long walk to the river and Joe was disappointed when they got there. He liked Sparrow's chatter and her sense of self-importance and when they reached the river, he realised he hadn't thought about Becky for the last ten minutes.

Sparrow was familiar with the cradle and helped Joe gather the gold from the ridges and put it in the bags he kept for the purpose. He marvelled that she could maintain her chatter and work at the same time. There was never any need of a response from him. She chattered away as though confident she always had his undivided attention. Other diggers moving around stopped to observe he had a new helper, or to comment how lucky he was to have the "singing angel" as his assistant. Sparrow would smile broadly when anyone commented on her and Joe working together.

When they had finished, Joe suggested they sit and have a spell while they waited for Jim and Susie.

"Do you think they'll be long?" asked Sparrow.

"Not long, I think," said Joe, looking at the sun. It moved from behind some clouds and Joe observed out loud that it might rain soon.

"Then I don't have a lot of time," said Sparrow.

"What do you mean?" asked Joe, a little nervous. He wasn't sure what this little imp had in mind.

"I'm glad we have a chance to chat. Just you and me."

"Yes. Me too."

"Do you remember that I saved your life?"

"How could I forget it?"

"I read in a book that if you save someone's life, they belong to you."

"So, you can read as well as sing?"

"Don't change the subject," said Sparrow, petulantly.

"Sorry."

"That's better. Now, I'm eleven, so when I'm sixteen, I think we should get married."

Joe looked at her and was struck by her serious demeanour. They sat beside each other on the riverbank, the water bubbling across some rocks nearby and the wind soughing through the oaks. Sparrow's hands were crossed in her lap, in just the position Becky's hands would be had she asked the same question.

Joe's mind was in a turmoil. He knew he had to take the proposal seriously as she would expect nothing else. He also knew he had to respect what Jim and Susie would expect him to do. The silence stretched out to a minute.

"Well? Cat got your tongue?"

"Oh Sparrow, perhaps you'll find someone else? Somebody younger than me? Besides, isn't the man meant to ask the woman?"

Sparrow couldn't help a little smile of pleasure when Joe called her a woman.

"I think this is different because you belong to me."

She came a little closer and put her head on his shoulder.

"I've dreamed of it being like this, you know," she said. "I've thought about you every day."

Joe couldn't help himself. His chest felt tight, his lips trembled, and tears weren't far away. His loss of Becky, the love that might have been and the adoration of this wonderful little girl became too much.

Sparrow sat back and stared at him.

"Are you crying, Joe? I've never seen a man cry. I didn't think they could."

"No, I'm not crying," he said, but his voice trembled.

"I'm glad, but you look upset. It's just a marriage proposal. People do it all the time."

Joe couldn't help but smile at the irony. The grown man trying not to cry like a child and the child speaking like an adult.

"You're upset about someone else, aren't you?" asked Sparrow, with insight beyond her years.

Joe just nodded.

"Do you love her?"

Again, Joe just nodded. He didn't know if it was true, but it seemed the best answer.

"Does it mean we can't get married?"

"I think so."

"That's ruined all my plans. What's the point of owning someone if you can't marry them?"

"Perhaps the book you read wasn't right? Perhaps you don't own someone if you save their life?"

Sparrow drew her knees up under her chin, put her hands on them, rested her chin on her hands and looked at the water.

"Perhaps," was all she said.

Joe had no idea if the matter was settled, or if he'd handled anything the right way. It was his first and he suspected his last, marriage proposal from someone like Sparrow. He liked Sparrow immensely and hoped he hadn't done anything to ruin their friendship, or that of Jim and Susie. This love business was turning out to be much more complicated than he'd ever thought.

It wasn't long before they heard Susie call out, "How goes the cradling? What are you two doing? I thought there was work to do?"

"We've finished," said Sparrow, jumping to her feet. "Are we going home now?"

"In a moment."

"Where's Daddy?"

"He's waiting back there," said Susie, waving a hand behind her. "He's got the supplies. He didn't want to carry them down to the river and back again."

"Sensible," said Joe, getting to his feet.

"You all right?" asked Susie. "You don't look so good."

"Just tired. That's all, just tired."

"Will you come and visit with us? We're not hard to find. Only a few hundred yards up Nuggety Creek."

"I will."

"When? Tomorrow night?"

"I can't tomorrow night."

"Sunday then?"

"I'll try."

Susie knelt and whispered to Sparrow, who waved goodbye to Joe and ran up the track away from the river.

"What did you say to her?" asked Joe.

"Her father has a present for her."

"Is it true?"

"In a manner of speaking. I wanted to talk to you. What's happened? When I left, I heard her talking up a storm and now she's as quiet as a mouse. Did she upset you?"

"In a manner of speaking," said Joe and smiled.

"She loves you, you know," said Susie, at first laughing and then serious.

"She told me."

"Ah! Did you know how to handle it?"

"Not at all. Made a mess of it, I'll warrant. She may not want to see me again."

"What did you say?"

"Told her I'm in love with someone else."

"She'd know if that's not the truth."

"It's the truth."

"Who is she? Where is she? Oh, Joe, I'm so happy for you! Don't worry about Sparrow. It's a child's crush, that's all. She'll get over it. Oh, I'd love to meet your lady! Will you bring her Sunday?"

Joe couldn't help himself this time. The tears started and he sobbed uncontrollably. Susie held him until he gained control.

"Joe, what's happened?" asked Susie as she held Joe at arms' length.

"It's a long story."

"I've the time."

"I haven't. I've got to take the gold to town."

"Come and see us after. I think we need to talk about what's happened."

"I'd rather not. I'm embarrassed to be like this."

"Nonsense. We all have feelings."

"Perhaps I'll come by on Sunday."

"If you don't, we'll come looking for you."

"All right," said Joe, Susie kissed him quickly on the cheek and headed down the track to join Jim and Sparrow.

Joe watched her for a few moments, then turned and picked up the bags of gold to put them in the saddle bags. When he opened one of the bags, he noticed some cloth. He didn't remember putting it there. He pulled it out and unwrapped it. It was the locket! There was a piece of paper that he unwrapped and read.

Joe. It's a wonderful gift, but I can't keep it. I'm sure you will find someone else. Becky.

Someone else? Is it that easy for her to let go? What a fool he'd been!

But it didn't diminish his loss and grief. Even a fool can hurt.

He re-wrapped the locket and put it in the bag, followed it with the bags of gold and mounted his horse. Riding into town, he thought he would have to get himself under control. Even now his face burned with embarrassment at what Susie must think.

Gold buyers were easy enough to find, but the price was too low, so Joe decided to send the gold to his bank in Bathurst via the mail and the Government armed escort. The price might have been certain, but the process wasn't. The Government charged a fee but took no responsibility for the consignment reaching its destination. However, the buyers knew that Joe sometimes was prepared to suffer the clumsy, time-wasting and uncertain alternative, so mostly it enabled him to receive a reasonable price.

After weighing and packaging his gold at the rundown, badly managed excuse for a Post Office, Joe headed back to his claim. He briefly thought to see Hannah, but he'd had enough emotional stress for one day. Hannah would be sure to press him for details and he knew he wouldn't be able to avoid her questions or satisfy her curiosity.

Back at the camp, Joe helped Sam for what was left of the day and headed off for a restless sleep with dreams troubled by images of Dan, Becky and Sparrow. Luckily, he could remember nothing of his dreams when he woke to pouring rain on the Saturday morning.

"I doubt we'll be diggin' today," muttered Sam, peering out at the weather. "This looks like its set in for the long haul."

"No breakfast either," said Joe, pointing at the fireplace. They cooked on an open fire, a space surrounded by stones on which they could balance pots and pans and a triangle of legs with a hook on which they could hang a billy. "I doubt even Thomas Farriner could start a fire out there."

"All, right," muttered Sam. "Who's Thomas Farriner?"

"I thought everyone knew," said Joe, looking at Sam briefly to see that he was serious. "King's baker. Started the Great Fire of London."

"Where's Thomas when you need him?" asked Sam, smiling broadly. "Why don't we wait until it stops or at least slows a little, then head off to town? Might as well go to the pub."

"Sounds good to me," said Joe, looking at his horse standing under a lean-to that he'd built with bark and wood. *Might take you and put you in the stables behind the pub. At least you'll be out of the rain and get a good feed of oats and hay,* he thought.

"He looks unhappy," said Sam, also looking at the horse.

"It's not much better in here," said Joe. They'd built the floor using some saplings and straw laid on the ground, but the rainwater was already making its presence felt.

"It'll be a mess in here later," said Sam. "Only thing worse than a funeral in the rain," said Sam, "is bein' somewhere like here. I wonder sometimes if the gold is worth it."

"I wonder that all the time."

"I think you need a whisky. Let's not wait. Let's go now. Besides, we can get some breakfast in town, so there's no point in waitin'. We'll collect Alan and Bert on the way."

"They might not want to come so early."

"At least you've still got your sense of humour," said Sam and laughed out loud.

They had some pieces of canvas to wrap around their shoulders to keep the rain out. It wasn't much good, but better than nothing Alan had once said.

Joe slipped the bridle on the horse and led him away from the camp in the still-pouring rain. It was uncomfortable walking, their boots sloshing in the water and mud.

"It's no good up here, but it'll be worse down on the river. The claims will be washed out again," said Sam.

"We wondered where you were," said Alan when they told him they were off the breakfast and the pub. "Thought you'd be here much earlier. Nearly went without you."

They all headed down the track and found there were other diggers with the same idea. Sam's prediction about the river turned out to be true and they could hear the rushing water long before they got to it.

"Luckily, we don't have to cross it," said Alan as they and about twenty others plodded along the road beside the river.

"Forget the river," said Bert. "Might not be any room at the pub. Looks like everyone has the same idea."

"That's the trouble with good ideas," said Alan. "They catch on."

"We can always get a bottle and sit under a tree," said Bert.

"I doubt that one will catch on."

When they reached the pub, there was no one there and the publican was more than happy to open. He waved at Joe when he asked about stabling his horse. "You know where it is!"

Joe saw to his horse and returned to the pub to find the others enjoying a cuppa with some lamb, cheese and bread.

"We should do this every day," said Joe, enjoying being out of the rain and having something different for breakfast.

They finished and Alan ordered four whiskies. Remarkably, they still had the bar to themselves.

"I wonder where everyone is?" asked Bert.

"Scared of the rain," said Sam.

"Might be," said Joe. "If the river gets up, they might need to move tents and things."

"It's a good chance to find out about Wallaby Rocks," said Alan, smiling. "You haven't told us what happened. Did you find your quarry?"

"Maybe later, Alan," said Joe tersely.

Alan looked at Sam as though he might add further information, but Sam shook his head briefly.

The publican asked if they wanted him to light the fire and help them dry out.

"It's too hot in here," said Alan. "We'll dry out soon enough. Anyway, a couple more whiskies on board and we won't notice."

"That's all right," said the publican, "just thought I'd ask."

"Will there be some cards later?" asked Sam. "I doubt the police will be out on a day like this."

"I'd rather not take the chance," said the publican. "I've a few black marks against me already and don't need anymore."

"It'll be a long day without cards or somethin'," said Alan.

"It's better than bein' in the rain," said Sam. "I'd just as soon sit here and drink whisky."

There was some idle chatter about the rain, the worst storms any of them had endured and some light banter about whose storm was the worst.

"I found her," said Joe in a moment of silence, deciding he had to get his tale over and done with and better to do so while they had the bar to themselves. The others were instantly silent, and alert and Joe realised they'd all been hoping for this moment.

"Was she all right?" asked Alan when Joe had been silent for too long. He must have known Joe was unsure how to continue.

"She was, but she had another feller."

"Did you try to get her back?" asked Bert, genuine concern in his voice.

Joe looked at the faces of the three men at the table. None of them showed anything other than genuine concern. Joe knew then that he was amongst friends whose only interest was his welfare. *And a little curiosity*, he thought ruefully.

"It wasn't as easy as that, Bert. She'd already told this other feller that she'd marry him, and she wasn't about to go back on her word."

"Did you meet him?" asked Bert.

"I did. He was there. As it turns out, I'd met him before."

"I think I read a book once where two fellers fought over a lady."

"I wouldn't bother with a book like that," said Sam.

"Why not?" exclaimed Bert. "It was a good book. Why wouldn't you bother with it?"

"What's the point of fightin' over a lady? Most fellers I know fight with 'em," said Sam.

"Fightin' over 'em is good practice for fightin' with 'em," said Alan.

"No, it's not," said Sam. "The rules are different."

"Good point," said Alan and they all laughed. Joe was glad they weren't too serious about it all. He didn't want to become emotional and embarrassed.

"What will you do now?" asked Bert.

"What do you mean?"

"Will you go back and see her again?"

"What would be the point of that?"

"You could be friends."

"You need to get out of the gold fields, Bert," said Sam. "Where'd you get a foolish notion like that?"

"I don't think it's foolish. My ma said you have to be friends first. She said if you're friends first, when love goes you can be friends again."

"My wife and I were only ever friends," said Sam. "So, when the friendship was over, there was nothing."

"You had a wife? I hadn't heard that!" said Bert.

"I don't tell everybody," Said Sam, staring at Bert. "Mostly, I only ever tell people who forget."

"I thought we were friends," said Bert.

"Oh! Oh!" exclaimed Alan. "You said *friends first*, Bert. You got an interest in Sam here that might go further?"

"You're just tryin' to embarrass me, Alan!"

"Who's trying to embarrass you, Bert?" called a voice from the doorway.

Joe looked and saw a dapper man standing there. Tall, elegant, fresh pressed pants, a waist coat, coat and cravat, tall hat and cane and smoking a long, thin cigar. He held a dripping umbrella behind him, shaking the water from it. Joe hadn't seen him before.

"The toff!" shouted Bert and Alan at the same time.

"Where've you been?" called Alan. "Come and join us!"

"Don't mind if I do, but I'll leave this outside. Will you keep an eye on it, my good man?" he asked the publican, holding his umbrella out for the publican to see.

"No," said the publican. "It's yours to look after. I won't be responsible for it."

"Then I have no choice but to bring it inside."

"What's the harm in that?" asked the publican.

"It will drip water on the floor."

"Be my guest. It's had worse."

"As you wish." The man shook a little more water from it, folded it and placed it against a wall before removing his hat. This revealed a head of sparse, grey hair, very thin on top, but not in any way making him look undistinguished. Joe thought there was something about the man that made him a man of the world. He took a chair from another table and joined them.

"Bert, Alan, how are you?" he asked, shaking hands. "And who are your friends? I would take it as an honour if you'd be so kind as to introduce me."

"This is Sam," said Alan, indicating Sam to whom the toff offered a broad smile and said, "I'm Alistair." His eyes sparkled and the skin around them crinkled as though it had a long-term obligation to accommodate a smile.

"And this is Joe," concluded Alan who also got the broad smile.

"Gentlemen, this is indeed propitious. I awoke this morning and thought the inclement weather could bring nothing but misery. I thought after a wonderful breakfast tenderly prepared by the love of my life to venture forth and prove myself wrong and I have indeed been fortunate to do so. May I purchase a round of drinks? I'm sure the good man over there is fully aware of your preferences and I have only to indicate my intention and it will be fulfilled expeditiously."

Everyone, including the barman just stared at Alistair. Finally, the barman spoke.

"I think you asked for a round of drinks?" he said.

"Yes, yes, of course. And I'll have a whisky."

The group remained silent as the barman prepared and brought Alistair's drink and filled the rest from a bottle.

"That'll be six shillings and eight pence," said the barman.

"Cheap at twice the price," said Alistair, counting out the money. "Now gentlemen, where were we?"

"You were going to tell us where you've been," said Alan.

"So, I was. I went back to Bathurst for a month or so. Left my family here, so I'm sure you'll all understand I'm delighted to be back."

"What was happening in Bathurst? Why did you go there?" asked Bert.

"No doubt about you, Bert. You're a man with an eye for detail. Straight to the heart of the matter, so there's no point in telling falsehoods. You'd see through them before I could establish a credible reason. No, the truth is the editor was on leave and I took his place."

"Editor?" said Joe.

"Yes, Joe. I work for a newspaper. I'm a journalist. I came here at the start of the gold rush. I have a wife and child and we were fortunate to find suitable accommodation. I decided to take the temporary posting to Bathurst alone for fear of losing it. Are you from around here?"

"Yes. I'm Sam's partner."

"Ah, then you are well familiar with the vagaries and intricacies of the gold fields."

"Perhaps I would be if I knew what they were," said Joe, smiling. He had a good notion of what Alistair had said but didn't want to put himself above his mates who all looked confused.

"Indeed, Joe. Indeed," said Alistair, looking at Joe intently as though understanding the reason for Joe's reply. "Alan and Bert," continued Alistair, "how are you both? Are you doing well at the auriferous accumulation?"

"By all the saints, Alistair. You'll need to at least meet us halfway with your speech," laughed Alan.

"By that I think you mean that I'll have to use prose. Oh well, so be it."

"Joe and Sam. I'm sure you've worked out by now that Alistair practises his trade regardless of his company," said Alan.

"An astute observation," said Alistair.

"He's also a man that's seen a lot of our world and has many stories to tell about the people in it. A student of mankind, you might say," continued Alan.

"You are also a man of letters when you put your mind to it," said Alistair.

"Nonetheless, we'll enjoy a whisky or two more and Alistair will no doubt remember some of those stories and our day will not be wasted."

As predicted, it wasn't long before Alistair said, "Did I tell you the time about…?" Joe found that every story started in such a fashion. He also found that when addressing a larger group, Alistair was more inclined to use the vernacular. Other people had come into the bar, and everyone listened to the stories and Alistair gave every impression of enjoying the audience. The barman was obviously delighted to have free entertainment for his patrons but would sometimes be slow to serve when a story had reached a critical point.

"C'mon, c'mon," muttered one frustrated drinker who had just arrived and had failed to understand what was going on. "Man could die of thirst in 'ere."

"I'll only be a moment," muttered the barman. "You can have the first one on the house."

The man smiled and became respectfully and appreciatively silent.

"Did I tell you the one about the time I was staying in a hotel in Singapore? I'd been sent there by a newspaper to cover some stories about unrest between the local races. Singapore is hotch-potch of different peoples, and I was so excited to go. However, the trip there was nothing to write home about and the place was hot and humid. Local custom was that we of the British colony had to dress appropriately, and I spent most of my time over-dressed and bathed in perspiration.

"On the second or third day, I came back to the hotel planning to have a siesta and approached the front desk to be escorted to my room. The young lady behind the desk was young, inevitably dark-haired and with exquisite features. I was captivated, so much so that I embarrassed her by staring.

"'Is there something wrong?' she asked." Alistair used a higher pitched voice than his own.

Joe had not ever heard a person from Singapore speak and it would seem he was not alone in the audience as everyone looked intrigued.

"'No, nothing,' I hastened to assure her.

"'Where you from, then?' she asked me.

"'Australia,' I said.

"'Ah, kooka!' she exclaimed.

"'Yes,' I said, marvelling that she knew one of our native birds. I thought I'd confirm her knowledge with a demonstration."

Alistair was already standing so he could more easily be seen by the growing audience. He placed his arms out by his sides, hands in front and elbows bent so they looked like wings. Hopping from foot to foot, he put his head back and imitated the cry of a kookaburra. Joe had heard a kookaburra of course and marvelled how much like one was the sound emanating from Alistair. Undaunted by his ridiculous appearance, Alistair hopped from foot to foot, bounding about to the cheers and laughter of his onlookers.

"Well," said Alistair when he stopped and the room quietened enough for him to continue, "she just stood there staring at me. I thought, like you, that I'd done an excellent job of mimicking a kookaburra and couldn't understand her lack of appreciation.

"'No, no!' she exclaimed. 'Captain Cooka!'"

The room roared with laughter and Alistair took a moment to have a sip from one of the many drinks that were lined up by his appreciative audience. Joe could hear calls of, "More!", "Another!" and "Who is he?" from the now large crowd that filled the bar.

"Just one more," called Alistair, "but I'll take a moment to wet my whistle first. And I hope you fellers don't mind if the lads at my table help me with the whisky. I welcome your generosity, but I fear I lack the capacity or stamina for the task you have all set."

The noise in the room became deafening as the patrons took a chance to reflect on what they'd heard, or to catch up on other matters.

"How are you fellers?" asked Alistair, taking a chair and showing obvious relief at a chance to sit. "Here, have some of this whisky." He poured the contents of some of the glasses into those of his companions.

"We bought those for you," said a gruff voice. "If you don't want 'em, give 'em back."

Alistair stood and looked at the man, showing no sign of intimidation. Joe thought it would be a mistake to underestimate the man owning the gruff voice. He wasn't tall, but in every other respect he reminded Joe of a barrel. His tired clothes and huge hands spoke of hardships in the gold fields. He looked like a man that had no patience for transgression.

"Ah, my good man. I fear I have upset you and offer you my profound apologies. Which of these glasses might be yours so we can restore it to its rightful owner?"

"Mister, I think yer mockin' me," said the big man, putting his own glass on a nearby table.

"Ah, my not-so-jolly companion, what a shame you take offence when none is intended. Perhaps I can buy you a drink? Would that restore our heretofore convivial relationship?"

"Mister, I got no idea what yer talkin' about!" slurred the man, already bunching his fists.

"I offered to buy you a drink. That's all."

"That's not enough. I've a mind to bust you one!"

The room had become silent, all the patrons intent on the confrontation.

"No fighting in here!" shouted the barman. "If I have to, I'll get the police."

"Leave the toff alone!" shouted a voice, "unless you can tell stories too!"

"This is none of your business!" said the gruff-voice man. "I'll bust you too, if you don't mind your own business!"

"Dear me!" said Alistair. "This has already gone too far! There's no need for argument, nor any need for pugilism! Don't worry, barman. I have no wish for fisticuffs. C'mon," he continued, turning to his antagonist, "let me buy you a drink and join us and let's all speak of happier times."

Joe marvelled at Alistair. He showed no sign of fear, but clearly had no chance against the digger. They'd both had too much to drink, and the digger was at least twice his size. There was no doubt in his mind that if a fight began, they'd all have to help Alistair.

The barman pushed through the crowd.

"C'mon, mate," he said to the digger. "Enough's enough, I think you'd better leave."

The digger felled him with a single blow. The room went completely quiet. No one had expected anyone to hit the barman. He'd usually be off limits. Joe supposed the digger usually drank somewhere else as he'd be barred from this pub forever.

Alistair looked down at the barman and said, "Would somebody please help this unfortunate man? I doubt he's been done any serious damage, and it would be of service to all of us if he could be revived as soon as possible. On the other hand, perhaps someone else can take over his duties?"

"Let's get on with it!" shouted the digger.

"My good man, what's the rush? We'll attend to our business soon enough. Looking at you suggests a little patience would do the world of good to your blood pressure."

Joe continued to be amazed by Alistair's complacency. He'd just seen the barman knocked out with a single blow and Alistair seemed to treat the matter as trivial.

"There's also the matter of where to stage our altercation. The man you recently sent to sleep has suggested it should be outside. I think despite your unruliness, we should respect his wishes. After all, it's his establishment."

"Outside, inside, it's of no matter to me."

"Then, I suggest outside, but under the roof where we'll be granted some protection from the elements."

The two men walked outside, Alistair going first and showing his back to his opponent. The other patrons fought with each other to get out and find a vantage point. Their rush showed they expected the battle to be one-sided and brief.

Once outside, Alistair stopped and faced the digger. It was like he saw him for the first time. A quizzical look appeared on his face, and he cocked his head to one side before speaking.

"This might take a while," he said. "Do you mind if I remove some of my outer garments? The expensive ones, I mean. The coat, waistcoat and the like. I can see you don't so burden yourself and I fully comprehend why. I only seek your permission as I would hate for you to start before I'm ready."

"I'll wait," growled the man, "but stop this bloody talkin' and let's get it done!"

"That's most generous of you," said Alistair, removing his coat, waistcoat and cravat. "Here, Alan, I wonder if you'd mind holding these for me?"

"Finally," said Alistair, once Alan had taken his clothes, "there's the matter of the rules."

"Rules?" blurted the digger, incredulous.

"Yes. We're not ruffians, are we? If you want a free-for-all, then I suppose I'll have to agree, but I'd prefer we fight like the gentlemen I know us both to be."

"There's no bloody rules!" shouted the digger and charged.

Alistair simply stepped to the side and the man rushed by, crashing into the spectators. They all went down in a heap, much to the amusement of the rest of the crowd.

The digger got to his feet, pushing any spectators roughly aside and glanced around briefly to orient himself and to find his opponent.

"Remember," called Alistair, "no rules." He put up his fists into a boxing position causing Joe to think that Alistair might know what he was doing after all.

The digger charged. Once again, Alistair stepped aside, but as he did, he kicked the digger hard in the knee. The digger fell, then struggled to his feet, favouring the leg that had been kicked. A smile flickered around his mouth. It looked like he'd formed a plan and Alistair would be in trouble.

There was no charge this time. Still favouring his leg, he walked towards Alistair. It was clear his intention was to back his opponent against the wall of the pub. Alistair smiled too, causing a brief look of concern on the digger's face.

"Oh dear! Who's that?" called Alistair, pointing behind the digger. The digger looked behind him and Alistair kicked him in the other leg.

"You should have opted for rules," said Alistair. "But I have to agree with you that it's more fun without them."

The digger charged, holding out his arms, trying to grab Alistair in a bear hug, but neither leg worked properly, so he stumbled rather than making an effective, direct charge.

Alistair evaded him easily and kicked a leg out from under him. The man collapsed, groaning and hit his head on a veranda post. Alistair kicked him again in the same leg as he lay on the ground. The digger lay there for a few moments, trying to recover his strength and probably to formulate a plan to deal with his unexpectedly skilled opponent.

The digger got to his feet, red in the face and clearly fuming with rage. He stared at Alistair but made no move. Then a small smile appeared on his face as though he'd finally formulated a better plan.

"C'mon, old boy. This is boring," said Alistair. "Time for us to put on a show." Holding up his fists, he turned slightly sideways and stepped towards the digger. Even when discussing it after with Sam, Joe was never sure what happened next.

One minute the digger was standing, half smiling with his fists out front, doing his best to imitate Alistair. The next he was flat on the ground. Sam said Alistair stepped forward, then to the side to miss a clumsy blow from the digger at which point the digger's head was completely exposed and Alistair took advantage of it slamming a left to the chin and a right to the head. Joe couldn't be sure what happened. All he was sure about was that Alistair was no stranger to boxing.

"Show's over," said Alistair, taking his clothes from Alan and thanking him for taking such good care of them. "Let's go back inside or somewhere else if the barman hasn't re-joined us."

"I sent the barman home," said a voice beside Alistair, "but it won't matter. I'll take over."

"Ah, Davey," said Alistair, "good to see you. It would behove you to manage your own establishment anyway. Have you met my friends? This is Sam and Joe."

"Yes, we've met," said Davey. "Regulars now. This fellow won't be though," he added, touching the still unconscious man with his foot.

"It's a shame. I still owe him a drink," said Alistair.

Everyone trooped back inside, and it took a while to settle everyone down and serve drinks to those that needed them. Alistair and his table were served first and there was no argument.

They were about to review the fight when a voice called from the doorway, "So? What're you doin' 'ere? Just goin' out for some smokes, you said."

A large woman filled the doorway. In fact, it looked to Joe that she might not get through it if her intention was to enter the pub. She wore a coloured apron that complemented the rosiness of her cheeks. Her hair was held in place by a scarf, but tendrils of hair had escaped and fell about her face and neck.

"Oh, darlin'!" shouted Alistair. "Fortune favours those who wait. I was just saying to my companions here that I must be going soon, but I was hoping you'd come by so that you can reacquaint yourself with Alan and Bert and indeed meet Joe and Sam for the first time."

"You bin gone fer hours!"

"It must seem like that precious, but I'm sure it's only been minutes. Why, I purchased the cigars and as luck would have it, on emerging from the store I bumped into Alan and Bert. I'm sure you remember them?"

"Which of you fellers is Alan and Bert?"

Alan and Bert waved.

"No, I don't remember 'em and as far as I can see, they aren't all that memorable."

"And these other two are Joe and Sam, friends of Alan and Bert."

Joe and Sam waved. Joe wondered at the silence and looked around to see the whole bar mesmerised by the exchange. Alistair was once again putting on a show. There was no doubt it was his day.

"Same goes for them."

"I'll be home directly, my lamb. In renewing our acquaintance, Alan and Bert insisted on each buying me a drink and it was the least I could do to return their generous hospitality."

"I'm not goin' witout choo."

"Where's young Alistair?"

"He's with Mrs McGillicuddy."

"A fine neighbour. None better in my view, but she may be worried. Perhaps if you go back now that you know of my imminent departure, you may be able to allay her fears."

"She's not worried."

"It's unseemly dear for you to be occupying the entrance to a drinking establishment."

"Doesn't bother me."

"Perhaps you could have some concern for the owner and his patrons?"

"Don't care about any of 'em."

"That is a shame. Gentlemen," said Alistair standing, "allow me to finish my drink in unseemly haste as my presence is required elsewhere."

He finished his drink in a single gulp, fetched his umbrella from the corner against the wall, returned his hat to his head and went to the doorway. He looked back, waved his arm with a flourish and taking the woman's arm, disappeared.

The bar was silent, everyone still focused on the doorway as though the woman and Alistair might return for an encore.

"Is that woman his wife?" asked Joe of his table, unable to keep the astonishment from his voice.

"Why wouldn't she be?" said Bert, cautiously.

"Just not what I imagined his wife to be like," said Joe.

"And what did you imagine his wife to be like?" asked Alan, but there was no accusation in his voice.

"Well, I don't know how she understands him. I don't most of the time," said Joe.

"She's a wonderful wife," said Bert. "Looks after him somethin' fierce. Cooks for him, makes sure he's well dressed and doesn't smoke too many of those cigars. He gets away with a bit, but not too much. She'd know he wasn't goin' out for smokes and when to come lookin' for him. It was a lucky day for him the day she came into his life."

"Then I'm beat!" exclaimed Joe.

"Who said you wasn't?" queried Alan and they all laughed.

It had turned out as Alan said it would, a fun day at the pub. However, it was a sorry and drunk foursome who struggled back to the camp through misty rain towards the end of the day, leading a horse that was confused because the men seemed to have forgotten the way.

The next morning Joe nursed the biggest hangover he'd ever had, but gratefully remembered there was more good than bad in his life.

42. THE PROPOSAL

Early afternoon on the Sunday, Joe thought his stomach well enough to handle the trip to visit with Susie, Jim and Sparrow. He'd decided the sooner the visit was behind him, the sooner things would get back to normal. The idea of normal was immensely appealing.

He rode his horse carefully down the track. It was wet and slippery from the previous day's rain. There wasn't much noise from the diggins. Most of the diggers were chatting quietly, enjoying their pipes and tea or maybe doing small repairs to problems caused by the rain. Some waved to him, but most ignored him. The dogs kept up a clatter the whole way and he wondered if he'd ever get used to them.

It no longer bothered him to ask directions, but he didn't need much guidance to find Nuggety Creek. He'd never been along the river away from the town further than Big Oakey, so if nothing else, the ride was interesting. He followed the river most of the way, the road obviously serving the needs of the diggers spread out along the ridges and flats. The number of diggers, tents and huts was a revelation. He was glad that he and Sam had a good claim, and he wasn't down here competing with so many others.

The country had opened after a while and there were fewer trees and hills. There were several small herds of horses and Joe wondered if diggers put their horses here for safekeeping or these herds were runaways. He decided on reflection the latter made no sense as runaways would be stolen or in the town's pound.

"Here he comes!" shouted Sparrow when he wasn't far up the creek. There'd been a few creeks that he thought might have been the Nuggety, but he'd been informed to the contrary by idle diggers.

He rode up and dismounted. It was a much better campsite than his own, being more open, but the trees were sparse and provided little shade. The area was not unlike the one that Jim and Susie had occupied at Ophir. He'd be willing to bet they got on with their neighbours here too.

"She's been waiting for you all day!" announced Susie, hugging Joe fiercely.

"Hold on you two! What's going on here?" queried Jim in mock affront.

"And where's mine?" demanded Sparrow. Joe gave her an awkward hug.

"You're not much of a hugger, are you?" declared a disappointed Sparrow.

"I suppose not," said Joe.

"You might need to be taller," said Jim. "Susie got a pretty good hug."

"I noticed that" said Sparrow with a hint of jealousy.

"Can I ride your horse, Joe?" asked Sparrow, this time with a hint of guile. "I was hoping you'd bring him."

"If Joe says it's all right, let's you and I go for a ride," said Jim. "I have to be sure you'll be good enough to ride your own horse one day."

"Oh, good!" shouted Sparrow. "Let's!"

"That's all right with me," said Joe, understanding that the whole thing had been arranged by Jim and Susie.

"It's not fair," said Joe, quietly to Susie after Sparrow had ridden away, led by Jim with the reins held firmly. Joe thought his horse didn't look so happy. Perhaps he'd been looking forward to a rest.

Susie fussed at the fireplace, organising some tea and damper.

"What's not fair?" she queried, looking at him quickly with a knowing smile.

"You arrange for us to be together and alone so you can find out more about my love life."

"I was hoping not to be so transparent! Anyway, it wasn't hard to do. I'm not sure which of you Sparrow loves most. You or your horse!" Susie sat opposite Joe. "Tea and damper won't be long."

"Shouldn't we wait for the others?"

"There's plenty there and they'll get theirs when they get back."

Joe said nothing and studied the sky, the tent, and the distant hills.

"Do I have to torture you?" asked Susie. "I will if I have to."

"It's all right," said Joe. "This is torture enough."

"I'm sorry. I only want to help." She reached forward and touched his arm, briefly and withdrew her hand. "Besides, you're going to have to get used to talking with your mother-in-law."

Joe looked at her sharply, hoping she wasn't serious. She wasn't.

"Will she get over it?" asked Joe, sadly. "I haven't hurt her, I hope."

"She's all right. She told me that you're in love with someone else and she's making other plans."

"She's lucky. I wish it was so easy. Making other plans, I mean. No. Let me take that back. I had a good day yesterday and I found things today aren't so serious."

"I think that's how it works. My mother wasn't so old when she died, but she told me on her deathbed that during her life, looking back she always had a different perspective. She realised that nothing really matters. Many things happen and we think we can't cope, but we always do."

"I think friends and family matter."

"We wouldn't be sitting here now if friends didn't matter. I know you know that's not what she meant."

"I know, I was just trying to shift the conversation away from me."

Susie laughed. A deep, throaty laugh that Joe hadn't expected. It was catching. Within moments, he was laughing too. After a few moments, he had no idea what he was laughing about, but they continued to laugh uncontrollably. Some of the diggers at the other tents looked over to see what had happened.

"Thank you, Susie," said Joe when he was able to stop laughing. "That's the best I've felt for a long time."

"I'll get your tea and damper. Help yourself to the sugar."

She poured two pannikins of tea and cut off part of the hot damper. Joe marvelled that she could handle it straight from the pan.

"I think you make better damper than Sam," he said after taking a bite from a slice liberally spread with golden syrup.

"I hope so."

"Do you want to know what happened?"

"Only if you've a mind to tell me. It's your business, Joe. It's only anyone else's if you choose to make it so."

"I met a girl in Ophir. She and her brothers had a claim near mine. I liked her, but we didn't talk about that. I only met her a couple of times, but I liked her from the first. They moved over here and when my claim ran out, I thought I'd follow her."

Susie studied Joe and he thought she might ask a question. She didn't, so he continued.

"I'd been here a while before I went looking for her. I found her last Tuesday at Wallaby Rocks. Unfortunately, she has another feller and they're to be married."

"That's a shame."

Joe liked the understatement, and that Susie chose not to make more of it. He smiled briefly.

"There's one thing," said Susie.

"Oh?" queried Joe. "What's that?"

"Sparrow thinks you're unavailable, but she's wrong."

"There is that, so now I'm looking forward to being a son-in-law to you and Jim."

They both laughed again.

"What's that about Jim?" asked Jim, leading Joe's horse with Sparrow riding. They'd come up the track behind Joe who hadn't heard them due to the noise of the cicadas.

"Nothing," said Susie. "Come on you two. I've some tea and damper, so get it while it's hot."

"Where's your claim, Jim?" asked Joe.

"Just there, not far up the creek," said Jim, indicating a spot along the creek. "I'm doing all right, but there's a lot of competition. I'm potholing, so I have to move every few days. I started further down the creek and I'm working my way up. The further up I go the better it gets."

"I told Daddy to start at the top, but he doesn't listen," said Sparrow.

"Still thinking on it," said Jim. "If I do, I'm a long way from the river and I don't have a horse."

Joe smiled at Sparrow who coloured brightly.

"It's not because I want a horse!" she snapped at Joe. "I'm glad we're not getting married!"

"Ah, my little bird," said Jim, softly.

"I'm sorry, Joe. I didn't mean it," said Sparrow contritely. "I would like a horse, though."

"Perhaps I'll give you mine," said Joe.

"Are you leaving, Joe?" asked Jim.

"Not just yet, Jim. We're still doing all right, but this won't last forever."

"What did you do before you came looking for gold?" asked Susie.

"I was in the police force," said Joe. "I was a policeman. I don't tell too many people. It seems the police aren't too popular."

"Your secret's safe with us," said Susie, "but you could always go back to it. There's always plenty of need for the law."

"Especially around the gold fields," said Jim. "Just last week they caught a feller robbing tents at night while the diggers slept."

"What did they do with him?" asked Sparrow.

"Gave him to the police. I think he was glad to be handed over."

"Why?" asked Sparrow.

"I think he thought the police might treat him better than the diggers."

"Is it like Ophir?" asked Joe. "Everything run out of the Commissioner's tent?"

Jim nodded.

"Then I don't think I'd like to go back to it."

"Might be better in Bathurst," said Susie. "There's the prison and courthouse there, too."

"I think I'm ready for a change," said Joe. "Might buy some land. I could raise some cattle or sheep."

"Then you'll still need your horse," said Sparrow, sadly.

"Have you had any experience with cattle or sheep?" asked Jim, smiling at Sparrow.

"No, but I could hire someone to help me."

"You have done well," said Susie. "We haven't done much better than make a wage."

Joe shrugged, wishing he'd said nothing.

"Don't worry, Joe. We all take our chances out here and if you've done well, good luck to you," said Susie.

"I'd best be getting back. It'll be dark soon."

"Thanks for coming," said Jim, stretching out his hand. "Come as often as you like."

"Thanks, Jim," said Joe, shaking his hand and doffing his hat to Susie and Sparrow.

"Don't be ridiculous," said Susie and gave an embarrassed Joe a hug.

"Me, too," said Sparrow and did the same, although Joe had to bend down to return it.

Joe mounted and rode off into the dying light of the day, pleased with the afternoon and glad that it was now over and done with and everything could return to normal. He did regret saying he'd been a policeman and realised he may have created a reason to leave. At least he didn't say he'd been in Sydney. Chances were he'd never be associated with the events at the pawn shop, but life had already taught him the thing you should expect most was the thing you expected least.

43. CHRISTMAS

They went back to the pattern of work that suited him and Sam best. Sam digging and Joe cradling. Towards the end of the week, they agreed over supper to have a look at the claim together the next morning. Joe said he wasn't getting as much gold from the dirt he took to the cradle.

"Dirt still looks the same," said Sam.

"I agree," said Joe, "but there's not as much gold."

Sam said he thought they were digging in an old creek bed. He thought the creek might have moved about over the millennia, depositing gold in different places and it was their good fortune to find one of them.

"There's no point in digging for a few colours," said Joe. "We've done well so far, so best to move to somewhere else if it looks like running out."

They sat by the fire, enjoying some tea. It was a pleasant evening, a gentle breeze blowing after the heat of the day.

"Might be time to give it away," said Sam. "There's a lot of diggers about. We might find it hard to get another claim."

"Some of them will go home for Christmas. It'll be easier then. Do you know which way the old creek runs? We might be able to pick it up on the other side of the Big Oakey."

"I thought that too, but it doesn't seem to work like that. It seems to have dumped the gold in holes. I suppose the same as it's done in all the other creeks the diggers are workin'. Perhaps what we're workin' used to be the Big Oakey."

As they walked down to the claim the next morning, Sam said that he was glad they'd reinforced the claim with timber, especially after the recent rain because the tunnel was now deep.

When they reached the claim, Joe was shocked how far in Sam had dug. He'd just been collecting the bags that Sam left and hadn't bothered to check inside the tunnel. He couldn't supress a gasp and a feeling that they'd been tempting fate, going in so far, especially with water from the creek sometimes flowing into the tunnel with the recent rain.

"What's wrong?" asked Sam.

"I think it's too deep. I think we're tempting fate."

"It's all right. See? It's well reinforced. And I haven't used all the timber you brought, so while ever it's deliverin', I think we should work it." He held the candle up to cast more light to reinforce his confidence.

More light only increased Joe's concern and he couldn't contain a sense of foreboding. Memories of pulling George from the tunnel came back and he shuddered.

"I'm sorry, Sam. I don't like it and I think we should abandon it. We're not getting enough gold from it to take any risks."

"How much gold did you cradle yesterday?"

"A few ounces."

"It's not much, but it doesn't bother me, Joe. I'm happy to keep diggin' here."

"Did I tell you about pulling Becky's brother out of a collapsed tunnel?"

"Not that I remember."

"I think it's time to abandon it, Sam. We don't know what affect the creek water is having on the sides. For all we know, the whole thing could come down at any minute."

"It's part of bein' a digger Joe. Feller's got to take some risks."

"Let's go back, have a cuppa and talk about it."

"All right. It's not as though the gold's goin' anywhere."

When they emerged from the tunnel, Sam pointed at the other diggers spread out along the creek, working both its bed and its sides.

"See? The other fellers are hard at it. You sure you're not over reactin'?"

As they walked, Joe told Sam about George. The story took more telling than the walk back to camp, so Joe finished it as they prepared and sipped their tea. Sam didn't interrupt and listened intently.

"He died anyway? That's sad," said Sam when Joe finished.

"Is that all you got from the story!" snapped Joe.

"Take it easy, Joe. I just thought it was sad that you got him out, but he died anyway."

"The point of the story is that tunnels are dangerous."

"You're not tellin' me somethin' I don't know, for God's sake. Everyone knows that tunnels are dangerous. Just tell me if you don't want to look for gold anymore. You don't have to blame the tunnel."

"Do you think that's it? I'm done with gold and looking for an excuse?"

"Well? Are you?"

"Of course not! I don't want to fight about this, Sam. You're taking all the risk and I'm getting half the benefit. If nothing else, it's not fair. So, if we keep digging in that tunnel, we share the digging fifty-fifty."

Sam looked at Joe, the expression on his face showing that he was confused by Joe's reaction, perhaps even concerned that he had been taking a bigger risk than he thought.

"All right," he muttered resignation in his voice. "Christmas is soon, and I want to go home to see my parents. Let's dig our claim until Christmas, sharin' the diggin' fifty-fifty if that's what you want. There's still some gold there and we might be lucky to find another good pocket."

"What'll we do after Christmas?"

"Prospect. Find another claim, perhaps up this creek or even another. Read the papers, hang around the pub and find out where diggers are havin' success."

"I can do that over Christmas, while you're away."

"I have a better idea. Why don't you come with me? Meet my parents. You'll like them, they'll like you. We can have some decent food, take a few days' break and have a rest."

"When will you go?"

"No, when will WE go?"

"I haven't decided to go yet."

"Then, I'll decide for you. You're comin'."

"How will you get there?"

"Coach to Bathurst, then try to get a ride. There's a mail coach three times a week and lots of carts between Bathurst and Carcoar."

"I haven't been there. Where is it?"

"About forty miles south-west of Bathurst. It's a pretty town. They raise cattle, sheep and horses there. There's grain, too, but mostly towards Bathurst. And there's talk of copper mines, but I don't know much about them."

"How will I find you?"

"Good. You'll come?"

"I will."

"It's about eighty miles from here, so maybe three days' ride. I'll come to the Royal Hotel every afternoon at around four o'clock startin' on the third day after you set out."

"How do you know you'll beat me there?"

"I'll be in Bathurst much faster than you, but after that it's anyone's guess. If I'm not there at four o'clock on the day you arrive, stay at the Royal. You could do a lot worse."

Joe was pleased they were no longer fighting about the claim and very pleased to be invited to Sam's parents' for Christmas. It would be good to get away from the gold fields, the memories of Becky and even the daily grind of looking for gold. The only problem was that he would have to endure a half-share of digging in the tunnel and the thought of it was enough to make him sick with dread.

They started out doing about fifty-fifty share of the digging, but eventually Sam convinced Joe to do less. Sam said Joe was better at cradling and he had the horse, so it was a more logical choice for him. Joe didn't put up much of an argument. He hated the idea of going into the tunnel and as much as he worried for his friend, he knew Sam was more efficient in there and likely to find more gold.

As it turned out they did find some more good pockets of gold and as much as they were each sure steady gold was almost exhausted, they were pleased their claim was fruitful almost to the time they stopped digging.

They'd decided to stop digging on the Friday before Christmas. If they both left Sofala on the Saturday morning, Joe would likely be in Carcoar on Monday evening the 22nd of December 1851. That would mean that even if he or Sam took a day longer, they'd be in Carcoar in plenty of time to spend Christmas day with Sam's parents. Joe fretted about a gift for Sam's ma but decided to solve the problem in Carcoar. Whatever gift he bought would then certainly be in better condition on presentation. He momentarily thought he could give her the locket, but quickly dismissed the idea. Becky was right. The person to whom he gave the locket should be special.

Even though he was headed to Bathurst on the Saturday, he sold all the gold in Sofala on the Saturday morning. He wasn't sure he'd get to Bathurst in time to sell the gold there and he didn't want to be carrying gold on a trip of three days. The bank's agent was still in town, so everything went well and according to plan. He saw Hannah and Pat briefly and was grateful they didn't ask about Becky. He was sure their lack of curiosity was due to Alan who he knew visited their store from time to time. They both fussed over some sweets for Sparrow, but eventually he followed Hannah's recommendations. There was a bar of soap for Susie and a small anxiety that she may mistake the intent of such a gift.

He hurried back to see Susie, Jim and Sparrow. His presents turned out to be a huge hit and both were embarrassed they had nothing to give him in turn. He couldn't have cared less and was relieved that his simple gifts had been well received. They waved goodbye amid demands that he call on them as soon as he came back.

On the way back to the camp, using his horse he dragged the cradle into some bushes far enough away from the river that a flood wouldn't get to it and deep enough in what was left of the bushes so as not to be found.

There'd been discussion over how they might have a whisky with Alan and Bert, but finally decided that it would only be possible at one of their camps. Alan told them to pack up everything but their beds and the tent, bring it down to him and Bert and have supper with them. Joe kept some supplies for the journey to Carcoar and they gave the rest to Alan and Bert. Sam had some whisky, and they had a pleasant evening talking about the fun they'd had and how pleased they all were to have met.

"Steady! Steady!" said Alan at one point. "This isn't goodbye, is it? You fellers are comin' back, aren't you?"

They all laughed.

Joe and Sam spent a last night in the tent and as the dawn broke, struck it and took the canvas to leave with Alan and Bert. It would be unlikely the beds would be there when they returned, but it would be easy enough to make more. They were simple wooden structures of saplings and bark and would probably finish up in someone's fire while Joe and Sam were absent. The remains of the hut would likely meet the same fate. Sam remarked as they were leaving that a lot of the diggers had already gone, probably with the same idea as themselves. "There's something about Christmas with your family," he said, a hint of sadness in his voice.

They walked into Sofala together, Joe leading his horse by the reins. It was easier to talk that way, although they did little talking. It was very pleasant to walk in the early morning between the times the mosquitoes left, and the flies arrived.

The cool of the previous night was still on the light breeze, the sun winked between what remained of the trees and once they came close to the river, birds called to each other to welcome the day. Cicadas hadn't yet started their incessant chatter and it was more like spring or autumn than summer.

Sam was in plenty of time to catch the stage to Bathurst and Joe didn't wait with him. He knew he'd be passed on the road but wanted to at least get to Bathurst in the day. He thought he would stay at the Shepherds Inn and set out early on the Sunday morning. If he could then make Blayney in the day, he'd have no trouble meeting with Sam in Carcoar at 4pm on the Monday.

He was about an hour out of Sofala when the stage thundered by. Joe marvelled that he didn't read about people being killed in them every day, such was the reckless speed at which they travelled. Sam gave him a brief wave from a window, but he was soon lost in a cloud of dust. There were other travellers on the road, mostly heading away from Sofala. Joe supposed that diggers were heading home or away for Christmas and doubtless some would be looking for greener pastures.

There was no point in stopping anywhere, so Joe kept up a steady pace all day. Nevertheless, he couldn't supress his excitement when he neared Bathurst. The prospect of a bath, a proper meal and a good bed caused him to push his horse the last mile or so. There was still enough heat in the sun, flies to spare and a drying hot wind that without encouragement, Joe's horse almost ran down the lane past the Shepherds Inn to the stables.

Next morning the Blayney road was new to Joe, but easy to follow as was the road from Blayney to Carcoar.

About midday Monday, he topped a rise and saw what he hoped was Carcoar in the valley ahead. He knew from Sam that the Belubula River ran through the town, but even from the distance it didn't look more than a creek. The town was very pretty, being made up mostly of wooden buildings, but there were some of stone. It was wedged neatly between the hills and Joe imagined the town layout was mostly dictated by the hills and the river.

It was early afternoon when Joe rode up to the Royal and wearily dismounted. His horse hadn't worked so hard in quite a while and looked sad, exhausted and dejected when Joe dropped the reins and walked into the bar. He didn't expect Sam to be there, and he wasn't. However, Joe now had a dilemma. There was no point in checking into the hotel since if Sam arrived, he'd only have to check out again. Nor did he want to leave his horse standing in the street. He needed feeding, watering and a good rub down. He'd done well on the trip and should be rewarded. Joe decided it would be a good way to spend an hour or so if he could find some stables.

Joe asked at the bar.

"You stayin' here?" asked the man. He was fair-haired, about thirty with a serious disposition and an air of authority.

"Might be, don't know."

The man looked at him as if he'd spoken a foreign language.

"Do you know a feller called Sam?" Joe was embarrassed that he'd never asked Sam's full name.

"I know lots of fellers called Sam."

"This one's been over at the Turon."

"You his partner?"

Joe nodded.

"I saw him in town this morning. Said his partner might be by."

"I'm going to meet him here later. In the meantime, can I use the stables for my horse?"

"If you want. Use the stables at the back. Only cost you a shillin'."

Privately, Joe thought it expensive, but also decided it would be a good way to spend his time before Sam arrived. He paid the money, went outside and led his horse to the stables at the back. There were plenty of oats and hay, so Joe put some in a trough and rubbed his horse down while he ate.

"You're a good horse," he whispered while he worked.

The time passed quickly, and it seemed like only minutes before Sam called his name from the doorway.

"Heard you were back here. You done?"

"I am," said Joe, "but I think my horse would appreciate a little longer. Can I buy you a drink in the bar and you can tell me what I've let myself in for."

"It's nothing to worry about," said Sam, "but the drink sounds good."

Over a drink Sam told Joe that his parents lived on the edge of town, only a few minutes' walk. They had two horses in a paddock behind the house, so Joe would be best to leave his horse there but could pay to leave him at the Royal if he preferred. Joe said that he would take his horse as he would appreciate the company.

"Bit of a holiday for both of us," he said. "There's the matter of presents, too."

"For the horses?" asked Sam, a twinkle in his eye.

"Yes," replied Joe, looking serious. "For the horses."

Sam looked confused, then burst out laughing, realising he'd been had.

"Seriously," said Joe, "I'd like to buy something for your ma and pa."

"You don't need to. They're happy you've come."

"I know I don't need to, but I'd like to."

"There's a couple of good stores in town. Buy something for Ma, if you wish. I'm sure she'd appreciate it."

"I'm open to suggestions."

"At this point you're on your own. Tolano's store has lots of things. If you can't find something there, I'd be surprised. You best get to it, though. He'll be closing soon."

"Does he have a store in Ophir?"

"I think so. Why?"

"There was a store there they said was owned by him."

"Can't be anyone else, but I'm sure it doesn't matter. He'll be just as closed soon whether he has a store in Ophir."

"Where's his store?"

"Next door. You can't miss it. I'll stay and have a drink with James."

"Who's James?" queried Joe.

"Me," said the bar tender, "but Sam knows he'll be drinkin' on his own. It's not to my likin'."

"You don't need to drink, James. I know you don't, so your conversation is all I'm after. Now, refill this glass like a good publican while Joe here does his shoppin'."

Joe hurried next door to a small shop frontage, fortunately still open. He walked inside out of the heat and was immediately addressed by a slight, young man with blonde hair, a shop-keeper's smock and a smiling visage.

"I do believe you'll be my last customer this day," he said. "I was about to close, but I'm happy to be of any service I can."

"I want a present," said Joe.

"A present?" asked the man, looking confused.

"I mean, I want to buy a present for someone."

"Ah! You'll need to give me some details of the intended recipient."

"It's for Sam's ma."

"Sam? Who's Sam? Am I meant to know Sam?"

"No. I mean it's for someone's mother."

"How old is she?"

"I don't know."

"How old is Sam?"

"About my age."

"That gives me some idea. We have all sorts of things, but some scented soap might be best. I haven't been doing this job too long, but I've noticed scented soap is a favourite. It's for Christmas, I suppose?"

"Yes. For Christmas."

"Follow me."

The man walked deep into the store. Goods were stacked on shelves, platforms and stands and in some cases, simply piled on the floor.

"It's a bit of a mess," said the man.

Joe had to agree. He walked carefully to avoid bumping any of the shelves or piles. As they went deeper into the store, his nostrils were treated to some welcome and wonderful smells.

"All sorts of things back here," said the man. "Soaps, oils, cloths, clothes and hats. I don't know much about them. You'll just have to find something you like or think she might like."

"The soap will do," said Joe, already overwhelmed by the variety of goods.

"I've some combs. They're two shillings each. There're some ladies' work boxes, too."

"What's a ladies' work box?"

"You know. Where they put needles, wool, pins and things like that. I'll show you one."

He reached up to a shelf and pulled down a box that was covered in patterned, coloured cloth. Joe took a few statutory moments to admire it but reaffirmed that the scented soap would be the best choice.

"I can let you have two bars for three shillings."

"All right."

"What about Sam's da? What are you going to give him?"

"I wasn't going to give him anything."

"That may not be right. His wife gets something, and he doesn't. I've got some cigars here I could let you have at a shilling each."

"I don't know if he smokes."

"It doesn't matter. If you buy him some and he doesn't smoke, he can give them to Sam."

"Sam doesn't smoke."

"Then get Sam some whisky. It would go nicely with the cigars. How many do you want?"

"Bottles of whisky?"

"No. Cigars."

"I'll take three."

"You should get six."

"Why six?"

"Six come in a box. Looks much better. They keep better in a box, too."

"I don't know if he wants them at all, much less six."

"It's Christmas, sir. I'll wrap all these things for you, and you'll enjoy the look of pleasure on their faces. Besides, I expect they aren't expecting anything, so you'll have to give them all something. You wait here while I wrap them."

He came back about five minutes later. During his absence Joe heard paper rustling and a quiet humming from the man as he worked.

"Here you are," he beamed when he returned. "I've put everything in this bag."

"How much?"

"Three shillings for the soap, six shillings for the cigars, five shillings for the whisky and a shilling for the paper and wrapping. That comes to fifteen shillings. You can have the bag for free."

Joe counted out the money and wordlessly turned to leave.

"Merry Christmas," said the man. "I hope they like their presents."

"What'll I do if they don't?"

"Oh, they will. Sam likes whisky, his pa likes a cigar, and his ma always admires the scented soap, but complains she can't afford it."

Joe couldn't help laughing.

"Merry Christmas to you, too," he said and left.

On his way back to the bar, he collected his horse from the stables. He pushed the bag into one of the saddle bags. Sam chatted amiably to James and several other customers.

"Oh dear! Didn't find anything?" said Sam, noting Joe's empty hands. "Will we have another drink, or would you like to go?"

"I'd like to go."

"We can come back later. It isn't far."

"All right with me."

Sam drained what was left of his drink, nodded to the others and followed Joe out into the sunshine. Joe stood by his horse.

"Just down by the river. Like I said, it isn't far."

After a short distance, they turned the corner and Joe could see a river crossing in the near distance.

"We don't have to cross the river. Ma and Pa live just there, this side of the crossing. They rent a place that backs onto the river," said Sam, pointing into the near distance.

They walked side by side, Joe leading his horse and a little nervous to meet Sam's parents. He wondered what they would think of him. Not that it mattered. He would only be there a few days at most. The sun was now low in the sky, glowing behind the trees that topped the nearby hills, but still hot enough to make walking uncomfortable. Joe had hardly finished the thought when Sam turned off the street and walked towards a small, wooden cottage. The gardens were neat and well-kept with some hardy spring flowers defying the summer heat. Some fruit trees blocked off the view of the commercial buildings to the right.

"So, this be him?" said a small woman, leaving her duties in a vegetable garden. "I've just collected some fresh vegetables for supper."

She stood in front of Joe, looking him up and down as though sizing him for purchase. Joe wasn't sure, but he thought she might be the smallest woman he'd ever seen. Yet, there was something about her that burst with energy, as though making up for her lack of size. Her smile was dazzling, drawing him close, and making him feel special. She held her apron out in front with one hand. It evidently contained what she'd just gathered.

"It's only a few things," she said, noticing Joe looking. "I'm sure they'll be a welcome change from what you lads've been eatin'."

She reached out with her spare hand and patted Joe on the cheek. He bent a little to make it easier.

"Mine's Kate and I know you're Joe. I can't tell you how much I've been lookin' forward to meetin' you. You boys out there in the bush with nary a woman to care for you. It isn't natural, but we'll fix that for a few days. Now, come inside. Pa's been hangin' out for a whisky."

"I'll look to the horse, Joe. I'll put him down back with the others," said Sam.

"I'll help. I'll need to take off his saddle and bridle," said Joe quickly.

"No, you go with Ma. I'll do that. It's all right. I know how," said Sam and smiled broadly. "Didn't know that did you?"

Joe untied his small carry-all from behind the saddle and took the bag and locket from his saddle bag. He wasn't sure why he took the locket. It didn't seem right to leave it somewhere that it could be stolen, so he put it in his pocket. He stood feeling foolish holding the bag of purchases in one hand and the carry-all in the other.

"C'mon, Joe," said Kate. "It'll be all right. Pa don't bite."

Joe felt even more foolish. He wasn't used to meeting people in their homes.

Kate led the way inside. Joe had to duck to go through the door.

"Suits us," said Kate without looking back. "I think it was built for midgets."

They went into a sitting room that occupied the whole width of the house. There was an unlit fireplace at one end, chairs along the walls and a small table and lounge at the other. A man on the lounge reading a paper leapt to his feet, dropped the paper on the lounge and strode quickly over to meet Joe.

"I'm Matt," he said, "and you must be Joe."

He shook Joe's hand vigorously.

The man was small, although not as petite as Kate. He had thinning grey hair, a receding hair line and a ready smile.

"We've been lookin' forward to meetin' you, Joe. Welcome to our home and you are welcome to stay as long as you want. We'll enjoy the company, won't we Ma?"

"I'll show you to your room, Joe," said Kate. "You'll be sharin' with Sam."

"I'm used to that," said Joe.

"I'm sure you are," said Matt. "Privy and washroom are out back. Ma'll show you them, too. When you're done explorin', come back and we'll have a whisky. I'm as dry as a parson's sermon."

Upon their return, all four sat in the parlour and the men had a whisky. Kate said she enjoyed whisky in puddings, but never on its own. Matt said that was a good thing, because it left more for him.

They sat for about an hour, enjoying the whisky and Joe and Sam entertained Kate and Matt with tales of the gold fields. Kate went out from time to time to tend to supper. Like Sam had said, Kate and Matt clearly liked Joe and he in turn liked them a lot. If he'd had any reservations before, he had none now and thought that he and Sam should stay more than the few days over Christmas.

"Supper's ready," said Kate when their glasses were empty. "It's only shepherd's pie and vegetables, but I expect you haven't had that too often."

Over supper, Matt told Joe he worked on a farm outside Carcoar. The farmer was a good man, although old and was looking to sell his farm. His wife had died several years ago, and he struggled to manage the daily work on his own. Despite Matt's help, he said he would sell if the opportunity arose. His daughter had moved back from Sydney about eight months previously, but she showed little interest in helping. Her child was often sick, and her living there probably made things worse for her father with the added worry.

"You'll get to meet them," said Kate when Matt finished talking. "Nathan and his daughter."

"Are they coming here?" asked Sam.

"No," replied Kate with a hint of a smile. "They invited us all around for a drink and supper on Christmas Eve. I think he wants you two boys to meet his daughter."

"What's she like?" asked Sam, Joe thought mischievously.

"She's all right," said Matt. "Bit of a worrier. Should let the child be out in the sun sometimes and play in the dirt. She frets a lot more about her child than I think she should. Bein' outside never hurt our little feller."

"Now, now Da. It's her child and she's free to bring him up as she pleases," said Kate in such a way that Joe thought it was a frequent admonition.

After supper, Joe tried to help with the dishes, but Kate wouldn't hear of it.

"I'll do that," she said firmly. "It's my job and I'll not have you takin' it. If I'm not useful, I'll be booted out."

Matt looked at her and smiled and Joe knew that Kate would never be booted out.

The men went to the parlour for a final whisky and Matt lit a pipe. Joe was relieved that the cigars would probably be welcome.

"What'll we do tomorrow?" asked Sam.

"There're a few things to be done about here that I can't do on me own. If it's all right with you and Joe, we can do those and get them out of the way. Be good to get them done. Been troublin' me somethin' fearsome."

Joe smiled. Matt didn't look like a man that would be troubled by anything.

"I told Nathan we'd all come out early day after tomorrow and help him with a few chores. I told him he wouldn't have to pay you two fellers. A Christmas drink would be payment enough."

"That's all right with me," said Sam.

"And me," said Joe.

"I'm pullin' your legs," laughed Matt. "I told him no such thing. He wants me for the day. Pays me three bob for a day's work, so I like to give him full measure. He's a good man. You fellers can come out later with ma."

The next two days went quickly. There was nothing onerous about the work that Matt had scheduled and there were frequent breaks for tea and scones. Kate kept fussing that no one had an appetite, forcing more food on Joe than he was accustomed to eating. He decided he wouldn't fit into any of his clothes when his stay was finished.

On Christmas Eve, Joe and Sam both woke late, neither one disturbing the other until it became too warm in their room. Over late breakfast, Kate talked more about Nathan and his daughter. She said that Nathan wanted to sell so they could move back to the city, or at least be near to a hospital. He worried about his daughter because she worried about her son. If he could get a reasonable price for his farm, he could afford the best medical help.

Joe only half listened, more interested in Nathan's farm than he was in the story. He did hear the bit about a reasonable price.

"What's a reasonable price?" he asked suddenly, interrupting Kate who looked at him in surprise.

"Are you thinkin' of buyin' it?" asked Sam, also abruptly showing more interest.

"I might be," replied Joe, nodding. "I've done all right at the digging, so it might be time to do something different. I don't want to be a digger all my life."

"I don't either," said Sam. "We could buy it together."

"I hadn't thought of that," said Joe, in a tone that held little prospect that he would.

"We'll be out there in a while so you can ask Nathan. I'm sure he'll suggest a fair price."

"It's better to know beforehand. I've always found the buyer thinks the goods are worth less than the seller."

"Nathan might surprise you," said Kate. She was holding her head to one side as though evaluating Joe as the farm's new owner and possibly Matt's boss.

"He might at that."

"Da will know," said Sam, clearly recovered from the disappointment at being rejected as a part owner.

"Let's not say anythin' about it. Let Nathan volunteer information if he has a mind to," said Kate. "Now, we better get ready. It's already afternoon."

"How will we get there?" asked Joe. "Will I need my horse?"

"No. We'll borrow our neighbour's gig and all squeeze into it," said Kate. "I know he's not usin' it. So we'll use our other horse. It's not too far, but too far to walk. Besides, I've brought some presents for everyone. I'm thinkin' to hand them all out this afternoon. Might be more fun than doin' it tomorrow with just us."

"I've got some things too Ma," said Sam. "Should I bring 'em?"

"I would," said Kate. "This'll be such fun!"

"I'm guessin' that Joe's got some things too!" exclaimed Sam. "You better bring 'em too, Joe!"

It took Kate longer to get ready than Joe had expected. He and Sam had been ready for an hour or so before Kate was ready to leave. Sam had taken a horse and returned with the gig which he parked under a tree and out of the afternoon's heat and sun. They were all dressed in their best which in Kate's case was a floral dress and bonnet and in the case of Joe and Sam, the best of their meagre wardrobe. Joe had brought the bag with his presents and had popped the locket in a shirt pocket for safe keeping.

"Shoulda got better things from the shop," muttered Sam when Kate reviewed their appearance before their departure.

"No matter," said Kate. "Da will be straight from workin' and Nathan always looks like he's just rolled in the dust."

As they drove up to the farmhouse, Joe couldn't help evaluating it for purchase.

It wasn't a big homestead, but big enough. It was made of stone and timber with a big veranda along the front. It faced north, so the veranda provided ample protection from the afternoon sun. Big trees grew all around and lined the short drive from the road. It was a pretty place and Joe could easily imagine himself living there.

They pulled up out front and all got down. Matt and Nathan had been sitting on chairs on the veranda, both smoking, but Joe couldn't see any glasses, so the party had not started yet.

"Hello Nathan," said Joe without waiting for an introduction. They shook hands. Joe saw an older man with kind features and a face that had been badly treated by many a sun. *There's something of the leprechaun about him*, his mother would have said. Indeed, his eyes flashed with mischief as though what Joe had just said might have a hidden, humorous meaning. As Kate had said, his clothes looked as though it had been a long time since they'd seen the inside of a shop and not long since they'd been in active farm use. "I'm Joe."

"Matt here has told me. Welcome Sam, Kate. Been too long, Sam. Goes it well in the gold fields?"

"Good enough. Joe here is my partner."

"So I hear. Come on in out of the sun. We thought we'd have a drink on the veranda before supper." He waved away some flies. "Flies permittin' of course. Matt, see to the horse. If you don't mind, that is."

"I don't mind. Sam, will you help? Be easier with two."

"Just before you do," said Nathan. "Sally! Sally? You there? All our guests are here. C'mon out and meet 'em."

Sally came out carrying a child on her hip. The child couldn't have been much more than a year old, thought Joe, but looked pale and listless. Sally had pretty, dark hair that she let grow long, dark eyes that held a sadness and regret that took Joe off-guard. He had an instant feeling of a need to protect this woman, to try to ease whatever burden she carried. He glanced at Nathan and couldn't understand why Nathan didn't help.

"Here," said Kate, reaching out. "Let me hold your little one. He's a bonnie laddie now!"

Sally passed her child across with what looked to Joe like a feeling of relief. In an instant, Joe realised Nathan didn't offer to help because if he did, he would always be expected to help.

There was more to moving to the city than being near to medical help, thought Joe. *Sally wanted all the help she could get.*

It was obvious to even a childless Joe that Sally's baby was a burden. Yet, the baby remained listless in Kate's arms, ignoring Kate's coo's and ahh's.

"Sally, these boys are Joe and Sam. Sam's Matt and Kate's boy. He's been away diggin' with Joe here at the Turon."

Sally brightened up when introduced. "I hear it's good at the Turon," she said, "but you're the first people I've met that've been there. Have you done well? The gold, I mean."

"We've done all right," said Joe.

"Joe worked at Ophir first, then we joined up to work the Turon," said Sam. "We decided to come home for Christmas."

"I expect a lot of diggers do that," said Sally, then laughed. "Although, this is their first Christmas, so I don't know why I think that."

"I agree," said Kate. "Christmas is a special time."

"See to the horse now, will you Matt? I'll see to the drinks. Perhaps you'll help me, Joe? I'd appreciate it."

"Glad to," said Joe and he was. Perhaps Nathan would talk about his farm.

The men went inside. There was a hallway, with doors to two rooms on both sides.

"Four bedrooms," said Nathan. "All big too, although mine's at the front with windows to the front and sides. I get the early mornin' sun. Used to be good when I was younger as it woke me up. Not so much these days. I couldn't keep the place without Matt. He's a godsend."

They walked out of the hall into a large living room.

"This here's the living room. Good and wide, plenty of space for a big family, although the Lord didn't ever see fit to bless me with one. Me and the missus that is, God rest her soul. You married Joe?"

"No, not yet."

"Too busy makin' a fortune, I suppose. Anyway, there's plenty of time. Sally's lookin', if you want to know. Drinks are over here. There's some sherry for the women and whisky for us. Do you like whisky, Joe? I hope you do. It's all I've got, unless you like sherry that is."

"I prefer whisky," said Joe, preferring to address only the matter of the drinks.

"You take the tray with the glasses. I'll get the bottles. That door at the back goes to the kitchen, washroom and privy."

"It's a good place," said Joe. "You must be very happy here."

"Not so much, Joe. Missus is gone and Sally's little feller is a bit crook. Her husband's gone too, so we make a fine pair. Moonin' about and feelin' sorry for ourselves. I think if someone came along and offered a fair price, I'd take it."

Joe was about to ask what Nathan thought a fair price would be when Sally came in.

"Sorry Pa," she said. "I was just talking with Kate and not thinking to help. I suppose sometimes I still think Ma is here. What can I do?"

"It's all right darlin', Joe 'n' me 'ave got it under control. We'll be along directly."

"I should ask you if you need some help Joe," said Sally. "Pa's a great one for doing everything on his own."

"I'm all right," said Joe. "I've got the glasses and Nathan's got the bottles."

"I've got a jug of water here too," said Sally. "I'll grab that and bring up the rear."

"Righty-o!" exclaimed Nathan.

Joe controlled his frustration, hoping there'd be another chance to raise the topic again with Nathan.

When they arrived back out front, the sun had settled lower in the sky and most of the heat had gone from the day. Joe knew it was only a matter of time before the flies left and the mosquitoes arrived. Sam and Matt had returned from putting the horse in the stables. Joe wasn't sure he would have bothered for the few hours they planned to be there, but then he wasn't privy to the plan. Perhaps they were expected to stay the night.

The women elected to have sherry as predicted, although Joe noted that they sipped at it as though they'd accepted more out of duty than want. The men on the other hand thoroughly enjoyed Nathan's whisky. Joe would have liked to fetch his own bottle but wasn't sure of the protocol.

Darkness had fallen and the mosquitoes were swarming. The women noticed, but the men not at all. Sally's baby had become restive, and she put him in a room near to the front where he could be heard if he needed attention. She said there was a net in the room to protect him from the mosquitoes.

Kate and Sally went to the kitchen announcing they would get supper before the men lost all interest. For his part, Joe enjoyed talking with Nathan about the "old times" on the farm. He clearly missed his wife as most of the anecdotes involved her. He clearly loved Carcoar too and Joe thought at one point it would be a mistake for him to sell and move away from an area he so closely identified with himself.

Joe was glad when Kate announced it was supper time. He'd already had too much whisky on an empty stomach and welcomed the idea of some food. The women had laid out the table inside with an assortment of things that could be eaten cold. Hams, lamb, breads, pickles and some cheese. Everyone was cheery and full of banter. The meal went quickly, and Nathan suggested they all stay inside, away from the mosquitoes. When they were all settled, the women still sipping on the same sherry and the men with their glasses refreshed, Kate announced that she had gifts for them all. She was obviously one of those people for whom the giving was the greater pleasure.

The gifts were simple, but everyone welcomed them with such a fuss that Joe thought they might be the first presents ever received by them. Kate sure had a way to liven things up.

When it was his turn, Joe made a similar display of presenting Kate with the soap, Matt with the cigars and Sam with the whisky.

"I haven't forgotten Nathan," said Joe, slurring his words and standing unsteadily. "Matt, you have to share the cigars and Sam, you have to share the whisky."

"Will I share the soap?" queried Kate. "I had a peek and there's several pieces."

Joe pretended to think carefully.

"No," he said. "I haven't forgotten Sally."

He had decided to give her the locket. The person didn't have to be special at all, just someone who would be delighted to receive it. He expected she would be overcome with gratitude, so he reached into his pocket and with a great flourish, presented her with the locket.

44. THE LOCKET

Sally took the locket and sat unmoving, staring at it. Joe tried to focus. He'd expected astonishment, delight, or gratitude. He didn't expect the wooden, frozen figure who held the locket in trembling fingers.

"What is it?" said Kate. "What's wrong?"

Joe shook his head in a vain attempt to clear it. Something had happened, but he couldn't begin to guess what it might be. The evening had collapsed. One minute they were all laughing, having fun, enjoying each other's company and now they all focused on Sally and the locket.

"Yes, what's wrong?" asked Joe. He looked at the others in the hope they might know something. Everyone else, including Nathan looked dumbfounded and stared at Sally and the locket.

Sally clicked the locket open and peered inside, squinting in the half light. She looked at Joe. Her face was pale, paler than Joe thought a face could be on a living person. No sound came from her mouth, but it formed a perfect O.

"Where did you get this?" she finally stammered, no longer looking at Joe, but at the locket. She stared at it, as though wanting it to talk, to tell her where it was from.

Joe's mind was a blank. He shook his head again as though he could clear the whisky, but he knew he couldn't. *He had to think. What did she know about the locket? How could she know about the locket?*

"I asked, where you got this?" demanded Sally. This time there was no stammer, only firmness and the sense of a right to know the answer.

Joe looked around the room. No one moved, no one spoke and all had a look of expectation.

Where did you get this locket?

"From a pawn shop," said Joe, finally. He had no idea of what else to say.

"A pawn shop?" replied Sally.

"Yes," said Joe, nodding.

"Where?"

"Sydney."

Sally studied the locket again, closely as though it spoke to her. Then she was nodding as though understanding what it said.

"What did you do in Sydney, Joe?" asked Sally, quietly and firmly as though she already knew the answer. "Before you became a digger?"

Joe had no idea how Sally knew about the locket or his connection with it, but instinctively he knew any lie would only make things worse.

"I was a policeman."

Sally nodded. The rest of the room remained silent. There were only two people now involved in what was playing out. It no longer mattered that other people were there, or what role they thought they had to play.

"So was my husband," said Sally and began to quietly cry.

"Darlin'," whispered Nathan and started to get up, to reach for Sally.

"It's all right Pa," said Sally. "I've always wanted to tell you. I just never found the words."

"Tell me what?" stammered Nathan, the colour gone from his face now too.

"About how Marcus died."

"Marcus?" exclaimed Joe, the question loud and out of place where the others spoke so softly.

Sally just nodded, as though the intrusion of Joe's question was enough for the moment. Her child whimpered in the front room.

"I'll see to him if you like," said Kate.

Sally smiled. "He's all right," she said. "I've given him enough to let him sleep for a while. I thought supper and everything might take a while, so I doubled the dose."

"The dose?" stammered Nathan.

Once again, Sally just nodded.

"I pawned the locket, Joe. Somehow, everything was my fault. Our baby couldn't sleep. Cried all the time. I was at my wits' end. I'd seen some doctors, but no one could help. Then, I was told about laudanum."

"Laudanum?" whispered Nathan.

"Pa. We're going to have to work on your vocabulary. These one-word sentences are not flattering," said Sally. She smiled at her father, but there was no humour in it. Joe saw only sadness and resignation.

"I'm just tryin' to help, darlin'."

"I know Pa. I'm sorry. I didn't expect this to come up tonight. I thought I'd left it all behind."

She looked around the room.

"Sit down Joe. I want you to hear this too. I want everyone to hear it."

"If it's private," said Kate, "you don't have to tell us."

"That's right," said Matt, "it's none of our business."

Sally shook her head gently.

"I'm not getting anything I don't deserve," she said. "You see, Pa, I'd left Marcus when I came home."

Joe thought the shock on Nathan's face showed he'd had no idea. And it was dawning on Joe that Sally didn't know his role either. *What a mess!*

"Marcus brought the locket home. He said someone had found the locket and handed it in. I took it and pawned it to buy laudanum. It's a miracle drug."

Sally nodded her head towards the front room. "He's quiet now, most of the time."

"Is that what you use to keep him quiet?" asked Nathan, an edge to his voice.

"It is. I knew I wouldn't get more on Marcus's salary, and I knew I needed more. I was going mad. So, I came home. I knew I'd get some money from you, Pa."

"Can't the doctors help? What about your idea to take him to a doctor in the city?"

"The only reason I want to go to the city is that we might find some help to look after him."

"So, you pawned it, and Joe here bought it? Is that what happened?" asked Nathan.

"I suppose," said Sally. "Marcus said he had to get it back. Talked about trying to get some money to redeem it. I suppose that's what he was doing the night he was murdered."

"Murdered?" gasped Kate.

"Yes," said Nathan. "The police came here and told Sally her husband was murdered. I thought they might have been tryin' to find out if she had somethin' to do with it, but they couldn't deny her shock on receivin' the news. It was obvious she knew nothin' about it."

Unlike me, thought Joe. His mind was in a turmoil. Of all the people to present with the locket, he had to choose Marcus's wife. Still, it was obvious she knew nothing about his role. If he could keep his wits about him, he might be able to put the night behind him with the others thinking his clumsy gift of the locket was simply misfortune.

"How was he murdered?" asked Kate, her voice unsteady. It was clear her curiosity and dread were in conflict.

"The police didn't know," said Nathan. Sally gave him a little smile of gratitude. She obviously preferred him to address the question.

"They said the murder scene was odd. Both the pawnbroker and Marcus were shot with the same gun. They think there might have been a third person there who'd attempted a robbery, Marcus caught him in the act and paid for the interference with his life."

"It must have happened when Marcus went to get the locket back! It's all my fault!" wailed Sally.

"Goodness!" gasped Kate. "What a terrible business!"

"Well at least the robber didn't get the locket," said Sam. "That was good luck for you, Joe."

"The police thought the robber might have taken it. They said it was in the pawnbroker's book, but it was missin'," said Nathan.

"I didn't know the police knew about the locket!" gasped Sally. "They didn't mention it to me."

"No, they told me about it outside as they were leavin'. I asked if anythin' had been stolen."

"Why?" asked Sally. "What did that have to do with it?"

"I was curious. They thought there'd been an attempted robbery and I reckoned if somethin' was missing, then the robbery would be real and not just attempted. However, they said only a locket was missin' and they doubted anyone would commit murder for a trinket. I presume now it was that one, but if it's missin' and not purchased, how did you come to get it, Joe?" Joe thought there was something more than curiosity in Nathan's voice.

"How would they know it's missin'?" asked Sam.

"The police said a pawnbroker must record in a book everything he buys and sells. They could see where he'd bought it, but not where he'd sold it," explained Nathan.

"I can only guess that the pawnbroker hadn't had time to write it up," asserted Joe lamely. He knew he didn't sound convincing.

"Then you must have been there just before the robbery!" shuddered Sally. "Oh, I wish you'd still been there when the robber came. You might have been able to help."

"Just a minute, darlin'," said Nathan. "Joe, I think you know more about this than you're lettin' on. You said you were a policeman in Sydney? Where was your watch-house?"

"Druitt Street."

"Sally, where's the pawnbroker's shop where you pawned the locket?"

"Kent Street."

"I don't know Sydney very well, but those two places are close, aren't they?" said Nathan, looking at Joe.

"They are," said Joe. "The pawnbroker's was on my beat. I knew him well enough."

"Marcus said he was sly," said Sally.

"What's that mean?" snapped Nathan. Joe wondered at Nathan's change of temper and didn't like where this was going.

"It means he didn't mind breaking the law," said Joe. "A few were like that. We kept a close eye on them for stolen goods."

"Why'd you buy the locket, Joe? Did you have a sweetheart?" asked Kate, not unkindly.

It was oppressively hot in the room now. Joe could feel the effects of the whisky wearing off and struggled to resist the temptation to take a sip from his untouched glass.

"You look uncomfortable Joe," said Nathan. "Why don't you tell us what you know?"

"I didn't have a sweetheart," said Joe.

"That's not what I meant," retorted Nathan. "What do you know about Marcus's murder?"

"I don't know anything about it," said Joe shaking his head. "I knew Marcus. He was from Bathurst Street watch-house. I didn't know him well. I'd seen him at the Court House sometimes. They told us he'd been shot. We never liked to hear of a shooting. We always wondered if we'd be next. I'm sorry for your loss, Sally. And I'm sorry I gave you the locket. I had no idea of its history."

"Why'd you buy it if you didn't have a sweetheart?" persisted Nathan.

"Frankly Nathan, that's none of your business. What I buy is my own business."

"Except when it involves my daughter!" roared Nathan. The shout shocked Kate and she gasped out loud.

"I'm sorry, Kate. I didn't mean to startle you."

"Let's all settle down," said Matt. "It seems to me this whole business is a terrible coincidence."

"I'm sorry, Matt," said Nathan, "but you need to see this from our point of view. I can't help feelin' Joe here knows more'n he's tellin' us."

"I can't help that, Nathan," said Joe. "If I knew anything, I'd tell you."

"You said you were a policeman," said Sally. "Why'd you leave?"

"Gold. I left to look for gold."

"A lot of us did that," said Sam.

Joe looked at the faces in turn. He could tell Sam was still on his side. He wasn't sure about Kate and Matt, Sally looked so sad and her face still showed the tears she had shed earlier. Nathan looked like a cat with a mouse. He looked ready to pounce, to restrain Joe and force from him what he knew.

"When did you leave Sydney?" snapped Nathan, staring at Joe aggressively.

"Nathan, I know this is your house, but I didn't come here to be interrogated. I'm ready to go now. I'm afraid I've had enough."

"Oh dear," said Kate wistfully. "The evening's been ruined. It was such fun earlier."

"Why don't you answer the question?" asked Nathan, his eyes blazing and almost frothing at the mouth, getting up and standing over Joe.

Joe also stood, and Nathan took a step forward, their faces almost touching.

"Step back, Nathan, and give me some space," said Joe quietly, his demeanour remarkably contrasting Nathan's.

"All right, but I'm waitin'."

"Nathan, it's of no consequence. Who cares when I left Sydney?"

"I care!" shouted Nathan, looking like he was about to step forward.

"Why?" asked Joe, again quietly.

"Because you might be the robber!"

Ah! There it is, thought Joe. Somehow, he'd known he'd have to confront the accusation before leaving, almost from the time Sally had identified the locket. It had been too long in coming and now that it was there, Joe felt completely at ease.

Again, Joe looked at the other faces. It was obvious that Nathan's conclusion hadn't occurred to anyone else. All the faces were stunned, staring at Joe as though he was someone else. A robber masquerading as their friend Joe.

Joe chuckled. Only Sam smiled, obviously relieved that the man in front of them wasn't a robber. He was his friend Joe. Kate and Matt looked startled, and Sally looked shocked. Perhaps no one had ever taken her father lightly. Nathan looked like thunder. Joe thought that if Nathan had a gun in his hand now, he would most likely be shot.

"Nathan, I think you'd better sit down," said Joe. "I haven't been accused of being a robber before. I don't like it. It's a serious accusation especially to a man who was a policeman."

"I will not!"

"Please do as he says, Da," said Sally.

"This is my home, and no one tells me what to do in my own home!"

"As you wish," said Joe. "But since it's your home and we are your guests, I think we should top up all our drinks."

"You impertinent bastard! If I had a gun, I'd shoot you for that!"

"I do believe you would," said Joe, "but then you'd be a murderer. What's worse? A murderer or a robber?"

"Then you are the robber?" shouted Nathan triumphantly.

"I don't know why you'd even suggest it. I told you I bought it. Why wouldn't you believe me? In any case, most crimes are committed by opportunists."

"What does that mean?"

"Like you said, you needed to be holding a gun and unable to resist the impulse to shoot me just now. What circumstances could you imagine where it would be a good opportunity for me to steal that locket?"

"I've no interest in your word games! I'll go to the police in Carcoar tomorrow! I'll tell them all about you!"

"Tomorrow might be a problem being Christmas day. However, leaving that to one side, what will you tell them?"

"That you were here, and you gave my daughter the missin' locket!"

"I bought the locket from a pawnbroker that failed to record the sale. I don't think they'll be too interested. Besides, I was a policeman."

"It puts you at the scene of the crime!"

"The man ran a shop. There were lots of people at the scene of the crime."

"Enough, Da! Enough!" shouted Sally. "This is getting us nowhere. I stole the locket and pawned it! Marcus was furious. He said he was only looking after the locket until he could find the owner. I tried to convince him that we could keep it.

I'm not blameless in this sorry affair! Poor Joe here bought the locket in good faith, and you accuse him of being a robber and perhaps a murderer! This has gone far enough."

Kate hurried over and held Sally. They were both sobbing now. "Oh Sally, Sally! What a nightmare for you!" sobbed Kate.

"It's the boy," whispered Sally. "I wish he was normal. It's all his fault."

"You don't mean that! You're just upset," sobbed Kate.

"I do mean it. I wish he'd never been born."

Kate gasped.

"We'll go," said Matt. "I'm sorry Nathan."

"It's not your fault, Matt. I'm sorry Kate. I overreacted. Things haven't been easy, you know," said Nathan. "But you Joe, I'll think more about you."

"I'm sorry too, Nathan. I ruined your evening," said Joe.

"No, you didn't," said Sally. "But here, take the locket. It's yours. I don't want it. I never want to see it again."

Joe took the locket and slipped it into his shirt pocket.

Once outside, Joe welcomed the cool of the night air. He asked if he could ride Matt's horse home, explaining that he wanted to be alone. Joe saddled the horse while Sam and Matt harnessed the other horse to the gig. They worked in silence. Joe knew there'd be more questions over breakfast and needed to clear his mind to be sure of consistent answers.

Joe rode slowly, ruminating on the night's events. He was grateful that everyone had parted on better terms but didn't doubt that Nathan would follow up with the police at some point. Sally had calmed things by pointing out that she was in fact a robber, but Nathan would know that an approach by him to the police would not be a danger for Sally. Nathan had other problems, of course. Things that would prey upon his mind and give reasons for him to forget about the locket. The fact that Sally had wished her son had never been born for one and the fact that Sally was continually treating him with laudanum. Yes, Nathan had reasons enough to worry more about the living.

A pale moon lit his path, the silvery light calming his troubled mind. He'd thought the events of that night months ago were long behind him. He should have known from his time as a policeman that fate cared little for the wants of men. Despite the stressful evening, he was able to focus on what to do next. No doubt being alone on a bush track with nothing but nocturnal animals for company contributed to his feelings of well-being. His horse plodded on faithfully, taking small and confident steps.

She's a good horse, he thought. *Nearly as good as his own, but not good enough to take instead of his own.*

The idea came and went. He couldn't just leave. If he did, Kate, Matt and Sam would be disappointed. No, they were more important than that. They'd been good to him and deserved better than desertion. Especially Sam.

He stopped the horse for a moment and looked at the hills around him. It was like he saw them for the first time. He admired how well they were crafted by nature. Rolling from one to another, joined by creeks and gullies, home to countless animals and birds. It was a pretty place that he'd come close to calling home. Now it wouldn't be, and he fretted momentarily that an event from months ago may well be an impediment to him ever being part of anything.

Sighing, he set the horse in motion again, feeling lonelier than he ever had in his life. There was no sign of light or life when he got back to the house. He stripped the horse, put the saddlery in the shed and went through the open back door. The room he shared with Sam was on the left and easy to find by the moonlight that came far enough into the house.

He undressed, put on his night shirt and crept into bed. There was no sound from Sam and he knew from experience that he must still be awake.

"You didn't say you were a policeman," said Sam's voice from the other side of the room.

"I know," replied Joe." Does it matter?"

"I suppose not. Pa wondered why I didn't know."

"What did you say?"

"That I'd never asked you."

"It's close enough to the truth."

"We talked about things coming home."

"I thought you would."

"Is that why you came home alone?"

"I wanted to be alone."

"To think?"

"Yes. Get some sleep. We'll talk about it in the morning."

Kate was her usual ebullient self in the morning. There were the usual pleasantries at the table, but everything seemed forced. It was as though no one wanted to be first to raise the matter of the previous evening.

"It wasn't your fault, Joe. Last night I mean," said Kate. She sat opposite Joe. They were all sipping tea, the meal finished except for the tea. Joe looked at Kate and smiled.

"Thank you, Kate, but I can't help feeling it was all my fault."

"You couldn't help that the locket had special meaning for her," said Matt. "How could you have known? I'm sure you would have expected a woman to be grateful for such a present."

"I would have liked it," said Kate.

"Would you like it now?" asked Joe, reaching for his pocket.

"Lord no," said Kate. "Could you imagine what would happen if Sally or Nathan saw it again?"

"It'd be red rag to a bull," said Matt.

"I think I'll leave today," said Joe.

"But it's Christmas!" exclaimed Kate. "Won't you stay for Christmas?"

"Where will you go?" asked Sam. "Back to the Turon?"

"I'm not sure."

"What's wrong, Joe?" asked Matt. "You don't have to go. You haven't spoiled anythin' for us, and you won't see Nathan or Sally again. There's no need for you to go."

"I wish you'd stay," said Kate. "It's wonderful to have you both here. If you go, Sam might go too."

"I won't, Ma. There's no need for me to go. I've come home for Christmas."

What is wrong? thought Joe. *Was it that his past had caught up with him?*

Joe looked at the three people. One had come to mean a lot because they'd shared danger and adventure. The other two he'd just met, but he felt like he'd known them all his life. If they knew what he was really like, he doubted he'd be welcome. He'd changed a lot in the gold fields. Those changes and the respect of these people had come to mean so much.

A gentle breeze moved through the open doors. Joe could feel it cool on his cheek, like the kiss his ma used to give him at night when she put him to bed. He missed his ma and wondered where she was now. For all he knew, she could be dead. Perhaps her guiding hand would have prevented all this from happening.

"I do know more, Matt. Things of which I'm ashamed. Oh, nothing the police would really care about. And I do know what happened to Marcus."

"Oh, you mean the police in Sydney know everything already? I thought Nathan said they still had questions," said Matt.

"That's the point. They don't know what I know. It was too complicated to explain. So, I left and came gold digging."

"Are you the robber?" asked Kate. Her face was tense, and Joe knew she hadn't expected the conversation to go in this direction.

"Yes," said Joe. "I stole the locket."

"Then you lied to Nathan!" almost shouted Matt.

"I don't think so. I only asked him why he'd think it. Besides, he threatened to shoot me for impertinence, so there might be more to Nathan than meets the eye."

"You a robber, Joe? I would never have thought it! How? Why?" whispered Kate, her hands to her face. "Oh Joe! Why?"

Joe studied his tea looking for inspiration.

"I don't know, Kate. Sally was right, the pawnbroker was sly. We'd worked a few schemes together. Simple things that didn't involve too much. Marcus was too honest, and the pawnbroker wanted him to be compromised. When Sally pawned the locket, I guessed she had pledged it for Marcus. I didn't know she was his wife, I thought she might have been a friend or a neighbour. The pawnbroker thought it nothing short of a miracle when I told him where Marcus had got the locket, so the pawnbroker seized the chance to blackmail Marcus."

"You told the pawnbroker how to blackmail Sally's husband?" said Sam.

Joe nodded.

"Wouldn't the police be interested in that?" exclaimed Matt.

"They might, but I doubt it would keep the Commissioner up nights. I think Marcus is the only honest policeman I've ever met. Most of us worked the system when we could. It was what we did."

"Did you know who Sally was?" asked Kate. "Before tonight, I mean."

"No. The pawnbroker only referred to the person that pawned the locket as a woman."

"How did Marcus get killed?" asked Matt.

"He and the broker shot each other. I tried to stop them fighting but couldn't."

"You saw it happen. Wouldn't the police believe you?"

"I didn't see it happen. The broker was shot, and I went to get help. They were both dead when I got back. There were too many things that were too hard to explain. I thought it was time to go looking for gold."

"Who shot Marcus? Was it the broker?"

"I presume so," said Joe. "They were lying on the floor reaching toward each other. Both had a grip on the gun. Maybe they fought over it or maybe the broker shot Marcus in revenge."

"Revenge for what? Did Marcus shoot the broker?" asked Matt.

"The broker thought so, but no. I did. It was dark and we were all fighting for the gun. I squeezed the trigger hoping it would frighten them enough to stop them fighting. It went off and the broker was wounded. Mortally as it transpired."

"It was an accident!" exclaimed Sam and Matt nodded.

"How did you get the locket?" asked Kate, her face ashen.

"Picked it up as I left. It was there and I took it. I regret it, of course. I wish I'd never seen it."

"Why did you tell us this?" asked Matt softly. "You didn't have to say anything."

"I know. I thought you deserved the truth."

"What about Nathan and Sally? Don't they deserve the truth too?" asked Kate. Joe thought he heard admonition in her tone.

"They wouldn't be able it leave it alone. Oh, Sally might but you saw Nathan. If I told him what I just told you he'd be off to the police at the first opportunity."

"And we won't be?" asked Matt. "How do you know we won't go to the police?"

"You can if you want. I don't mind. It's up to you."

"Why don't you care?" gasped Kate.

"Oh, I care all right. The police might get excited about me leaving the scene of a crime, but there's nothing else there for them. If you told them, they'd probably take some notes and that would be the end of it. Nathan on the other hand would badger them until they acted. In fact, they'd probably only take action to get rid of him."

"Nathan might find out eventually."

"He would if you go to the police or tell him, but I don't think you will. I think you believe me."

"You took a gamble Joe," said Sam.

"It's only a gamble when you have something to lose," said Joe in a soft voice. "Right now, I feel like I've lost everything."

"We can go back to the Turon and stake another claim", said Sam. "There's plenty of gold left."

"You haven't lost everything Joe. We believe you, don't we Pa?" said Kate.

Matt nodded. "Yes, Joe. None of us will speak about what you've told us today. Will we?" he added, looking at his family.

"It's none of my business," said Sam. "Especially if it means we can still be partners."

"Stay for Christmas," said Kate. "Please Joe. I've some wonderful food for lunch today. Things will get better I promise. There'll be no more talk of this. Christmas is for family and fun. Last night got away from us, so let's not lose today as well."

"And I've got whisky!" almost shouted Sam.

"And cigars!" shouted Matt.

"And soap!" screamed Kate at the top of her lungs.

"All right, all right!" shouted Joe out loud and they all laughed together like old friends sharing a familiar joke.

45. THE DEPARTURE

Joe got up early and left the next morning. It was still dark, but he'd planned well the day before and left his saddle, bridle and saddle bags where he could easily find them in the shed. Sam snored loudly as he left the room, and the sound masked any noise he might make. His horse came readily from the back paddock, and it took no time to saddle him up. He led the horse quietly towards the side gate.

The previous afternoon had gone so well Joe almost decided to stay but knew he couldn't. He'd burdened Sam's family with knowledge that would weigh more heavily with each passing day. He doubted any of them would go to the police, but Matt had to face Nathan almost every day so he might be tempted to tell Nathan what he now knew. It didn't matter either way to Joe, but he respected Sam, Matt and Kate too much to let them agonise over what they might see as betrayal.

As he neared the gate, he heard a rustle in the bushes. All his instincts went onto immediate alert. There was no moon like the previous night, and everything was a shadowy blackness. He couldn't challenge as he would alert those in the house to his departure. The sensible thing to do was to stop and let the threat come to him. He cursed himself that his revolver was in his saddle bags. There'd been no reason to think there would be any danger at this time of the morning. Could it be the police? Had they been alerted? Or possibly Nathan?

"Joe?" whispered a soft voice. "It's me. Kate."

"Kate! What are you doing out of bed?" He walked towards her shadow.

"I came to say goodbye. Something tells me we won't be seeing you again."

"That something might be right."

"You have nothing to fear from us Joe. I'd like us to be friends. What happened with Nathan and Sally doesn't matter to us."

"That's not the point."

"I know it's not the point, but I'd like it to be. You're a good man Joe. We all do things we're not proud of, so it's way past time for you to be worrying about such things."

"I'll start again somewhere."

"Somewhere that your past can't find you?"

"Hopefully."

"You can come back one day. We'll be somewhere around here, so you'll be able to find us. Nathan and Sally will probably move to the city, so it will be safe here. I hope you try. Sam will miss you. He said your common sense with tunnellin' probably saved his life more than once."

"I'll miss him. He's a good friend. They don't grow on trees."

"Then don't go."

"Goodbye, Kate. Thanks for your hospitality. You, Matt and Sam. It's been a wonderful Christmas. And your friendship. Yesterday meant a lot to me. I'll never forget you all."

"Goodbye, Joe. Lean down here so I can give you a kiss. It'll need to be a good one to last you the rest of your life!"

Joe leant down and Kate kissed him on the cheek, just like any mother. She pulled him close and whispered, "Take care of yourself, Joe. May the road rise to meet you and the wind be always at your back."

"And may the good Lord always hold you in the palm of his hand."

"Oh Joe, I'll sure be missin' you! You are a better man than you think. A brave one too!"

Kate took Joe's hand, held it fiercely and whispered, "Take good care and get goin' you spalpeen 'fore I put the dogs on you!"

Joe led his horse out the gate, mounted and rode off into the night. He turned left into the main street heading in the direction of Bathurst. He had no plan and didn't care. The shocking thing was how easily his past could find him. He didn't like who he'd been and preferred who he'd become. But who he'd been was as much a part of his life as the air he breathed. It really wasn't possible to become someone else.

He rode first to Blayney where he bought supplies. There were plenty of towns, so there was no need to buy more than he would need for a few days. From Blayney he turned towards Millthorpe, then headed towards Gulgong. There was no reason, they were just the names of places with which he was now familiar.

After a few days the weather turned cold. It wasn't unusual for it to happen, even in summer. He was glad of the old jacket that he'd kept from Ophir. Stopping his horse, he dismounted, pulled the jacket from his saddle bags and pulled it on. As he did, he felt the weight of the locket in his shirt pocket. He took it out and studied it imagining that his bad fortune had started with the locket. He hadn't been able to give it away. Perhaps the locket should belong to no one. Perhaps it was possessed by something evil.

There was a momentary impulse to throw it away. The damn thing had brought him nothing but trouble, dogging his heels at every turn. Remembering its value, he thought better of it and put it in his jacket's pocket. There's be a woman soon enough that would be pleased to take it if only for its value. The wind picked up suddenly and the chill in the air deepened. There was a rumble of thunder in the hills and heavy drops of rain began to fall. He took shelter in a nearby stand of trees.

It wasn't long before he saw a woman in the distance. This time, he'd find a way to get rid of the locket for sure.

46. CAROLINE

Caroline woke. What a nightmare she'd just had!

Fearful, she looked and was relieved to see her baby sleeping in the cradle. How long had she been asleep? It felt like days. She looked at the locket clutched tightly in her hand and dropped it onto the nearby table. Could any of what she'd just dreamt be true? How would she ever find out? And the man she just met on the road? Was that the man in her dream? And the locket! What would she do with that?

Tom would know what to do and she missed him and longed for his return, more than she thought she could bear. Her dream had been sad, so full of lost love and loneliness that she couldn't control her own emotions. A single tear coursed slowly down her cheek, and she swiped it irritably away.

There was a noise at the door. She looked at it fearfully, but her fear turned to joy when she saw Tom standing there, his clothes wet from the rain.

"Oh, Tom!" she shouted and ran to his arms.

ABOUT THE AUTHOR

Peter Clarke is only one of many Australians who are intrigued by the stories of the immigrants who helped create a nation. Where did they come from? Why did they come? Why did they stay?

Born in Mudgee and raised in the Blue Mountains, Peter is familiar with the challenges of drought and fire, but these challenges are nothing compared to those faced by the early pioneers.

A working life in the computer industry has not in any way prepared Peter to write about the pioneers. However, a lively interest in early Australia and an adequate Irish heritage has contributed to a curiosity that has only been in part satisfied by several trips to Ireland. Thus motivated, Peter used the new technology to surf world history and events, to create a story of one man's journey which reflects the difficulties of the time.